WALTER
TIMES TWO

WALTER TIMES TWO

ANNIKA CHAMPENOIS

Sunny Laughs Press

Chapter One

"OF COURSE, no one would suspect I was volunteering at this science fair with ulterior motives." Aurelia Jackson, editing intern and devoted story-dreamer, leaned over to straighten a stack of flyers while she listened to a penetrating fifth grader's voice nearby. When her blonde hair fell forward, she let it frame her view of the elementary school's assembly room.

Her roommate, Jackie, tsked beside her. "You don't have ulterior motives. Don't be *dramasacious*."

Aurelia stiffened at the rogue word. Jackie liked to torture her by recreating adjectives with wrong endings. "Do you mean 'dramatic'? You do realize I'm here to eavesdrop on children, right?"

"For the sake of your stories." Jackie's cocoa-colored ponytail swung as she picked up a pile of science camp flyers and added it to the dwindling stack on the table. "All of us are here for our own motives, but they're not ulterior. They're just *reasons*. I'm here because I want to get the kids excited about science." She turned in the direction of the next table. "Hey, you. Why are you here?"

The university student Jackie had hailed blinked in surprise. "Excuse me?"

"Besides wanting to be nice and help out, what made you want to come help with the fair?" Jackie clarified.

"Oh." The girl relaxed her shoulders. "I grew up nearby. Some of these children are my neighbors."

"Cool. What about you?" Jackie asked one of the guys as he crossed the room with a beaker in his hand. Sunlight streamed through the window and lit up his hair, blinding Aurelia when she looked in his direction.

"Why did I want to come?" His voice perked up like Jackie's did when she talked about chemistry. "Science is my life. Here I get to relive where it all began."

Aurelia jotted down a quick note with her pen. She could use this guy's passion for one of her characters—perhaps a friendly, sometimes overly excited science teacher.

"See?" Jackie turned back to her roommate. "Reasons. You have them, just like everyone else. You're here to help and to spy."

Aurelia raised her brows at the last word. "And spying is totally not ulterior, right?"

"BYU's science programs," Jackie called, flapping a flyer at a sixth grader and his interested parents as though she hadn't heard the question. "Chemistry camp for kids!"

By the time their replacements arrived, Aurelia was ready to get home and write.

"Is your song ready for tonight?" Jackie asked as they stepped outside into the September heat. Utah was, as usual, in the middle of a drought, and the mountains behind the school displayed wilted brown and red fall colors.

"I know it from beginning to end," Aurelia answered and paused. "Will people think I'm weird?"

"They already know you're weird."

"Individual *friends* know, but not the whole ward." She didn't even know half the people in her church unit, although tonight's activity should help with that.

Jackie was unconcerned. "It's a talent show. Sing your French song and shine. You know, for someone who loves words, it's ironic that English can't keep your attention."

"English is great, but it's not enough on its own," Aurelia argued as they crossed the wide street of 900 East, the buildings of Brigham Young University obscuring their view of the west mountains in the distance. "More languages equal more words. Wonderful words. Stories—"

"Maybe you'll even attract a guy."

Aurelia nearly scoffed but reconsidered and decided to let herself dream. "With beautiful brown hair."

"No, he'll be blond. But if I approve of him, I'll help him out and give him a wig," Jackie said wickedly, making Aurelia sputter. In her mind, there was simply nothing more attractive than a guy with rich brown hair. Nothing. But seriously, *a wig*, just to change his hair color?

She protested the finer points of wigs as outlined by Jackie while the two of them headed up the stairs of the Elite apartment complex, a red brick building just off the side of the road.

"Is the Cursed Room clean?" Jackie broke off to ask.

"I haven't touched it since Julie left." They stepped inside, Aurelia breathing a sigh of relief as she passed through the cool breeze blowing from the AC. The sparsely furnished apartment welcomed them with a couple of African safari posters Jackie had gotten hold of at some point. Aurelia looked toward the open hallway that led to their shared bedroom, the bathroom, and the Cursed Room. "What's our new roommate's name again?"

"Um, Shannon, I think." Jackie grabbed her backpack and rifled through its contents.

Aurelia pulled out her laptop. "How long do you think she'll stay?"

"Less than a month."

Aurelia snorted. "That's a pretty safe bet."

"Hey, that one girl stayed for almost two."

"Yeah, but that was five roommates ago."

This was their second year living together in Elite, and for one reason or another, the other bedroom never stayed occupied for long.

Julie, the latest roommate, had barely spent time with them as it was, always off to the pool for swimming practice. When a place had opened up with one of her teammates two weeks into the semester, she had jumped at it.

Jill, the girl before her, had left when she got married. That was pretty normal for BYU.

Before that, Mary had gotten arrested. *That* had been a shock.

And the list went on and on. Although it was supposed to be a shared bedroom, the Cursed Room never attracted more than one resident at a time. Even so, there was no shortage of candidates for the room when it was empty. Someone new always moved in not long after the previous girl left —and then she moved out, making room for the next girl.

"Make sure you let her in when she shows up," Jackie said.

"Of course. Why wouldn't I?" Aurelia frowned, but already her mind was drifting to the grade-schoolers at the fair. After today, she had a better feel for their voices. She opened a Word document, her fingers itching to rewrite some of the conversations in her story.

"Because you get so immersed in your stories that you forget the world around you."

"What?" Aurelia made an effort to focus on Jackie's words. "No. I mean, I never get so distracted that I don't hear the doorbell."

"Fine, fine. See that you don't," was Jackie's bossy response before she left.

* * *

"See?" Aurelia said out loud to herself that afternoon while she put down her laptop to answer the doorbell. "I pay attention. Take that, Jackie."

She swung the door open to a tall young man with excitement in his smile and energy radiating off him. Obviously he wasn't the new roommate.

His striped polo shirt looked dusty, his jeans were torn, and he had stubble on his face that could get him kicked off campus if he were to venture that way. BYU's Honor Code was adamant about that clean-shaven look.

His hair—oh, his hair. Aurelia was tempted to lean against the door and sigh. His hair was a gorgeous brown and stood up like soft grass on a well-cropped lawn. His eyes, set in a firm, oblong face, sparkled with the same merry brown shade and held hints of green.

The man dropped down on one knee and held out a velvety red box, which opened to reveal a bejeweled ring.

"Aurelia Michelle Jackson, will you marry me?" he asked.

The world skidded to a stop. Her mouth opened, but she didn't know what to say.

"Huh?" She stared down at him. The scene in front of her didn't change. There truly was a stranger kneeling in front of her, presenting a ring and waiting for an answer. "Who are *you*?"

He winced and answered in a tenor voice, "I know I left abruptly, but I didn't have a choice. I came back as soon as I could. Will you marry me?"

How did he know her full name, or any part of her name, for that matter? Who did he think he was?

The world resumed its rotation while Aurelia grew hot all over. With a glower at the stranger, she slammed the door shut.

"Wait," his muffled voice called out. Before she could lock the door, he flung it open and advanced. "Aurelia, come on."

With a gasp, she grabbed the shoehorn Jackie had once received as a white elephant gift and brandished it at him, stepping backward and willing him not to move farther inside. Her heart beat so fast it hurt. "What do you think you're doing?"

"Aurelia?" He looked confused. "Don't you—wait, are you serious?" He whispered the last part, his eyes widening as if at some sudden revelation. He looked down at his watch and back at her.

She tightened her grip on the shoehorn. Not the sturdiest of weapons, but if she hit him in the neck . . .

Wait, she had seen him before—just a bit ago, at the fair. He was the guy who mentioned revisiting the roots of his love of science.

What was he doing here now?

He took a step toward her but seemed to think better of it and held out his hands. "You do know me, right?"

"I saw you today at the science fair," she blurted.

He frowned. "The science fair?" Then he jerked and yelped, "*Today*? Are you sure?"

"You need to leave," she said, her voice shaking.

Instead of obeying, he brought a hand to his forehead while his eyes glazed over. "I went back too far."

How could she talk the lunatic into leaving? She cleared her throat, only to have his eyes refocus on her, freezing her to the spot.

His brows knit, and he took a step backward. But only one. He still filled the doorway. "I'm sorry. Aurelia—I shouldn't even know your name yet—but I do. How do I fix this?"

She bit her lip and indicated the exit. "Go?" Her voice was high-pitched.

He stared at her and the shoehorn she wielded. "Right. Yes. I'll leave. Forget, um, what happened. Sorry." He cleared the doorway at last.

Aurelia hurried to lock the door, then crouched beneath the curtained window to peek outside. He was walking away, throwing a glance or two back at her apartment, his posture dejected.

She shuddered and walked on silent feet through the living room, singing quietly to herself in French. Should she call the police? She grabbed a bag of broccoli from the fridge and wandered around, peeking out the windows of each bedroom, popping broccoli in her mouth at intervals, and practicing the Indila song she would perform at tonight's talent show. Her voice sounded scared and wispy, but there were more important things to worry about.

She chewed on the inside of her cheek. Could it have been a joke? The guy shouldn't have known her name, but someone else could have told him and set this up. Why would they do *that* though? For that matter, who in town even knew her middle name?

The doorbell rang, making her cry out and clap a hand to her mouth. Heedful of anyone looking in the window, she got down on the floor and crawled to the dining table, reaching up for her cell phone. With 911 dialed and her finger near the call button, she crept to the window to get a glimpse of whoever stood outside.

It was a tall lightly freckled girl with a suitcase. Aurelia scanned the walkway but saw no one else. When her gaze returned to the door, she found the girl staring at her through the window.

Aurelia coughed and opened the door. "Hey. Are you Shannon?"

"Yeah. Um, what's your name?"

"Aurelia."

"Oh. Nice to meet you." Shannon shifted her weight.

"Can I help you with your stuff?"

Shannon hesitated for a moment before she relaxed. "Sure. I have three bags in my car."

Aurelia tensed at the thought of going outside, then reminded herself that the proposal might be a prank. In fact—she stuck her head out the door to reassure herself the coast was clear—someone must have dared their friend to pull that stunt. Someone who knew her full name. If she found out who it was, she would give them a piece of her mind.

Shannon's gaze flickered from Aurelia to their surroundings and back.

"I'll help. The Cursed—" Aurelia nearly bit her tongue. "I mean, your room's down the hall, on the left."

* * *

"I'm glad I get to meet the ward tonight," Shannon said, although she looked nervous as they walked to campus. "Do they have a lot of activities?"

"Family Home Evening activities on Mondays, and then monthly activities like tonight." In a church ward for single people, ages eighteen to thirty, the "family" part of Family Home Evening referred to the ward members rather than blood relatives. The only person in the singles' ward who was married was their leader, the bishop, which made sense. The man needed all the experience and wise spousal support he could get when it came to providing the spiritual and material help everyone came to him for.

"What made you move to our place?" Aurelia asked, hoping the question wasn't too intrusive. Maybe if she learned early on why her Cursed Roommates had left their previous apartment before moving to hers, she could try to keep the same thing from being a problem here.

"Noises." Shannon hunched her shoulders. "Sometimes I thought I saw . . . movements. The place before that—I think there was a bad spirit or something. And the place before that—well, anyway." She clutched her hands together. "Your place is pretty safe, right?"

If by safe, you mean strangers feel like they can come over and propose, then sure. Aurelia didn't voice the thought. Instead, she answered, "Um, it's a nice place. How long have you been at BYU?"

"Three years."

"Me too," Aurelia said.

"And you're studying . . . ?"

"Editing. I actually have a campus editing internship instead of classes this semester, so you'll see me working at home all the time." When she wasn't editing, she was usually working on a story, so either way, Shannon would see her working at home.

"That's cool." Shannon followed her up a short set of cement stairs. "What do you like to do for fun?"

"Listen to music." Aurelia didn't usually tell people she wrote. She had story ideas like crazy, but none of them were ready to be made public. She could talk about music though, so she began discussing songs and artists, making an effort to befriend Shannon.

Maybe Shannon would break the Cursed pattern and stay the rest of the semester. If Aurelia could make herself believe that, she would be a good, friendly roommate, and they might end up friends for life, still keeping in contact when they were both in their seventies and had fifty grandchildren each.

Make that sixty-something. Hmm, no, what was a good number?

"How many grandchildren do you want? I mean, children?" Aurelia changed the question to a slightly less unheard-of one, well aware that her author mind had gotten ahead of itself as soon as Shannon furrowed her brow. "Actually, never mind. Um, we're almost there now."

They entered the Wilkinson Center, a six-story campus building full of shops, common areas, and "classrooms" that were used for church and various activities but rarely for actual classes, to Aurelia's knowledge. Shannon returned to small talk, but the uncertainty that had hung about her since she arrived at the apartment was back in her voice, and Aurelia silently cursed herself for being the cause.

They entered the designated room, a square space that would have been empty if not for the people, the piano in front, and the rows of chairs that had been set up. Aurelia caught sight of Jackie in the front row, homework in her lap and two open seats on her right. Good. Jackie could help put their new roommate at ease. "There's our roommate, Jackie."

Aurelia smiled her way through the crowd and arrived at the front. "Hey."

Jackie looked up. "Hey yourself. Oh hi, are you Shannon?"

Shannon took the middle seat, and Aurelia claimed the far seat, looking up at the projector in front while the other two began to chat. Knowing the projector screen would soon show her music video, she swallowed and began running lyrics through her mind. Her heart thudded as she tried to prepare herself to sing in front of all these people.

A group of guys sat down behind her. She turned at the sound of their voices and went rigid.

The guy who had proposed on her doorstep sat two rows behind her.

Chapter Two

Cold washed over her. How was it possible? How had he found her again? Her heart beat an impressive tap dance as she watched him.

There was no way this was a prank. No one in their right mind would prank her like this, not even Jackie. The guy had shown up to all three places Aurelia had been today: the science fair, her apartment, and now her ward activity.

He was stalking her.

The culprit looked comfortable as he talked with his seatmates, James from the ward and someone Aurelia didn't recognize. He had shaved, and his clothes were clean, but it was definitely him. He raised his gaze, caught Aurelia looking at him, and smiled. Then he shut his eyes and folded his arms.

Aurelia faced forward and joined in the opening prayer for the evening's activity.

After the prayer, she threw a wild look at Jackie. Could she clue her in on what was going on? Shannon sat between them, her foot tapping nervously. It didn't seem like a good idea to make her even more nervous. Or to talk about the guy behind them while he could overhear it.

Aurelia squirmed and sneaked backward glances throughout the show. She missed most of the jokes from her ward's stand-up comedian, and she was distracted from the dueling banjos that would normally have captured her attention. She did finally close her eyes and relax during a piano solo that took her down a soothing waterfall of music. Maybe the guy's presence needn't shake her. With all these people around, most of whom she knew by sight if not by name, she was safe.

She forgot to be nervous about her own solo until her name was called. Taking a deep breath, she walked up to the front and accepted the microphone.

"This is 'Tourner Dans Le Vide' by Indila, my favorite French artist. It speaks of an interesting love story"—she cleared her throat and tried not to look at the guy in the room who had proposed to her—"as you'll see in the music video."

Her hands shook as she helped the DJ ensure that the muted music video and the karaoke version of the music on her phone would begin in sync. Then she faced the audience under the tinkling sounds of the opening notes and began to sing.

Jackie gave her a broad smile and two thumbs-up. Beside her, Shannon's smile was encouraging. Involuntarily Aurelia's eyes flicked to her visitor from earlier that day just as he straightened in his seat to watch her.

Her breath hitched in the middle of the phrase she was singing, but she quickly picked up the melody, trying not to let his attention faze her. His eyes didn't leave her. She swallowed and tried to focus on the novelty of Indila's world, but goosebumps rose on her arms the longer her would-be suitor watched.

By the end of the song, she felt terribly turned around, just as the lyrics spoke of. Leaving the scene to two ballroom dancers, she stumbled to a seat at the front, on the opposite side of the room from her stalker.

It was grueling to sit through the last few performances. As soon as applause for the final number dissolved into general chatter, she sprang up and headed for the dessert table. Her nerves were strung tight, and she needed something to calm them.

High-calorie sweets decked the table, disappointing her. Where were vegetables when she needed them? She snatched a lone cookie and a napkin and looked around for Jackie.

"Aurelia, great job on your song." Katie, her ministering sister, stepped up to her. "Do you know what all the words mean?"

She relaxed, feeling better with a friend at her side and infinitely grateful for the church's ministering system, which assigned people to keep an eye out for and care for someone else. Katie was an angel in a time of need. "I've only looked up half of them so far," she replied. "Wasn't it interesting though?"

"Yeah, that guy in the painting was *dreamy*, and the ending gave me chills. I put the song on my watchlist. Hey, how are the Costa Ricans?"

Aurelia managed a smile. Her dad had been called away to Costa Rica as a mission president three years ago. Aurelia's mom and two younger siblings had made the move with him. The mission had been extended till the end of the year or so, and she couldn't wait to see them when they came home. "They're doing well. President Jackson runs a tight ship, but he hasn't had to keelhaul any of his missionaries yet."

Katie's eyes sparkled. "Probably because it's against the rules for missionaries to play in the ocean, right?"

They were laughing when Katie's friend called out to her.

"Sorry, gotta go," Katie said and stepped away.

"See you later." Aurelia turned in Jackie's direction again. She turned right into a male chest that wasn't supposed to be there.

"Oops," she mumbled, stepping back and looking up. Then she froze.

"Sorry. Hi. You sang really well," her stalker said.

Up close, his brown hair and eyes were even more breathtaking than before. Up close, it was also clear that he was several inches taller than her, and he was definitely sturdier. She gulped.

"Are you in choir?" he asked.

"Uh, n-not right now." She twisted the napkin in her hand and dropped a large piece of her cookie. Her eyes darted toward the bishop and back.

The guy smiled, which made his eyes shine. "But you have been?"

When she shrugged, he shoved a hand through his thick brown hair. A nervous reflex? She swallowed and looked away from the hair.

"Do you know French?" he persisted.

She shook her head. "I wouldn't—mind learning it." She bit the inside of her cheek and stepped back, ready to escape this conversation.

"I know BYU has great language classes."

"Yes. There's never really room in my schedule," she replied in a tight voice, cutting herself off from explaining other reasons such as her inability to pick the language she would most like to learn. He didn't need to know that. He didn't need to know anything about her. In fact, he already knew far too much about her.

"What's your name?" he asked.

"'Scuse me?"

"I know they announced it before you sang, but I don't remember. What's your name?"

She stared at him hard. "You know my name."

He blinked and gave her a weak smile. "Okay. My name's Walter." He held out his hand. "What's yours?"

"Aurelia, good job on your solo," someone called out nearby. "It was awesome."

She nodded at the person, keeping her eyes mostly on the guy in front of her.

"Aurelia." Walter smiled. Not that she knew for sure his name was Walter. He could be lying about that.

She felt herself heat up again, the way she had outside her apartment. "What are you doing here? This isn't your ward." Her hands stilled. "Is it?" *Oh, please don't let him have moved into the ward.*

"No. James from your ward invited me and my roommate. Um, you like music, right?"

"Yeah." She edged away from him and toward the person who had called to her—and who was now, unfortunately, turned away.

"I have two tickets to an a cappella concert this Friday," her stalker continued. "Would you like to go?"

Her mouth opened. Her eyes narrowed.

Go somewhere alone with him? Maybe even give him her phone number and have him pick her up from where he already knew she lived?

Her mouth snapped shut. Instead of dignifying him with a response, she glared and strode away.

"Nope, I've never had a porcupine," Jackie was telling a group of confused-looking guys.

"I need to talk to you," Aurelia interrupted her friend. "Actually, I need to leave. Are you ready to leave?"

Jackie stepped away from her potential admirers and looked around. "I am, but what about Shannon? Hey, Shannon," she called out as she caught sight of the girl behind them, "are you ready to go?"

Shannon frowned before gazing up at the guy she had been talking to.

He put a hand on her arm. "I can walk you home when you're ready."

"Really? Thanks, Simon." Shannon smiled at her roommates. "I guess you don't have to wait for me." She returned her attention to the guy before they could answer.

"And just like that, she's lost to the masses," Jackie murmured as she and Aurelia left. "She'll probably never speak another two words to us if she's already found a boyfriend."

"Don't say that. We could still become friends," Aurelia protested, but even she felt her enthusiasm fading. Shannon was probably moving out soon anyway. The Cursed Room was too powerful.

She didn't speak on the short walk home. With the sun setting, the ninety-degree day had cooled to eighty-something, making it easier to breathe. She glanced around, her senses alert, as they approached the door and let themselves in.

Jackie misinterpreted her silence. "If you're mad at me for not contributing to the talent show, I told you I would have done it if I'd had more time to prepare something," she began in annoyance.

"It's not that. Did you see the guy I was talking to?" Aurelia snatched a container of carrot sticks from the fridge.

"You mean at the talent show? Which one?"

"I only talked to one guy. Remember the guy from the science fair?"

"Uh . . ."

"The one who said science is his life?"

"Oh yeah."

"He was there tonight."

"Oh hey, doesn't he have brown hair?" Jackie's face broke into a wide smile. "You like him. Did he ask you out?"

"No. I mean, yes. But he also asked me to marry him." Aurelia stuffed a carrot stick in her mouth and crunched down on it.

Jackie looked confused. She seemed to debate with herself about how to reply. "Well, good for you," she finally said and headed for the back hall.

"No, wait." Aurelia spoke through her mouthful. "Jackie, he was outside our apartment a few hours ago. He knocked on the door and proposed to me."

"Proposed?"

"With a ring and everything." She chewed, trying to free up her mouth for speaking.

"Don't eat when you're stressed," Jackie snapped, her voice sharp with sudden worry. "It's a bad habit. Do you know this guy?"

"No, I've never spoken to him. But he called me by my name. My *full* name."

Jackie wrinkled her nose in concern. "That's weird."

"It's not just weird, it's—and then he shows up at the talent show."

"Did he say anything strange over there?"

"Well, yeah." Aurelia leaned against the counter. "He acted like we hadn't met, and he even asked what my name was."

"Okay, describe the proposal scene again."

"He called me by name and asked me to marry him." The memory made her sweat. "He knelt and held out a ring. When I tried to shut the door on him, he broke into our apartment."

"He came inside?" Jackie shrilled. "How did you get away?"

"I kept him talking, and—after a bit, he left."

"He's psycho." Jackie wiped her forehead, and Aurelia nodded fervently. "But he didn't do anything this evening that caught people's attention, did he?"

"No, he acted kind of normal. Although he wasn't good at taking the hint that I didn't want to talk to him." Aurelia breathed out hard. "Jackie, I don't want a stalker."

"Did you call the police?"

"Not yet. I didn't want Shannon to know about him. Can you imagine how she'd react?"

There's a stalker guy proposing to girls he doesn't even know? That's it. I'm happy with my high school degree. I'll go home and flip burgers.

Aurelia could totally see her edgy roommate doing it. "If we lose her in less than twenty-four hours, *I'll* consider leaving."

"Aurelia." Jackie stared at the carrots and slowly reached for one, then put it in her mouth.

"What?"

"Do you think it could have been a hidden camera prank?"

Aurelia shook her head. "I thought so at first, but he would have told me at the end, right? He would have had to, and he should never have forced his way inside. That part is too creepy to be legal."

"So, 911?"

Aurelia bit her lip. She wasn't so sure she was up to talking to the police tonight. "Maybe I can go to campus tomorrow and report him. I don't know that it's an emergency."

"Unless we all get murdered in our beds tonight."

"Unless that happens, yes."

"Or unless you get dragged from your bed by a brown-haired maniac with a ring."

"Then you'd better defend me," Aurelia said.

"Honey, I ain't defending no one," was Jackie's swift response. "We can put furniture against the door and windows, but once I'm asleep, I'm not waking up for—"

Her words cut off as Shannon entered, and the three of them eyed each other in silence.

Shannon was the first to speak. "Um. Good job on your song, Aurelia."

"Oh. Thanks."

"Good night." Shannon edged around them and went to her room.

Aurelia and Jackie looked at each other, wordlessly continuing their conversation.

Aurelia shrugged.

Jackie rolled her eyes.

Aurelia sighed.

Jackie put her hands on her hips. "Well, this is a *ridiculative* situation. That's all *I* have to say."

Chapter Three

IN THE END, both Aurelia and Jackie went to bed without moving any furniture.

"Don't let in any strangers today," was Jackie's parting words the next morning.

Aurelia yawned over her cereal, regretting her sleepless night and wishing she had gotten an earlier start. She could have gone with Jackie to campus to report her stalker. Instead, she watched the door until a click on the other side announced that Jackie had locked it.

After breakfast, she turned on her laptop. She definitely wasn't going anywhere alone.

Shannon entered the living room with her backpack slung across one shoulder. She waved and headed the same way Jackie had gone.

"Bye," Aurelia called and frowned at a sentence in the article she was editing. She considered several rewordings while voices sounded at the door.

"Aurelia?" Shannon called back to her. "Someone wants to talk to you."

Aurelia mechanically moved her laptop to the table, still thinking through the sentence. Then her eyes widened as Shannon's words sank in together with the memory of yesterday's visitor.

"Wait!" She sprang to her feet and rushed to the entrance, not wanting Shannon to be gone by the time she got there in case it was . . .

Walter. There he stood, three feet from the door and looking just as intent as yesterday.

"You *have* to say yes to the date," he said, stepping forward while Shannon disappeared out of sight. "You did the first time. We can't change that."

"No!" Aurelia backed up, which unfortunately put her out of reach of the wide-open door so she couldn't shut it. "I thought I told you . . ." No, she hadn't, had she? "I'm telling you to stay away from my place."

"Look, I'm sorry." He pulled a hand through his hair. "I made a big mistake coming here yesterday, but if you'll get to know Walter—go on that date with him—I'll leave you alone. I promise."

She couldn't believe the gall of him. "*You're* Walter. I'm not going *anywhere* with you."

His vibrant eyes clung to hers as though he thought he could persuade her with the power of his gaze. "But the Walter you met at the science fair and at the talent show has never been to your apartment and freaked you out, and *I* only did that because I timed it wrong."

Aurelia clenched a hand at her side. "That doesn't make sense. It also doesn't make sense that you would come to my talent show and pretend we'd never met."

"That wasn't me. I mean, it *was* me, but it was the original me, the one you should be talking to, the one you should be going on a date with on Friday."

She held his gaze, edgily wondering whether he was one of those predators one should keep eye contact with or look away from. "Look. Walter," she said carefully.

He waited.

"See? Your name's Walter. The guy last night was Walter. You look exactly the same. I'm not an idiot." She already felt dumb for explaining how he was the same person, as though she had for even a moment thought he might not be. Her annoyance gave her the courage to step forward and grab hold of the door.

He took a deep breath. "The thing is—"

Aurelia slammed the door and locked it. Her heart beating fast, she stepped back, congratulating herself. He hadn't managed to wrench it open.

Now, to find her cell phone . . .

"Aurelia, I can't let it end like this." His desperate voice came through the door.

"Then let it end with a restraining order," she tossed over her shoulder, "because I'm calling the police."

"You don't understand. There are two of me right now, and I messed up things yesterday, but we have to fix it."

Where had she put that phone?

"I traveled back in time," Walter shouted through the door.

Silence overtook the apartment. Only the humming of the fridge could be heard.

Aurelia turned, slid open the long window on the left, and looked down at the guy crouching in front of her door. "What?"

He stood and came over to stand in front of the window screen. "I went back in time yesterday. I thought I had gone back one hour, but . . . I was wrong."

She moved her mouth, but nothing came out.

Walter sighed. "I'm a research assistant for a physics professor at school. Our team's trying to create something with the right composition to provide a means for time travel. You'll hear about it from me—*him*—when you start spending time with him," he corrected himself and paused as if to gauge her reaction.

Time travel? Was he serious?

"Long story short," he continued, "I ended up going back in time yesterday. I went straight to your place without realizing it was a different day. Now there are two of me, and the one who freaked you out is me, but Walter Version One, the one from the science fair and the talent show who just met you, is totally innocent of all this."

She crossed her arms. "If he's innocent, why did he just happen to show up at my ward activity and ask me out? He sounds an awful lot like you, since he's showing interest in me."

His mouth quirked. "He asked you out because he's already half in love with your looks and your singing voice. That's not so rare. It happens in Disney all the time and in real life too." He was actually amused. Oh, she wanted to wipe that annoying smile off his face.

His voice turned earnest. "But he'll get to know your personality and fall more in love. That's how it happened when I asked you out the first time, after hearing you sing in French. You said yes, and we started dating. We can't change that now."

"I think you're a very disturbed person," she said slowly.

It probably wasn't smart to tell a very disturbed person that.

"I'm not going on a date with you," she said in a firm voice.

"You don't have to." His voice was placating. "But if you'll go out with him . . . I'll have to figure something out. Make sure you cross paths again."

Oh no he wouldn't. Aurelia slid the window shut, then turned away, raising her voice. "I don't believe in time travel."

Movement outside was followed by Walter's voice coming through the door again. "How much broccoli do you have in the fridge?"

She stopped in her tracks. "Huh?"

"How much? And how much asparagus in the freezer?"

She glanced involuntarily toward said appliance. "This isn't helping," she exclaimed. Why in the world would he ask . . . But she *did* have broccoli in the fridge and asparagus in the freezer, as well as several other vegetables. A shiver worked its way through her body.

"Aurelia, I know you," Walter said through the door behind her. "I know you snack on vegetables because I've been here a lot, hanging out with you."

She hugged herself. "Nuh-uh. Knowing my dietary habits doesn't prove you know me in the future. It just shows you've been stalking me."

"You're writing a story about . . . No, wait. I don't think you got the idea for that one yet. I won't ruin it for you."

She swallowed and began to turn around. Was she supposed to believe she had told him she wrote stories?

Of course she hadn't. She would have remembered it if she had.

"You like to climb trees." This time, he sounded like he was grinning.

She tried to think of the last time she had climbed a tree. It had been at least a year. He couldn't possibly have spied on her for that long and only now emerged from stalker-hiding to face her. Could he?

She jerked the window open anew.

"Who did you talk to?" she demanded. "Who told you these things about me?"

He stood and shook his head sadly. "It hasn't happened yet. But it has to. It can't *not* happen."

She huffed. "None of this is making sense, and I need you to leave."

His expression was earnest. Either he was a great actor, or he really believed what he was telling her. "I'll leave," he said. "I'll leave you to take this in. Aurelia, you're the only one who knows there's something wrong about me being here."

"There's something *very* wrong about you being here," she interrupted.

He nodded, somber, and backed away a step. "I can't talk to the other me about it. I don't know what'll happen if I meet myself. But I can't let our love story not happen because you won't go out with him anymore. That's why I'm trying to talk to you. Please try to at least think about it. Please?" he repeated when she said nothing.

Her jaw tightened. "I'll think." If it would make him go away, she would promise just about anything.

He let out a breath. "Thank you. Goodbye." His eyes lingered on her before he turned away.

Aurelia watched from the window, waiting until he was out of sight and the sound of his steps long gone.

She resumed the search for her phone and was relieved when she found it on the floor. Picking it up, she took a deep breath. "This is it. I'm gonna do this."

She looked up contact information for the campus police and dialed their number.

* * *

IT WAS USELESS. She had reported him, for all the good it did, yet she was stuck in her apartment all day, afraid to go outside and annoyed with the whole situation. At least she got some work done, although she wasn't sure how well she did it.

"Good, you're here," she exclaimed that afternoon, grabbing Jackie's arm the moment she came home. "Will you go shopping with me?"

"Clothes? I don't have time for that."

"No, groceries."

"Oh. Sure." Jackie's tone changed completely. She dropped her backpack off at the entrance and fell into step with Aurelia, heading toward the Creamery on Ninth. "Did you report him?"

"I tried. I called the campus police, but . . . I don't know Walter's last name."

Jackie groaned. "What are they gonna do, then? Hope he comes around again so you can call for help while he's there?"

"They asked me to come in tomorrow. I think they're looking through a list of Walters who have declared some sort of science major, and then they'll match him to my description and to whatever images campus surveillance has caught. Then they'll have me come look at pictures in their office."

"Good. Lunatics like him shouldn't be allowed to run around and scare people."

"And then excuse himself with lies." Aurelia shook her head. "He says he's not the same guy who asked me out last night and that I should say yes to that guy."

"What a load of rubbish. 'Go on a date with me, 'cause I'm not me.'"

"Yeah." Aurelia rolled her eyes.

Jackie's steps began to drag. "Wait, when did he say that?"

"Um. This morning. He came back to our apartment."

"What? And you're still alive?"

"Of course I am." Aurelia hunched her shoulders, the insinuation that Walter's visit should have left her dead making her feel even more scared than she already was. "He didn't make it inside this time."

Jackie shuddered. "Good. If you hadn't already reported him, I would go to the campus police with you right now. Did he tell you he has a twin or something?"

"Huh?" Aurelia grabbed a shopping cart at the entrance.

"That's the only way he could be telling the truth. If he had an identical twin, it could have been the other one who asked you out."

Aurelia nodded and moved toward the middle aisle of the creamery. "I guess that's possible."

"Even so, that means one of the twins is crazy, showing up out of the blue with a ring."

Unfortunately, that was true.

"How about this?" Jackie began. "What if you identify him and the police find out it was a hidden camera prank or something else—something non-dangerous. They can give him the scolding he deserves and a warning not to do it again. Problem off your shoulders. We need brussels sprouts."

Even with the twin theory, there were still problems, as Jackie had pointed out. Aurelia thought it over as she lay in bed that evening. If the

Walters were two different men, one of them was crazy. Hopefully it was only one of them that was crazy.

She tried to imagine the scene from the talent show under the assumption that that Walter had never talked to her before. In this scenario, he wasn't acting crazy.

Then she remembered how her visitor this morning hadn't corrected her when she called him Walter. If they were twins, they couldn't both be named Walter.

The thought propelled her out of bed and onto the floor on her knees, where she prayed fervently that she had been the victim of hidden camera.

She vowed to haunt the internet the next day looking for videos of herself being proposed to. Either that or the police visit had to give her some peace.

Chapter Four

Officer Sanchez handed Aurelia a sheet of paper from across the otherwise empty table in the sterile room. Not even a computer graced the desk. "Can you identify your stalker?"

Jackie's chair squeaked as she leaned in to look at the page with her. Five "Walters" smiled up at them from the photo lineup, but Aurelia knew immediately that it was the one on the far right she had met.

"This one," she said, putting her finger on the photo, and Jackie agreed.

"How about here?" The officer gave her another sheet.

Again, it was easy to tell. The first guy had a facial shape similar to Walter's, but the eyes were wrong and the hair was curly. Another guy had dark brown hair but definitely wasn't him.

"The one in the middle." He looked innocent and cute. She set her shoulders against the deceitful appearance.

"This is the guy you saw in all four instances?" Sanchez wanted to know.

Aurelia nodded. "At the fair, on my doorstep, at my ward activity, and then at my place a second time." Listing off the occurrences made her feel flushed all over again. She really did have a stalker.

"And he kept showing up after you asked him to leave you be?"

She confirmed it, and the officer took back the sheets, his gaze steely. "We'll reach out and have a talk with him."

Aurelia's heart was beating fast by the time she and Jackie left the office. The police would put a stop to Walter's appearances. If they gave him a restraining order . . . Who knew this kind of thing could happen in *her* life?

Jackie pulled her into a tight hug, surprising her. "Stay safe. If I have to beat up these Walter twins, I'll do it. Keep me on speed dial."

"I will." Aurelia felt some of her worries wash away in the hug. She watched Jackie leave and then, squaring her shoulders under her backpack, she continued along the crisscrossed lawn and entered the campus library. This was where she would work today. She would be safe among other students, even if her favorite spot did tend to have few visitors.

She headed upstairs toward the third floor, where she liked to study near rows and rows of books that were too nonfiction to distract her yet gave her the homey feeling of being in a library. Turning over her visit with the police in her head, she wondered if she could pull off writing a mystery novel now that she had firsthand experience with law enforcement. Her breath caught in wonder, and her steps quickened. That would just about make it worth it, wouldn't it?

On the designated floor, she plopped into a sturdy chair at a heavy wooden table and pulled out her laptop. Her mind itched for story time, but she only gave herself a few minutes to jot down notes from the interview with the police. Then she stretched her hands, opened up an article, and winced at the first sentence.

The world was ignorant of the difference between em dashes and en dashes. Oh well. At least it gave her a job.

It took her a while before she was satisfied with the article, but finally she summed up her notes and sent them off. Massaging the back of her neck, she looked up and jerked at the sight of a familiar face fifteen feet away. A hesitant Walter bypassed the bookshelves and approached her table.

"Hi. Did I say something offensive at the talent show?"

She opened her mouth and shut it. What made him think he could keep coming up to her? At least they were in public again. If he did anything strange, the guy studying two tables away would notice.

"Because . . ." He sat down next to her, making her stiffen. "I don't want you to feel offended. If I did something wrong . . ." He trailed off.

She clenched her jaw, ready to leap from her seat if she had to. "Why did you pretend you'd never seen me before?"

He sat up in surprise. "So you *were* at the science fair. I thought I recognized you, but I didn't know if it mattered bringing it up since we hadn't talked at the fair."

Why would he bring up the science fair? She was referring to the scene on her doorstep. Had he really not been there, or was this part of an elaborate scheme to make her think he had nothing to do with it?

She stared at him, honestly trying to understand. If there was any possibility he wasn't the same person who had proposed, she wanted to know.

His eyes were wide, warm, and brown with green flecks. Aurelia had never understood how characters in books read others' emotions by looking in their eyes, but it did look like the guy was confused.

He cleared his throat. "You're still welcome to come to the concert. If you like a cappella."

"Don't try too hard," she snapped, her own irritation catching her off guard. Just as she had started to, unreasonably, think he might somehow not know about the proposal, he was asking her out again. In her mind, she heard that same voice asking her to marry him.

"I'm not dating you, and I'm not marrying you," she exclaimed.

He reeled backward, nearly sending his chair to the floor. Getting up quickly, he sent her a look. "I didn't ask . . ." He huffed, his face flushing. "Bye."

The back of his neck was bright red as he strode off and disappeared into the multimedia lab. Hopefully he would be in there a good, long time while doing homework or would at least use the stairway outside the lab when he left, rather than walk past her.

Not that she should count on either option. She started to gather her things.

"Hey."

Her laptop clattered onto the tabletop, and the warped wire of her spiral-bound notebook stabbed her in the wrist. Walter emerged from behind a bookshelf near the door through which he had just disappeared.

He dropped into the chair he had recently vacated. "That didn't go well. I told you you've got to accept his invitation. I didn't even know you would run into me—I mean, him—this soon again. It was a perfect opportunity. But now we're back to square one. You don't believe any of it yet, is that right?"

She glared. "I don't want you spying on me."

He held out his hands. "If I'm the same guy that just left, I can't have been spying just now, can I?"

"Who are you, his twin brother?"

He actually looked delighted at the idea. "I don't have a twin," he said with a smile.

She stared at his shirt. Thin yellow stripes separated the green and black stripes on his polo shirt. A moment ago, he had worn green and black . . . but no yellow.

He frowned. "Does he even know your name yet?"

"Yes, he doe—I mean, *you* do." Her mind was churning. Maybe she remembered his shirt wrong. Surely there was only one of him. "Don't you remember when I told you my name at the talent show?" she lied.

He shook his head. "I didn't go to the talent show. I was hanging around near my place when he came home, and I overheard my roommate asking about his conversation with the singing girl. His answer was grumpy. Since I knew I asked you out after your performance, it was pretty obvious you had rejected me. Him."

That was interesting. She hadn't told him her name at the show. Someone else had called it out, yet he seemed to take it at face value that she had told him.

No. She shook herself and held up her hands. "Okay, stop. Enough is enough," she declared, as much to herself as to him. There was no way she could believe the crazy things he told her. She took a deep breath. "Go away, or the police will have a real serious talk with you."

He deflated. "I'm really sorry I came on Monday, but Aurelia, I promise I'm not a bad guy. I just need things to happen the way they did the first time. We *both* need things to happen the way they did. Now I have an idea." He folded his hands on the table. "I remember that first date, a Vocal Point concert. I picked you up, but I don't have to do that this time. You could meet him there and arrange with someone—maybe with Jackie if she isn't too busy—to meet you afterward and walk you home. Meet in a public place, say goodbye in a public place. It can't hurt, right?"

She sighed and spoke with deliberation. "Walter, I said leave. When a girl says leave, you do what she says."

He blinked and paused. With a look of—regret? Sadness? No emotion whatsoever?—he stood and walked toward the stairs by the multimedia lab.

Aurelia was just starting to breathe easier when he stumbled to a stop and skittered to the right, disappearing among the bookshelves.

So that he could come back around from behind?

I don't think so. She stood and picked up her laptop.

Someone appeared from the staircase landing on the left.

She fumbled to catch her laptop but dropped it on the table again, making the guy at the other table jump. Furious, she glared at Walter, who walked by decidedly not looking at her, his expression tight and his cheeks flushed. Aurelia's eyebrows relaxed slightly from a glare to a frown as she focused on the stripes on his shirt. She had remembered right. There was no yellow.

Her heart pounded. When she could no longer hear his footsteps, she grabbed her things and hurried to the stairs for a quick look.

The stairs she had hoped Walter would use in order to avoid her were a regular construction zone, blocked by a rope and two signs.

"He probably wanted to avoid you, but he couldn't leave that way," a voice said behind her, making her spin around to face yellow-stripe Walter once more. "I saw how he didn't look at you. We have a problem if he's afraid of you."

She put her hands on her hips. "Walter, what are you doing here?"

He blew out his breath. "That's a good question. I honestly thought I'd go back to my own timeline the first time I fell asleep, but obviously that hasn't happened. I'm still here in the past. It makes me wonder if we'll all relive what's already taken place until we get to when the other me goes back in time—and then I guess the world will resume from where it left off." He reached back to rub his hair. "That means he can't deviate from the things he did the first time around. If he does things differently and doesn't end up going back in time like I did, we might be stuck with two of me."

Aurelia felt sick, like the day she had tried and regretted a ride in a theme park drop tower. Walter had walked past her less than a minute ago. Then all of a sudden he was behind her. There hadn't been time for him to retrace his steps, much less change his shirt. Nor had there been time earlier when she watched him disappear behind the bookshelves on the right and reappear from the staircase on the left.

"There may be two of you," she said, proud that no tremble came across in her voice, "but you'll have to come up with a more plausible explanation than time travel."

They had to be twins. If they were two separate people, they must be identical twins, and at least one of them—in fact, the one who currently stood beside her—was unstable.

She turned to leave. Walter reached for her hands, which made her squeak and jump back even while he quickly drew away.

"Sorry, I forgot," he said. "I'm used to us being close. But Aurelia, you've got to go on that date with him. Tell him you'll meet him there if that makes you feel safer. Just please go to the concert tomorrow."

"Why don't *you* go with him if the concert is that important to you?" she asked angrily, storming toward the same exit Wal—the other guy had gone for.

As she slowed on the stairs, he fell into step with her and grimaced. "That wouldn't be a good idea. I don't think he should be aware of me. I wish *you* weren't aware of me, but unfortunately I can't undo that."

"You can stop coming around."

"But I can't." His voice turned pleading. "Don't you see? You and I dated the first time around. We fell for each other, hard. We talked about the future, and I was sure you would say yes when I proposed. You're the love of my life, Aurelia, and even though it sounds funny for me to say it, *I'm* the love of *your* life. But now? If you refuse to go out with him because I scared you, all this'll never happen. You and I will never discover we were meant for each other. I can't give us up like that."

Aurelia shook her head as they walked side by side across campus. How could he say such things to a stranger? It was a good thing the police would be talking to him soon.

Walter continued. "Of the two of you, you're the only one I feel I can talk to since you know about me. I made a blunder, but you have to know that I—and he—am a good guy, and you and he have to get to know each other. Will you please, please promise to say yes when he asks you out again?"

The word "when" stuck in her mind. "When," or better yet, "if."

"To the concert?" she clarified.

"Yes, tomorrow's concert."

"Sure," she said, and he stumbled.

"Really?"

"Yes. If you'll leave me be now."

His face fell. "Right. Okay. But you'll say yes when he asks you."

"Yes."

He paused and smiled. "Thank you. I'll leave now. Have a good day, Aurelia."

She hid a smile as he walked away.

Not that she owed him anything, but she could easily keep her promise. Apparently, there were two Walters—two look-alikes that went by the same name. She swallowed at the thought. Well, the one that was supposed to take her on a date wouldn't ask her out again. He had been far too embarrassed and upset after she said no to the date *and* to marriage. If a Walter found her before tomorrow evening and asked her out, she would have to assume it was the one who had extracted her promise, and she would accuse him of pretending to be the other Walter. There would be no need for her to say yes.

Better yet, she would steer clear of either Walter. If she could avoid them both until tomorrow night, the concert would begin and end without her, and Walter should have nothing else to bug her about.

The thought made her breathe a sigh of relief. After tomorrow, life would get back to normal.

* * *

By the time she reached the apartment, Aurelia's plan was in place. First, she called Dr. Eunice, the professor in charge of her internship, hoping she could cancel today's meeting. It was short notice, but to her relief, Dr. Eunice allowed her the change of plans and told her she would email out another assignment.

Next, Aurelia called her friend Kylie and asked for permission to come over for a visit and stay the night.

"Oh, would you?" Kylie exclaimed, true to her usual enthusiasm. "Would you stay Friday night, too, and house-sit? I've been wanting to visit my cousin in Idaho for her birthday, but I haven't been able to find anyone to watch my dog. Will you stay two nights and watch Chicha for me? We can hang out tonight, and I'll come back on Saturday."

"Yeah, sure. That fits my plans perfectly."

"Thank you, thank you," Kylie gushed. "Come right over. I'll bake something, and we can watch a movie, and . . . just come," she finished with a laugh.

Aurelia packed a bag, sent a text to Jackie, and fled to the south part of town with a feeling of triumph. If Walter couldn't find her, she would be safe through tomorrow's concert.

On the doorstep of her friend's inviting white brick home, she took a bracing breath before ringing the doorbell.

The door banged open, and a five-foot-tall woman with flaming curls flung herself at Aurelia.

"I haven't seen you in *months*," Kylie squealed, squeezing tight.

Aurelia staggered backward. "It's good to see you too," she managed to say over the top of her friend's head, the deep breath she had taken before announcing her arrival saving her. It was hard to believe her friend was a working woman with a company job and a mortgage. Surely Kylie held back some of her natural zeal at work, though it was hard to imagine.

Kylie released her, only to grab her arm. "My dessert book is open and ready. Come pick something for us to make."

Aurelia hadn't realized how much she needed her friend until that moment. Friendship, dessert, and a safe place—what could be better?

They chatted their heads off as they whipped up a batter, took Kylie's chihuahua for a walk, and ate a spicy dinner. Aurelia felt like she was in a different world.

"Do you remember how George would impersonate Star Wars characters?" Kylie asked, her cheeks red from laughing while she tried to eat her slice of cake that evening.

"C-3PO was the best," Aurelia giggled, although she had mixed feelings about her memories of George. He used to hang out with her and Kylie and their other roommates back when they lived in the Arcadia apartment complex. Eventually he gravitated toward Aurelia and took her on dates, but she always felt like she had been a comfortable choice. It never felt like he saw her as more than a buddy.

"The way he would gaze at you like a lovesick puppy was adorable," Kylie said. "He would have married you on the spot if you'd dropped Italian and learned to sing something in Ewokese."

Aurelia rolled her eyes. "There wouldn't have been time. I was busy learning the meaning of all the words in 'The Prayer.'"

Kylie grinned. "And then in the next Italian song you came across."

Aurelia chuckled. "And the next after that."

"George didn't have operatic taste, huh?"

"Nah. The lovesick gazes were a joke anyway. He liked hanging out with all of us, and he enjoyed our dates, but he was never into me." That seemed to be the pattern of her dating life. Either there was little interest, or the interest started out strong but waned on his side or hers after a few dates.

"Are you sure? Well, at least he asked you out." Kylie waved her fork and nearly knocked over her cup with her enthusiasm. "That counts for something, right?"

Aurelia savored a bite of chocolate cake. "It does." It *was* great when a guy had the courage to approach a girl. Just so long as the first question out of his mouth wasn't whether she would marry him.

* * *

THE NEXT MORNING, Kylie left for Idaho, blowing kisses from her car. Aurelia took Chicha for a good, long walk and came back refreshed, ready to face the day. Over breakfast, she texted Jackie to find out how things were at home.

Jackie sent her a pouty face and a Marco Polo of her cry-singing "All by Myself." Apparently, all was well.

Without Kylie around, thoughts of Walter were quick to return. Work held Aurelia's attention captive for a while, but as the afternoon wore on, her eyes kept straying to the clock. The start time for the Vocal Point concert drew nearer.

She checked on Chicha's food bowl, ate her own dinner, checked her watch, picked up a book, and had just decided to go for a walk with the suddenly antsy dog when her phone rang.

She picked up. "Hello?"

"Miss Jackson, this is BYU Campus Police."

"Hi." She looked down at Chicha as he ran circles around her, whining.

"We had a talk with the Walter you pointed out, but he was in class Monday afternoon at the time you specified. We confirmed with his teacher and several students that he attended class that day. I'm sorry, but it was someone else who came to your apartment."

"Oh." Aurelia rubbed her face and took a step toward the couch, only to nearly step on Chicha, who let out a squeak. "Sorry, Chicha."

"What?" The policeman on the other end sounded confused.

"Oh nothing. Just the dog." Her apology appeared to have no effect on the chihuahua, who barked and raced to the glass door and back again.

"Right. Well, we take cases of harassment very seriously. If he comes near your home again, don't hesitate to call us. Call while he's there if possible."

Chicha's barks continued, punctuated by whines.

"Okay. Thanks for talking to him."

His "Of course" was almost drowned out by the chihuahua. Aurelia hung up and headed toward the backyard but was again stymied by the dog.

"Easy, Chicha. I can't let you out if you trip me up." She frowned at the thought of the two Walters. The police had talked to the wrong one. Of course they had. The crazy one wouldn't attend the other guy's classes or be at his apartment, now would he?

Frustration gripped her, but when she glanced at her watch, a wave of satisfaction relaxed her shoulders. The concert was about to begin, and she wasn't there. At least one thing was going right today.

She made it to the glass door, and Chicha scratched at it urgently. When Aurelia slid it open, he sped outside like a bullet.

Strange dog.

She stayed in the doorway where the air conditioning reached her. A neighbor in the opposite yard waved at her, and she returned the gesture. Chicha turned around in the grass and barked at her, sounding crazed.

Aurelia smiled. "What, no 'thank you' for letting you out?"

Yip, yip, yip.

"You want me to join you?" She shook her head and stepped farther back into the cool living room. "I'd rather—"

Pressure exploded in her ears, in her stomach, everywhere. She had a sensation of falling forward, but she got stuck mid-fall, leaning against nothing while nothing seemed to lean back against her.

A painful pressure in her arms and her head took over, and she gasped. The world turned black and immaterial.

Chapter Five

HEAD THROBBED. Stomach queasy. Bed soft beneath her.

Aurelia opened her eyes to a cautious squint. A white room surrounded her, and a nurse with a cleft chin and elegant cheekbones appeared in her line of sight.

"Hello. How do you feel?" The woman looked like the picture of the Italian actress Sophia Loren that once adorned the wall of Aurelia's grandparents' home. Turn her black and white, and Aurelia would worry that *she* had gone back in time.

"Um. My arms are itchy," she answered and looked down at the culprits as they became itchy to the point of pain. They were bandaged.

"Yes, they're lightly burned. Some of your hair was singed off."

"From what?"

Nurse Cleft Chin gave her a gentle smile. "I think the police will talk with you about it after the doctor checks you out. Your emergency contact has been notified as well. We'll give you time to talk to your family in a bit."

Aurelia lay still, feeling the sore spots from her fall while the nurse checked her vital signs. The doctor arrived, and following her examination, a police officer joined them.

"Miss Jackson, please tell me in your own words what happened," Officer Hayward said after a short introduction.

She did her best, although she hoped to get answers from the officer and not the other way around.

"Did you have any warning? Did you notice any strange smells or noises?"

She thought about it. "No." Then she caught her breath. "Kylie's dog! Is Chicha all right?"

"Mr. Kohler's watching the dog."

"Mr. Kohler?"

"One of the neighbors. When he saw you fall, he rushed over to check on you, and he called emergency services."

It must have been the neighbor she was waving to just before the explosion. Thank goodness he saw it happen.

"What about the explosion itself?" Hayward continued his interrogation. "Did it make any noise?"

"No, it just . . . happened. How damaged is the house?" she asked and braced herself.

The man blew out his breath. "There's no damage. A couple of things fell over on the shelves near the door, but nothing's broken. Our forensics team is studying the chemicals from a thin layer of dust near the glass door. The dust would suggest a bomb of sorts, but there's little else to indicate that possibility. We haven't yet ruled out a gas explosion."

A bomb? Aurelia felt queasy as her phone went off on the bedside table. She craned her neck to see an incoming Skype call from President Jackson.

The officer finished his interrogation while Aurelia's phone continued to go off.

"Let us know if you think of anything else," he finally said. "We'll be in touch."

"Okay." Her head was beginning to hurt again, but she answered her dad's third call as Officer Hayward left the room. "Hey, Dad."

"Honey, what happened?"

It was a group call. Dad was in his car with his phone, and Mom and Rachel and Rowan joined from the mission office. Rachel was crying, and Rowan's eyes were large and round.

"You guys, I'm okay," Aurelia said quickly. "Rachel, don't worry."

"Your head is bandaged," she wailed.

"Oh. Well. It got a bump, but it doesn't hurt much." An uncomfortable heat grew in her stomach, reminding her of when she first passed out, when it felt like her insides were on fire. But the moment passed. She gave the nurse a sideways glance. The woman hadn't noticed anything.

"Tell us everything," Mom ordered, looking ready to take on anyone who might have had a finger in Aurelia's near demise. "Your dad and I haven't stopped praying since the hospital called."

Aurelia appreciated that. She could use extra prayers after the crazy week she had had.

* * *

BY THE TIME the hospital processed the results of her tests and declared her healthy, Aurelia's body had stopped throbbing. She had slept in between exams, and now the sun shone through her window, announcing a new day.

"You're free to go," the discharge nurse said and lowered his clipboard. "Everything appears to be fine, but call us if you have any worries."

"Thanks," Aurelia said while Jackie picked up her purse for her. Jackie had arrived a few minutes ago and seemed surprisingly calm and collected.

Aurelia's legs were stiff for the first few steps, but she soon stopped thinking about them as she walked through the spacious halls that smelled like antiseptics and overall cleanliness. What had exploded last night, and why? It couldn't be related to the other strange events of her week, could it?

When she stepped outside, Jackie led the way to her car and opened the passenger door. "Here. Make sure you're comfortable."

Aurelia got in and buckled up, appreciating the soft seat.

Jackie came around and took the driver's seat. She started the car, pulled out of the parking lot—and broke down at last, crying up a storm as she drove.

There was the Jackie she knew, warm and caring and a little scary. "I'm okay, Jackie," Aurelia tried to reassure her while the scenery outside flashed by.

"No, you're not," Jackie sobbed, stopping at a red light Aurelia had been sure she was about to blow through. The light turned green, and Jackie took off again, making a jerky right turn on the next corner. "Stop trying to comfort me. Who plants bombs in people's houses, anyway? Maniacs."

"They're not so sure it's a bomb at all," Aurelia reminded her, but she couldn't tell if Jackie heard her.

She breathed a sigh of relief when they parked. Hobbling from the car on her stiff legs, she held her breath when Jackie put a hand on her arm to assist her.

"I called our ministering brothers, so they'll be by soon to give you a blessing." Jackie wiped her nose and stomped her way up the stairs, her pace a little more violent than Aurelia might have wished until they entered the apartment. "Well, one of them will. The other's out of town. I should have thought about that last night. Then we'll Skype with your parents, or if you're too tired, *I'll* Skype and make sure they get an update. Do you want to lie down on the couch or go to bed? It'll have to be the couch. We can't let the ministering brothers in your room. Shannon hasn't responded, but I'm sure she's gotten my text about you. She's at a friend's place."

"I don't need to lie down," Aurelia tried to tell her. "I slept most of last night." Even so, an ache in her stomach made her sit on the velvet couch.

Jackie went to the kitchen. "I'm in touch with Kylie too, so don't worry about texting or calling her. You need to rest." She came over with a bag of green beans and plopped it on the sofa table. "Here." Before Aurelia could make a move, Jackie snatched it back up. "No! No stress eating," she ordered, ripping the bag open and cramming three beans into her own mouth. "I'll return this to the fridge."

"I don't feel like eating anyway," Aurelia mumbled.

"What?" Jackie's eyes widened. "Are you sure?"

Aurelia lay down and fell asleep.

* * *

BY NOON, though, she had had enough of sleep. Her stomach stopped hurting while she received a series of visitors from the ward, and the pain in her arms faded to an itch and stayed there.

"Try moving your tower," Jackie suggested after the latest visit while she eyed the black-and-white chessboard.

Aurelia pursed her lips. "Should I trust you to help me or expect you to sabotage my chances?"

"I just want you to make a move. I don't have the patience for chess. Okay, how has Shannon not checked her phone by now? Doesn't she care that you got hurt?"

It *did* appear like Shannon couldn't be bothered to so much as send an "Oh no" text, but Aurelia tried to shrug it off. "With you here to care for me, she doesn't need to. Oh, what I wouldn't do for some sprouts right now."

Jackie looked torn. "Mine are gone. I'll have to buy some, but I can't leave you alone."

"We'll probably have another visitor soon, and then I won't be alone. I never knew we had such a nice ward."

"The news spread like wildfire." Jackie's tone was dry. "I'm not sure if it's because people are helpful or because they think it's cool what happened. *Curiositivity* killed the cat and all that."

Aurelia winced at the rogue noun. "I don't even know what *did* happen." She wanted to take the bandages off her itchy arms. At this point, she merely looked sunburned beneath the bandages, and it hadn't hurt much while she ate her soup an hour ago, although Jackie had been ready to hold the bowl and spoon-feed her. "So far as I know there wasn't a bomb involved. But obviously *something* exploded. It's so weird." She sighed. "You can't blame the ward for being curious, but they're genuinely concerned too."

"You're right. I can't believe your family can't do more than Skype you though. It's awful to have this happen while they're away on a mission."

"It's not like I'm badly hurt. I took a nap I wouldn't normally need, and now I'm sitting on the couch with a sore head and itchy arms, that's all."

There was a knock on the door. "Stay," Jackie said, pointing a severe finger at Aurelia before striding to the door and pulling it open.

A shock went through Aurelia when a brown-haired young man rushed inside.

"Aurelia, are you all right?"

* * *

SHE HAD GONE to Kylie's to avoid him. She had reported him to the police. She had lain awake in bed worrying about when he would show up next.

Before she could speak, Walter was at her side, enveloping her hands in his warm, firm ones and kneeling in front of the couch. "I can't believe this happened," he exclaimed. "I didn't even think about—I am so, so sorry. How do you feel?" he asked in deep concern, the green flecks in his eyes holding her own eyes captive.

"Uh," was all she could think to say. His actions and concern seemed so natural that in that moment, she couldn't think whether she ought to shake her hands free or just go with it.

"Is this Walter?" Jackie came up behind him.

Aurelia nodded and feared her confirmation would cause Jackie to make a quick decision for her and throw him out the door. Jackie stepped into Walter's line of sight and crossed her arms menacingly.

Walter stood. "Can I get you something? What would you like? Maybe cabbage? Shredded?"

Jackie's mouth fell open.

"No, I, uh, actually wanted sprouts," Aurelia said lamely. She had to give him credit though. Cabbage suddenly sounded good.

"*I* was going to buy that for her," Jackie said with a glare, as if the very idea of someone else taking over the task was offensive.

"I can get it," Walter insisted and asked Aurelia, "Where did it happen? Where were you when the explosion took place?"

"At—a friend's house."

"Which friend? Kylie?" His voice cracked.

She blinked. "Yes?" Her answer came out like a question. "How would you know that?"

He rubbed a hand over his face. "I'm an idiot. I knew there was an explosion at her place that night. You and I went to the concert. The next day, you learned your friend Kylie had been in the hospital because of some strange explosion at her home. We went and visited her together that day."

He must be talking about what "should" have happened before he traveled back in time and changed things.

"*Really,*" Aurelia drawled, skeptical. "We hung out two days in a row?"

"Yeah, you agreed to lunch the following day because the concert hadn't given us much of a chance to get to know each other. Then you found out about Kylie, and we went there instead. Where *is* Kylie? Is she in the hospital?"

"No, she was in Idaho when it happened," Aurelia answered. Kylie had hurried back to Utah that morning, bringing with her a flood of tears over what had happened in her house, of all places. It took some doing to comfort her and assuage her misplaced guilt, but eventually, Kylie had to return to her home to check out the damage, or lack thereof, and to talk to the police.

Aurelia thought about how Kylie would have been home and might have gotten hurt if Aurelia hadn't pet-sat for her. Technically, Walter's story checked out—but he was a stalker and a Walter look-alike, not a time traveler. Time travel was science fiction.

"I should have—" Walter cut himself off. "I promised to stay away when you said you'd agree to the concert, and he was supposed to have come across you again and asked you—I didn't realize you'd get hurt. Still, I should have remembered Kylie and gotten her away from her place that night. That would have been smart."

He finished that last sentence with a growl of annoyance. Pressing his lips together, he glanced at the door. "I better go." He edged away. "I told James to come get me at my place and take me to see you, so they'll be here soon. Get well. And it's good to see—*meet* you, Jackie." He gave both girls a wave, and then he left.

Jackie gaped after him. "What . . . was that?"

Aurelia bit the inside of her cheek. "That was someone who thinks there are two of him."

"That makes zero sense."

"I agree."

After a minute, Jackie shook her head. "The boring chess game awaits."

"You know, we *could* play something else."

"I don't want you to exert yourself."

"UNO would be exerting myself?"

"Yes. Now, stay seated like a good girl, and—"

Another knock on the door cut her off. Aurelia stood, rebellious and tired of being babied. Still, she was too slow for Jackie, who sprinted for the door to save her injured friend the trip.

"He-llo." Jackie stumbled over the word. She almost sounded angry.

"Hi, we came to check on Aurelia. Tim told me what happened." James caught sight of Aurelia as she appeared in the doorway. "Are you okay?"

Next to him, Walter stood with his shoulders hunched, his gaze flickering about as though he were embarrassed. He wore a purple-and-white polo shirt instead of the green shirt Aurelia had seen just minutes ago, and his chin was rough and unshaved, which gave her pause. Besides his appearances in the library, this was the best proof she had so far that there were two of him. That was, two people who looked the same. She stared in awe.

Jackie, who hadn't scrutinized Walter like Aurelia had the last few days, didn't appear to notice the changes. "Aurelia, you need to sit down," she ordered, putting a hand on her shoulder.

Ugh. She had spent enough time on that couch already. "Standing is good for me," she quickly improvised. "It helps with my oxygen flow."

Jackie gave her a suspicious look but turned her attention to the visitors.

"What happened?" James asked.

Aurelia forced herself to give him a recap while Walter's gaze took in the bandages on her arms. He caught a glare from Jackie and looked away with a start.

James let out a breath. "That's crazy. I'm sorry that happened." He turned to his friend and waited, but Walter's eyes were focused somewhere near Aurelia's feet. James prodded in a hiss, "You wanted to talk to her."

Walter looked up at his friend with a puzzled frown. Then he looked toward Aurelia, though he didn't quite meet her eyes. "I'm sorry too."

It came to her that this Walter, possibly ignorant of his look-alike's actions, had been rejected at the talent show, rejected in the library with a line about marriage, and had then been picked up by the police and accused of stalking her. That would be enough to make any innocent person nervous.

"Um," Walter continued when no one spoke. "You said it wasn't a bomb?"

"Yeah. Or it was an incomplete one. It 'lacked some of the critical components' of a bomb," she said, quoting the latest update from the police.

"What did it feel like when it exploded?" he asked, a line between his eyebrows.

Aurelia opened her mouth and then stopped to ponder. Suddenly, she didn't want to describe it in the terms she had given the police. The lack of warning or the direction she fell were not as interesting as what it really felt like. A flutter of excitement took hold as she imagined how she would describe it if she were to put it in a book. "It—it was like I got stuck as I fell. Something pushed back at me, and I leaned against it."

Ugh, rough draft. She was spouting this off in rough draft form, out loud.

New words, better ones, formed in her mind, and her excitement grew, along with a familiar warmth and love of words. "It was a war of gravity. I never heard the noise of an explosion. The world had gone silent, and I couldn't breathe, but I didn't feel the lack."

Both visitors gazed at her, James in confusion, and Walter in concentration.

War of gravity. Aurelia savored the words. She needed to get a pencil *now* and describe what it was like to be caught in an explosion. "I've gotta go."

James blinked and took a step back. "*You've* gotta go? Do you mean, uh, that *we* should get going?"

Walter whispered to him, "Maybe she needs to, you know—*go.*"

As in, go to the restroom? Aurelia almost laughed out loud. "No, I just remembered something I need to do. Thanks for visiting."

"No problem. And seriously, if I can help with anything, let me know," James told her.

"Bye," Walter mumbled, moving backward and accidentally catching Jackie's gaze. He gave a little jump because her glare was still going.

Poor guy, Aurelia thought as her roommate shut the door on him. All the same, she happily seized the moment to hurry to her room to write.

Within a minute, Jackie entered and leaned against the desk. When Aurelia didn't acknowledge her, Jackie cleared her throat.

"For what it's worth, if Walter is two different guys, or two different versions or whatever, I like the first one best."

Aurelia's eraser stopped. "The first to visit today? Are you kidding me? He's the one that proposed."

"I know, but you have to admit, his confidence is hot. He wasn't even touched by my death glares. The second guy was timid."

"Because I rejected him. For . . . apparently no reason, from his point of view." Was he aware of his doppelganger?

"I'm just saying." Jackie grinned and put her hands in her jeans pockets. "If you'd met him, this first guy, normally, and if you two were dating, it seemed perfectly natural—and hot—the way he ran to your side and got down and held your hands."

Aurelia's cheeks heated. "That's not natural at all. I don't hold hands with guys until I've dated them for a while."

"How can you be a writer and not be a romantic?" Jackie asked incredulously. "Holding hands, kissing—those are *importatious* things. You've gotta do some of them."

"No, I really don't." Aurelia wrote the word "important" at the top of her page, correcting Jackie's word in writing.

"You should." Jackie leaned over and spoke in her ear. "For research. How does it feel to kiss a guy? You've gotta do it so you can show in your books how it feels."

Huffing, Aurelia pushed her away. Sure, she had never gotten much farther in a relationship than she did with George, but she also hadn't had strong feelings for any of those guys. She certainly wouldn't kiss someone she didn't care for.

Jackie laughed until a knock on the door made her roll her eyes. She went to open up for the bazillionth time, and with a long-suffering sigh, Aurelia laid down her pencil and returned to the living room.

"I'm back." Walter entered with a grocery bag in his hand.

Jackie followed behind, helplessly trying to strike him down with her eyes. He didn't take notice.

"Did he visit? Me and James?" Walter asked.

Aurelia rolled her eyes in exasperation and plopped down on the couch. "Yeah, he did."

"Did anything happen?" He sounded eager.

"They said hi and left," she said, choosing to go with the shortest version she could think of.

"Oh." His shoulders fell. "Well, here are your sprouts." He placed them on the dining table. "And here." He pulled out a colorful box of triangular ice pops. "I bought you ice pops, Jackie."

"*What?*"

Aurelia winced. That wasn't the sound of gratitude, and Walter could tell. He turned to Jackie, whose face had gone pale.

"How do you know this about me?" She raised a shaking finger and pointed at the man who held a box of her favorite treats. "How do you know Aurelia eats all those vegetables? What makes you think you can walk in here and do whatever, whenever?"

He looked like a deer caught in the headlights. "Sorry. I just thought that this is a hard day for you, too, and it might be nice for both of you to get something. I didn't mean to . . ." His voice trailed off at the sound of running steps outside.

Shannon burst in and skidded to a halt. "What happened? Jackie left a message saying something about an explosion. What was it, a bomb? *Where* was this?"

"On the other side of town," Aurelia answered. She felt ready to forgive Shannon her earlier lack of concern now that she could see how shaken the girl was.

"Here in Provo." Shannon sounded disgusted. "Right here in little happy-bubble Provo, we have a bomb go off. What's so safe about Provo?" Her voice rose into the higher octaves of hysteria. "A bomb! In Utah! I'm going home. There are other places I can go to school."

She strode past the others and slammed her bedroom door behind her.

A confounded Jackie turned to Aurelia. "What's she doing?"

"Packing." It was Walter who answered.

"Does she even care that you got hurt?" Jackie whispered to Aurelia, the shock in her voice turning to anger.

No one answered. Noises from the Cursed Room confirmed that their newest roommate was, indeed, packing.

Walter sighed. "She left last time too."

Jackie jerked her head to look at him. "What?"

"When Kylie got hurt in the explosion. Never mind that she doesn't know Kylie. When she heard about it from Aurelia, she freaked out and left town." He looked gloomy. "You won't like the next one."

"The next what?" Jackie asked nervously.

"The next roommate." He shuddered. "Neither will I."

Aurelia watched him. "How long will she be here?" she asked, not sure if she wanted reassurance of a short period of misery or if she wanted to test him and see how his "prediction" worked out.

He shrugged. "It's never very long, is it?"

Aurelia pursed her lips. "If we won't like her, I hope it won't be long."

Walter blinked—and then he blinked some more. His mouth spread in a wicked grin that made Aurelia blush without knowing why. She could swear his eyes twinkled as he replied, "I hope so too."

With a last look in the direction of Shannon's room, he bid the girls goodbye. Then he left.

"What was that about?" Jackie asked, frowning at the door.

"I don't know." Aurelia shifted on the couch. "He's psycho."

"True." Jackie let it go with a shrug and held up the bag Walter had brought. "Sprouts?"

Chapter Six

Sunday dawned clear and bright. Aurelia gingerly moved around getting breakfast. Jackie was in the bathroom, and Shannon was already a memory, fully moved out, leaving the Cursed Room empty as ever.

Rather than call attention to her freshly bandaged arms, Aurelia went to church in a long-sleeved dress, which she hoped wouldn't kill her when she walked home in the heat afterward. She was already tired of feeling like everyone's invalid. Today she would feel beautiful in her turquoise dress.

Upon entering her ward's assigned room in the Wilkinson Center, Aurelia found herself swarmed by people who wanted to know how she was since the explosion. When she and Jackie sat down, the seat on her left didn't remain empty for long.

"How are you feeling?" Walter's familiar voice asked as he plopped down.

Aurelia glared at him. He wasn't supposed to be here. "I don't approve of ward hopping."

His lips tugged into a smile. "I know. I'm not ward hopping though. I'm actually in my own ward right now, but I can't very well have both of me there, and I don't want to miss out on church just because the other me is there."

Aurelia frowned. Walter leaned forward and winked at Jackie.

Winked!

Jackie looked at Aurelia and winked at *her*, wriggling her eyebrows.

Aurelia felt her cheeks go red as she remembered how Jackie had approved of this particular Walter yesterday.

"How were the ice pops?" Walter asked.

Jackie sat up ramrod straight, all winking activity forgotten. "I haven't eaten all of them yet," she said, the picture of dignity.

Aurelia choked on a laugh just as the bishop's counselor spoke into the microphone to start the meeting. Walter looked pleased that his present had been accepted.

Sitting next to Walter during that first meeting was unnerving. Aurelia's circulation worked overtime, keeping her very, very awake. She made up her mind to tell him to sit with someone else during Sunday School but was surprised when he got up and wandered over to join James of his own accord.

During the lesson, she stole more glances at him than she cared to admit, but she scowled every time she caught him stealing a glance at her. He wasn't shy about adding his own comments to the lesson. She thought it terribly unfair how much she liked the thoughts he shared.

When the class ended, Walter made his way toward her.

She grabbed Jackie. "Let's go."

"Aurelia," Walter's voice called out behind her, "is there any way I can prove—"

"No." She pulled Jackie toward the doorway.

"—or convince you to—"

"No."

She chanced a look back just as he stopped, his expression less than happy. But something firmed in his face, and Aurelia had the feeling he wasn't giving up.

Jackie made a face at Walter just before Aurelia succeeded in pulling her around the corner.

Aurelia huffed as they walked, remembering Jackie's earlier, more enthusiastic reaction to Walter at church. "I don't get you today. Is he winkable, or is he grimaceable?"

Jackie looked at her in surprise. "You're making great progress in English. Must be my influence."

Aurelia rolled her eyes at the ceiling.

"And I honestly don't know," Jackie conceded. "I'm still trying to figure it out myself. Is he a stalker, or is he crazy?"

"Again, neither option is great." The time travel story was too ludicrous to even share with Jackie. Instead, she led the way to the main floor and stopped in front of a bulletin board covered with notices. Her eyes scanned the papers until they found the pale yellow one that had caught her attention this morning. "Jackie?"

"Huh?"

Aurelia cleared her throat. "Do you wanna go with me to a science lecture tomorrow?"

Jackie stared at her. "Since when are you interested in science?"

"This one's . . . different. It's about time travel."

Jackie raised her eyebrows and turned to peruse the poster. Aurelia could see her gears churning as she considered whether that was even scientific or not. Finally she nodded. "That should be interesting."

Aurelia let out her breath. She had been embarrassed to ask.

Jackie's phone pinged, and she dug it from her purse to check her email. Her eyebrows rose higher still. "Here we go again. We have a new roommate, and she's moving in tomorrow."

Aurelia grabbed her own phone and checked her matching email. "What makes all these people so desperate to move in the middle of the semester?" she exclaimed.

"No one knows the answer to that better than us." Jackie put her phone in her bag. "The question is, how do we make it stop?"

* * *

AURELIA TOOK off her bandages for the last time the next morning. Her head no longer hurt, and her arms had faded from red to a pink that wasn't far off from her usual color, as though the mystery explosion wasn't that big of a deal.

If only she could tame her mind the way time tamed her injuries. She struggled to focus on work that morning in the living room, and it wasn't the Walter situation or the as-yet-unsolved explosion that bothered her.

She needed a new story to absorb. Her mind cried out for a book, and she fervently wished she had thought to get something from the library the last time she went for a drive. A bowlful of snap peas didn't help her thinking. Two trips to her room for chocolate didn't help. The music she played on YouTube didn't help.

When the doorbell rang, it was a relief to set aside her laptop. She hurried to answer, ready for a break from the morning's monotony, even though she could guess who was outside before she swung the door open.

There stood Walter in all his glory, self-assured and determined, his green-flecked eyes fixed on her. Jackie called him hot, but Aurelia decided then and there to call him confident.

"How are you feeling?" Confident Walter asked.

"Dandy." She was thoroughly tired of the word "fine" after everyone and their uncle had asked her the same question for two days straight.

"Good." He held out a book. "This is for you."

She found herself taking it, surprise warring with excitement and then disappointment. "A Louis L'Amour book?" Her dad loved L'Amour's Westerns. Aurelia had tried to read one before but had gotten stuck. She would probably like it better if it was from a girl's viewpoint.

"I think you might like it. The main character's a girl."

She snapped her gaze up, but Walter was already turning away, saying, "I'll let you get back to work."

She stared at his retreating back.

He had just given her a book, assumed she would like it because the main character was female, and left without giving her a chance to reject the book. How did he know her so well?

She was halfway through the first page by the time she made it to the couch.

* * *

SEVERAL HOURS LATER, she left her mentor's office, fuming.

"This doesn't prove anything," she muttered fiercely.

Dr. Eunice had asked her to study up on cowboy literature in preparation for editing a batch of short stories set in the Wild West. Had Walter given her that book to be nice, or was he trying to prove he knew the future? But it proved no such thing. If anything, it further proved he was a stalker. Had he broken into Dr. Eunice's office or hacked her email account to find out what she was working on?

Aurelia growled and threw her hands in the air, earning the attention of a startled couple studying in the hallway.

She arrived early at the classroom for the time travel lecture, pulled out a bag of snacks, and crunched down hard on a carrot. By the time she finished it, she felt slightly calmer.

Some older men sat down on her right, discussing the lecturer's credentials among themselves. Jackie arrived and dumped her heavy backpack on the floor next to Aurelia. When a group of students walked down the aisle, Aurelia scowled at the sight of Walter among them. She had known he was likely to be here, but it was still annoying.

He and his friends were talking about something science-y.

"The negativity on its own can't do it," Walter told the others. "We can't create a zone potent enough . . ."

He broke off at the sight of Aurelia and blinked, looking from her to his guy friends and back. "Hey." He hesitated, his gaze on her face in general but not focused on her eyes. "How are you feeling?"

She shrugged. "Fabulous."

He blinked and gave her a half smile. "I'm . . . glad." He hurried to sit down with his friends.

"That was friendly," Jackie observed.

Aurelia shook her head, remembering the book currently banished to her backpack. Given to her by the *other* Walter. Infuriating though it was, she was already looking forward to the end of the lecture when she could go home and see what happened next in the story.

A teacher stepped to the podium to introduce the speaker. Jackie joined politely in the applause as Dr. Littlewater took the floor. Aurelia merely narrowed her eyes at the man.

"Let's see what you can tell me," she muttered. Not that Dr. Littlewater's insights could do anything to confirm Confident Walter's explanation. He had *not* traveled back in time.

Jackie gave her a strange look. Aurelia realized she was being the cynical one today, while her roommate was a polite attendee. That wasn't the usual way of things.

Dr. Littlewater picked up the remote control for his PowerPoint presentation and jumped right into things.

"Is time travel possible? Absolutely. We're already doing it. All of us travel forward in time, sometimes at different speeds."

Aurelia frowned. Jackie opened a heavy chemistry book across her lap.

"Airplanes traverse time zones. A passenger can arrive at San Francisco Airport an hour before his scheduled flight left Japan."

Aurelia tapped her foot.

"Time is relative. It moves faster or slower based on gravity and speed. Astronauts at the space station age slower than we do. Time passes faster on top of a mountain than at sea level. The question is not whether we can travel in time, the question is whether we can travel to the past, and that, my friends, is something we do not currently have the means to do. What we *can* do is speed up time or slow it down as . . ."

Really? Aurelia crossed her arms. Sure, she would never have believed him if he had claimed people could travel back in time. Still, what was up with drawing people to a lecture with the tantalizing title of "Time Travel Lecture," only to tell them that traveling to the past was impossible?

She sneaked a glance at Walter, who was nodding and taking notes.

". . . in the medical field, vitrification . . ." Dr. Littlewater continued.

Jackie looked up repeatedly, increasingly more intent on the lecture than on her homework.

Aurelia had to admit it was interesting. Organs were "turned off" or frozen, then turned back on in working order at the end of surgery. She wouldn't have thought of that as time travel, but the rather disturbing story of cat brains being frozen for seven years and then restored—with slower activity than before but still working—was something for the books.

Wormholes, negative energy, and electron guns sounded interesting as well, though she feared half of it went over her head. Cosmic strips completely lost her as she stared at the PowerPoint picture of fake-looking, lighted strings that were supposed to be one-dimensional.

The presentation ended with applause. As the room dissolved into movement and conversations, Aurelia and Jackie squeezed out past the men on their row.

Aurelia found herself just across the aisle from Walter. She probably should have let it go, especially since this was the Walter who appeared to respect her boundaries, but she called out, "Hey, Walter" and watched him turn and look at her in surprise.

Ignoring Jackie's gaping mouth, she approached him. "That was interesting. So there's no traveling back in time, huh?" *If you tell me there is and that you've traveled . . .*

He looked relieved at her apparent friendliness. "Not now, no, but I'm part of Dr. Jude's research team, and we're working on some of those methods Dr. Littlewater mentioned, like negative energy and an alternative to the cathode ray tube, to create a space that can transport something back in time. It'll probably be years before we'd dare try to make something alive go back in time, *if* we can get this to work for inanimate objects within the next year or two, but we're hopeful we can make some real breakthroughs with our project."

Aurelia blinked at him. His excitement was completely, innocently ignorant of her sarcasm and made her think of a puppy, besides.

"Oh," was her response.

"Yeah," he agreed. When she didn't say anything else, the light in his eyes flickered, and he looked away uncertainly. "Sometimes I go on about things others don't care about. Um. It was a cool lecture." He looked around and saw his professor wave him toward Dr. Littlewater. "I'm gonna talk to the lecturer. See you. I mean, have a good day."

"And there goes Nervous Walter," Jackie announced in a low, dramatic voice, making Aurelia jump. "Pity. I'd like to see Hot Walter talk to you again."

"Don't call him hot. Or this guy nervous. He wasn't that nervous," Aurelia defended him. "Not until the end, anyway. You didn't hear him talk about his research project, did you?"

"Nope. Did he light up when he spoke science? I forget, he's the guy who said science was his life. I agree with him there."

He *had* lit up, and Aurelia admitted to herself that it was attractive seeing him speak of something that fascinated him.

"Wait a minute." Jackie tapped a finger to her cheek. "Was that Hot Walter or Shy Walter who said that about science?"

Aurelia shook her head. "He's not shy, just . . . reticent."

Jackie stared. "Open a thesaurus and tell me 'shy' and 'reticent' aren't synonyms."

Aurelia winced. "Sure they are, but 'reticent' has a different connotation." *Time for a distraction, quick.* "What did you think of the lecture?"

Jackie, like Walter, brightened. "It was cool. Hold on, I want to talk to our speaker. Maybe I'll give Walter a few death glares while I'm up there and see if I can scare him off."

With a wink, she left before Aurelia could protest. If she had wanted to, that was.

She stepped back, narrowly avoiding one of the men who had sat by her. He and his friends passed by, their conversation even more science-y than the worst part of the lecture had been, and left the room. Behind them, Walter reached the doorway, sent a hesitant look in Aurelia's direction, and left when she gave no encouragement.

Jackie rejoined Aurelia and they started home, Jackie growing animated as she discussed the presentation before moving on to fiction.

"If time travel to the past ever became a possibility, there would be two of the same person running around at the same time," Jackie said as though the thought was exciting. "That could get messy."

"Yeah," Aurelia said gloomily.

"So would things somehow fall into place the way they did the first time, or would they change completely?"

"I don't know."

"And then you see how it happened in Harry Potter, with Hermione and the Time-Turner."

"That was something in between those two options," Aurelia said. "Things happened the same way the second time, but they wouldn't have happened that way if Harry and Hermione hadn't traveled back in time and done what they did."

"It must have happened differently the first time," Jackie reasoned, "but they only remembered how it happened the second time because the changes their doubles made overrode whatever would have happened otherwise."

"Yikes," Aurelia said softly as she imagined her mind being wiped of previous memories. The Time-Turner method did seem in line with what Walter had hinted at in the library: the past repeated itself but with changes made by the person who had traveled. Meanwhile, that time traveler relived the entire past up until the time his or her other self went back. She shook her head. "But you know what, if this were real, what was supposed to happen would happen. We know there's a God, and he would make sure of that."

"True," Jackie replied thoughtfully.

"And because God exists, I don't believe in time travel."

"Now, hold on, didn't you learn today that time travel is very scientific?" Jackie protested. "God works with the laws of science."

"Yeah, but didn't we learn that the Harry Potter kind of time travel will never be a thing?"

Jackie debated both sides of the point until they arrived home. "Anyway, thanks for inviting me. It was *educationing*." She plopped her backpack on the dining table.

Aurelia coughed. "That begs for a snarky reply."

Jackie turned to face her. "What reply would that be?" she asked sweetly.

"Oh, I wasn't planning on saying it."

"Maybe you should."

"Nope."

"Were you thinking I need more education?"

Aurelia tilted her head. "That's what *you* just said. Not me."

Jackie opened her mouth but stopped at the sound of a key inserted into the lock on the front door.

Aurelia tensed. The door opened and revealed a very pretty girl.

The girl's makeup was a bit overdone, but her long, highlighted brown hair with elegant curls at the bottom, her small figure accentuated by a fitted denim shirt and white jeans, and her tan face with purple eyeshadow above large blue eyes were stunning.

"Welcome." Aurelia had completely forgotten that the new roommate was moving in today.

"Oh, hello," Jackie greeted while the vision swept inside.

"Hi." The new roomie's voice was deep and throaty. She dropped her purse on the dining table and faced them. "I'm Meana."

"Meh-ah-na?" Jackie repeated slowly. "Wow."

Meana sniffed but looked pleased. "Yes. Help me bring in my stuff?"

She was halfway out the door before Jackie or Aurelia could say anything. They looked at each other and followed.

Outside, they found the new girl opening the trunk of a shiny yellow sports car. It was stuffed to the brim but wouldn't have been too daunting on its own. Unfortunately, there was also a pickup truck next to it. A guy jumped from the truck and began to unload it.

Aurelia took a look at it all and wished the lecture had ended an hour later.

"Here, take my suitcase." Meana shoved the large wheeled item toward her. "And you, you can take this," she told Jackie, pointing at a large box.

Aurelia headed up the stairs. Behind her, Jackie answered, "Nah, I'll take this instead." It was obvious she didn't care for the way Meana tried to boss her around.

At ten trips of luggage-carrying, Aurelia stopped counting, and Jackie stopped letting her help, worried she would have repercussions from her recent fall. Aurelia couldn't help her anxiety when Meana's coffee table was given a spot in the living room. The place was perfectly fine and well-furnished without it, and she didn't like having to rearrange the couch to leave space for storage behind it. Still, she ought to be accommodating enough to accept some changes.

Meana spoke throughout it all. "I know this isn't a great place, and it's tiny, but it'll be better for me than where I lived before. I could not *stand* my roommates anymore. Here, if we move that dresser against the corner, there should be room for mine. I really can't use just any old dresser that dozens of renters have used and dirtied."

She kept up a monologue sprinkled with ample orders while Jackie responded with a grunt here and there until everything was finally inside. Meana gave the guy with the truck a sensual hug, wrapping her arms around his neck and leaning her head against his, before letting go and waving him away with her fingers. Aurelia almost expected to hear her say "toodles."

"Well," Aurelia began, catching her breath and feeling like she needed to say something to further welcome the new roommate, "if there's any—" She intercepted a look from Jackie that was probably meant to be a warning. Or maybe it was her own regret that caused her to imagine it. It was too late to stop now though. She finished the sentence. "If there's anything we can help with, let us know." She braced herself for more requests from Meana.

"By the way, I'm Jackie." Jackie redirected the conversation and subtly scolded Meana for not having asked her roommates' names yet. "This is Aurelia."

Meana looked at Aurelia and raised an eyebrow. Silence stretched out between them.

"Lovely," Meana concluded coolly. She spun away from the two girls. "This will do *much* better than my previous place. Ta-ta."

Aurelia stared as the girl disappeared inside the Cursed Room.

Jackie grimaced. "This should be fun."

Aurelia shook her head in wonder. "She said 'ta-ta,' Jackie. If you ever hear her say 'toodles,' I need to know. This is surreal."

"*You're* surreal," Jackie countered with laughter in her voice. "I'll pay attention to her words, though I hope she doesn't utter too many in my presence. Hot Walter was right. It won't be a picnic living with her."

Chapter Seven

AURELIA HAD NEVER SPENT SO much time talking to the police before, but apparently, they still hadn't solved the mystery of the explosion. They called her in the next afternoon for another interview, but she was unable to give them any new details.

The interview made her antsy. So many things were strange in her life right now, and she needed an outlet. On her drive home, the sight of the elementary school she and Jackie had visited last week made her pause.

It was surrounded by a park with pine trees. *Climbing* trees.

She parked at home, dropped off her things, and hurried toward the school, a rare breeze blowing through her hair.

It was a perfect day to be out. The sun was milder than usual, and the sky was a deep blue. Aurelia reached the park and was quick to pick out a tree.

She grabbed the lowest branch and swung herself up. Sap stuck to the palms of her hands as she climbed. A twig caught in her hair and drizzled yellow pine cone pollen on her as she freed herself, already reaching for the next hold, her cares falling away as she moved higher and higher and got closer to the sky.

Stopping near the top, she took a deep breath of fresh air and looked out at the cottony clouds and distant blue mountains. On her far right, she could see Mount Timpanogos, with its little bit of snow that never quite melted. When she turned on her heel, she faced Y Mountain a couple of miles to the east, the mountain that carried BYU's iconic letter. She was surrounded by towering guards, and she loved it.

At last, she directed her attention to the people in the park.

The four teenagers on the tennis court took a break to drink from their water bottles. When they returned to the game, the girl in the yellow shirt looked as enthusiastic as anyone else, but what if she was hiding a world of pain under her happy exterior? No one knew what she endured at home. Tennis with her friends was her only real getaway, her . . .

Stop, Aurelia commanded herself. She had so many ideas for stories and not enough time to write them all. If she allowed herself to come up with a new one, it would have to go on the backburner as number twenty-four or something like that.

The tennis ball clanged against a racquet and bounced on the ground. Branches rustled above her, and a jogger's shoes slapped the pavement at the edge of the park, the sound muted by distance.

Aurelia's story maker was on, and she couldn't turn it off. She finally relented and gave it free rein.

The woman in the grass was timing her "nap" perfectly so that no one would suspect she had been at the crime scene in question.

The jogger was an agent who worked together with the woman hidden in the pine tree. He would pass by her tree without looking at her, but the stripes on his polo shirt were a signal to her that . . .

She nearly swallowed her tongue as the jogger approached. It was Walter. Exquisite brown hair, kind-looking, oblong face, damp polo shirt. Walter.

Now he was walking, slowing down. To her dismay, he stopped near her tree to stretch. His movements were slow and distracted. She guessed— hoped—that his gaze was unfocused, because unfortunately, the direction of his gaze was not to Aurelia's benefit.

She wanted to melt into the branches. If only she could move down to where the branches were thicker, but movement would be a big mistake when she wanted to go unnoticed.

Walter appeared to shake himself from his thoughts before he raised his head toward the sky, stretching his neck.

Then he lowered his head slightly and looked straight at her.

He stared from the ground, and she stared back.

Well, this was just wonderful. Would he walk over and call up to her? Walk away? Come and climb up to her?

That last option was unacceptable. Taking preventive action, she climbed down quickly and jumped from the last branch onto firm ground to face Walter. He was now less than ten yards away, and his grin was fading fast.

"How's your jog?" she asked loudly, not waiting for him to speak first. She was in control, not him.

"It's, uh, good." Apparently, this was Reticent Walter. His cheeks turned red as he spoke. "Sorry, I didn't know that was you. I thought it was fun someone was—You like to climb?"

"Yes, I do," she said, keeping her gaze on him. It seemed to make him uncomfortable. Conversely, looking at his deep brown eyes softened her.

He, as usual, didn't look her in the eyes exactly, although he did keep the conversation going. "What makes you like it?"

She blinked and thawed further. She knew how to describe this. "It's pure freedom. You get to stand high above the ground and look out at the world through a frame of green needles and prickly branches. You smell the sap, feel the breeze, look at the expanse of sky and the faraway mountains, and you wonder about those people on the ground who'll never know you were there." She looked at her grimy hands, then at Walter. His gaze was finally focused on her.

She continued, "Your hands get scraped up and dirty, and you get bark and needles in your hair and on your clothes, but who cares? It's good to play outside and get dirty now and then."

He bounced on his heels. "It's so much better than holing up in the house with technology, right? You really enjoy it, huh?" He sounded impressed with her speech rather than weirded out. "You described it well."

She blushed and ducked her head. "I've often described it to myself. I can't make up something that good on the spot."

He tilted his head. "You like words."

"Yes." She watched him in sudden suspicion. Would he make fun? "I guess I'm weird that way."

"Weird? You like words. I like science. It's cool," he said simply.

Of course she had to look into his warm brown eyes again just then. Maybe she hoped to see whether he was sincere, but instead of reading his mind, she got caught in his gaze. He really did have nice eyes.

"I don't know if words are more of a passion or a hobby to you, but I think it's great," Walter was saying. "For me, science is, well . . ." He faltered, and his eyes flickered about. "But, um. I should get going."

She was surprised and, strangely, disappointed. With their track record, he likely thought he had pushed his luck far enough by talking to her this long.

She shifted, breaking the spell of his eyes. "I should go too."

"It was good to talk to you." He turned away.

Just as she was thinking his departure helped proved him harmless, he turned back. "Hey, Aurelia? A mission friend of mine is hosting a karaoke night on campus tomorrow. Do you wanna come? As a friend? I know you can sing, and you'd probably enjoy it. It's at seven." He raked a hand through his hair, which he really shouldn't be doing. Did he know how much she liked that hair?

"Where is it?" she found herself asking.

His shoulders relaxed. "In the Wilkinson Center. I don't remember the room number. I could text it to you—or I can look it up right now if you have another minute," he said quickly as she frowned at the idea of giving him her phone number. "Hold on."

Aurelia stood by as he pulled out his phone.

"Here it is. Room 3023."

She typed it into her own phone, wondering at what point she had become crazy enough to accept an invitation from Walter, even if he was the sane Walter and probably—hopefully—safe. She *definitely* wasn't accepting out of an obligation to his other self, who wanted them to date. If friendship or something else were to bloom between her and this Walter, it would be on her own terms, not prodded on by Confident Walter's wishes.

She drew a deep breath. "I think I'll be there."

He looked pleased. "See you then." He turned and picked up the pace, resuming his jog.

Surely he was harmless, right?

* * *

Walking in on Meana chugging a bottle of orange juice in the kitchen reminded Aurelia she had a new roommate whose schedule she didn't yet know.

"How were your classes today?" she asked when Meana finally finished the bottle.

Meana gave her a look. She wore jeans with rhinestones and a bright white jacket, which was unbuttoned to reveal a hot pink tank top underneath. "Who even asks that? Does anyone like school? No."

Shocked, Aurelia cast about in her mind for another subject. "Do you get home this early every day?"

"It depends." Meana raised her eyebrows. "*You* should talk. *Aurelia,*" she drawled.

Aurelia blinked repeatedly while Meana headed to her room, leaving the empty bottle on the counter. The "you should talk" must have referred to how early she was home. Meana wouldn't know Aurelia didn't have classes this semester.

The way Meana had said her name, though, and the reason behind that attitude was harder to decipher.

She wished Shannon still lived here. There had been more potential for a friendship with her.

Unnerved, Aurelia grabbed an apple and bit into it. Then she grabbed her purse, deciding she might as well go shopping.

At the sound of someone out front with a key, she walked to the entrance, flipped the lock, and opened the door for Jackie.

"I have a date tomorrow night," Jackie said brightly.

"Really? Who is he?"

Jackie's eyes shone, and Aurelia started to feel better. "He studies in the Benson Building all the time. We don't have classes together, and he doesn't have chemistry classes this semester. Poor thing, right? I've noticed him before, but this is the first time he's talked to me. His name's Rodney, and he's studying astrophysics."

"Of course he is." Aurelia lowered her apple. "But Jackie . . ." She gave her friend a very serious look.

"Yes?"

"Can you associate with a guy who doesn't major in a branch of chemistry?"

"Oh, stop it." Jackie shoved her.

"Because astrophysics isn't *nearly* good enough." Aurelia tried to scoff, but her own laughter was getting in the way. "Do you like him? What are you doing for your date?" There would be no telling Jackie about tomorrow's karaoke night now. It wasn't fair to have Jackie text her during the date with Rodney, but Jackie would insist on checking up on her if she knew about Walter's invitation.

"Get this—we're going to a water balloon activity." Jackie rubbed her hands together. "It should be fun. And there'll be barbecue. I like him so far. He's interesting to talk to," she continued while she grabbed an ice pop from the freezer. "Anyway, I have to head back to campus." She paused and tilted her head at the purse hanging from her friend's shoulder. "Where are *you* off to? Sneaking out to see Walter?"

Aurelia choked on her last bite of apple. "I'm not giving up vegetables for life, am I? What kind of a question is that?"

Jackie waved her hand. "You think he's cute. I think he's hot. But mark my words, if he turns out to be an axe murderer, I won't let you marry him."

"Gee, thanks."

"You're welcome."

"I'm gonna go now," Aurelia grumbled and walked past her.

"Tell Walter hi for me," were Jackie's cheerful parting words.

* * *

"'Tell Walter hi,'" Aurelia scoffed as she wandered the aisles of Macey's. "I'm not seeing him. You'd do better to tell me to connect with our new roommate. *That's* going to be difficult." She paused in front of the pork roasts, pondering. Confident Walter had said she wouldn't like the new roommate, but Aurelia liked people. She raised her chin. She would like Meana too. One or two unpleasant encounters wouldn't deter her. She just had to find something to talk about that Meana liked, which evidently wasn't school.

She eyed the roasts. Maybe she should make dinner for her roommates. That would be a good starting point.

"Another bad spot. Imagine if someone were to go through here," grumbled a man's voice as Aurelia selected her meat.

"We can't be picky about the location. I don't see us creating a spot from scratch, and the air's strong here."

"Air's strong"? Strange wording. Aurelia looked up with interest. Three men appeared at the end of her aisle fifteen feet away and brought their cart to a halt halfway out of view.

"'Strong.' Pish. We need a more specific way to measure." The man lowered his voice. "Those kids have better instruments."

"Get one from the kids, then," the salt-and-pepper-haired man said shortly, his words barely audible. He spoke with some sort of eastern US accent—Boston, maybe.

"They'd notice and report it," said the man she couldn't see at all.

Aurelia frowned. Report it? Were they talking about stealing?

"Then we'll get by with what we have. For now." The third one circled the area and came back. "It's strongest here, all right."

Aurelia gave a start and turned away as he looked in her direction. She was hearing things out of context. Trying to ignore the strange conversation, she took a step down the aisle and fumbled to pick up her last-minute shopping list.

"Stop right there."

She jumped and looked behind her, thinking they were talking to her. None of the men paid attention to her though.

One of them held his hands in the middle of the cart. She couldn't see what he was doing, because the cart was piled with food that blocked her line of sight, and the largest of the three shoppers now stood on her side of the cart with his back turned to her, blocking even more of the scene.

"Okay, pump it again," said the larger man in a quiet voice. "Slowly."

She folded and refolded her list, trying to calm her heartbeat. Should she pay attention to what they were doing? If some children were about to be robbed—but the men had said they wouldn't do it, whatever it was.

"That's enough now."

She sneaked a look back at them. Behind the other man, the one engaged with the cart lifted his hands, and something metallic disappeared into his bag.

"Let's go pay," said the Boston guy, and the three of them walked off, their voices fading away.

Aurelia shifted her weight. Was this her semester for meeting crazy people? Her imagination must be going into overdrive. Whatever they had "pumped" and whatever they had been doing—it probably wasn't any of her business. So long as *they* didn't show up on her doorstep and spout nonsense at her.

Putting her list in her pocket, she headed for the pumpkin crate by the entrance.

* * *

When she got home, she picked up a grocery bag and hurried up the stairs, her stomach growling for dinner.

At the top, she stopped dead in her tracks. Walter was bent over in front of her apartment, the perfect icing on the cake of her ominous evening. No one but Confident Walter would lurk like this.

Aurelia spoke up loudly. "Look who's creeping outside my door."

He paled and straightened. "I wasn't. I was only leaving a note for you."

In no mood for excuses, she strode over with her keys in her hand. He backed away to make space for her and watched her in silence before he cleared his throat. "If you'll read it, I'd appreciate it. And, uh, I'll get going now. Good night." He started to leave while she pushed the door open.

She paused to consider him. "Where are you going?"

He stopped. "Home, more or less."

How cryptic. She picked up the envelope, keeping her eyes on him and listening to the sound of someone walking through the apartment. Jackie was home, then. Or Meana. Or both. Aurelia was safe.

"What is it you want?" The words fell from her mouth, surprising her as much as Walter.

The guy had proposed to her. Professed his love. Asked her to date a carbon copy of himself. He had shown up at her apartment, and now that she was here, he was . . . leaving?

"You're not going to stay and beg me to date the guy you say is you?" She raised her eyebrows at him. "Or hang around hoping I'll let you talk to me?"

He walked up to her but didn't enter. Aurelia caught her breath and leaned back against the doorframe as Walter stood close to her, half a head taller, like in a romantic scene in a movie, spoiled only by her fear that he was a psycho and by Jackie's appearance on the other side of the doorway.

"I would love to talk to you," he said earnestly, undaunted by Jackie and her crossed arms. "But—"

"Walter? Is that you?" A voice sounded from the living room.

A pained expression crossed his face.

Meana answered her own question, making her way to the doorway and gushing, "Of course it is. Aren't you a sweet boy, coming to see me at my new place."

Aurelia had to step backward into Jackie to avoid getting elbowed by Meana.

"What?" Walter asked halfheartedly. "No, no one told me you live here."

"I moved here yesterday. It's so good to see you."

"Welcome to your new place, then," he said, stepping backward as she made a grab for his arm.

Her hand sliced through empty air, but she gave him a sweet smile. "You should—"

"Aurelia and I were . . ." Walter interrupted loudly, but then he stopped and dragged a hand through his hair, looking frustrated. "I guess not yet," he murmured and looked at Aurelia.

"Let me just get my—" Meana began.

"Sorry, I have to go. Let's continue our conversation later, okay?" Walter asked Aurelia. "Good night."

He headed for the stairs with long strides, digging his hands into his hair as he went.

Meana leaned out past the doorway. "Good night, Walter," she called in a clear, beautiful voice. Aurelia's eyebrows lifted in response, but she quickly subdued them.

"What conversation?" Jackie asked Aurelia.

Meana turned to her as well, her voice going flat. "What are you to Walter?"

"Um." Aurelia stared at her, possible answers running through her mind. She was the girl he had proposed to. The girl he drove crazy. The one who had called the police on him.

Meana raised her nose in the air. "Walter and I are dating."

"You . . . are?" Aurelia looked back toward the door. *This* Walter didn't appear to have feelings for anyone except her, but she supposed the other Walter could be taking Meana on dates. Meana *had* appeared possessive.

"Yes." Meana's voice was sugary sweet. "I don't mind if he has friends like you though. It's good for him to have a few platonic friendships."

Jackie gasped, but Meana ignored her, turning on her heel and going to her room.

As soon as she was gone, Jackie rounded on Aurelia. "Why didn't you tell her Walter likes you?"

"Well—it's hard to know where I stand with him." Their relationship was far from platonic, but Reticent Walter had made an effort at friendship today. Meana's attitude did leave a sour taste in Aurelia's mouth though.

"Yeah, but that girl—ugh. What did Walter want?"

"To leave me a note." Aurelia looked down at the white envelope with her name on it.

"Really? What does it say?"

"I don't know." Aurelia walked to the couch, keeping her back turned to a curious Jackie while she ripped open the envelope and pulled out two pieces of paper. "Oh. There's one for you."

"For me?"

"Yeah." Aurelia handed it over. At least that should make it easier to read her letter in private.

She sat down and unfolded it.

Dear Aurelia,

I'm so sorry I freaked you out when I showed up on your doorstep. Please forgive me, and please give the other me a chance. I promise I'll leave you alone if you spend time with him.

She shook her head at his plea. The next time she saw him, she might just want to let him know she had begun to spend time with his "other self." Then she would see if he kept his promise.

I won't be around much at your place while the newest roomie is around. Meana and I used to live in the same apartment complex, and she always tries to get me to go out with her, and she acts like we're a couple when I've never given her reason to think we are. I've learned how to be firm with her, but the other me hasn't learned it yet, and I guess I'd better let him learn it. Not that he'll run into her much while she lives with you, unless you start inviting him over.

Oh, this is such a mess. I am so, so sorry for messing things up. Please forgive me, and try to believe my explanation, even if it is crazy.

You're wonderful!

Walter

Aurelia laid down her note. So Walter had a stalker, and it was Aurelia's new roommate? That was actually . . . kind of funny.

"The plot thickens," she muttered and looked over at the sound of Jackie's giggle.

"Look at this." Jackie shoved her note into Aurelia's line of sight.

Aurelia looked at the collection of letters, subscripts, and arrows. "Is that a chemical formula or something?"

"Yep. It's a chemistry joke."

"And it doesn't freak you out like his gift of popsicles did?"

"Of course not. Everyone knows I love chemistry. Or *should* know it."

Aurelia felt herself grin. "I don't know why, but that makes me happy."

"What did yours say?" Jackie asked nosily.

"He's begging for forgiveness."

"Ooh, Mr. Darcy style? Does he have an explanation for his strange behavior?"

"Not Mr. Darcy style, and Mr. Darcy's never been a favorite of mine anyway." Aurelia sniffed. "He's rude for most of the story, even for someone who's shy in public."

"There you go again, you hopeless nonromantic," Jackie groaned.

"Let's just hope you have a hopelessly romantic evening with your Rodney tomorrow," Aurelia said, refolding her note.

Jackie snorted and then beamed. "Not a chance. Water balloons, remember? I can't wait."

<h1 style="text-align: center; font-style: italic;">Chapter Eight</h1>

THE NEXT AFTERNOON was filled with ringing gunshots and dusty plains, courtesy of a John Wayne movie Dr. Eunice had recommended. From the couch, Aurelia intently watched the exchange between a cowboy and the boy who brought him a message. It was nice to focus on something other than the crazy conundrum that was her life these days.

The front door opened and shut, followed by springy steps that stopped near the TV.

"Cowboy movies? You're watching Westerns while I slave away at school?" Jackie asked in disbelief. She located the remote control and paused the movie. "Oooh, hot cowboy."

Aurelia stared at the frozen screen. "'You got a name, kid?' Why do they ask that? To sound cool, I guess, but really, that's not the question. Every-one's got a name."

"You and your words," Jackie said in amusement.

What if someone actually *didn't* have a name? Aurelia bit her lip, pondering.

"You got a name, kid?"

"No."

In Aurelia's mind, the cowboy's face lit up.

"All right. I'll call ya Dan."

*He had always been ready to bestow names on whoever answered in the
negative. It had just never happened before.*

No, she didn't want it to be goofy. She tried again.

"You got a name, kid?"

"No," the boy answered softly, not meeting his eyes.

She could build a story on that, all right. Now she just had to find out
why the boy didn't have a name. Already, the possibilities were filling her
mind. Had he grown up with parents who didn't care for him and who had
never called him anything? Maybe Mom had passed away, and Dad had
never been the same and had ignored his own child. Or had the boy grown
up walking the streets, taking care of himself?

"You're in an author mood," Jackie observed. "You're hard to rile up
when you're in the zone, like now."

Aurelia ran her roommate's words through her mind, making an effort
to focus on them. It took a minute before they registered. Then she had to
ask, "What exactly are you doing to rile me up?"

"For one, I stopped your movie. Don't you want to watch it anymore?"

It took her another moment to answer. "No, actually. And by the way,
I'm *not* lazing off while you're at school. This is work."

"Bingo. That was the other thing I did, or implied, to get you riled up."

Meana's bedroom door opened down the hall, and Aurelia started. She
had thought herself alone in the apartment until Jackie came home. When
in the world had Meana arrived?

The pretty brunette strode into the kitchen and put popcorn in the
microwave. As the appliance hummed, she leaned against the counter,
crossing her legs at the ankles and looking through Aurelia. Not past, but
through.

Once the pops began, Aurelia saw little point in trying to have a conversation over the noise. She looked awkwardly from Jackie to Meana, who
continued to act as though she were invisible. An excruciating minute later, the
popping noises slowed, and Meana retrieved the bag and returned to her room.

"I don't think she likes me," Aurelia whispered.

"I have a theory," Jackie announced, her voice at normal volume. "Honestly, I don't think she likes people in general, but I think she specifically
disliked you from the moment I introduced you."

"Ouch." When Jackie said nothing else, Aurelia asked, "Why?"

"I get the distinct impression she wants to be the only princess around."

"I'm confused."

Jackie tsked. "Her name. Your name." She gestured. "Both of you have fancy names. She's used to being the princess wherever she goes. I think she dislikes you purely because of your name."

Aurelia's jaw dropped. "Wow. You . . . could be right."

"If she's outright rude to you at any point, tell me. I'll beat her up for you." Jackie's expression was grim.

Aurelia winced. She wouldn't be telling her any such thing.

"Well," Jackie continued, "I've got homework to do, and then I'm off to the barbecue."

Aurelia smiled. "You mean, off to your date. Is he picking you up?"

"Yep, so get out your shotgun."

* * *

JACKIE'S DATE WAS A TALL, gangly young man with piercing eyes. The eyes reassured Aurelia this guy could be both intelligent and interesting enough to keep Jackie engaged.

After they left, Aurelia headed to the Wilkinson Center.

She arrived five minutes late to the karaoke activity. Music played as she entered, but no one was singing yet. A dozen people sat or stood around, and Walter chatted with a guy by the dessert table.

He broke off and came over to greet her. "Hi. What are you planning to sing?" he asked with a full-blown smile, his right cheek dimpling.

She liked the effect but kept that to herself and pretended surprise at the question. "Me? Sing? I just came to listen."

"I guess that's an option." He gave a half smile as though unsure whether she was teasing and whether he dared tease her back. Then he turned to his friend who had followed. "Brian, this is my friend Aurelia. Aurelia, Brian."

"Nice to meet you," she and Brian told each other.

"Over there"—Walter pointed at a guy who sat up front with a computer—"is Elder . . . I mean, Roy. We were never companions, but we were in the same district twice on the mission."

The opening strains of an Adele song played. A tall girl picked up the microphone and stepped forward.

The computer guy's voice boomed out. "This is Lena, singing 'Rolling in the Deep.'"

Someone cheered. Aurelia took a seat, and Walter sat next to her, Brian on his other side.

It helped to have Brian there. Walter really was acting like a friend. Sort of. Aurelia only felt a little nervous about sitting next to him.

She pulled out her phone and texted Kylie to let her know she had arrived and was safe. With Jackie on her date, Aurelia had roped Kylie into checking up on her at the beginning of the karaoke activity and again an hour or so into it.

Behind her, a girl whispered to her guy friend, "You be Jasmine, and I'll be Aladdin."

In a falsetto, the guy whisper-sang "A Whole New World," making the girl snicker. Aurelia's mouth twitched, and she relaxed a little in her seat.

Walter nudged Brian and whispered something, making Brian respond with a shove. The two of them teased each other until Walter ended the banter with a "Sssh" and leaned back to listen. Aurelia's lips quirked again. She was tempted to remind Walter that he had started the conversation in the first place.

A few songs in, she went and got a drink from the dessert table. No one followed her, which helped her relax further.

On her return, something made her stop behind their row of seats.

Humming. Walter was humming along to a Backstreet Boys song.

She couldn't hold back her smile. When she sat, his humming faltered, and he turned red.

Aurelia giggled and clapped a hand to her mouth. Walter cut her a sideways glance. She avoided his eyes and kept her mouth covered. He smiled. Then he started humming again.

Her mouth spread in a grin as she removed her hand. Oh, she would have to tell Jackie about this. He was seriously cute.

The song ended, and a rap began. Aurelia tapped her foot to it and looked up at the lyrics screen, her heart pulsing along with the beat and then stuttering in her chest as the lyrics sank in. Her smile froze. She looked away from the awful words on the screen, but the girl continued to sling out her rap.

Feeling almost panicked, Aurelia looked to Elder—whatever his name was—at the computer. Surely he would protest and ask the girl to pick a different song. He had to realize how inappropriate this one was.

He stared at the screen in front of him. Aurelia couldn't tell if he was embarrassed and avoiding looking at the performer, or if he didn't care.

Her pained smile melting away, she glued her gaze to the floor to keep from reading the screen. Even so, she felt miserable as the lyrics became worse, planting disgusting images in her mind.

Walter's arm nudged hers. "Are you ready to go?" he whispered.

She looked up quickly, feeling a rush of gratitude as he stood. With his head lowered, he made his way past the others in their row, and she followed him from the room.

He fell into step with her, looking as miserable as she felt. Aurelia struggled against a burning in the back of her eyes. Why had she stayed and listened? She would probably remember phrases from that horrible rap at random moments for years. Ugh. She hated how her mind did that.

Walter raised his head. "I bet there's someone playing the piano on the terrace downstairs. Do you want to go listen?"

Hope warmed her at the idea. Good music would help chase the rap from her mind, so she nodded.

He rested a hand lightly on her shoulder and led her toward the stairs. Earlier that day, she would have moved away from his touch, but at the moment, the contact was a comfort.

As they approached the terrace, she realized with a sinking heart that she hadn't heard any piano music. Sure enough, when the piano came into view, it was player-less.

She stopped and fought down a rising tide of emotions. If only she hadn't come tonight. If only *she* had been brave enough to get up and leave earlier.

Walter kept walking. He reached the piano and sat down on the bench. Opening the hymn book that stood on the rim, he positioned his hands.

A group of reverent chords filled the space between him and Aurelia. Recognizing the song "Abide with Me; 'Tis Eventide," she listened, shocked to discover that Walter, lover of all things science and sometimes stalker of Aurelia, played the piano.

He ended the song, lengthening the last note and looking at her. When she didn't speak, he turned to a different hymn.

She stepped closer to the music of "Praise to the Lord, the Almighty." It touched something inside her, releasing a tension she had been feeling in her stomach.

He took a deep breath and, to Aurelia's surprise, sang along on the next verse. His voice cracked once as though he were nervous, but his tone was spot-on.

At the end he asked, "What song would you like?"

She smiled at the kindness in his brown eyes. "Number 219."

An answering smile flitted across his face. He flipped to "Because I Have Been Given Much" and again sang along. Aurelia listened with growing contentment before joining in, her voice clear and pure, everything she wanted to feel like. Her soprano and Walter's strong but gentle tenor were beautiful together. It gave her thrills.

"Now which song?" he asked.

She smiled but shrugged. "You pick."

His gaze still on her, his fingers moved across the keys. She recognized the beginning of "A Whole New World" just as Walter said, "You be Aladdin, and I'll be Jasmine."

She laughed out loud. Aladdin's part began, but Aurelia was chuckling. Walter sang the first line and broke off, whispering urgently, "I'm singing your part right now." He sang the next few words and whispered loudly, "Come on. I'm trying to help you out."

Through laughter she sang the next bit. When it was Jasmine's turn, she closed her mouth, and to her delight, Walter continued on in a piercing falsetto.

Her phone buzzed, interrupting a great moment. She remembered that Kylie was supposed to check on her. "I have to answer this," she said.

Walter responded by playing a series of chords that made her feel like she was moving through running water. Enjoying the sensation, Aurelia closed her eyes for a moment before she checked Kylie's text.

Everything all right?

Yes. Thanks for checking. She hit send and seated herself on the edge of the piano bench. Walter scooted over to make more room.

"Requests?" he asked. "I've memorized a lot of Disney songs and popular soundtracks. You can test me. Or we can go back to the hymns."

"Do you know any Harry Potter music?"

Without skipping a beat, he began a Hogwarts piece. Aurelia put her phone under the bench. When she straightened, Walter's hands paused.

"I'm sorry about tonight," he said in a low voice.

"It wasn't your fault," she told him. He couldn't have known someone would pick a song like that. She hadn't been smart or brave enough to leave, but *he* had. He had acted, and he had left.

"Still, I'm sorry." His hands touched the keys, and the music resumed.

Between Disney songs, Harry Potter soundtrack music, and a few more hymns, Aurelia was in turn entertained and touched. Walter's presence beside her felt good and safe in spite of their history. The space between them was somehow reduced to an inch or two by the time the end of a song left her deliciously tired.

She sighed. "I should probably get going." She turned to him, and her heart lurched at his proximity. "Thanks. That was fun."

"I'm glad we were able to do that," he agreed, smiling at her.

She looked away, feeling warm. Now who was being reticent? The wall clock caught her gaze, and she sprang to her feet. "It's nine thirty!" Had they really spent two hours at the piano? She picked up her phone and straightened to find Walter frowning at the nearest exit.

"It's dark outside," he said. "Should I . . . Can I walk you home?"

She bit the inside of her cheek in indecision. "No-o, I'm good." Maybe it was ridiculous to refuse to allow him to walk her home when she had just spent hours singing with him. She was just so used to being nervous around one of him that it was hard to trust that he was safe.

"Are you sure?" His eyes stayed on her more than they usually did, though not as much as Hot Walt—no, *Confident* Walter's always did.

"Yeah, I'm fine." It would be awkward to change her mind now. She started toward the east doors but had to stop and turn. "I—appreciated you playing the piano. That really helped me. Thanks, Walter. Good night."

He smiled at her. She turned and left at a brisk pace, butterflies in her stomach and a smile on her lips.

Chapter Nine

RODNEY WAS WALKING AWAY from Elite when Aurelia arrived. She gave him a smile and a wave. Then, once he was out of sight, she booked it home to interrogate Jackie.

"How was your date?" she asked as soon as she entered.

Jackie was stepping out of her sandals. She smelled like barbecue, and her tie-dye shirt had wet splotches on it. She gave Aurelia a curious look. "Where were *you*?"

"At a karaoke night." Aurelia felt a sudden twinge of sadness. Already, her evening was becoming a treasured memory—and one she likely wouldn't repeat. She might never get to sing with Walter at the piano again. And after tonight, she wanted to.

She shrugged back her melancholy to focus on Jackie. "How was Rodney?"

Jackie's smile was immediate. "Great."

Aurelia huffed at the lack of details. "And?"

"Get this. He's going to India next year to help build a playground that'll generate electricity for the community."

"Whoa."

"And last summer, he lived at a ranch and drove cattle across the plains."

"Adventurous." Maybe Aurelia should interview him before she got too far with her Western novel. Or maybe she should spend a week at a ranch herself. "Did you get him drenched?"

"Not *drenched*, per se," Jackie said modestly. "We worked as a team during the water balloon fight, but I did turn on him a few times."

"How'd he react?"

"Tried to get me back."

Aurelia broke into a grin. "'Tried.' You got him more wet than he got you?"

"Probably," Jackie replied with a Cheshire-cat grin. "I'll see him tomorrow when we study between classes."

"Get ready for a second date." At least someone was having luck with her love life.

Jackie shrugged but looked happy.

* * *

ONCE HER ROOMMATES left the next day, Aurelia went to release the stowaway.

With it still being September, she was probably one of the first people to buy a pumpkin this year. She needed it for something other than Halloween though. The children in her story were getting rowdy, and she needed to see how messy they could get.

Opening the trunk of her car, she stood looking at the heavy orange melon.

"Do you want help with that?"

She startled and whirled to face Walter, her heart beating fast.

He wore blue and orange stripes today as well as a backpack. Was he pretending to merely pass by on his way to school? That was a new tactic, but it wouldn't win any points with her.

"What are you doing here?" Her voice was sharp.

"Oh—um, I actually came by to find out if you brought your phone home with you last night."

She blinked. "My phone?"

"Yeah." He shifted his weight. "I remember you put it under the piano bench, but I don't remember seeing you pick it up. I went back to the Wilk to look for it, but it wasn't there. Do you have your phone?"

She stared at him in bemusement, trying to realign in her mind which

Walter she now faced. This was Reticent Walter, the one who had saved her evening last night and made her long for more time with him. He, of all people, had come up with an excuse to come by after things had gone so well between them last night. It was flattering, even if it was somewhat reminiscent of the other Walter's behavior. Was it safe?

He cleared his throat. "So, do you?"

"Do I what?"

A dimple flashed in his cheek. "Do you have your phone?"

"Oh. Yes, thanks for checking. And sorry I was rude. I thought you were someone else."

"Really?" He stared at her for a moment.

She cleared her throat. "It's complicated. Maybe I'll tell you more about it some other time."

"Oh okay. Well, I guess if you have your phone, I'll go. Unless you need . . ." He eyed the pumpkin.

"Do you have ten minutes?" she blurted out.

He brightened. "I have half an hour."

His ready answer made her smile and point at the monster vegetable. "I'm going to smash that, and then I need help with cleanup." Her smile froze, and her gaze flew to Walter, whose eyebrows were now raised. "Um, that is, I'm writing a book about some kids, and in one scene, they smash a pumpkin and it gets all over an adult. I need to know how it breaks to make sure nothing's wrong with my scene," she finished and held her breath.

This was it. He thought she was crazy. It wouldn't have mattered much to her two days ago, but now—

Walter's mouth split in a grin. "I think that's great. Let's do it."

"Really?" She let out a laugh, relieved at his reaction.

"Yeah. That's super cool that you write. Where's your equipment for cleanup?" he asked, almost bouncing on his toes.

His enthusiasm allowed hers to grow. "It's inside, and I have a coat rack that'll serve as the person who gets splattered." Explaining her plan, she let him in the house, pausing only for a minute to send Jackie a text. In spite of last night, it seemed smart to let her roommate know Reticent Walter was visiting and to ask Jackie to check up on her in a bit. Aurelia's nerves hummed at Walter's presence in her apartment, but he was a perfect gentleman as they put together a cleaning bucket and took it outside, along with the white plastic-wrapped coat rack she had prepared beforehand.

They put the rack in the parking lot below and returned to the top of the stairs where Aurelia laboriously picked up the pumpkin.

She took a deep breath. "Here goes," she said and dropped it over the banister.

Splat!

For a moment, she gauged the damage: orange splatter on the plastic-wrapped rack. Pieces of pumpkin strewn along the ground.

She looked at Walter, only to find him looking at her. "Why do people smash pumpkins? It's not that exciting."

He laughed, a musical sound that did something funny to her insides. "Maybe you should put *that* in your book."

"Or cut the scene." She frowned, thinking it over. "But it ties in so well with everything else. I'll decide later. Let's get to work."

With her notebook in hand, she darted around in the parking lot, taking pictures and measuring with Walter's help how far throughout the parking lot the larger pieces of the pumpkin went and how far up the "person" any orange could be found.

Walter seemed to find her idea fascinating. "You're going about this like a true scientist."

She shook her head, pushing a wisp of hair from her face. "Like a crazy author. Okay, let's get rid of the evidence." She picked up a garbage bag and shook it out.

"After last night, I feel like I should be singing something," Walter said as he began pulling splattered sacks off the coat rack. "Do you do this a lot?"

"What, smash pumpkins?"

"No, experiment."

She dropped a large piece of pumpkin into her sack. "You and Jackie. You can't help but think in science terms, can you?"

He pretended to be perplexed. "Why would we need to? Tell me, what else do you do for your stories?"

"Um." She took a wet rag from the bucket and scrubbed at an orange stain on the sidewalk. "I sat in on some of my high school football team's practices. I needed to know what kind of things their coach tells them to do. And sometimes I spend time with children just to help me get their dialogue right." She frowned. Those two things didn't sound very impressive. "There are more things I'd *like* to do than what I've done."

"Like what?"

"Try out farm work. Spy. Go to Iceland." After all, she had recently fallen for another song, "Husavik," and its chorus was in Icelandic. It would be amazing to write a book set in Iceland.

"Hold on. *Spy?*"

"Yeah." She backtracked to her earlier answer, leaving behind the fantasy of glaciers and rolling fields. "I love spy stories and mysteries. They're—"

Her phone rang. Picking it up with a soapy hand, she found Jackie's name illuminating the screen. It was time for Aurelia to check in.

"Sorry, I have to take this," she apologized and accepted the call.

"Having fun?" Jackie's voice said in her ear.

Aurelia blinked. "Yes?"

"Good. I figured I should call instead of text, because if he had knocked you out and heard an incoming message, he could have texted me back pretending to be you, and I wouldn't know the difference."

Aurelia sneaked a glance at Walter, grateful the conversation wasn't broadcasted on speaker. "I guess that makes sense. Thanks, Jackie."

"You're welcome. But if the apartment is trashed when I get home, he's gonna get it."

"Why would—" Aurelia began, but Jackie had hung up.

It was a good thing Jackie didn't know they had desecrated the parking lot. And, of course, politely cleaned it up.

"I can't find any more stains," Walter said and picked up a trash bag. "Oops, we forgot to sing while we cleaned."

"What would you have sung?" Aurelia was still trying to come to terms with the musical side of the guy who had caused so much confusion in her life recently.

"'It's the Hard-Knock Life,' of course." He grinned. "What was the name of that French singer, the one whose song you performed? I've been wanting to check out her other songs."

"I'll look up one of them for you when we get inside." She was only too happy that he wanted to hear it. Walter threw away the evidence of their unusual activity, and the two of them returned indoors to wash their hands. Aurelia opened the browser on her phone and took a bag of peas from the fridge. "Do you want any?"

"Sure."

He took a couple of peapods, and she popped one in her mouth while a YouTube ad played. Then the Indila song started, and they put their heads together to watch the music video.

Aurelia didn't remember when she had last felt this happy—besides last night at the piano—as she stood in the middle of her living room munching peas with a less and less reticent Walter and listening to music in French.

They were halfway through the video when the door opened.

Meana skidded to a stop.

"Walter." Her voice was pure sugar overload. "So good to see you again. You should have texted me and let me know you were coming."

"What?" He looked at her in confusion. "But—you don't live here."

"Of course I do. I told you that already."

"But you live at Heritage Halls?" His statement came out as a bewildered question.

"I *lived* in Heritage Halls. I moved here this week, as you well know. *Wheah is yore memory, boy?*"

Aurelia jerked at that last sentence, intrigued. Some sort of Southern accent had appeared. It wasn't "toodles," by any means, but it was still a sentence and an attitude she hadn't expected to hear in real life.

Meana seemed to realize she had deviated from her charming approach. She quickly changed her tone. "I appreciate your visit though."

"Oh, well," he fumbled, "I was actually visiting—"

"I need a smoothie after the day I've had," she interrupted and grabbed his arm. "Let's go."

"But . . ." He looked over his shoulder at Aurelia. "Will you join us?"

"I can't," she said, feeling bad for him. Confident Walter had told the truth in his note. This Walter was no more interested in Meana than the other one was.

"Aurelia has a lot of homework," Meana excused her, obviously unaware of her internship. "Come on, it'll cheer me up. You're so good to me, Walter."

Meana dragged him out the door, leaving Aurelia behind. The living room seemed suddenly large and empty.

She looked down at the paused song on her phone and sighed. Walter would have to hear the rest later.

Slowly she put away everything connected to the pumpkin experiment, glad her roommate hadn't interrupted *that*.

Poor Walter. He appeared too much of a gentleman to refuse Meana's request. Hopefully he knew Aurelia really couldn't have joined them. She frowned and wished she had made that clearer. She had a meeting with Dr. Eunice soon. In fact, with nothing to keep her here, she might as well leave early for campus.

Her shoulders slumped as she packed her bag and left, wishing Walter's visit hadn't ended that way. It wasn't fun having a stalker, was it? Although maybe Reticent Walter didn't think of Meana that way just yet.

* * *

HER WEEKLY INTERNSHIP meeting went smoothly. Dr. Eunice liked her insights on the short stories written in the Western cowboy period, and after discussing some of Aurelia's edits, Dr. Eunice promised to email her a batch of articles for the upcoming week.

When the meeting ended, Aurelia walked out of the office and stopped short.

Walter, sitting on one of the indoor benches, looked up from his textbook. "How was your meeting?"

"*Walter.*" Her low growl was icy. She had no doubt which Walter this was.

He winced. "You know, I want to say I love it when you say my name, but at the moment, that's not quite true."

"Don't even try to tell me it's a coincidence you're here," she said through clenched teeth.

"It's not," he said matter-of-factly, undaunted by the storm clouds hovering around her. "I was hoping we could—"

"How do you know my meeting schedule?"

He stood. "Aurelia, we dated for—some time. We got to know each other's sched—"

"We never dated," she interrupted again.

"Not yet anymore." He sounded regretful.

"We've *never* dated. Time travel isn't real. How can you—how can you believe in God and yet stand here and tell me time travel is a thing?"

He goggled at her as though she had asked why the world was flat. "Time travel isn't incompatible with God."

"Of course it is."

"Come with me to institute," he pleaded suddenly. "You'll see that I believe in God. I always make comments in class. I've been going to institute since I don't want to stop having a religion course during the week just because I have to avoid the class the other me attends. I can explain to you after class how I see time travel working with God. Please come. It's tomorrow and every Friday at seven in the MARB," he said, naming another campus building.

He gave her a pleading look, and she stared back at him, thinking.

Over the course of less than twenty-four hours, she had come to enjoy Reticent Walter's company. She didn't feel the same about Confident Walter, although he clearly had Jackie's vote.

Yet how could this Walter look and sound so exactly like the other Walter if he wasn't him? What if the two *were* the same person, present and future?

"If you can come to believe that time travel is real," he continued, "and that I really had gotten to know you before I went and proposed, then maybe we can start over and you can give the other me a chance."

He didn't seem to know that she had, in fact, given the other Walter a chance. She had willingly spent time with him twice now and enjoyed it. Should she go to institute and try to figure out whether this Walter was okay? Gauge whether his personality was any different than the other Walter's and whether he had a testimony?

For the sake of the Walter who had played the piano for her, she felt the need to.

"I'll come," she said.

Walter's smile started out slow and gentle, as though he feared anything bigger would be too much for her peace of mind. The smile grew, though, until his entire face shone at a hundred watts. It nearly pulled a smile from Aurelia in return in spite of her nervousness at what she had agreed to.

"And we can talk after class?" he asked hopefully.

She nodded.

"Okay."

* * *

THOUGH SHE HADN'T MANAGED to invite Meana to eat with her, it was high time Aurelia cooked the roast from Macey's.

She prepped it, though she was somewhat distracted as she wondered what time travel arguments Walter could possibly come up with. Anything *she* came up with only made her shake her head. As much as she loved fiction, it was just that: fiction.

By the time Jackie came home, the apartment smelled heavenly. Jackie breathed in and murmured, "Mmmm."

She said nothing else though. When was Jackie ever this quiet? Why didn't she interrogate Aurelia about Walter's visit? Then Aurelia noticed her roommate's dreamy expression.

Aurelia sidled up next to her and spoke slyly in her ear. "Did you enjoy studying with Rodney?"

Jackie jumped and pushed her away. "Don't startle me."

Aurelia laughed. "Well, did you?"

"Did I what? Oh yes. And you know what? I think I like him."

Aurelia laughed harder. "I sure hope so. If you get this distracted over someone you don't care for, I'd be worried for you when you actually liked someone."

"Seriously, I love the way he looks at me. And talks to me. And asks about my classes." Suddenly, she grimaced. "But when he talks about astrophysics, I don't always love it. It's a cool topic, but he's lost me a few times, and that gets really boring."

Aurelia tried to process that. "Okay. So he needs to remember he's not talking to an astrophysics major, and then you'll be good?"

"Yeah, if he'll teach me rather than talk about those concepts as though he's thinking out loud, that'll work."

"That's positive, right? You're not cooking tonight, by the way. Our roast is ready."

"Ahhh. Believe me, my friend, you shall hear no utterance of protest from me."

"Methinks she waxeth poetical." Aurelia grinned. "Maybe Rodney has an inspirational influence on you."

"The *deliciousity* of the feast before me is not quite overpowered by the *attractivation* of Rodney."

Aurelia made a face. "Ugh. Sit down and let's pray. It's your turn, and don't you dare use rogue words in your prayer. It would be sacrilege."

Over dinner, Jackie returned to correct English and even left cloud nine to ask about Walter's visit. "What was Walter's excuse for coming by?"

"He, uh . . . well, to backtrack a little, I went to his karaoke night last night."

"Wait a minute. *His* karaoke night?"

Aurelia squirmed and soon found herself telling Jackie how Walter had invited her to karaoke. As a friend.

"So we had karaoke yesterday." Aurelia didn't want to talk about the ugly song or even the amazing, healing music session they had had afterward. "Then he showed up this morning and said he wanted to be sure I had brought my phone home with me last night."

"HA," Jackie exclaimed so loudly that Aurelia jumped in her chair. "He's *definitely* not trying to be just friends. 'Did you bring your phone home with you?' Ha. If this is Shy-slash-Reticent Walter, I'll have to give him a different name. He's making real progress here." She considered. "Have you mentioned him to your parents yet?"

Aurelia shook her head. "They've got enough to worry about."

"They're going to need some warning before you go and get hitched."

"Excuse me?"

"Just saying." Jackie sipped her root beer. "He's lost his stalker status, right? If we've decided he isn't crazy, I should think you'd be about ready to throw yourself at him."

Aurelia's mouth hung open. In the end, the only argument she could come up with was, "He *might* still be crazy."

Yet she had agreed to join him for his religion class tomorrow. Her stomach turned over at the thought. Who was the crazy one now, and what would tomorrow bring?

Chapter Ten

AURELIA PACED in the living room, her breakfast dishes forgotten and her computer neglected.

Why had she agreed to go to institute with Walter?

Her mind couldn't wrap itself around the idea of time travel. She dreaded hearing whatever speech Walter had prepared to convince her of the impossible. If it weren't real, though, how could there possibly be two Walters? There *were* two of him. She had seen proof of that. Yet what if Confident Walter was unstable and dangerous? And was it possible Reticent Walter had known about him all this time?

The idea made her eyes sting. She badly wanted the Walter who had played the piano for her to be innocent.

By late afternoon, she had had enough. She called James in her ward and asked for Walter's address. She would be the one to surprise him for once. Maybe it would help her to see him in his natural habitat.

She groaned, thinking how both Jackie and Walter would tell her she sounded like a scientist.

Aurelia would have liked to say she marched right over to Walter's place, but the truth was that she nearly turned back three times. She half expected Confident Walter to pop up along the way and stop her, although that idea made no sense, since he had tried all along to get her to spend time with his other self.

She frowned. Where *did* Confident Walter keep himself these days? Reticent Walter would be the one at the address James had given, right?

With her heart in her throat, she reached his condo and knocked.

Walter opened the door and started in surprise. They stared at each other for a long moment before he smiled. "Hi. Won't you come in?"

This had better be Reticent Walter. Without taking her eyes off him, Aurelia entered.

There was an air of both uncertainty and excitement around Walter as he watched his silent visitor. "Do you wanna sit?"

"Mm-hmm." She took a seat at the dining table opposite the chair he must have occupied, judging by the way his open textbook faced. Walter took that seat and asked, "Have you worked the pumpkin smashing into your book yet?"

It *was* him. A load of fear dropped from her shoulders, and she brightened at the question.

"Not yet," she answered, "but I will." Inwardly she cheered. *This is Reticent Walter. This is Reticent . . .*

Her shoulders fell. She still had trouble with his doppelganger, and even the Walter in front of her continued to confuse her.

She bit her lip, and he waited for her to speak.

He looked so nice sitting across the small table that barely had enough room to keep his knees from knocking into hers. His hair looked soft and springy, his brown eyes curious.

She cleared her throat. "Do you have any plans tonight?" Did he know about her invitation to institute?

He blinked. His gaze strayed to his textbook and back up. "I have work at seven. It's close by. Do, uh, you have plans?"

"Yeah, I have a thing." With him. Not *for* him. She didn't have a thing for him. Well, actually, she kind of did, but that just made things more problematic.

"Okay." He sounded disappointed. It warmed her, which was also problematic.

She could have liked him so much if she hadn't been scared off by the proposal and the time travel story. If there had only been one of him all this time. Was it wrong to like him? Dangerous, even?

"Is something wrong?"

Aurelia rested her head in her hands. "I think I'm going crazy."

The room was silent for a minute.

Then Walter cleared his throat. "Well. It's not the worst place to be."

She looked up in surprise. He gave her an innocent look, and it nearly made her smile.

Unfortunately, the day's anxiety won out, flattening her lips into a straight line. Her emotions were on a roller coaster, and she couldn't trust the ups.

"I don't think I'll go to my appointment tonight after all," she said slowly.

Walter nodded. "I'm sure you don't have to."

Aurelia frowned, suddenly suspicious. Was Reticent Walter telling her on behalf of Confident Walter that she didn't have to attend institute?

Thunder rumbled outside.

She put her elbows on the table and looked directly at him. "Why did you visit me the day after that explosion? That doesn't make sense to me." Confident Walter had said he made James bring Reticent Walter to her place, but was that really true, or had he made it up because he happened to know the two of them were on their way?

He shrugged. "I honestly didn't know about the explosion. James showed up here and told me to get going. He was all mad I was in my PJs. It was weird. But when he told me about you . . . I didn't think you'd want me there, but on the other hand, he was insistent, and I was worried, so I got changed and came along with him."

She stared at him. It might make sense for Confident Walter as a stalker to tell her to go to the concert and then show up himself to take her, but it didn't make sense for him to get Reticent Walter to come visit her. He must seriously believe in this time travel thing if he was, in fact, trying to get her to spend time with this Walter. And since the two looked and sounded exactly the same—ought *she* to believe in this time travel thing?

Walter tilted his head. "So—if you're not going to your thing tonight, and I don't have work yet, do you want to stay for a bit?" There was hope in his voice as he glanced around the place. "I could, uh, order pizza . . ."

Her eyes filled with sudden tears. As much as she enjoyed spending time with this Walter, she couldn't let go of her confusion.

"Are you okay?" Walter asked, jumping up.

Aurelia stood, too, passing a hand across her eyes. "Yeah. Sorry, I need to go home." She moved toward the entrance, making a small berth around

Walter to discourage him from putting his arm around her in case he thought to comfort her that way. It was really too bad because it might have been nice to be comforted, but at the rate things were going, she would have flinched away from him.

"Is there anything I can do?" he asked, following behind.

Why did he have to be so nice? This whole thing would be easier if she didn't like him. Then she could write off both Walters.

"Stop being so nice to me," she answered out loud.

He stilled, and she missed his earlier hopeful look. Then suddenly his smile returned in full force. "Okay." He opened the door to a gray world and grinned at her. "I'll be mean the next time I see you."

Her mouth gaped open. "Wh-at?" His mischievous expression made her gasp out a laugh in spite of herself.

She left with a small chuckle and a lot of confusion.

The sky was cloudy, the sunlight dim. Aurelia leaned her head back, letting the breeze toy with her hair. It felt good, but she continued to feel bad inside.

Walter and Walter were harmful to her peace of mind. Did that mean Reticent Walter wasn't good for her? Even when he did nice things like walk out on a gross song with her, cheer her with piano music, and clean up pumpkin gore?

Even during this visit, he had made her smile or laugh, or want to, several times.

She paused and tried to piece together her memories of both Walters. Despite their identical appearance, it was strangely clear to her which Walter had been present at each encounter she had had.

As she compared her experiences with the two of them side by side, she was struck by a sobering thought.

She had already established that she liked Reticent Walter best. If the time travel story was somehow true, though, he was the Walter that would eventually travel back in time and would become, and leave her with, Confident Walter.

She forced herself to walk on, her throat working to swallow a lump. Time travel wasn't real. Something was wrong with Confident Walter, who either happened to have the same name as Reticent Walter or who pretended to.

Her head ached by the time she arrived home, where she stopped and stared at an uncharacteristic sight.

Jackie sat on the couch, her eyes red-rimmed, a bag of celery on the table and a green stalk in her hand.

A wave of cold swept over Aurelia.

Jackie looked up at her. "It's over," she said hoarsely. "I thought we had something going. I thought there'd at least be a second date, but he's already tired of me."

"Rodney dumped you?" Aurelia exclaimed, regretting the words the instant they were out of her mouth. She should have used a nicer word than "dumped."

"Yeah, he dumped me." Jackie sounded angry for a moment, but then she sagged back into the couch. "If you can even use such an active word to describe it. It's more like he just stopped paying attention to me. He told me he wasn't really 'feeling it.'" She made air quotes with her fingers. "He seemed so bored today when we studied, so dispassionate."

Her voice broke on the last word, almost breaking Aurelia's heart. Aurelia slumped onto the couch beside her and whispered, "I'm sorry."

Jackie sniffed.

"I went to Walter's place," Aurelia said in a dead tone. "Just now. I don't think I can do this anymore."

Jackie took a good look at her in spite of her own misery. "You can't deal with the two different Walters—is that what you're saying?"

"Something like that." Aurelia's voice broke.

"Oh, honey." Jackie gave her a hug. "Have some celery."

Aurelia eyed it with distaste. She ate celery when she was depressed, as Jackie well knew. It was a good pity-party food because it compounded misery upon misery. The stalk got stringy pieces stuck between a person's teeth, which gave that person extra reason to feel bad. And then there was the whole negative calories thing. Aurelia was slender enough that it wouldn't hurt her to put on a few pounds, but did celery help with that? No. When she ate something, she ought to be able to get some calories out of it. Celery added to her misery in more ways than one.

Jackie looked unhappily at the stalk in her hand, put the end in her mouth, and tried to bite off a clean piece.

"Reporting Walter didn't even help," Aurelia moaned and picked up a piece herself. "The police didn't find the right guy. And the worst thing is that I'd have liked him if he hadn't pulled that stunt."

"I know. I really think you would have hit it off with him."

Aurelia struggled to break off the celery hanging from her mouth. She freed it with several more cracks. "It's hopeless."

Jackie sighed and stared into space. "I didn't think I was *that* into Rodney. It's only been a few days. But it was exciting, and he was cool, and I thought we clicked. How is it he didn't feel the same way? We should have had more time to get to know each other. Maybe I would have decided I wasn't interested, but for him to end it this fast, before I got the chance to find out for myself—it's maddening."

"I think it's rude," Aurelia cried out, her eyes watering. "If he was bored, there's something wrong with him. No human being could get bored with you." She looked dejectedly at the uneven piece of greenery in her hand.

Jackie sniffed. "I guess I should be glad it's over so soon if it wasn't going to turn into anything." *Crunch. Crunch.* "But I'm not."

"Jackie."

"It feels so unfinished," Jackie wailed. "You know I rarely date. I don't have time, or no one asks me out, or I'm not interested in anyone. Now that I finally thought I was, it's already over. When will I get married at this rate?"

"Jackie," Aurelia repeated.

"I want to find my Prince Charming." Jackie tried to break the celery with her hands. "I bet it'll be years before I meet someone else who interests me, and then *he* probably won't care for me either." She looked at the twisted stalk in her hand, gathering courage for another bite.

"Jackie, this isn't working. We need ice cream."

Jackie looked up, a glint lighting her eyes. "We do?"

"Yes. You know what the problem is with celery?" Aurelia shook her stalk. "It clears your mind. You can't drown your sorrows in it, because it picks you up and tells you to start thinking and doing. I don't want to think or do right now. I don't want to problem-solve my impossible situation. I want ice cream."

"Are you sure?" Jackie asked, obviously uncertain about this departure from Aurelia's standard procedure.

"Yep. Put on your shoes. I'll get my purse."

A minute later, they stepped outside into pouring rain.

"Huh." Aurelia looked at the drizzly gray world. "Would you look at that?"

The two girls shared an umbrella on their way to the creamery, rain pounding above them. On their arrival, Aurelia shook water from the umbrella and proceeded inside. There was ice cream that needed picking out.

They chose three different gallon tubs and went to pay. Their freezer would be full for the next while.

The cashier glanced at the rainy outdoors and then back at the girls with raised eyebrows.

Jackie noticed his glance. Hugging the Graham Canyon and English Toffee cartons to her chest, she looked back at the cashier and whispered, "Never underestimate the power of ice cream."

Aurelia picked up the Chocolate Chip Cookie Dough bucket, and they trudged home.

They shut the door on the rain, retrieved spoons from the kitchen, and returned to the couch.

Jackie's eyes were still red. She blew her nose and asked, "So the Walters are off the list, are they?"

Aurelia felt a stab in her chest at the idea. "I don't know. They should be, but I just don't know. Did you know I was supposed to meet one of him tonight? But I'm not going to."

"He can't blame you in this weather." Jackie loosened several scoops of Chocolate Chip Cookie Dough.

"I wasn't going to go even in good weather, and I even told him so. Of course, it was the other Walter I told, so I guess I still stood him up."

"How many Walters are there again?" Jackie put a big spoonful in her mouth.

"Too many."

"So you have too many guys interested in you, and I have too few. Neither is fun, is it? I guess I have guys interested in me sometimes that I don't want to date. Am I as bad as Rodney, then? Do I break their hearts?" Jackie sounded heartbroken herself at the thought.

Aurelia knew there was a right answer. She just couldn't think of it. So she put a chunk of Graham Canyon in her mouth and let the honey-molasses taste take over.

"And here I am breaking Walter's heart," she said sadly. An image of Confident Walter's beautiful hundred-watt smile from when she agreed to meet up at institute came to mind. She groaned and worked the crunchy ice cream further into her taste buds.

"I'm sorry if I've put pressure on you to give him a chance when I shouldn't have," Jackie mourned. "I should have stuck to the death glares and a restraining order, but he seemed harmless in spite of everything. What's a woman to do?"

"He told me he traveled back in time," Aurelia confessed, staring at a spot on the couch. "After he freaked me out with the proposal and I turned down the other Walter at the talent show, the first one showed up again." With her brows drawn together, she looked up at her friend and roommate as she finally spilled the details. "He said he had traveled back in time and thought he had only gone back an hour, so he went and proposed. Then he found out he had traveled back to before we met."

Jackie paused with her spoon halfway to her mouth. "Seriously?"

"Yeah. He's been wanting me to go out with Reticent Walter, because apparently, the first time around, I agreed to a date at the end of the talent show."

Jackie stared. When the ice cream was about to melt off her spoon, she put it in her mouth. "But time travel isn't scientifically possible at this point," she reminded Aurelia. "The lecturer said so."

"I know. The other Walter said something to the same effect."

"I'm so sorry." Jackie shook her head. "I didn't even know what you were going through. Does that mean one of your Walters is crazy, or is there just one of him and he's doubly crazy?"

"There are two of him, but I don't know if one or both are crazy." Aurelia sucked on a spoonful. "That's why I'm eating ice cream," she managed to say with her mouth full. "I don't want to think about it anymore. Let's forget him and Rodney for now."

"Rodney," Jackie said disconsolately. "Who else will invite me to a water balloon fight on a first date? He was perfect. Have you tried the toffee?"

Aurelia tried it, and her eyes widened with pleasure. "Put the others in the freezer. If no other ice cream existed, I'd be happy with this one."

"No, no, we need the variety. See, a taste of Graham Canyon"—Jackie put a chunk in her mouth—"and a bit of toffee. Now a bit of cookie dough and a bit of toffee."

"Doesn't your mom make homemade ice cream? Has she ever made something with toffee?"

"No, but she has some good ones with strawberries. And chocolate. Lots of chocolate."

"How would you make it with toffee?" Aurelia wanted to know.

"Who knows? Let's look it up on YouTube."

The YouTube tutorial led to a Studio C sketch, which led to another. Aurelia and Jackie feasted and partied, completely forgetting to be sad.

At last they went to bed, stomachs full and the freezer stuffed with left-over ice cream.

Aurelia pulled up her covers, eyeing the window in the dark and listening to the crickets on the other side. She had needed this break. Tonight she would rest. Tomorrow she would face her situation again. Tomorrow was temple day, and she would get the clarity she needed. She would.

Chapter Eleven

It was a good thing Aurelia had regained some of her usual cheer before a chipper Kylie called her the next morning.

"Do you still go to the temple on Saturdays?" was Kylie's greeting over the phone.

Aurelia put a white dress in her bag and swallowed a laugh while Jackie turned over in her bed with a moan. Tiptoeing from the room, Aurelia set down her bag in the living room and answered, "Yes, I'm going in an hour." She hadn't made it last week, what with the hospital visit and all.

"Can I join you?"

"Sure. There might still be room in the session." She glanced at the freezer.

"Sweet! Now, how are you?"

"Fine."

"I mean, since the explosion at my place, *how are you feeling*?" Kylie asked significantly.

"Oh. Really, I'm good." Aurelia pulled a bowl from the cupboard. "I'm one hundred percent back to normal."

"Good." Kylie clicked her tongue. "I know this is weird, but . . . I think something similar happened at Macey's."

Aurelia paused. "What do you mean?"

"An explosion. One of my neighbors was shopping there yesterday, and she heard this crash. People went running to investigate. Someone saw several items fall off the shelves, and a lady nearby fell to her knees. She seemed okay but shaken."

"Macey's?" Aurelia asked anew. "As in, the grocery store?"

"Yes."

"Was it the one in Provo?"

"Yep. Well, I think so. It's weird, isn't it? Maybe it isn't the same thing, but it sounds kind of like what happened at my place."

"Yeah, that *is* weird," Aurelia breathed. Had it followed her?

"Anyway, I'll get ready now and meet you at the temple," Kylie announced.

"I'll see you there."

Two minutes later, Aurelia had ice cream and her open laptop in front of her. It only took one Google search to find an article about yesterday's incident at Macey's.

It was a short article, sparse on details. No one had been injured, but the blast was noticeable enough to make it into the news. Someone said the explosion itself hadn't made noise. What drew everyone's attention was the sudden crash of cans no one had touched.

She sat back, pondering.

Who would go to a grocery store and set off an explosion? Her thoughts strayed to the strange men who had been at Macey's at the same time as her. With all their talk of strong air and stealing instruments from kids, had those men set up a bomb of sorts? Or had someone shown up yesterday to cause an explosion?

If this was similar to what happened at Kylie's place, though, no one had set off anything. Right? No one had been at Kylie's place last Friday except for Aurelia and the chihuahua.

A feeling of discomfort ran down her back. She certainly hoped no one had been there.

Her nerves tight, she shut down the laptop and picked up her temple bag.

The temple was full of people that morning, but a spirit of reverence prevailed in spite of the crowds, calming Aurelia. She basked in the Spirit and took her time saying a silent prayer at the end. While she had prayed for nearly two weeks for Walter not to harm her, for herself to be wise and protected in her dealings with him, and even for him to get whatever mental help he might be in need of, this time, when she closed her eyes, she had the thought to pray for something new. She asked to be able to trust her own feelings when it came to the Walters.

This was it. This was the clarity she had been looking for, or at least the next step to gaining it.

She had enjoyed her time with Reticent Walter in the Wilkinson Center. Hopefully she wouldn't have felt that way if he were, in fact, dangerous. And if Confident Walter was somehow his future . . .

She prayed that her feelings would reflect what was right.

After the temple, Kylie invited her home for lunch. Chicha ran circles around both of them while Kylie bounced around in the kitchen, heating up a casserole.

"That was great! Let's do it again next week. I'll steam some vegetables along with this. We can still eat before the bug people get here."

"'Bug people?'" Aurelia fought a grin as she took a seat at the dining table, out of the way and safe from any overly exuberant movements. "Who else did you invite over?"

"Pest control or whatever they're called." Kylie waved away Aurelia's teasing. "They were here last week spraying for spiders. Today's their follow-up visit."

"Do you have to pay for both visits?" There was much Aurelia didn't know about the homeowner's world.

"I didn't even have to pay for the first one." Kylie dropped the steamer of vegetables into the pot and left the kitchen with a skip in her step. "It's a startup company trying to build a customer base. All I have to do is fill out a survey and give them permission to use any quote from me." She plopped into a seat across from Aurelia. "Now you have some explaining to do."

"I do?"

"Yes." Kylie raised her eyebrows. "Texting? Checking up on you?"

"Oh." Aurelia reddened. "That."

"You were on a date, right?" Kylie looked ecstatic. "How was it? Do you like him?"

"It wasn't a date, exactly," Aurelia amended. "We went as friends. He was nice though." The karaoke night hadn't been nice, but Walter had been. "I'm glad I went."

Kylie bounced in her seat. "You like the guy. I can positively see stars in your eyes. You're going to see your 'friend' again, right?"

Aurelia laughed. "I'm certain I will," she said, knowing the irony was lost on her friend. It was impossible for Aurelia *not* to see Walter again. He was everywhere, he kept dropping by unannounced, and he, or at least his "future" self, was stubborn about getting her to believe his story. "What about you? Any 'friends' in your life right now?"

The conversation stayed successfully on Kylie's life while they ate. They were arguing about doing the dishes for each other when the doorbell rang.

Kylie rushed to open the door. Aurelia dashed in the opposite direction to the kitchen, where she turned on the faucet and started scrubbing.

Voices sounded at the door, tugging at her mind and slowing her movements. Kylie and her visitors entered the living room.

"It shouldn't take more than ten minutes, twenty at the most if we discover anything that needs an extra spray."

Aurelia looked over her shoulder, her eyes widening. She had seen those two people before—at Macey's. The salt-and-pepper-haired man and his bigger companion were the same ones who had discussed taking something from children and wishing there were fewer people around.

What were the chances of meeting them here? And—should she be worried?

The men kept talking, and the water kept pouring. Finally she had the presence of mind to put her clean plate in the drying rack.

"Aurelia, I told you you can't wash my dishes," Kylie scolded, coming up behind her. "You're my guest." She took over, and Aurelia let her.

She hung around, not loving the thought of these two men being in Kylie's home. They had acted so strange in the store. Just what had they been "pumping" at Macey's? And why had they tried to hide it?

With a shudder, she glanced at the spot in the living room where she had lost consciousness last week. The men had been both at Macey's and in Kylie's home before the respective explosions. Was it coincidence, or was there a real connection?

Heavy steps entered the dining room, followed by a man's voice. "You'll want to go to a different room while we spray in here."

"Sure," said Kylie, drying her hands and then tugging Aurelia along.

When the men left at last, Aurelia hurried to the window to watch them get in their car. It was a company car with a magnified picture of a red spider on it. It looked legitimate.

She looked away from the unappetizing arachnid. The two men were just doing their job. Maybe they had been spraying insecticide at the store that day, trying out a spray before they bought it.

Antsy and annoyed with her own doubts, she told Kylie goodbye and left the house.

* * *

WHEN SHE CAME HOME, Jackie looked up from her textbook. "Guess what?"

"Uh. The ice cream's gone?" Aurelia hoped that wasn't the case.

"Nope. Try again."

She held up her hands in surrender.

"Walter came by—twice—and asked if you're okay."

Aurelia sank onto a chair. "Of course he did."

Jackie gave her a pointed look. "He wasn't wearing the same shirt the second time. Although," she added, "the shirts were similar. Your boyfriend might want to expand his wardrobe."

"His wardrobe is fine," Aurelia protested. "Who really cares about guys having variety in their clothes?"

"Oooh, defending the delinquent, are we?" Jackie sounded rather happy about it.

Aurelia stared at her, rolling the words across her tongue. "'Defending the delinquent.' That—is—a wonderful phrase."

"Thank you very much." Jackie took a bow. "Also, I hit on a new name for Shy Walter." She leaned her elbows on the table while Aurelia braced herself. "He's now Comeback Walter. He had his shy spell after you turned him down, but he's made a real comeback since then. Will you even be able to tell the difference between him and Hot Walter? Because he's—"

"Don't say it," Aurelia warned.

"*Confident* like the other one now," Jackie said in amusement. "Or at least getting close."

"Thank you." She hadn't used the word "hot."

"And hot," Jackie mouthed, with just enough voice to make it audible.

Aurelia stood abruptly, her chair screeching back. She paused, part of her mind glorying in the dramatic way she had stood. "Enough with the hotness," she said and raised her chin. "But I accept the name Comeback Walter. It's a good description. Any ice cream left?"

"I already told you yes." Jackie rolled her eyes. "You seriously think I could have finished it? I'm surprised you're not asking about green beans, though, or broccoli."

"Green beans sound good." Aurelia headed for the fridge. "I do have some in here."

"Well, I'm glad your little stint with depression is over," Jackie observed. "But we still have a time travel issue. Are you going to continue to consort with the Walters?"

"They're continuing to consort with me, aren't they?" Aurelia returned, picking out a bean. "Coming by to see how I am and so on. One of them must have been worried because I was all sad and confused at his place yesterday, and the other's checking up on me because I didn't show up for institute in the middle of a rainstorm."

"Yesterday was an eventful day," Jackie said.

Aurelia gave her a cautious look. "I'm sorry about . . . things with Rodney not working out."

"Who cares?" Jackie said nonchalantly. "We had seen each other for less than a week. We weren't even boyfriend and girlfriend."

Aurelia didn't say anything, but the way Jackie had lit up those few days had been real. It made Aurelia feel bad to have two guys, or one guy—from two different time periods?—pay so much attention to her, even if she didn't know what to do with that attention.

* * *

When Walter attended her ward the next day, she didn't get upset. When he greeted her and said he hoped she hadn't gone out in the thunderstorm, she was okay with it and didn't tell him that she had, in fact, ventured outside.

When he walked up to her after the second hour, her heart sped up.

"Can I talk to you?" he asked anxiously. "About the time travel thing and my faith? We could grab a booth above the terrace. Would that be okay?"

It really might get harder to tell the difference between Confident Walter and Comeback Walter. Confident Walter's confidence had taken a bit of a blow by now.

"How long will this take?" she asked.

"Maybe a few minutes. Maybe longer."

She frowned but turned decisively to Jackie. "I'll see you at home." It was time she heard his explanation, if for no other reason than to get it over with.

Jackie gave her and Walter an appraising look. "Don't do anything I wouldn't do," was her verdict.

Aurelia headed for the walkway that outlined the terrace from above. Below her was the piano. Longing stirred in her at the memory of sitting there with Walter, singing reverent hymns and animated Disney songs.

She had no such fond memories of the Walter currently with her.

Whirling to face him, she crossed her arms and glared at him. They stood near a booth, but she decided she preferred this conversation standing up, and she wouldn't be budged. Apparently, she was in a contentious mood. It wasn't a good sign if that was the effect he had on her.

"What do you have to say?" she challenged.

He shifted his weight. "Did you want to sit?"

"Nope."

He watched her for a moment. Then he paced away a few steps and came back, pulling a hand through his hair.

Her eyes flicked to the hair, but she forced them away and focused on the scripture case in Walter's hand. "Do you always use a hard copy of the scriptures?" she asked. She did herself, but she knew few others who did. The world didn't appreciate real live books anymore.

"No, I use my phone, but the other me has that. I grabbed these scriptures from my room when I wasn't home."

She felt a sudden urge to laugh. If the situation weren't so complicated, it would have been funny the way he spoke about himself.

He blew out a breath. "You know the scriptures say that time works differently for God, right? That time doesn't exist for him?"

She hesitated. "Yeah."

His gaze held hers. "Plus, what about all the prophets he's shown the entire history of the earth to and held nothing back from?"

Moses and Nephi popped into Aurelia's mind just before Walter continued, "I can't help thinking he might have taken them through the eons of time rather than shown them everything on some celestial screen or 3-D model. In some way or other, I think they went through time with him."

Her hands stilled. She had no idea if that was the case or not, but . . . she could believe it. Walter's thoughts made sense.

His voice softened. "If he can do anything in or outside of time, don't you think we mortals might be able to find a way, even if it's inferior to his, to move through time via the laws of the universe?"

She frowned. "It's one thing for God to bend time, but mortals?"

Walter smiled. "I honestly didn't know if we *could* make it happen, and I definitely didn't think it would be this soon, but it's been exciting to be on the research project and see how far we could get, and then . . . it was figured out, and I'm here."

It was figured out? As in, by him and his team, or by someone else?

He reached for her hand but stopped as if remembering how uncomfortable it made her. "That's all I have to say about the time travel thing. You kind of need to believe it's real in order to trust me and the fact that there are two of me, but that's not as important as you knowing I believe in Jesus and his restored church."

"What?" She straightened. Where were all his other arguments and explanations? Did he really think he could cover this in a few measly sentences and then move on to what mattered most?

"I said I believe in Jesus and his church." His gaze was insistent. "The plan of salvation. I believe it with all my heart."

She bit her lip. Something in her had started to feel, just recently, that his time travel story wasn't quite impossible. His short explanation helped further that feeling. Meanwhile, she couldn't help but admire the way he put forth the gospel as more important.

When her heart warmed at his last few words, was that the Spirit saying he was sincere, or did she only feel the Spirit because the words themselves resonated with her?

What had she told herself yesterday? *Pay attention to how you feel. Don't overanalyze.*

A reassuring peace grew inside her. She *was* feeling the Spirit, and she wouldn't second-guess it. If Walter was lying right now, she was sure it would feel wrong, but he wasn't, and it didn't. He believed the things she knew to be true, the things that mattered most to her. Both Walters did.

A seedling of hope sprouted at the thought of the other Walter, the one she had come to like, having this strength of testimony.

"Would you come to institute with me on Friday?" the Walter in front of her pleaded. "You can come judge for yourself whether I believe in God. Maybe if you get to know me—*me* me," he clarified, pointing at himself, "and if you eventually start to like me, you might decide you want to befriend the other me as well."

She watched his face as he revealed his newest plan. He clearly didn't know she *was* spending time with his other self.

Maybe she *should* get to know him. After all, she wanted to get to know his possibly past self. Still, she wouldn't make another promise she couldn't keep. Friday had been heart-wrenchingly confusing.

She cleared her throat. "I might go, but I can't say yes right now. A lot of things can happen between now and Friday." Like, she could change her mind back and forth a million times.

"Okay." He nodded, then added in a cautious tone as she made to step away, ready to go home, "And maybe we could do something during the week?"

Of course he couldn't wait until Friday. Aurelia felt a flicker of apprehension but also a tingle of butterflies in her stomach. After all, she had thoroughly enjoyed having his counterpart at her place. Would she enjoy spending time with Confident Walter as well?

"How about—" he began, but Aurelia interrupted.

"My place. Wednesday at seven. We can play games." *On my home turf,* she added in her mind, pleased with the idea. Jackie would be there, and so would . . .

His smile grew weak. "What if Meana's there?"

Her smile grew wider. "Then Meana's there." If they were going to spend an evening together, she needed to feel safe—and conversely, she might enjoy seeing him sweat.

Walter nodded resolutely. "I'll be there."

Aurelia struggled to keep a straight face. "I'll see you later," she said and turned away before he could ask about walking her home.

Chapter Twelve

When Aurelia entered the apartment, Jackie was scrubbing the frying pan clean, and a mouthwatering smell of meat and cheese emanated from the oven.

"How did it go?" Jackie wanted to know.

"Well enough. Do you want me to cut up greens?"

"And reds and purples." Jackie nodded at the tomatoes and red onions. "Did you say, 'Well enough'? You realize I'll be living my dating life vicariously through you. You have to come up with something better than that or move on from Walter."

Aurelia picked up a knife. "I invited him to come here on Wednesday."

"Well, well," Jackie said in a completely different tone. "You've accepted him, then? Get ready to write a romance, because you're about to get some firsthand experience."

"I'm not writing a romance." Aurelia scoffed. "You know I'm not romantic."

"That's about to change, my friend."

"Let me remind you I don't do well with sappy." Aurelia chopped away. "*Romances,*" she began, her voice dripping with sarcasm, "talk about things like noticing what the other person smells like. *His embrace enveloped her with the scent of leather and smoked wood,*" she improvised theatrically.

"Sounds like you've read a romance or two," Jackie interjected.

Aurelia coughed. "Reading isn't the same as writing them. Besides, so many of them are overdone. *He knew he would never again smell saffron without thinking of her*. Really? Take that to our era, and what have we got? People don't wear perfume these days. If a guy were to notice something I smelled like, it would be my deodorant."

"*Deodorant*?" Jackie moaned. "You're so not romantic, Aurelia. What about hair products though? Your shampoo smells like something nice, right?"

"It's supposed to, but I don't think it does anymore. I haven't been able to smell it in a while."

"Hold on." Jackie came around the counter and didn't stop until she had planted her face in Aurelia's hair, where she took a deep sniff that tickled. "Mmmm. The smell's still there. Strawberries, right?"

Aurelia giggled and pulled away from Jackie. "I must have gotten so used to it I can't tell anymore."

A knock on the door cut off Jackie's response. The two girls looked knowingly at each other.

Aurelia went and swung the door open. She wasn't sure whether to smile at him or glower because, while she had agreed to let one of him come over soon, it would be overkill for that same Walter to come over now, so soon after their talk at church.

Her eyes narrowed until she noticed his tie and relaxed. That wasn't the one he had worn at church today.

"Can I take a rain check on being mean to you?" he asked. "It doesn't seem right to do it on a Sunday."

She blinked, then felt herself smile. She had forgotten about Comeback Walter's promise to be mean when he saw her again.

"I guess that's okay." Butterflies took up a circuit inside her when he grinned. Suddenly shy, she looked down and wondered what excuse he would use the next time to avoid being mean. "Would you like to come in?"

"Sure." He followed her inside. "Hi, Jackie."

"Hi, Walter," Jackie answered. "Dinner's almost ready. Why don't you join us?"

"Really?" He looked shocked at her friendliness. "Are you sure?"

"I'm always sure." She sniffed as though he had offended her.

He looked at Aurelia.

"Yeah, you're welcome to join us," she said.

"Thank you," he told them. Then he put his hand on Aurelia's arm, making her start and look into his vibrant eyes.

"How are you doing?" he asked in a low voice. "Friday was a little rough, right?"

Heat raced through her body at his proximity and his concern. An impractical part of her rejoiced in the fact that she had worried him. "I-I'm doing better."

Jackie put her dishes in the sink and sauntered from the kitchen. "I gotta go to the restroom." She walked close by Aurelia, who backed away from Walter. "Romance," Jackie whispered slyly.

Aurelia set her jaw as her roommate disappeared. When she turned to Walter, he looked confused. Annoyance with Jackie pulsing through her, Aurelia put her hands on her hips.

"Walter, what do I smell like?" she asked, ready to prove Jackie wrong. If he had noticed a smell about her, it would be her deodorant, or so she hoped for the sake of proving her point.

He frowned. "I don't know, I haven't . . ." His frown gave way to a twitching grin. "Hold on, let's see."

He put a hand on her shoulder and walked behind her, leaning in close. Aurelia froze.

Having Walter in her hair was different from having Jackie in her hair. When he breathed in, her hair tickled her ear and her neck until she could barely stand it, and everything in that area broke into goosebumps.

"Some sort of red berry. Strawberries or raspberries?" He sniffed again. "Strawberries. You smell good." He stepped in front of her.

Certain her face was bright red, she swallowed and moved away. "Cool. Just wondering." What had she been thinking asking Walter about her smell? Although she hadn't realized he would take it as an invitation to investigate.

He smoothed a hand over his own hair and looked around, suddenly nervous.

Then he cocked his head at her, and she could see his mischievous side returning, plain as day.

"What do *I* smell like?"

The thought of him expecting *her* to smell *him* sent another frisson of heat through her, but she was amused at his audacity. The humor freed up her brain enough for her to think up a quick response and a way out.

"You smell like trouble," she said in a stern voice.

"Time for dinner," Jackie announced, making both of them jump as she walked back in.

"I'll set the table." Aurelia hurried to the kitchen.

A minute later, they were all seated, a meat pie teasing their noses. Jackie gave Walter a very direct look when she asked him to say the prayer. Aurelia broke in, declaring she would say it, and started praying before anyone could protest.

It would actually have been nice to hear Walter pray, but Jackie's invitation had seemed too much like a challenge.

After the prayer, they dug in, enjoying Jackie's cheeseburger pie with veggies served on the side.

"This is way good," Aurelia told her.

"Yeah, it's wonderful," Walter praised.

"I hope you didn't already have dinner plans," Jackie told him, and Aurelia looked at her in suspicion, certain she was fishing for information.

He shook his head and pulled something from his pocket. "This has been giving me trouble."

Aurelia looked at it. "Your student ID?"

"Yeah. When I went to the Cannon Center less than an hour ago, they wouldn't let me in. They said my card showed I'd already used it on my Sunday meal. The same thing happened last Sunday. I'm supposed to be able to scan it for a meal every day, but I think there's a glitch in their system."

Already used . . . Was he saying what Aurelia thought he was?

"It's not so bad if it happens during the week, but I haven't been keeping real food in my apartment, so when the card doesn't work on Sundays and I can't go out and buy something, I have to stick it out on whatever snacks I can find." He tucked the card back into his pocket. "Sorry, I don't mean to complain," he hurried to say, "and obviously I should be smarter with food storage. I might want to replace the card though."

"No, don't do that." The words were out of Aurelia's mouth before she realized she had spoken. "I mean, I'm sure it's . . . If it's the system that has trouble, a new card might have the same problems. Or even more problems."

"I guess that could be true," he said slowly.

Why hadn't it occurred to her to wonder more about how Confident Walter got by? If Comeback Walter lived in his student apartment, where did the other Walter sleep? How did he pay for his meals?

Did he have an exact copy of the student ID card?

If he did, a new card would make his copy void.

"I'll make sure to be prepared next Sunday," Walter continued. "But I really appreciate you two inviting me to eat with you." He gave Aurelia a warm smile.

"You're welcome." She squirmed under Jackie's sharp gaze. "We can't have you going hungry."

"She's glad you came," Jackie translated, making Aurelia redden.

When they put away the leftovers, Walter claimed the sink and took over dishwashing.

"Thanks." Jackie looked at Aurelia with a glint in her eyes. "Can we keep him?"

"Hey, Walter." Meana walked in from the back hall, her makeup perfect, a spring-green jacket hugging her top, and a white skirt swishing at her feet.

She smiled brightly while everyone else froze in surprise. Reaching the sink, she turned off the faucet and grabbed his arm. "Come help me with my car. I'm worried about a noise it's been making."

Stunned, Walter let her steer him from the apartment.

Aurelia blinked. What had just happened?

She turned to Jackie, who gaped at the door. "Did *you* know she was here?"

"No." Jackie shook her head in a daze. "She must have been here when I came home from church. Was she napping all that time?"

"Not *all* that time," Aurelia said logically. "She must have woken up and heard Walter, then fixed herself up."

Jackie frowned. "Comeback Walter has made strides, but he's not quite there yet. He's no match for Meana. Now, *Hot* Walter would have known what to do."

"That's not fair," Aurelia argued. "She caught us all by surprise.

Besides, she asked for help. Even Confident Walter might have had to give in to that."

Jackie nodded, but Aurelia couldn't tell if she was listening.

Suddenly, Jackie slammed a hand on the counter. "Can you believe the nerve of her?" she exclaimed as the situation caught up with her. She strode to the door. "I'm gonna turn things around on her so fast, it'll leave her dizzy."

"Jackie," Aurelia called out in sudden desperation, but the door had shut behind her friend.

Aurelia paused in indecision. She didn't want to make a scene. She didn't want *Jackie* to make a scene, but going outside to stop her might only add to the chaos.

The door swung open, and Jackie ran back inside.

Aurelia watched in silence as Jackie got out the cheeseburger pie and scooped a huge slice onto a paper plate. When she covered it with saran wrap, Aurelia figured that at least she wasn't planning on throwing it in Meana's face.

Was she going to give it to Meana though? That made no sense.

Jackie ran outside, the plate in her hand.

Hesitant, Aurelia at last stepped outside in her socks and leaned against the railing to watch the proceedings below.

Walter sat in the driver's seat of the yellow sports car, the door open and a covered paper plate in his hands. Jackie and Meana stood next to him, talking excitedly.

"Yeah, I know cars," Jackie exclaimed. "Scoot over, Walter. Let me take a look at this."

He scooted into the passenger seat, pulling his legs across the divide. Jackie quickly took the seat he had vacated and revved up the engine while Meana protested.

"Walter was about to figure out the problem."

"I've got it. No worries. I can definitely feel there's something funny here," Jackie responded.

"You can?" Meana sounded surprised and a little worried. "You don't have to help though," she continued, her voice turning sour. "We've got it under—"

"So far, so good," Jackie broke in, ignoring her. "It doesn't sound *too* bad."

"I think we should take it for a test drive," Meana suggested quickly. "Why don't you hop out, Jackie, and Walter and I'll drive around and see how it goes."

"You take that seat back there," Jackie told her. "I better stay in the front. I'll know what to do if there are problems."

"Oh, but . . . okay. Walter, won't you join me back here?" Meana scooted into the back seat.

"Actually, Walter, you need to take those leftovers home and put the pie in the fridge before it goes bad. Why don't you hop out?" Jackie told him.

"Let us drive you home, Walter," Meana said in a sultry voice.

The engine revved some more.

"Ugh, never mind, we should *not* be taking this for a test drive," Jackie concluded. "Walter, you need to go. You do know there's meat in that pie."

He didn't need to be told again. "All right, see you later. I hope the car gets fixed. Thanks for the food."

"But—" Meana began.

The engine noise increased, drowning out her words as Walter made his getaway. "Here we go." Jackie spoke loudly. "Meana, do you have tools in your trunk?"

"I don't . . . We don't need tools, do we?"

"Just in case. Hold on."

Meana let out a shriek as the vehicle moved. "I thought you said we shouldn't drive it right now."

"Sorry. Just a little back and forth to see how it does. What did you say was the problem again?"

Walter was nearly out of sight. Aurelia backed away from the railing.

"I thought you could tell what was wrong—Bye, Walter," Meana raised her voice in a desperate shout, then lowered it again to an angry pitch. "I thought you knew what was going on with the car."

"I mean, what tipped you off that something was weird? Noises? Problems braking? How long has it been like this?" Jackie fired off her questions.

"Ohh, I don't know." Meana's voice was annoyed. "Why did you have to . . . The car is fine. I'm sure it's fixed."

"Oooh, it does run nicely now."

"Stop moving the car and let me out."

"Sure," came the cheerful reply.

Aurelia returned indoors, her feelings jumbled. She was glad Walter had made his escape, and she wanted to laugh at how well Jackie had taken control, but her amusement pricked at her conscience the way many of her misgivings about Meana had pricked at her since the girl moved in.

Meana stormed inside, stomped into her room, and slammed her door hard.

A moment later, Jackie entered, chuckling. "Serves her right. I freed the hostage, meaning Walter. What's up?"

Aurelia was staring in the direction of Meana's room. "Do you ever . . . feel sorry for her?"

"For *that* drama princess?" Jackie stared at her.

"Yeah. I mean, she keeps chasing a guy who doesn't even like her—"

"Because he likes *you*," Jackie said in a smug tone.

"—and she hasn't made friends with us—"

"She's never *tried* to."

"—and we know she didn't get along with her roommates before us."

"Big surprise." Jackie put her hands on her hips. "What are you getting at? She has no social skills and no friends?"

Aurelia winced at the harsh words. Even Jackie winced. "People who don't get along with others usually have their reasons."

Jackie's eyebrows pulled together. "What do you think her reason could be?"

"It could be anything." Oh, the story maker was on and spiraling out of control. Aurelia gestured as she spoke. "Maybe her parents are as mean and unfriendly as she is, and it's all she knows from home. Maybe she was raised by relatives who didn't care about her." Was she going too far with her theories? "Maybe she dated psychotic, manipulative guys in high school who ruined her trust in people, and now she's wired for dysfunctional relationships."

Jackie shook her head in awe. "How do you think up these scenarios? And what if none of it's true? What if she's just mean?"

Aurelia shrugged. "Everyone can change. She probably expects us to hate her. Maybe if we treat her differently, she'll eventually start to open up to us."

Jackie squinted at her. "Kill her with kindness?"

Aurelia bit her lip. "Yeah. Only, that sounds a little violent."

"You want another phrase?" Jackie looked around and grabbed a bag of marshmallows. "Smother her with s'mores?"

That was still violent, but Aurelia couldn't resist the alliteration. "Stoke her with sweets?"

"Choke her with cheese puffs," Jackie shouted.

"Stop it," Aurelia begged, covering her mouth.

"No, no, you told me to be kind to her, so I will be." Jackie's voice was overly virtuous. "I'm putting cheese puffs on my grocery list."

Chapter Thirteen

AURELIA NEVER SAW Meana leave for school the next day, but when she went for a walk in the morning, the yellow car was gone.

She was jumpy that day, half expecting Meana to stroll in anytime, but neither Walter nor Meana walked in on her unexpectedly. She was okay with that. It gave her a chance to breathe.

On Tuesday, she was alone again until Jackie returned from classes.

"You're home early," Aurelia greeted with a smile as she looked up from her laptop.

"I decided to bless you with my presence as I do homework. Out loud. I have oodles of textbook passages and formulas to entertain you with."

Aurelia snorted. "I would love nothing more."

"It's a rare privilege." Jackie unzipped her backpack. "My only regret is that you won't understand the novelty of what I read to you."

Aurelia looked at her file and wondered if she should call it a day.

Jackie cleared her throat and began reading in a dignified voice. "Combustion—"

The doorbell rang, and Aurelia made an exaggerated scramble for the entrance to escape the out-loud homework session.

She pulled the door open to reveal the usual brown-haired culprit. She would be truly surprised to someday find a door-to-door salesperson on the other side.

"I'm here to be mean to you," Walter announced. "I figured I should do it sooner rather than later, especially after skipping it Sunday. Do you have time now? Can I come in?"

Aurelia's mouth hung open. She leaned on the door and accidentally swung it wider, which Walter took as permission to enter.

"Did you say 'mean'?" Jackie asked from the couch with a frown.

"Yes." Walter took off his shoes. "I realize it won't win brownie points with you, but it'll win brownie points with Aurelia, so I'll do it anyway."

"What?" Jackie mouthed.

"What's your least favorite song?" Walter asked Aurelia.

"Uhh." Here she had thought he would keep making excuses to avoid being mean to her. Instead, he was embracing the idea?

"What's a song you don't like?" he asked again, pulling out his phone.

Puzzled, she named one of the pop songs that came up at dance parties. Everyone else seemed to love it, but not her.

"Really?" Walter gave her a dimpled smile before turning his attention to his phone.

In another moment, the song started playing.

Aurelia opened her mouth in annoyance, but Jackie beat her to it.

"Hold on. What's going on?"

Walter turned up the volume and put the phone in his pocket. "It seems I've been too nice to Aurelia, so I'm making up for it."

Jackie gave up on him for an explanation and looked at Aurelia. "Which Walter is this?"

"CB," Aurelia answered, not wanting to call him Comeback Walter to his face. He looked from one girl to another in confusion before his face smoothed again.

"Thanks for dinner last Sunday," he told Jackie. "I'd like to take you girls out to dinner as a thank-you. I mean, I've gotta take both of you since you were both involved, right?" he asked Jackie with a cast of his head in Aurelia's direction.

Aurelia tried to ignore the music from his phone while he handed Jackie a baby pink card with a white lace pattern across it.

"You're invited to dinner at 'blank' on 'blank,'" Jackie read out loud.

"Right. Does Wednesday evening work for you guys?"

Confident Walter was coming on Wednesday, so Aurelia shook her head. "Thursday would work."

"Thursday," Jackie agreed.

"What time?" Aurelia asked.

"Sorry, what was that?" Walter cupped his ear. "Jackie, what did she say?"

"Oh, real mature. You won't talk to me now?" Aurelia folded her arms across her chest.

Jackie grinned and looked at Aurelia. "Six o'clock?"

Aurelia nodded, and Walter rubbed his hands together and grabbed the card back. "Do you like Brick Oven?"

"Oooh, yes," Jackie exclaimed. "You know you don't have to do this, right?"

Walter was writing on the card. "Of course I do. You were the perfect hostess to me. I'm your humble servant now—or on Thursday evening anyway." He gave back the card, and Aurelia came over to look. He had filled in the blanks with "6 pm" and "Thursday."

Jackie gave a bark of laughter while Walter retreated. Aurelia wondered whether he was leaving because she had come over.

"This card cracks me up," Jackie chortled. "Where did you get it? *Please* tell me you bought it in full view of everyone at whatever store you got it from."

"I don't remember anyone noticing other than the cashier." Walter smiled and looked around. "Aurelia, you need a piano in here."

"Uh-huh. Right. So you can play songs I don't like?" she asked, though her insides warmed at the idea of Walter coming over and playing in her apartment.

His response was to sing along to the party song still playing on his phone. She rolled her eyes. At least she was learning something new about him today. Apparently, he had a sense of humor and was willing to see a joke through to the end.

"So, Jackie, you were doing homework?" Aurelia stared pointedly at Jackie, who was kneeling backward on the couch, her arms leaning against the top as she watched in amusement.

"Yeah, but I better not do it out loud now. Walter would join in, and you'd be left out of the conversation. We have to include Aurelia, right, Walter?" she asked with a commanding undertone.

He put a hand to his chest. "I would never ignore Aurelia when you told me not to, Jackie. Aurelia, what are your pet peeves?"

She crossed her arms again. "Oh no, I'm not giving you any more ammunition."

He looked wounded. "Come on. I have to go soon, but I can still mess up a few things before I go. What annoys you? People drinking out of the milk jug? Moving the condiments to the wrong shelf? I could do anything you don't like."

"I think I'll pass."

He looked thoughtful and then shrugged. "Milk it is." He went and opened the fridge.

Aurelia moved quickly to intercept him. "Walter!" Chuckling in disbelief, she caught the door and tried to shut it, but he kept it open and grinned at her, his face inches away.

"Don't drink the milk, Walter," she ordered, trying hard to school both her face and her voice into sternness.

"But I'm thirsty," he whined.

Jackie burst out laughing, making both of them jump. She stood and grabbed her schoolwork. "I'll go to my room and leave you two to yourselves. Can't concentrate with all the drama."

Aurelia was of half a mind to tell her to stay, but Jackie made her escape before she could do it.

The refrigerator door was at a standstill.

Aurelia tried to glare at Walter. "You're a bad boy."

His grin softened. His eyes, flecked with green, smiled at her with sincere admiration.

Aurelia felt her heart speed up and her hands grow clammy. She released the fridge and stepped back, casting about in her mind for a way to change the mood and stop whatever he was trying to do.

The opening line of her despised pop song played. She suddenly realized this was the third time in a row the song had started over.

"*No,*" she exclaimed in an awful voice. "You've got it on auto-repeat? Give me that phone."

In the blink of an eye, he whisked it from his pocket and turned from her.

She made a grab around him for the phone, but he held it high in the air, and Aurelia cursed his few extra inches as she stood on her tiptoes, stretching to reach the device.

"Sorry." He didn't sound sorry at all. "The only thing I've been able to torture you with since I stepped in the door is music. I can't give that up now."

She let all caution and shyness fly and grabbed his forearm as high up as she could reach, then pulled down hard with both hands. With a startled laugh, he allowed his arm to drop, but it dropped sideways, locking across her middle and turning her with it.

Aurelia stopped, surprised to find herself breathlessly backed against him, holding on to his arm in front of her.

Walter stopped moving too.

Making quick use of the reprieve, she let go and grabbed his hand with the phone. They struggled for control of it, turning this way and that amidst panting and laughter while annoying lyrics blasted in Aurelia's face.

Finally, she managed to tear it from his hand and herself from his embrace. Quickly backing away, she turned off the song and held up the phone in triumph.

"All right," Walter gasped with laughter. "Have I been mean enough to you?"

"You to me?" Aurelia asked with raised eyebrows. "Yes. Me to you? Not yet."

"Oh no, you mustn't be mean to me," he begged. "I just need to know, do I need to act like this again the next time I see you? Or can I be nice from now on? I'll be whatever you tell me to."

Those were words he had better not tell just anyone. She shook her head to clear it. "You can stop being mean." She found the search bar on YouTube and started typing.

"Good. Um, can I have my phone back?"

She finished typing and held out his phone. He took it just as "My Little Pony" began to play.

"Aaaugh," he groaned, clapping a hand to his chest as though wounded. "How could you?"

"Just remember, that'll be in your search history now," she told him, feeling he wasn't nearly as upset as he ought to be.

He turned off the video, looking mournful. "My little sister might appreciate that." He grinned. "Eighteen years old and all that. Thanks for letting me visit. I have to say it was invigorating. I'll see you later."

Of course you will, she thought, not unhappily. "Do you want to come to dinner on Sunday?"

"I would love to."

"It probably won't be me cooking. Jackie cooks most of the time, although—maybe I'll make dessert." She swallowed before she could babble on. "I'll see you then. And on Thursday."

"Are you two okay meeting me at the restaurant?"

"That'll work." If he showed up here to pick them up, Meana might end up joining them. As much as Aurelia wanted to befriend her, she wasn't eager to have her wriggle her way into this. Likely, Walter had thought of the same thing.

"Great. See you, Aurelia."

She liked hearing him say her name. People didn't use names much these days. She had listened to entire conversations in which no one addressed each other by name, which was frustrating when she didn't remember what they were called and was listening to find out.

Of course, she was in no danger of forgetting her own name. She must like hearing him say it for different reasons.

She shut the door slowly, then turned around even more slowly.

"Don't be so glum," Jackie told her from the other doorway. "You'll see him on Thursday."

Aurelia stiffened. "I'm not glum."

"Yes, you are." Jackie plopped down on the couch with an armful of homework. "I swear you sighed as you shut that door. He's barely left, and you already miss him. It's time to sharpen that pencil and write your romances, my friend."

"I'm not about to turn into some misty-eyed miss," Aurelia insisted. "And you're not getting any sappy romances from me."

"'Misty-eyed miss'?" Jackie quoted with delight. "I love it. You should definitely have one of those in your next story. Maybe a Cinderella-type miss who's stuck doing the chores." She looked around, caught up a broom, and started sweeping it across the floor, singing, "I'm misty-eyed for my prince—"

The door opened, and Meana walked in and stopped to stare at her now sweeping, quietly humming roommate. "Jackie." She laughed, but the sound was spiteful. "You're always so . . . domestic."

Aurelia felt a burn creep up her neck. The words didn't sound like a compliment at all.

"How's your car today?" Jackie asked brightly.

Meana's fake smile gave way to a scowl, and she sauntered to her room as though Jackie and Aurelia had suddenly become invisible.

Aurelia and Jackie looked at each other, Aurelia trying hard not to laugh. This wasn't the way to kill her with kindness, but—

Jackie pulled her broom across the floor and continued her operetta. "And his name is Waaaal-ter."

Chapter Fourteen

AURELIA WROTE out a list that evening and added to it over the next two days whenever she remembered something she wanted to know about Walter. Her list contained questions for Confident Walter on the left side and Comeback Walter on the right.

She had begun to realize how little she knew about the guy. How many siblings did he have? How well did they get along? Where was he from?

And for Confident Walter, where in the world did he live, and how did he spend his time since he had to avoid Comeback Walter and even his friends?

Come to think of it, Comeback Walter knew little about her. He didn't know what she was studying or the fact that she was interning this semester. She knew he was into science and that he worked on a project that had to do with time travel, but those were only surface details.

It was a good thing Confident Walter was coming today. Unless Meana showed up, game night would provide an ideal setting for interrogating him.

By the time he arrived, Aurelia was ready to drag him inside. "Come in," she invited, trying to cover her impatience.

"Thanks." He entered far too slowly and looked around with caution but didn't ask about Meana.

Jackie sat with her things scattered across the dining table. She gave him a cheerful wave. "Sorry I can't join you. Too much homework."

Aurelia suspected Jackie had purposely secured a front-row seat to watch them. She wouldn't let it bother her though. Without preamble, she turned to Walter and asked her most urgent question. "Did Kylie ever have any more explosions at her house?"

If Walter *had* come from the future, she may as well tap his knowledge. Seeing two of the Macey's men show up at Kylie's place had continued to nag at Aurelia. If their visit to Macey's had anything to do with the explosion in the store, their first visit to Kylie's home would surely have been connected to that explosion as well.

In which case, their second visit might result in a new incident.

"Besides the one that took place during the concert?" he asked. "No. I'm sure you would have heard of it if she had, and you would have mentioned it to me."

"Good." How could those men have had anything to do with either explosion, anyway? It had been a far stretch. Although maybe she shouldn't trust Walter's answer, since time travel itself was still a far stretch.

She sighed and walked to the couch. She had almost gotten used to its position away from the wall since Meana moved in and rearranged things. Ignoring the pile of games on the sofa table, she proceeded with her questions. "Walter, where do you live right now? How do you avoid seeing the other Walter? How do you eat? Who else knows about you?"

He sat on the couch and held up his hands in mock surrender. "Whoa, give me a minute to answer."

Aurelia sat down beside him. "I'll give you ten seconds." She started to cross her arms but quickly realized there was little room to do so. Her position between Walter and the armrest barely left her breathing space.

"I admit to a stint of homelessness that first week until I secured a place with my uncle," he said while Aurelia scooted away from him and hit the armrest. How had she gotten herself trapped in a corner so quickly?

"I hope it doesn't change things too much between what happened the first time and what's happening now," he continued, "but what else can I do? It seems like I'm stuck in this timeline until we all get to the point in the future when I'll travel back. Anyway, I explained to my uncle, vaguely, that I was having trouble with the dorms. He and my aunt live in Provo, a bus ride or a nice, long walk from campus. I get to eat there, too, but I feel weird mooching off them, so sometimes I buy my own food or go to the student cafeteria."

She nodded. That explained poor Comeback Walter's problem with the cafeteria.

He paused. "So far, I don't think the other me has realized I'm using my credit card or student ID, which is a big blessing but makes me feel like a dunce. I guess I'm an easy victim for identity theft if I don't notice things like that."

Jackie snickered and left the room. Aurelia wondered whether this was more of her matchmaking maneuvering, giving the two of them time alone, or whether she now stood with her ear to the wall, ready to charge in if Confident Walter turned out to be the maniac they had first thought he was.

She continued her interrogation. "What about clothes?"

"I managed to smuggle a few days' worth of clothes from my apartment. I probably haven't noticed that yet either, and I don't think I will for a while, knowing me."

Aurelia snorted.

Walter's answering smile was broad, and his eyes danced as though they couldn't hold still, capturing her with their liveliness.

He wasn't supposed to make her laugh. What were her other questions again?

She became much too aware of being alone with him in the room.

"Um." None of her questions came to mind. She broke eye contact, only to find herself looking at his thick brown hair. That didn't help.

She stood and pointed to the other side of him, where there was more space. "I'm gonna sit over there."

"Oh, okay."

Walking past him would be a feat, she realized belatedly. She'd have to squeeze right up against him. Or maybe she could move the table? She leaned down to do so, and Walter stood quickly.

"Here, let me help."

"No, it's fine." She started moving in front of him.

"You're right, there's more room for you over there," he said, side-stepping.

"I've got it," she told him and sucked in a breath as he put his hands on her shoulders to help them switch places without colliding.

"I should have . . ." he mumbled apologetically.

The back of her knee hit the table. "Oops."

"Here, I'll just move over," he said, changing his mind and stepping back so she could stay where she had been all along but have more space.

"Oh, sure." Aurelia backed up against the armrest.

Meana burst inside and dropped her books on the floor while Aurelia and Walter froze.

"My teachers are so stupid," Meana complained loudly. Then she caught sight of the couch-navigators, and her petulant expression transformed into a smile. "Walter. It's so good to see you again."

"Hi, Meana," he replied in a neutral tone and looked at Aurelia.

"Thanks for coming to visit me again." Meana walked over and reached for him just as he suddenly walked to Aurelia's other side and sat down out of reach on the armrest. "I should have known you would do something that thoughtful, especially when I'm having a rough day."

"I didn't know you would be here, but it's too bad you're having a bad day."

"It's all better now," Meana answered in a voice that actually made Aurelia want to gag. The beautiful brunette decided to sit on the opposite armrest, where she would have a good view of Walter once Aurelia sat down to make it less awkward.

Not knowing what else to do, Aurelia plopped down. Somehow, she now sat even closer to Walter than she had before.

"I'm sure it helps to be home. Aurelia has a great place," Walter said, looking down at Aurelia as though that would help hide his face from Meana. It was a more intimate setting than Aurelia was used to, and she half regretted sitting that close to him, although a part of her liked it. Had he been Comeback Walter, she knew she would have enjoyed it. "Did you meet with Dr. Eunice today?"

"It's not like Aurelia owns the place," Meana broke in, displeased. "But it's fine living here."

"Did you meet with Dr. Eunice?" Walter repeated.

"No, that's tomorrow." *As you well know, stalker*, Aurelia added in her mind. It wasn't her fault that her inner voice was a little breathless.

"How's your internship going?" he asked immediately, leaving little time for Meana to speak.

Aurelia's answer, however, was too slow. The pixie-like girl stood and walked behind the couch, then put her head between Aurelia's and Walter's, forcing Aurelia to lean back.

"Thanks again for that concert, Walter," Meana purred, sliding a hand down his arm. Aurelia quickly scooted away, embarrassed and a little grossed out. "When are we going on another date?"

Walter blinked and frowned.

Aurelia stood. "Well, I don't wanna be a—"

The words "third wheel" didn't make it out of her mouth, because Walter leaped to his feet and interrupted. "Where are you—we—going?" He sounded almost desperate, but his grip was light when he took hold of Aurelia's arm. "The store?"

Meana's smile turned sour.

"Um, yes." Aurelia experimentally moved her arm, freeing it from Walter's grip. When his arm fell away, she gave him a small smile. She would have been disappointed if he had refused to let go.

"Did you hear my question?" Meana asked stubbornly.

"Right. Sorry, Meana, but I don't think we've ever been on a date." Walter's voice was carefully devoid of emotion as he watched the flirtatious girl out of the corner of his eye, as though he were afraid he would turn to stone by looking at her directly.

"Of course we have." She scowled. "Vocal Point, right? You invited me. We—"

"I did *what*?" Walter looked her full in the face, and his eyes widened. Actually, they did more than widen.

Aurelia suddenly watched him with keen interest, storing away in her mind the revelation that Meana had taken her place at the concert. This might be the closest she would ever come to seeing someone's eyes bug out in real life. Eyes bugging out was a phrase she had thought to ban from her own books because she didn't believe it was real. Now she might have to rethink that.

"And I had the *best* time," Meana began, although her voice was at odds with the words. She was beginning to look really annoyed at Walter's denseness. Aurelia, for her part, wondered what had made Walter take her now-roommate on that date. *Did* he have any interest in her? The thought pricked her heart, although she really had no claim on him.

Jackie entered the room, zeroing in on Meana. Aurelia sensed chaos in the making, but before Jackie could do anything, Walter spoke.

"That's it," he said and turned around.

Meana reached out again, but Walter had already bounded across the living room. He grabbed his shoes in one hand and ran out the door.

Meana stared at the exit. Then she turned to Aurelia with a glare that made her stiffen.

"You scared him away," Meana said. "Couldn't you have given us some privacy to talk? Sheesh." She stalked off to her room, sending Jackie a baleful glare on the way.

Jackie rolled her eyes. She moved a hand across the air in front of her face, and her features relaxed. "There. I've forgotten her. Where do you suppose Walter went?"

Aurelia let out a groan of frustration, unable to clear up her feelings as quickly. "I don't know. Maybe to talk to himself?"

Jackie tilted her head and considered. "Yeah, I would too."

Chapter Fifteen

THE APARTMENT SHONE like a new penny. Aurelia had vacuumed, scrubbed, and washed, first working through her annoyance over last night and then trying to distract herself from nerves over the upcoming dinner. She and Jackie would be spending the evening at Brick Oven with the Walter she liked.

She gave the floor beneath her another scrub with her rag.

Jackie walked in and stared. "Am I allowed to walk on that?"

Aurelia sat up and looked at the wet floor. "Oh. Um, sure."

Jackie made her way to the couch, keeping her arms out for balance. "Thanks for cleaning. This is pretty nice, especially if Meana walks in and slips and falls."

"Jackie!"

"I'm kidding. Are you ready for your date?"

"Yes." She dumped her rag in the bucket. A look at the clock revealed they still had half an hour before they needed to leave.

"I'll go clean the bathroom," she muttered.

* * *

AT FIVE TILL SIX, the girls arrived at Brick Oven despite Jackie's protests that they ought to arrive "fashionably late."

"I suppose we should also have arranged for spotlights to shine on us as we enter?" Aurelia asked dryly.

"Yes." Jackie clapped her hands. "And you should wear a floor-length ballgown. He would look up at you and be unable to take his eyes off you all evening."

"We need stairs as well, then," Aurelia remarked as they entered. "If he's going to look up at me."

She scanned the people and chairs lining both sides of the corridor leading to the front desk. Her gaze fell on Walter just as he stepped away from the wall with a muted smile. He looked pale.

"Walter," Jackie greeted him imperiously.

His smile turned crooked. "Miladies." He bowed.

Jackie held out her hand. "You may kiss my hand."

Aurelia nearly choked, and Walter's eyes widened.

"On second thought, don't." Jackie withdrew her hand. "But you may kiss Aurelia."

Aurelia coughed and glared at Jackie, who beamed at Walter, effectively avoiding her gaze. Embarrassed, Aurelia forced herself to face Walter, whose eyes were now sparkling. "Don't mind Jackie. Should we get in line?"

His brown eyes were steady on hers. "I already got us a spot. It'll be our turn soon."

"Okay." She kept looking at him, paying more attention to the face this time than to the hair. She had seen that smile of his light up the world, and even now, it swelled to a grin.

"To be honest," he said, "there are times I would be happy to mind Jackie."

Aurelia's face heated. Jackie mouthed something in triumph and pumped her fist.

"Walter, party of three," the lady at the front desk called.

As they followed their assigned waiter, Walter fell in next to Aurelia. His arm settled against her back, and he started to hum.

The arm across her back distracted her from whatever she had been thinking. The humming, in turn, distracted her from the warm feelings evoked by his partial hug.

In an instant, she recognized the song. "Are you humming 'My Little Pony'?" she asked incredulously.

He gave her an innocent look. "For some reason, that tune has played in my mind almost every time I've thought of you the past few days."

"How often have you thought of her?" Jackie was quick to ask.

He paused. Aurelia thought he might retreat into blushing and reticence, but instead he said, "Oh, I lost count a long time ago."

"How about an estimate?" Jackie persisted. "You've gotta have some idea. Fifty times? Hundreds? Thousands?"

Walter shook his head. "The brain's estimated to have sixty to eighty thousand thoughts a day. The hundreds are definitely too low."

Jackie looked delighted as they sat down, though Aurelia didn't know whether that was due to his little science fact or to the high number of times he had confessed to thinking about her. Knowing Jackie, it was probably both.

As they talked over the menu, Jackie leaned in to advise Walter, "Buy her love with the Mediterranean pizza. It has tons of veggies."

"Are you vegetarian?" he asked Aurelia in surprise.

She raised her eyebrows. "If I were, would I have pointed out the Meats-A-Pizza?"

"No, no, we're talking snacks here," Jackie corrected and began to explain Aurelia's love of vegetables, which was strange to hear, since the other Walter had announced it to Aurelia what seemed ages ago.

After a mouthwatering consultation, Walter ordered the Mediterranean and the five-meat pizza in the largest sizes, plus fruit pizza for dessert.

"Two large pizzas?" Aurelia stared at him. Did he really eat that much? Was that normal? What would it be like cooking enough to feed him all the time?

Of course, that last question was entirely hypothetical.

With all the innocence of a serpent, Jackie turned to Walter. "Given how much you've thought of Aurelia, why did you take Meana to a concert the other day?"

Walter choked on his ice water, and Aurelia jolted and hissed, "Jackie! That's none of our business." She and Walter weren't dating. He was certainly allowed to take out other girls.

Walter set down his glass and looked at Aurelia. "Actually, I'd like for you to know. I don't want you to have the wrong impression."

"Oh. Okay." She clasped her hands together and watched him in nervous anticipation.

He settled back on the bench and sighed. "It all started the day I went to a friend's talent show and saw a beautiful girl with a beautiful voice who, intriguingly, sang a song in French."

Aurelia blinked rapidly, her cheeks warming.

"I walked up to this girl and tried to ask her out, but she acted like I'd done something terrible and walked away. That, um, hurt." He didn't meet either girl's eye at the confession of vulnerability. "I saw her again in the library and thought maybe I could figure out what I had done wrong, and maybe she would give me a chance, but again, I was rebuffed."

Aurelia felt bad. She also privately savored the word "rebuffed." Sure, it was a negative word, but it was unusual in conversation. She had rebuffed someone. Wow.

"Then along came a beautiful girl who has hunted me for months. She waylaid me, as usual, and told me she had nothing to do that weekend and was terribly lonely, and I, well, buckled. I offered her one of my concert tickets. In the back of my mind, I had the idea I could stay home and not use the other ticket—although I'd looked forward to the concert—but she jumped at the offer and gushed her thanks and told me when and where to pick her up and left before I could get in a word."

"She would," Jackie muttered.

Aurelia nodded and felt her shoulders relax. It was a relief to know for sure that Walter wasn't into Meana. It also didn't hurt to learn a little more about her new roommate from his story.

"Are you okay with that?"

She looked up at Walter's anxious question. "Yes, of course. I mean— you didn't do anything wrong." She fumbled with her napkin. "I'm sorry I rebuffed you those first two times. There was something else going on, and I had my reasons."

He answered in a sober voice. "I know you did."

Jackie straightened in her seat, her eyes narrowing with suspicion. Aurelia stared at Walter. "How would you know that?" she asked weakly. This *was* CB. Right?

He chewed on his lip. "I had a talk with myself."

Aurelia and Jackie looked at each other. Was he saying he had met himself? Or was this just a way of speaking for him?

"In fact, he—I—barged into my apartment last night."

Aurelia leaped to her feet, hitting the table with a thump and grabbing it for balance. "He did *what*? I mean . . . *who* did?" she finished slowly and stared at him. He stared back, his face as pale again as it had been when they met inside the entrance.

She waited, just in case her save had somehow come in time.

"There are two of me," he said, dashing her hope. "And you two know all about it."

They stared at each other until Aurelia couldn't take it any longer. She stepped out of the booth and paced in front of it, causing several diners to look her way. She didn't care. Confident Walter *had* gone and confronted himself. What was he thinking?

The Walter on the bench followed her with his eyes, and Jackie looked worried.

Aurelia stopped. "Why would he visit you?"

"He wanted to know the same thing you guys did. Why I took Meana on a date."

"But—*why*?" She threw him a wild look and paced on.

Walter got up and caught her hands. "I'm sorry. I don't mean to upset you. And I didn't mean to upset you. In the past. Or the future. I guess I'm really gonna mess things up." He frowned. "Well, in the future, I'm gonna go to the past and mess things up. Which I already did."

She stared at him and squeezed his hands, not sure if she did it for comfort or to punish him in some small measure. "He didn't want you to know about him." The thought unsettled her. "Won't this make things worse?"

"I don't know. Honestly, I'm still reeling from the news."

She took in his haggard expression. Of course he was reeling. This wasn't fair to him. Although technically, he was the one who had given himself a shock. That made feeling bad for him complicated.

"Is that why the police talked to me?" Walter asked. "They thought I had been bothering some girl. Was that you?"

"Yeah. I'm sorry it was you they talked to. I had to report him for stalking me." Her throat began to burn as she remembered the day Confident Walter showed up on her doorstep with his ring box. "Um. What did he tell you about our first encounter?"

He gave her a searching look. "He said he showed up at your door and acted like you were a couple, and it was the same day I tried to ask you out. It was pretty bad timing for me to approach you that evening."

Confident Walter hadn't mentioned his proposal, then. With a sigh, Aurelia sank back onto the bench.

Jackie patted her hand. Fortunately, she didn't bring up the proposal either.

When Walter sat down beside Aurelia, her heart sped up. She hardly knew what to do with herself following his revelation. Their food arrived in steaming pie pans, but no one seemed inclined to eat. Even Jackie sat wordless in her seat.

Walter was the first to speak. "Um. If you don't mind me asking . . ." Aurelia held her breath, wondering what he would say now. "What's your major?"

She blinked. "My major?"

"Yeah. I actually don't know very much about you."

She let out her breath and almost laughed in relief. "I realized the same thing several days ago."

Her appetite began to return as she answered his questions. Pretty soon, she found herself in a conversation akin to what would take place on a normal date while a plethora of meats competed with cheesy veggies for space in her mouth.

Walter was intrigued to learn about her internship. Aurelia found out he hoped to study analytical chemistry in graduate school, and he talked about some of the things he was doing to prepare for it now.

"So you want to be a chemist?" she asked.

"Among other things. There's so much we still don't know about our earth and the universe, and I want to discover as much as I can so my children will know more and the generation after them even more. What about you? Do you want to be an author and an editor?"

"I want to be a full-time mom." She had learned to bring that up early in conversations when she liked a guy. "If I can be an author on the side, that'll be a second dream come true."

"Very cool. My mom's been a full-time mom most of my life, and she did an amazing job."

Jackie snickered. Walter's face took on a funny expression, and then he spread his arms wide. "As you can tell," he joked.

Aurelia hid a smile. She was glad he supported her choice and glad she was getting to know him. "By the way, would you be okay sharing your schedule with me?" she asked. "It'll help give me an idea of when you or the other you might come by."

He winced at the reminder of his other self but took a pad of sticky notes and a short pen from his jeans pocket and wrote out his schedule for her. "Here. Now, what about *your* schedule? Could you write down when you have those meetings with your instructor?"

"Yes, but you might want to stay clear of me before and after my meetings. Walter knows the when and where and might show up to talk to me." She gave him a sideways glance before taking the note and pen he offered.

He rubbed his face. "This'll take some getting used to."

"*I'll* say," Jackie broke in. "With any luck, one of you'll be gone before we get used to it. Although it'll probably be years before we get 'used' to it, so that's not much comfort."

Years? Aurelia imagined having two Walters for several years. She liked to think she could get to know and fall in love with the right guy in less than a year. In months, even. Would she have to date Walter for several years before he proposed? She wrinkled her nose at the thought.

"Thanks for dinner." Jackie stood, surprising her. "And thanks for answering my question about Meana. I can't blame you for taking her out, since you weren't dating my roommate yet." She wiped her hands on her napkin. "Now that I think about it, I don't believe you've taken Aurelia on a single date, which is really too bad. Also, I have an errand to run, so I'll take off, and you can give her a ride home. Cool? See you later."

"Wait a minute," Aurelia squawked in outrage and moved to stand, but Jackie was already halfway across the room.

Walter's hand settled on Aurelia's arm. "Might as well wait a few minutes, right?" He watched the exit as Jackie disappeared. Their server must have been watching, too, because he hurried to their table as though worried everyone would leave before paying.

Walter handed over his credit card with the bill. When his card was returned, he looked at Aurelia, trying not to laugh. "Would you like a ride?"

She wasn't nearly as amused.

"What does she think she's doing?" she exclaimed as they stood. "I mean, it's obvious what she thinks she's doing, but *why* is she . . . Okay, I know the answer to that too. But she needs to stop."

Walter tried to look sympathetic. "Yeah, this is rough. She shouldn't, uh, force us to spend time together."

"She *shouldn't*. She needn't. It's heavy-handed." Aurelia fumed her way out of the building. "I mean, I love Jackie. She's . . ." Her lips quirked. "She's Jackie. But honestly, I don't think we . . ." She trailed off, blushing.

"You don't think we what?" Walter's eyes were wide.

She forced herself to finish the sentence. "We don't need encouragement to spend time together. We'll spend time together with or without Jackie's interference. I think," she added, worried she was being too presumptuous.

Walter breathed out. "Yeah. Yeah, we will." He led the way across the parking lot, the trees around them turning golden red in preparation for October. "She does have a point though. We haven't gone on any dates, and I'd like to if my, um, appearances haven't scarred you too much." He opened the passenger door to a dark blue Nissan and looked at her. "Will you—will you go to dinner with me on Tuesday?"

The other times he had asked her out hadn't gone over well, but Aurelia no longer wanted to rebuff him. Locking gazes with him, she was reminded of the day she had looked into his eyes in the library. She was struck again by his green-flecked eyes, his brown hair, and his earnest but eager expression. More than that, though, she was attracted to the personality and humor he had shown over the last week. However, the timing of his question worried her.

"Why exactly are you asking me out?" Her voice was quiet. "Is it because the other you told you to? Or because Jackie wants you to?"

"No." His tone left no room for doubt. "It's because I noticed an extremely cute girl at a talent show the other day, even though her apparently justified rejection—*rejections*," he corrected, emphasizing the plurality, "stung. Since then, she has proved interesting, great to talk to, and a lot of fun to do things with."

Her lips turned up. "I would like to go to dinner with you," she answered and ducked into the car. Walter shut her door, his face alight.

When he entered on his own side, he asked with a hint of a laugh in his voice, "In the interest of full disclosure, why did you say yes just now to going on a date with me?"

Aurelia's face heated, but it was only fair that she answer the same sort of question she had posed to him. She cleared her throat. "Similar reasons."

"You think I'm extremely cute?"

"Sure," she answered lightly in spite of the way her heart beat at his flirting.

"And I'm fun to do things with?"

She nodded and hesitated, feeling shy but wanting him to know his efforts that evening in the Wilk had meant a lot to her. "After the karaoke fiasco, I loved our time at the piano. Thank you for that."

His gaze softened. "I enjoyed that too."

The drive home was marked by a strange level of peace. Aurelia's butterflies filled her with an energetic awareness, but she felt peace nonetheless as they talked.

When they arrived in the parking lot, Jackie's car was in its usual spot.

"So much for her errand." Aurelia turned to Walter, her harmony broken up by annoyance. "You're still coming to dinner on Sunday, right?"

"I wouldn't miss it."

"You can bring a friend if you like."

"Thanks. If someone comes to mind, I'll invite him. That's nice of you."

Nice? Not exactly. Having an extra person there would curtail Jackie's obvious efforts to leave the two of them alone together.

Not that she hadn't enjoyed the fruits of Jackie's efforts. The moments in her apartment when Jackie left them—remembering those scenes made Aurelia blush. Walter had smelled her hair. They had fought over his phone, with her basically trapped in his arms. She had liked it.

Still, she didn't want Jackie to strong-arm them into spending time together. Hadn't Aurelia and Walter just agreed they would do it without encouragement?

Aurelia smiled back at Walter, hiding her thoughts. Jackie did *not* need to play her tricks on Sunday.

Chapter Sixteen

WHEN SHE FOUND Confident Walter at institute the next evening, Aurelia wondered whether he knew that she knew that his other self knew about him.

"Hi," he said, which told her nothing.

"Hi," she answered, giving nothing in return.

If he didn't know, it might be fun to keep it secret, especially given how nervous he now looked.

"I'm sorry I ran out on you last time. I was in shock," he said.

She nodded.

"And you should know I'm not interested in Meana." He cleared his throat. "Neither of me is. I know myself. I'm sure it had to do with the pain of rejection when you said no to going to the concert."

Funny. He had phrased it so as not to let on that he had spoken to himself about it.

"I'm sure it did." Was she smiling enigmatically? She hoped so.

His comments in class for the next hour were sparse, and he kept giving Aurelia searching looks. It felt good to have the upper hand for once. By the time class ended, though, she was ready for more open communication.

"I thought you had decided it was a bad thing to meet yourself," she told Walter while the students around them left.

His brown eyes widened. "He told you? *I* thought—that is, I didn't know you'd been spending time with him, and I can't believe you didn't tell me."

"Because you promised to leave me be if I spent time with him?" She watched him, remembering why she had agreed to come to institute in the first place. She wanted to get to know the other Walter, and if this Walter was his future, she really should get to know him too—even if he made her heart beat in a different, less enjoyable way than did Comeback Walter.

He nodded and took a deep breath. "Does this mean I have to leave you be from now on?"

That was the compromise he had come up with. However, she was ready to propose something different, so she raised her chin. "No, but you'll have to back off when I say so. If ever I say no to something, then it's a no. If I say leave, you leave."

He was already nodding emphatically. "Of course."

The classroom was nearly deserted by now. Aurelia wavered between relief that he had accepted her deal and uncertainty about being alone with him in the classroom. "And, uh, I gotta go now."

"Can I walk you home?" Leaving the room, he ignored the refreshment tables and mingling crowds as she moved toward the exit.

"No. But thanks."

"Okay." He sounded disappointed.

She stopped with her hand on the glass door. "Don't come around on Sunday. Walter's coming to dinner."

His smile came slowly, but it brightened his entire face the way it had last week. "Okay."

Surprised to feel an answering smile on her face, Aurelia quickly told him goodbye and walked out into the cool evening.

Once out of sight, she shook her head at his enthusiasm, but she couldn't stop smiling. Who knew a grin could be so contagious?

She was halfway across campus before she saw the familiar silhouette and her step hitched.

One of Kylie's bug sprayers walked ahead of her. Even in the fading light, she saw enough to recognize him as the man with the Boston accent.

She watched him in dismay. What was he doing here? If he hadn't been so unaware of her every time she saw him, she would wonder if he was stalking her, just as Walter had.

A vague feeling of déjà vu floated through her. It was as though she had seen him before—even before Macey's.

Biting her lip, she tried to shake the discomfort that dogged her. What was he up to? His strange conversation at the store and the timing of the explosions sat heavy on Aurelia, making her worry there was more to him than met the eye.

She could follow him.

Her eyes brightened with anticipation and a dose of fear. Would spying on him be wrong? She did have reason to be suspicious though. He had been in Kylie's home. Walter had said there were no more explosions at Kylie's place, but who was to say the man wouldn't go back and hurt her somehow? Not to mention that things could happen differently now. According to Walter, it was Kylie and not Aurelia who got hurt before.

At the fork in the road, she turned and trailed behind the man, keeping a good distance.

Surely she would be safe following him for a minute or two. Just till the edge of campus or so. There was no need to follow him through Provo in the dark.

In the meantime, she could gain some spy experience.

Her heart fluttered with excitement. She would follow him like the main character in her secret agent story would do. This was a chance for her to feel what her character would feel, to practice and play around with countersurveillance techniques.

A grin spread across her face, and her step quickened so as not to lose the man.

What was the first thing a spy needed to keep in mind as she followed her quarry?

Don't stand out, she told herself. *Look like you belong.*

Schooling her features into something less excited, she strode on with purpose. If the man were to turn around and look her way, she wouldn't falter. She wouldn't hesitate.

What else did she need to keep in mind?

Don't be recognized.

He might not remember her from Macey's, but he had seen her at Kylie's home. How had she looked that day? What had she worn?

She found a scrunchie in her pocket and wrapped her hair in a ponytail. Her hair had been down the other day. She wished for a cap to change her style and obscure her face, but maybe she had the next best thing: a light jacket she had brought in case the walk home was chilly.

She put it on and debated raising the hood. It was probably too warm for it to look natural if she put it on.

Her quarry passed the Joseph F. Smith Building and descended a small set of cement stairs. She walked across the JFSB courtyard, trying to look comfortable and unhurried. He reached the Eyring Science Center. She took the stairs.

He entered the Eyring Center, and Aurelia stopped.

The lit-up building should have been inviting, but instead, it felt like a trap. She moved closer, watching the door through which the man had disappeared. She could walk inside and have a real live spy experience, but reason told her no. Her senses told her no.

She jumped at the sound of wingbeats and, hand pressed to her chest, glared at a bird landing on the roof.

Looking at the building again, she took a deep breath and, disregarding reason, forged on.

As the door closed behind her, she saw the suspect walking down the hall. Adopting an unaffected expression, she strolled in the same direction, chanting to herself, *I'm a student. It's natural that I'm here. I'm a student.*

Her footsteps echoed on the floor, and she listened to the heavier footsteps ahead of her while she passed lab room after lab room with keypads on the doors. Strange-looking equipment hung from the ceiling in one of them, visible through the narrow window near the top of the door. Maybe Walter's lab was in this building. Peering in through one of the rooms that had lights on, she wondered what the equipment for *his* research project looked like.

For now, though, she must focus on the man ahead of her. She needed a good cover story if he were to notice her. She pulled out her cell phone and bent over it—just in time.

The man looked back. As he paused, Aurelia's eyes focused on her phone. Slowing her walk, she moved her fingers as though she were scrolling through social media posts. Whatever she did, she mustn't look like she was tensing up.

At last he continued on, and she breathed out in a silent puff.

He sped past an open corridor from which voices sounded. When

Aurelia reached it, she peeked down the hall and nearly stumbled, then sped out of sight as well and leaned against the wall to catch her breath.

"You need a break from your homework, Walter," Meana was saying twenty feet away.

"Actually, I think I'm about ready to go home," he answered.

"Great." Meana took it as an invitation. "I'll walk with you."

High-pitched, electronic beeps reached Aurelia's ears. Still within sight, her suspect was keying in the code on a door. Remembering her cover, Aurelia gulped and pretended to type something on her phone until he entered the room and let the door shut behind him.

Now what? Walter's and Meana's voices were fading into the distance. She almost wanted to go after them, but this whole evening had been so weird that she wouldn't know what to say to Walter, and Meana's presence would only make things worse.

She scowled at her phone. The Macey's men were getting on her nerves. How had this man gotten the code to one of the labs?

Suddenly, she slapped her forehead. What if the man was a professor? She may have just followed a teacher to his lab. If so, there was nothing at all suspicious about seeing him on campus.

On the other hand, it seemed strange for a professor to spray bugs as a side job.

Keeping her steps as quiet as possible, she made her way to the room the man had entered, throwing a casual look in the window as she passed. There was little to see, and she didn't dare let him catch her looking in, so she kept going and started searching for a way out.

Finding a set of stairs, she took them with the relief of someone escaping a prison. By the time she made it upstairs and found an exit sign, she had a new plan in mind.

If this man were faculty, she should be able to find him online. All she had to do was look up the website for BYU's science department when she came home. It would show pictures of each faculty member, and she could scan through them until she found this man and possibly even his friends. How hard could it be?

* * *

Two hundred forty-three. BYU's life sciences department had two hundred forty-three faculty members, and four of them didn't have photos.

Aurelia pushed away her laptop and rubbed her eyes. She hadn't found any of her culprits among the pictures. Maybe she could abandon the search in favor of working on one of her stories. That would be far more enjoyable. Or she might go to bed. She wasn't usually on her laptop this late in the evening.

No. Determined, she returned to the list of degrees at BYU.

Further research revealed another department, physics and astronomy, which also made use of the Eyring Center.

She moaned and put her head in her hands.

Meana wandered past, and Aurelia looked up. They had spoken little to each other this week, but Aurelia still wanted to make an effort at friendship. "How was your audition on Wednesday?"

"Oh, that?" Meana scoffed. "I'll be getting one of the lead parts after my performance. I always do great at these things."

Aurelia blinked. "Congra—tulations." She tried not to make it sound like a question. Had Meana gotten the part, or was she just assuming she would?

Meana raised her eyebrows. "You're such a fake."

"The irony of that statement is overwhelming," Jackie said as she entered the room. "The question is, which kind of irony? Is it dramatic irony, or does Meana recognize it herself?"

Meana blushed a dull red.

Jackie fixed a glare on her. "Don't harass my roommate."

"Hey, we're all roommates," Aurelia protested and tried to smile at both of them. "Meana, do you wanna—"

"No." Meana cut her off and headed for the front door, her nose in the air.

"—hang out and watch a movie?" Aurelia finished.

Meana opened the door and looked back at her. Then she sniffed. "Fake."

The door swung shut behind her.

"Don't let her treat you like that. How can you still be trying?" Jackie huffed. "I've told myself to be nice, but she's always rude before I can say anything polite, and I refuse to reward that."

It was impossible not to feel offended by Meana's rejection, but Aurelia was stubborn. "I won't stop trying."

Jackie groaned. "Just don't be too *sweetful* to her." Aurelia cringed and grabbed a cushion, ready to throw it at her friend, but Jackie's next words stopped her. "By the way, there was an explosion at Day's Market this morning."

"What? Were you there?"

"No, I ate out for lunch, and it came up on TV. Two people got hurt. Not badly hurt, but one passed out, and both got singed. There was no fire, and they hadn't found signs of a bomb by the time I saw it on TV. This is really weird."

"Yeah, it is." Aurelia dropped her cushion and started a Google search. "There's already an article about it online. How many explosions have there been now?"

"Three, right? That we know of. Yours, the one at Macey's, and this one."

"There might have been more." Aurelia looked up after a quick scan of the article, feeling anxious. "My explosion didn't make it into the newspaper. There could be others like that. Some might even have gone unnoticed by *anyone*. If I hadn't been at Kylie's when hers happened, she might never have known about it. A few things fell off the shelves. She could have blamed it on her dog." She shivered. "What if it's happened in other places, and it's gone unnoticed and unreported?"

"What if?" Jackie repeated. "There's nothing you or I can do about it, right? It's up to the police to investigate."

Aurelia frowned. She wanted to do *something*, but what could she do that the police couldn't? She certainly couldn't go back in time to stake out Day's and find out if the three Macey's men had been there recently. Typing in "science of explosions" in her search box, she opened the link to what turned out to be a terribly long academic paper. After skimming over the first few paragraphs, she stopped, disheartened. What could she contribute besides what she had already told the police about her own experience?

She minimized her browser, faculty lists and all, unsure she could focus right now. The idea of these explosions continuing to happen without warning made her skin crawl, shadowing the itchy feeling she had had after her incident at Kylie's. She suspected it was akin to experiencing an earthquake and then feeling phantom earthquakes afterward, imagining again and again that another one was beginning.

Chapter Seventeen

It was a long shot, but maybe she could get information from Walter, even if he didn't know what it was about. Sunday dinner would be a prime time to try.

When she opened the door at a quarter past three that Sunday, her heart sped up at the sight of a worried-looking Walter.

"I hope we're in time for dinner," he said. "You didn't eat it all already, did you?"

Aurelia relaxed into a chuckle, accepting his joke about arriving much earlier than dinner warranted. "I guess I should have told you what time to come." She opened the door wider.

"I brought my friend Brian. You've met him already, if you remember," he said as they entered.

"Nice to see you again." She remembered Brian being at the karaoke night, but she didn't bring it up. Not the greatest of memories.

Now, *post*-karaoke memories—those were great.

"Thanks for having me," he replied.

"Something smells good." Walter sniffed the air. "Gingerbread?"

"Yeah, I didn't know what kind of dessert you like, but I made gingerbread cake." It had cooled just in time for her to put together the layers before the guys arrived—apricot preserves between the two round cakes, and chocolate icing on top.

Walter followed her gaze. "That looks amazing. I can't wait to try it."

Aurelia smiled in relief and turned to the kitchen where Jackie was washing her dishes from the last few days. "Hey Jackie, this is Brian, Walter's friend."

"Hi, Brian." Jackie flashed him a grin. "Safety in numbers, huh?"

"What?" He looked disoriented.

"Want some Aurelia-snacks?" Jackie offered.

"Aurelia-snacks?" Walter looked at Aurelia with humor, and her face heated.

"Vegetables," she said quickly, indicating a plate of carrot sticks on the sofa table.

"Aurelia-snacks sound better." His smile was broad. "Jackie, want some help in the kitchen?"

"Not yet. You guys should play a game."

"I can play until my family calls on Skype." Aurelia ducked from the room and picked up a pile of games from her closet.

The three of them settled on UNO, nice and simple. And bloodthirsty, within minutes of starting. There seemed to be no end to the mean cards, and all three were quick to use them.

When Aurelia's turn was skipped, she looked up at Walter. "Do you know Professor Jared Young from the life sciences department?" That was one of the male professors who hadn't had a photo online.

Brian laid down a plus-four card, snickering.

Walter tilted his head and added another plus four. "I don't think so."

"Or Keaton? Or Hemingway?" *Was* the man from Macey's a professor? She laid down a third plus four, and Brian groaned.

"No." Walter turned to his friend, who shrugged as he filled his hands with cards and said, "Me neither." Then he turned back to Aurelia. "Why?"

"I still need to take a science elective class." That wasn't a lie.

He brightened. "I can give you plenty of recommendations for teachers."

Aurelia hid a smile in spite of the dead end she had hit on her line of questioning. She was starting to adore Walter's love of science and academics. "Thanks. Maybe I'll ask you more later."

When her family called, she moved to the armchair with her laptop, leaving the boys to destroy each other.

"How has your week been?" Mom asked while Dad slid out of the picture. He probably had someone he needed to talk to. "Do you still hurt anywhere?"

"No, I'm totally recovered," Aurelia said.

"How many of those do you have?" Brian exclaimed, and Aurelia looked over to see Walter place a reverse card on top of the pile.

Mom's eyes narrowed. "Do you have someone over?"

"Yes, we have company." A little nervous, Aurelia turned the computer around. "This is Walter." He put down his cards and waved. "And Brian." Brian waved as well.

"This is my mom and Rachel and Rowan," she told the guys.

Her family members called out greetings. Aurelia turned the laptop back around, but Mom wasn't done.

"Who are they? Walter and Brian?"

Aurelia didn't know what to say. She watched Brian lay down his cards and wander off to the kitchen to see if he couldn't help with something after all.

"Walter and I," she began, her mind churning, "are going on a date on Tuesday. Brian's his friend."

"A date? And yet he's there at your place now. How long have you known him? How come you haven't told us about him before?" Mom fired off her questions.

Walter came over to stand behind Aurelia and face the interrogator. "That's probably my fault, Mrs. . . . ."

"Jackson," Aurelia whispered.

"Jackson. Hopefully after our first date, I'll be worth talking about." He winked at Aurelia, and her cheeks warmed.

"Well," Mom said with a smile, "you know the way to Aurelia's heart is . . ."

"What?" Walter leaned in closer and Aurelia prepared to roll her eyes.

"Being fully converted."

Aurelia blinked rapidly. She had expected a joke. Instead, she was touched by her mom's words pointing to what mattered most to her: being dedicated to God.

"Good," Walter said with emphasis. "I wouldn't have it any other way."

"Walter." Fourteen-year-old Rachel giggled. "You have nice hair. I especially like the color."

Aurelia went rigid. In the kitchen, Jackie had a cough attack.

Aurelia's family knew all about her attraction to brown-haired guys. Had her mom been thinking about that from the moment she saw him? How embarrassing.

Walter was taken aback for only a moment. "Thank you." He fluffed his hair. "I was thinking about dying it purple, but maybe I'll leave it be for now."

"Rachel, don't hit on Walter," Aurelia scolded and tried to come up with a different subject. "Um, so there have been more explosions in town."

"Really?" asked Rowan, her eleven-year-old brother. "Cool!"

"Where? How many?" Mom asked swiftly.

"Just at stores," Aurelia answered. "Two other explosions. The police can't tell what caused them."

"Maybe Utah will lead the world into a zombie apocalypse," Rowan suggested.

"Ew, Rowan." Rachel wrinkled her nose. "But seriously, that's kind of cool. Well, if it doesn't give Mom and Dad nightmares."

Mom fanned herself. "I think just about anything you tell us at this point will give me nightmares."

Impishly Aurelia decided to test her statement. "You should know I studied scriptures this morning. I went to the temple yesterday, and I went to church today. Oh, and I eat nice, square meals. Jackie cooks all the time."

"Just trying to fatten her up, Sister Jackson," Jackie hollered dutifully.

"Will that give you nightmares?" Aurelia asked with feigned concern, then laughed at her mom's grimace.

"Aurelia Jackson, stop teasing your mom," a deep, rumbling voice said as Dad appeared on-screen, his face clearly showing his amusement.

"Yes, sir, President Jackson." Aurelia saluted.

Rachel sighed. "You *always* go to church, and you *always* go to the temple on Saturdays. None of that's new."

"Really?" Walter asked with interest. "You go to the temple every week?"

"Yeah." She turned to him and was again struck by his brown eyes—and by the hair he had fluffed at Rachel's earlier comment. She cleared her throat. "It started out as a thought that I could kind of serve a mini-mission by attending every week while my family serves in Costa Rica—Dad's mission president there—but now I'm thinking I can keep going with it even when they get back. I've come to love it." It was the most spiritual place she could be, and doing ordinances for those who didn't have a chance to receive them in this life was always exciting to her.

"Just wait until you're back in school," Jackie called out and accepted the dishtowel from Brian, who had finished drying the last of her dishes.

"Hey, Walter," Rachel said seductively, "are *you* looking for someone who's fully converted?"

He laughed. "You betcha."

"I *am* in school," Aurelia called to Jackie and looked back at Rachel, wondering how to deal with her.

"Well, just wait until you're married to homework again," Jackie returned.

"Is that what you are, Jackie?" Walter asked.

Jackie sighed deeply. "My husband is the worst taskmaster."

This whole conversation was beyond ridiculous. It had taken no time for things to get derailed, and they didn't get any better in the next few minutes. Aurelia vacillated between exasperation and laughter until the call ended.

"Your family's great," Walter remarked. "I had no idea they were on a mission. How long have they been there?"

"A little over three years. Their mission got extended because of some health complications the next mission leader is dealing with. They're coming home in January."

"And where's home?"

"Orem," she said, mentioning the city next to Provo. "They're renting out the house while they're away, but once they get back, they'll be close enough for me to visit anytime." Thinking about it almost hurt because of how much she looked forward to it.

Jackie called from the kitchen, "It's time to make lasagna."

Walter and Aurelia jumped up to join her, ready to take orders. Jackie directed them to mix the cheeses while she and Brian made the meat sauce. Soon, the room filled with the smell of sizzling meat.

"Ready for compilation," Jackie announced, wiping a smear of tomato sauce from the side of her face. "Brian, spread some of the sauce in the pan."

As soon as he did, she placed pasta on top and put her hands on her hips. "Now, Walterelia, one-fourth of the ricotta mixture."

"Walterelia?" Aurelia's voice was strangled.

"I think that means we have to spread it on together." Walter chuckled, his cheek dimpling. "Here, hold the spoon, and I'll put my hand over yours. Let's start by dividing it into quarters in the bowl."

"We really don't need to do this," Aurelia giggled, but it was too late. Her hand was trapped.

"Oops," said Walter. "Sorry. Were you trying to make a line there? I was about to divide it the opposite way. I'll follow your lead. There we go. Wait."

"This is ridiculous," Aurelia groaned, well aware that they had an audience. "We could at least have had one of us divide it up before we joined hands. Sheesh. There, it's in quarters. We're picking up the bottom left portion," she told him, and they managed to spread it across the pasta without too much pain.

"Now, if you two are done flirting, I'll spread a layer of mozzarella," Jackie said severely, as though she hadn't encouraged the flirting herself. She spread her handful of cheese like the sower in the parable and turned to Brian, who watched her almost worshipfully. "Meat?"

He obeyed. Jackie followed it up with pasta and looked at *Walterelia*. "A repeat performance of your spreading skills, if you please. I must see it again to judge the efficiency, grace, and overall aesthetics."

Aurelia wanted to dump the bowl of remaining cheese mixture over Jackie's head, but Walter, his lively eyes dancing, picked up Aurelia's wrist and placed the spoon in her hand before placing his hand on top of hers.

"Marvelous!" Jackie exclaimed with a pompous accent as they worked. "Phenomenal!" she said as Brian took over with the mozzarella. "Superb!" she cried out as she herself added to the growing lasagna.

Several layers and exclamations later, the last layer of the last ingredient was added, and aluminum foil was spread theatrically across the top.

"In the oven!" Jackie cried, doing a twirl with her hands in the air while Brian positioned the pan. "Now, games."

Brian seemed unable to tear his gaze from Jackie while they played, and Aurelia watched him on the sly. He remained quiet, perhaps trying to get a feel for Jackie's ways and humor. Or maybe he was shy? Probably not the kind of guy Jackie would go for, unfortunately. Either she was unaware of the effect she had on him, or else she ignored it.

When the smell of lasagna filled the air, they cleared away their game to set the table. Aurelia retrieved milk from the fridge, and Walter caught her eye and gave her a devilish smile. He had to be thinking about their stalemate over the fridge the day he was "mean" to her. She reddened but grinned back at him.

They enjoyed the lasagna in full. Then, finally, they sat back with large slices of gingerbread cake.

"This is amazing," Walter said, spearing another piece with his fork while Brian nodded his assent.

Aurelia ducked her head, smiling. "It's my mom's recipe."

"I need to have you bake more often," Jackie said.

"So long as you keep cooking, I'm happy to."

"Is it just the two of you that live here?" Brian asked.

"Nope, there are three of us. We have a Cursed Room, and it currently has an occupant." Jackie wiped her mouth with her napkin. "But she can't possibly be home right now, or she would have sniffed out Walter and left her room."

"Whoa," Walter began but couldn't seem to think of a feasible protest. Probably because she was right. "What do you mean, 'cursed'?"

"No one stays there for long," Aurelia took over. "Our third roommate always moves out for some reason or other. Another one moves in quickly after that. Meana's our third roommate this semester."

"If you ask me, the room is more cursed than ever with her living there," Jackie confided.

"Come on," Aurelia protested.

"But Aurelia's determined to be nice to our roommate, so I'll try to speak nicely of Meana, even though she's determined to make us miserable."

"Cursed Room," Walter muttered. "Wow."

"I seriously think it'll break the curse when either Aurelia or I leave. At least it'll change *something*." Jackie stood, picking up her plate.

Brian followed her to the kitchen. "I'll do the dishes."

"Oh sure," Jackie said, pleased, while Walter moved to help as well.

Jackie took up position behind Brian to offer a running commentary on his dishwashing. Aurelia pulled up a tall chair on the living room side of the kitchen counter and watched from a more respectful distance.

"Soap it up good," Jackie said. "Way to scrub. Ooh, three at a time. Ambitious." Brian looked flushed, but his smile grew, and Walter shook with laughter by the time they finished.

"Looks like we're done here." Walter put the last plate in the dish rack.

"Come back on Sunday," Jackie told him.

"Thanks."

"Thank you all for a great evening," Brian said as they returned to the living room, where he picked up his bag. "Jackie, you were enchanting." He bowed and handed her a paper animal.

"I was?" she asked as if struck.

"Most definitely."

She blinked at him.

Aurelia looked from one to the other. Hoping she wasn't being too impulsive, she said, "Brian, you should come on Sunday too."

"I'd love to," he said.

Jackie just stared at the gift he had handed her: an origami giraffe.

Was that what he had been working on during their games when it wasn't his turn to play? Aurelia had paid more attention to how he looked at Jackie than to his hands, but she had noticed him folding up paper.

Walter opened the door and flashed a smile at Aurelia. "I'll see you on Tuesday."

A thrill ran through her at the reminder of their first actual date. Walter followed Brian outside, leaving the two girls alone.

Aurelia turned to the still-immobile Jackie and squinted at her. "You look a little . . . frozen in place."

Jackie looked up from the giraffe. "No one's ever said that to me." Her voice was full of wonder.

"That you're enchanting?"

"Yes. Also—he gave me a giraffe."

Aurelia laughed. "So what are you going to do about it?"

Jackie tapped a finger to her lip. "I suppose I'll test his origami skills next Sunday."

Aurelia rolled her eyes. "It's okay to say it if you think he's cute."

"Nope." Jackie's tone brooked no argument. "Not until he's made me an elephant."

Chapter Eighteen

"Guess who?" Aurelia muttered to herself when the doorbell rang the next morning. All things fair, though, Walter hadn't come by unannounced in several days. It could be someone else.

She opened the door. Nope, it was him. Having memorized his schedule, Aurelia knew Comeback Walter had a class about to start. This was Confident Walter.

"Do you want to go jogging before it gets hot outside?" he asked brightly.

She blinked. "Um."

"Morning exercise. Who can say no?"

Was he always this hyper in the morning? Aurelia was more awake than some, but she wasn't exactly bouncy.

Dare she run with Confident Walter? There was a time she wanted to run *from* him when she saw him. Would she feel unsafe jogging at his side?

He ran in place. "I promise it feels good."

One corner of her mouth tugged upward. "I don't really jog. If I come along, it'll probably have to be a walk."

"A walk sounds good. With maybe a little bit of jogging. What do you say to five minutes of jogging?"

She shook her head and leaned against the doorframe. "Ten seconds."

He caught his breath on a laugh. "I'm having déjà vu. Although the first time around, you said five . . ." He caught himself. "Come on, you can commit to more than that. How about four minutes?"

"Nah. Thirty seconds." She had had this conversation with him "the first time around"?

"Two minutes?" he pleaded.

"Forty-five seconds."

"Okay, so you want to do it for a minute," he concluded.

"No, I want to do it for, like, thirty seconds, but I'm committing to forty-five."

Mischief danced in his eyes. "Let's round that to a minute."

The *hotness* Jackie kept referring to was back. He was confident and self-assured, and somehow his insistence and their bargaining made Aurelia want to laugh rather than retreat. Maybe he was growing on her.

"Where are we headed?" she asked as she followed him down the stairs.

"I normally go to Kiwanis Park, but you're welcome to choose."

That's right, the other Walter had been jogging in Kiwanis the day he found her climbing trees.

"Kiwanis sounds good."

She fastidiously checked her watch as they went, not trusting him to tell her when a minute was over, and switched to a walk as soon as possible. When they reached the park though, she couldn't resist speeding up, and Walter was happy to follow.

The trip turned into a mixture of walking and jogging. As they walked anew, Walter asked, "How was Sunday dinner with me? Do I need to take myself to task for anything?"

She gave him a suspicious look. "Is that why we're jogging, so you can interrogate me about our relationship?"

"Mainly, it's because I miss you." There was no denying the sadness in his face as he looked at her.

Aurelia wasn't sure how to respond. She didn't *not* believe in the time travel story anymore, but she wasn't yet ready to picture his side of the story enough to empathize with him.

Her eyes followed the winding path ahead of them. Already, it was bringing them back toward the school and 900 East. "Sunday was fun. We invited you and Brian to come again."

He cocked his head. "Who's Brian?"

She blinked. "Uh. Your friend?"

"I have several friends named Brian."

"Well . . . Didn't he come to Sunday dinners with you the first time around? No, never mind, I guess we started inviting your double over because you're using your student ID for meals." She thought about it for a moment as they left the park behind. "Brian was at the karaoke activity."

"Oh. Was that a couple of weeks after we met? I remember one of my friends invited me, and I considered taking you, but I wanted to do something more date-like."

Aurelia rubbed her forehead. "So we didn't go to the karaoke activity?"

"That's right."

She bit her lip and looked up at him. "What other things are different this time around?"

His forehead creased. "That's a good question. Maybe we should compare notes."

She nodded as they crossed the street. Among all the things that had happened since they met, what was she most curious about? "Did you catch me climbing a tree at the park?" she asked, remembering how this Walter had mentioned her hobby with a grin the first time he told her he had traveled back in time.

"Yes," he said with the same grin.

"What did we do instead of karaoke?"

"We went to the Good Move Café."

She had heard about the place. It was a restaurant where people could play board games and eat. A great date idea—but she had never been, not this time around, anyway.

Would she feel any sort of déjà vu if she were to go there? Would she feel déjà vu about anything she had experienced before Walter went back in time? At the moment, nothing tugged at her memory.

"I'll have to think up other questions to ask," she told him. They were getting close to her apartment, and in spite of their camaraderie on their jog, she was beginning to feel nervous. "You think of what you want to know too. But I better go now. We can split here. I'll see you later."

He opened his mouth and then closed it, his shoulders slumping. "Okay. See you."

Aurelia moved away from him and argued with herself the rest of the way. Why did she avoid having him walk her to the door? She had left the apartment with him, but now they couldn't walk back together?

He was the same Walter as the other Walter, and she trusted the other one. By default, she ought to trust this one too. Yet something about the idea of walking to her apartment door with him brought back fears of him forcing his way inside and assuming stalker behavior.

She locked the door behind her and wondered if she would ever be quite ready to trust him. Would she get there naturally given time?

She hoped so. Meanwhile, she could barely wait for tomorrow.

* * *

WHEN SHE OPENED the door to Walter the next evening, her heart fluttered. Tall, dark, and handsome all applied to him, though he wasn't the sort of mysterious, somber man who usually earned that description. He looked eager and was smiling hard enough to show dimples in both cheeks.

"You look great."

"Thanks." She warmed under his admiring gaze and resisted the urge to touch her hair. Half of it was braided across the top of her head while the rest hung loose. She wore dark jeans and a light gray blouse, the color of which always seemed to make her blonde hair shine.

"Are you ready?" he asked.

"I just need to get my shoes on." She bent down, covering up her nervousness. This wasn't the Walter-is-a-creepy-stalker kind of nervous. No, now that she was going on an actual first date with the guy, she felt almost giddy.

Finished tying her laces, she stepped outside, hyper-aware of her surroundings and most especially of Walter.

They had almost reached his car when a voice behind them called, "Walter."

Aurelia swung around. Meana was rushing across the parking lot toward them. She must have just come from campus.

"Walter, my mom's unwell. She might need to go to the emergency room." Meana grabbed Walter's arm. "Come see her with me. You'll know what to do."

Aurelia's breath hitched as Meana tugged him a step away. Would he postpone their date for Meana and her mom? This was different than Meana asking him to take her out on a rough day. But what if Meana was making it up?

Walter frowned. "Wait."

"She just called me. Walter, come on."

"Meana, I can't go." He planted his feet firmly. "I'm with Aurelia tonight."

Meana let go of him and stared. "But—I need your help to evaluate Mom's condition."

Breath returned to Aurelia's lungs. Walter wasn't leaving. Her fear melting away, she took a step forward.

He put his arm around her and continued in a mild voice, "I can't. If you think she needs the emergency room, take her there or call for help." His forehead creased. "If you need someone to visit her with you, I'm sure you can get someone else to go."

"What?" Meana exclaimed.

"Jackie might—" Aurelia began, but Meana interrupted with fury.

"You've always been a nice guy, so I'll forgive you for your lapse of judgment today." She stomped around Walter and marched up the stairs.

Aurelia stared after her. How far would Meana go to spend time with Walter? She turned and looked up at him, tensing when she realized how close they were, as his arm was still around her.

His breath tickled her hair. "Do you think her mom really does need help?" he asked in a low voice.

She swallowed. "Probably not. She seemed more concerned about having you there than about her mom."

"That's what I thought too." His brown eyes were searching. "So what I did was okay with you?"

A feeling of lightness spread inside her. She nodded and smiled. "Thank you." This was the most she had seen him stand up to Meana. The line between being a gentleman and being firm might worry him, but Aurelia had no fears he would ever be unkind to anyone. While she might err on the side of being too agreeable when it came to Meana, Walter didn't need to let Meana take advantage.

"Well, then." He smiled and indicated his car. "Shall we?"

"Where are we going?" She moved to the passenger side, and Walter's arm brushed hers when he reached past and opened the door. Meana's tactics seemed to fade into a distant eon, lost in the face of the upcoming evening.

"Someone told me you might like Indian food. Have you ever been to Bombay House?"

She watched his dancing eyes and felt a rush of anticipation. "No, but I'm sure it's good."

Based on the smells in the restaurant when they walked in ten minutes later, it was more than good. Aurelia couldn't contain her excitement as she looked over the menu, oohing at every other item.

"If you want to try everything, we'll have to come back ten more times," Walter said, not sounding at all displeased at the prospect. "I think we may have our next half dozen dates planned already. What do you want to drink?"

"Water's fine. This is expensive enough as it is." Her phone rang, but she ignored it.

"You should pick a drink. You've gotta like lassis, right?"

"They're pretty amazing," she admitted.

"Mango, strawberry, or rose?"

"Strawberry. Thanks."

Walter made their orders and asked for a rose lassi for himself.

"What does the rose taste like?" she asked when they were alone at their table.

"We'll find out soon."

"You've never tried it?"

"Nope, and I figured you hadn't either. You'll have to try a spoonful when it arrives."

She shook her head. "I need a bigger vocabulary."

"You need a . . . Why?"

"Because I keep wanting to say 'thank you,' but if that's the only thing I can say, it'll make for boring conversation."

Walter leaned back his head and laughed. "How about if you learn to say it in other languages?"

"Right. *Takk,*" she joked, using one of the polite Icelandic phrases she had learned after the song "Husavik" inspired her to check out some online tutorials. Her phone rang again. "Sorry, I'll turn off the sound." She dug out her phone, but Jackie's name on the screen made her pause. Just a few weeks ago, Jackie would have been quick to call 911 if Aurelia hadn't picked up while she was with Walter. Aurelia felt safe now, but what if Jackie didn't feel the same?

"Um, I don't normally answer the phone on dates, but maybe I'd better this time," she said. "Jackie might have her reasons."

"Okay."

She picked up and asked, "Hello?"

"I'm calling to check on you," Jackie said cheerfully.

"Thanks. Everything's fine."

"And I wanted to know if you had candles."

"Candles?" Aurelia parroted.

"On your table. And a quartet nearby. On a scale of one to ten, how romantic is it? Please tell me eleven," she begged.

Aurelia groaned and switched to a brisk, professional tone. "No, thank you, I'm not interested in buying a vacuum. Have a nice day, sir." With that, she hung up.

"And that's how you end a conversation you don't want to have," Walter said in amusement.

"Well, we're on a date."

"True, and I think you've run out of roommates who can interrupt us."

"I sure hope so," she said but couldn't help laughing at the way he said it.

Their waiter showed up and placed their dishes on the table, creating a bounteous display. This was one interruption Aurelia could live with. She breathed in the amazing smells of their curries and spiced naan breads.

Walter pushed his curry bowl near the center of the table. "Try some of mine."

He didn't have to tell her twice. "You'll have to try my lassi drink," she said, handing over her glass.

"And you try the rose."

It was the perfect way to enjoy as many of the menu items as possible. Aurelia savored the rich flavors in full. Walter was turning out to be a very thoughtful guy now that he was on a first date rather than running around proposing to strangers.

Chapter Nineteen

How could he possibly think the joke shop in Harry Potter was called Zorro's?

That was where their conversation had led, and all Aurelia knew as they drove to the library down the street and got out in the parking lot was that Walter needed to see for himself that the fictitious shop's name was Zonko's. They simply couldn't end the evening before they looked it up in the book. She took her Harry Potter trivia seriously. That, and she really liked to go to the library.

"So this is the Provo City Library," Walter said, looking up at the castle-like, corbel-roofed building that had once been a part of BYU. "This'll be a new experience."

"You've never been here? Unacceptable," Aurelia exclaimed in partially feigned outrage and grabbed his arm, pulling him along.

"Does this count as our second date?" he asked as they entered. "It feels like a second date. You sure move fast."

She gave him a disdainful look. "I move fast when there are books involved." With a sniff, she let go of him.

He reached out with his newly freed arm and caught her hand. "What should our third date be?"

"Focus. We need to get you acquainted with the library."

He brought her hand and his up between them, drawing her close to his side and leaning his head down toward hers. "I was kidding," he said in a low voice that tickled the hairs around her ear. "I've been here before. I even have a library card. I just wanted to see how you would react."

How she would react? To the warmth that spread through her at his closeness, his head intimately near hers while he held her hand?

Warm and soft and firm. That was how he felt. His eyes looked soft and inviting—

"Do you want to watch general conference with me on Saturday?" Walter asked. "My place? Jackie's welcome too. I know one of my roommates will be there."

Aurelia swallowed. *Conference,* she reminded herself, pushing through her hazy thoughts. October conference, when leaders of The Church of Jesus Christ of Latter-day Saints would speak to the world.

"I could come. I mean, I'd enjoy watching the second session with you." She stumbled over her words. "I promised to watch the first one with a friend and have lunch at her place. Jackie has plans for the second one."

"Second session, then. But if your lunch plans fall through, let me know," he said and moved his thumb across the back of her hand.

Let him know what? What it felt like when he caressed her hand?

She shook her head. He was reducing her to a ninny.

"Now, then." She tore her hand from his with some regret and looked in both directions, remembering her purpose in coming here. "Harry Potter. I never know whether those books will be in the children's section or the young adult section or even in the adult section. I think there are usually some in each. Let's try the young adult section first."

She turned on her heel and headed left. Walter strode to keep up with her.

Suddenly, she stopped and whirled to face him. "You said you've been here before. Where's your library card?"

"I don't have it with me."

She pursed her lips. "You're guilty until proven innocent. Better get that card ready to show me by Saturday."

"Yes, ma'am." He saluted and then pointed behind her. "That's the young adult section over there. See, I'm already starting to prove myself."

"Yes, because there's no way you noticed the signs on—" Movement caught her eye. When Aurelia saw the two men, she froze, and chills ran down her back.

"Signs? Oh yeah, it says 'Young Adult' on the shelves." Walter grinned before noticing her discomfort. "Aurelia?"

Breathless, she turned to him, keeping the people behind him in sight. For a moment, she considered him. "I'm going to ask you a question, and I need you to answer quietly," she said in a hushed voice. "How do you feel about spying?"

"Spying?" he asked in an acceptably low tone.

"Yes." She watched the men behind him—the bigger guy from Macey's and the rather nondescript one who had "pumped" something that day. "I need to find out what those two are doing here." Walter turned to look. "The middle-aged men over in general fiction D and E. I'm going closer to hear what they say."

He gaped at her. "Is this another experiment?"

She started toward them, not prepared to answer.

Walter caught up and grabbed her arm as she rounded the help desk. "Why those two, of all people?" he whispered.

She hesitated. This wasn't about experiencing what it was like to be a spy. Maybe that was an added bonus, but she really did believe there was something shady about these men. She just didn't have enough evidence to explain herself and sound credible.

"They look like my crooks," she said with an angelic smile, knowing it sounded like she was referring to someone in one of her stories.

"Let me show you some of my favorites," she continued at a normal volume and led an incredulous Walter to the suspense stories a few shelves from her targets.

Walter seemed bemused at first, but he caught on quickly, turning and pointing out some Wild West books that allowed them to face in the direction of the men. At Aurelia's insistence, they soon split up. As the two men walked down the aisle past her, Aurelia headed for the murder mystery novels that were now nearer her moving targets.

She picked up several books in turn, acting like she was reading the back of each, while her mind churned.

So far, their conversation and activity looked normal, but that could change. What if they decided to "pump" something again, like they had done at Macey's? Or to talk about stealing?

"—not my favorite," one of the culprits was saying.

"You need to expand your horizons," the other one chuckled. "Read more. How are things with your niece?"

"Pretty bad. I can't depend on her. We need to find a different distraction."

Aurelia bit her lip. She *had* seen them before Macey's, hadn't she? These two and the salt-and-pepper-haired man. The recollection was so vague that she had no idea where it had been. Running her everyday locations through her head didn't seem to jog her memory.

The men walked to a different aisle and stopped to talk. Aurelia picked two books and walked to the next shelf, where she bent to look through a row of novels while straining her ears.

Walter came around the corner at an alarming pace. "*What are you doing?*" he hissed.

She straightened and looked at him in surprise. "Checking out books." Surely there was no need to re-explain the fact that she was spying, especially since even her quiet voice might be overheard by her targets from this distance.

"But *why* . . ." He moved his eyes in the direction of the men and did a subtle nod with his head.

She watched him helplessly. "What are you getting at?" Then something registered in her mind. Walter wasn't wearing the same shirt as before.

Both of him were at the library?

"Please tell me you're not spying on them," he whispered.

She raised her chin, though her heart beat fast at her realization. "Why not?"

He winced. "I'm sorry, but you have to leave."

Her mouth dropped open.

"Please," he said. "Find Wal—*me*, and leave the library."

She gave her head a shake. "Why? Does something happen here tonight?" Like another explosion?

"Not that I know of, but I don't want you spying on those guys."

"Why not?" she asked, and even though her voice was a whisper, it held an edge.

"I'm sorry, but you have to go."

"You know something about them," she said in realization. "You know, and *you're* spying on them. But *I* can't?"

"I can't let you get involved." He put a hand on her shoulder as if to guide her away, but she stood stock-still, daring him to try to move her. Dropping his hand, he slid away to the end of the bookcase and disappeared behind the O and P shelves.

"*Let* me?" she whispered angrily. What was his problem?

She clenched her jaw and looked in the direction of the help desk, not facing the men but keeping an ear in their direction. Not that she was able to eavesdrop. A storm of irritability brewed inside her, drowning out nearby voices.

At a noise behind her, she did a one-eighty and watched Walter approach. He wore the right shirt. This was the Walter she was on a date with.

Quietly he walked up to her and put his hand on her arm. "Hey. I think we need to leave."

"Not you too," she said, her voice losing its whisper volume.

"I'm sorry. He said I need to get you out of here."

Get me out of here? It took her a moment to realize she was walking, letting him steer her toward the exit. "What's the matter with him—with *you*? You're the same person," she accused.

"Sorry. I just think we'd better listen to him."

They stepped out and started up the stairs.

"I would understand it if he needed us to leave because we shouldn't have both of you here, but that's not why he—or you—are making us," she complained.

Walter dug out his car keys and remained silent.

Aurelia fumed. "*He* can spy on them, but *I* can't. Why do I need to be protected?"

"Is that so bad, to protect you?" he asked cautiously.

She plopped down in the passenger seat. "No—and *yes*. Are these guys dangerous? What did he say to you?"

He got in and started the car. "He, uh . . ."

"What?"

"He said if I wanted you to be safe, I needed to take you and go."

"Safe?" Aurelia paled and turned in her seat, watching the library disappear behind them. Wavering between worry and anger, her pendulum soon made its choice.

"Classic male chauvinism," she huffed, folding her arms in defiance.

She should have run back inside when she had the chance. Made Confident Walter tell her what was going on, maybe even made him leave.

"Honestly, if those guys are bad—" Comeback Walter began.

"Then you shouldn't be running around following them through the library, should you? And yet you are, right now," she snapped.

He had no reply to that. Maybe because he didn't know why his other self had stayed, or maybe because he knew she didn't want to hear him defend himself. They drove in uneasy silence.

"What if he's in danger right now?" she blurted as they reached Elite. This was frustrating, being mad at the guy who was still at the library, wondering whether he was putting himself in danger, and blaming the guy next to her for what he was doing in the future in the present. "This is stupid."

"Sorry," Walter apologized as he parked.

She shook her head and got out. This was when she would normally tell him thank you for the date, but frustration held her tongue. Why did Confident Walter have to keep ruining things for her and Comeback Walter? How could she be mad at Confident Walter without being mad at his other self? She couldn't, not this time.

Walter came around to her side. "Can we talk about it?"

The bushes that lined the parking lot rustled in the evening breeze. If only she could be as tranquil as them. She clenched her hands and swung to meet Walter's gaze. "He won't tell me things."

"He won't tell me things either."

She huffed. "He's *you*. In the future, you'll rewind the world and not tell either of us anything."

He looked at the ground. "I don't know what to do about that."

"Shouldn't I be able to trust you?" Her voice came out forlorn. She was supposed to have dated Confident Walter for a while. How did that work if they didn't trust each other?

Comeback Walter jolted forward, his gaze earnest. "I want you to be able to trust me."

"But I can't." She bit her lip and softened her voice. "Not right now. It's too much."

He stared at her.

"I guess I need some time."

"Can we talk this over later, then?" His words came out in a rush.

"Yeah. Just give me a bit." She sighed. "I did have fun tonight—up until that point. Let's talk later, but right now, I need some alone time."

He nodded slowly. Aurelia stepped away and took the stairs, feeling like a deflated balloon. When she looked back, Walter was still there, his shoulders lowered.

They were parting on sad terms, and it made her annoyance rise again while she pulled out her key. By the time she entered her living room, her emotions had come full circle.

She started to pace. Yeah, yeah, Walter was a good guy and wanted to keep her safe. Yeah, something was awry with those men. She huffed. *Then why is he following them around himself?*

Her heart jumped into her throat at the sight of the face watching her from the couch. "Jackie," she exclaimed.

"Are you all right?" Jackie asked, her eyebrows raised.

Aurelia resumed walking. "Ohhh, he made me so mad."

She completed several more turns while Jackie remained silent. Finally, Aurelia stopped. "Why aren't you saying anything?"

Jackie shrugged.

"No, really. You've gotta have something to say. Something really Jackie-esque."

Jackie gave her an innocent look.

"Let's have it," Aurelia demanded.

Jackie complied. "Trouble . . . in paradise?"

Aurelia sank onto the couch. "There we go. That actually kind of helps. Why didn't you say that when I first walked in upset?"

"I don't think it would have helped then. So what's up?"

Aurelia's story tumbled out, complete with huffs and puffs. Then she had to explain to Jackie why she thought those men were worth spying on in the first place.

Jackie goggled at her. "You think these guys are behind the explosions in town?"

"I don't know, but it's suspicious they were at both Kylie's place and Macey's."

"Right. So are you mad that Walter wouldn't let you spy, or are you mad that he might put himself in danger?"

Aurelia sniffed. "Both." She hunched her shoulders and looked at the ceiling lamp. "I don't actually need to worry about him, right? I mean, really, would they be able to hurt Walter if they caught him at the library? I don't think so. So maybe I'm mostly annoyed that he's keeping me in the dark."

"Aurelia, what if there's an explosion at the library after this?" Jackie looked much more serious than Aurelia was used to. "If there is, you *have* to tell the police about these guys."

"Walter didn't seem to think anything would happen—although I didn't ask him directly." Aurelia bit her lip. "Actually, I shouldn't wait for an explosion. I should tell them now. Tell them to look into this bug-spraying company. Although the men didn't bring their spray equipment to Macey's or the library."

Or did they? They hadn't brought anything as large with them as what they used at Kylie's, but they had brought *something* metallic to Macey's that disappeared into one of the men's bags afterward.

She groaned and rubbed her head. "What in the world are they up to?"

"Who knows?" Jackie stared straight ahead. "Do you think you could have found out the answer if you'd stayed in the library another ten minutes?"

"Maybe," Aurelia was quick to say, but then she thought about it some more. Would the men have launched into an explanation of why they made things explode? Of course not. The most exciting thing that might have happened would be for them to pull out their metallic object and start "pumping" again. Either way, their visit to the library wouldn't mean anything to her unless there was a follow-up explosion. Hanging around for another ten minutes wouldn't have changed that fact.

"Maybe not," she muttered.

"Or what about if you spy on them elsewhere?"

She shook her head.

"So how can you find out?"

Aurelia looked around at the apartment. Meana was away or quietly hanging out in her room. The living room was lit up, but darkness pressed against the windows. A stack of textbooks decorated the otherwise empty table.

Finally she spoke. "Walter. He knows something. And I think I might know where to find him."

Chapter Twenty

THE NEXT MORNING, Aurelia stood in front of the second-best climbing tree, just off the path of Kiwanis Park, her arms crossed.

Comeback Walter had gone jogging here the day he found her climbing. Confident Walter had taken her jogging here in the morning. It made sense. He must have switched around his exercise schedule to avoid running into himself, but he still preferred this particular park. If he came today, she would be ready for him.

If he came.

As the minutes ticked by, her mind strayed into paragraph territory about the most miserable part of spy work.

Waiting: it's the killjoy of spies, she wrote in her mind. *It must be mastered, and worse, endured in . . .*

There. She brought her mind back to the moment and added steel to her posture when she caught sight of a lone jogger. Confident Walter.

He got close before he saw her. With a stumble, he stopped five feet away. "I looked for you at your apartment."

"What happened after I left last night?" Her voice was sharp.

He chewed on his lip. "Not much. They talked and . . . left."

"Who are they?"

His lips drew into a narrow line.

She looked around and hoisted herself up to sit on the thick, low-hanging branch behind her so she could gain a height advantage over him. "Walter, if you want a relationship with me, you need to trust me."

He came over to lean on a branch across from her. "The other me can't know about this."

"Tell me," she said.

He pulled himself up, bringing him nearer to her level. "I can't tell you much."

That didn't sound like he was ready to cooperate. She stood and grabbed a branch above her for balance. "I already know there's a valid reason to spy on them. You don't want me anywhere near them." As she pulled herself higher, an idea caught in her mind, and she felt a thrill of equal parts fear and excitement. "Do they end up kidnapping me or something?" she asked, looking down through the needles at Walter.

"No! No," he exclaimed as if horrified at the idea. Making his way to a forked branch, he faced her anew. "I don't think you were even aware of their existence. *I* wasn't. I don't like the fact that I am now." He dragged a hand through his hair, then stopped to look at his sap-sticky hand.

"But Walter and I *are* aware of them now," Aurelia reminded him. "So tell me what you know."

He looked at her for a long moment. Finally he sighed. "I can tell you they're thieves. And . . . they're okay with people getting hurt."

She sniffed. "I can tell you they work for a pesticide company, and they've been in Kylie's house."

"What?" He gave her a blank look.

She climbed higher, the scent of pine calming her somewhat. "I'm going to tell the police about them."

His voice turned panicked. "No, don't do that." When she turned to him, she found that his eyes had widened. "Aurelia, I need these guys in order to travel back in time. If that gets jeopardized, I might never become one person again."

That didn't sound good at all. She swallowed. "Then what do we do?"

"Keep it to ourselves. For another . . . while. The other me can't know these things either, or he might do things differently and not go back in time."

She shivered and rubbed her arms. "I won't tell him. But how long will it be until there's only one of you and we can talk to the police?"

Closing the gap between them, he settled against a branch beside hers.

"I'd feel bad telling you exactly when it is because . . . I was ready to propose the day I went back in time." Aurelia tensed at the reminder. "I don't want you to feel pressure that you, or we, are supposed to be at that point by a specific date."

She looked toward the sky. This was why Walter wasn't sharing. Aurelia *didn't* want to know when he would propose. A small thrill ran through her, but anxiety followed close behind.

When Walter spoke again, his voice was cautious. "Does Kylie know these guys?"

She shook her head. "They work for a pesticide company that sprayed her home."

"Which company?" His eyes brightened.

"I don't know, and I don't want you spying on them." If he could forbid her, she could forbid him, and for the same reason. She didn't want him to get hurt. "Is that what you've been doing when you're not hanging around me?"

"Only when I've managed to come across them. Mostly, I'm busy studying."

"Studying?" She accidentally knocked down a pine cone from beside her. "But the other you is doing that."

"Yes, but don't you realize how amazing it is that I can study twice as much material in the same amount of time?" He looked as excited as Comeback Walter had at the end of the time travel lecture. Not to mention at the science fair when he first brought up his love of science. "I can study ahead for other classes, sit in on some of the bigger ones where no one will know I'm not enrolled, and review material from my previous classes. My aunt and uncle are teaching me family history, and I've started looking into graduate schools and preparing application essays."

"Studying," she mumbled to herself, trying not to let his endearing enthusiasm get to her. She didn't want to let go of her annoyance with him so soon.

"The other me's pretty happy about it too," Walter continued. "He brought some of last semester's books over when my uncle and aunt were out of town the other day." He put a hand on his knee, then stopped to inspect the dirt and sap that stuck to his pants leg.

"Consequences of climbing," Aurelia said, keeping her voice aloof.

He shrugged and brushed his hands off on each other. "I've gotten dirty before. In fact, there was the time I wanted to test—" His words stopped, and he promptly shut his mouth.

"What?"

"Uh, never mind." His ears turned red.

She waited, sunlight streaming across her through the branches. When he didn't speak, she scooted closer. She couldn't resist prodding him to share whatever it was that embarrassed him. "I thought we were done keeping secrets?"

He opened his mouth and shut it. "It was a childhood experiment. I had read about Native Americans washing their clothes in the river, and I wondered how effective that was. I decided to test it on my little sister, Polly's, green lace dress."

"What?" Aurelia's eyebrows flew upward. "Why not do it on your own clothes, not to mention on something less . . . delicate?"

Walter looked guilty. "It was a one-time experiment, so it had to be a good one. In my mind, that meant I needed the most fragile piece of clothing. Besides, my sisters often let me use their things. I'd go exploring with their bows and Care Bear hair clips holding my knapsack together."

The image of little Walter walking around intent on business, girly hair ornaments on his belongings, was too much for Aurelia. She had to smile. "So, the dress?" she prompted.

"Right. First, I had to get it dirty."

"What did you do, throw mud on Polly while she wore her dress?"

Now his cheeks grew red. "Um. *She* didn't wear it."

Aurelia chuckled. "Don't tell me *you* wore it."

Walter was silent.

"You *wore* it?"

He cleared his throat. "I put it on and rolled in the mud at the bank of the creek. Then I tried to wash the dress." He rubbed the back of his neck. "Some of the stains wouldn't come out. Mom wasn't happy."

"What about Polly?"

"I think she would have joined me if I'd invited her."

Aurelia bit down on her lip. Her throat tickled, and she cleared it with a cough. "I better get back," she said and began her downward descent.

Above her, Walter followed. Aurelia placed her sap-scraped hands with confidence and closed her eyes when needles drizzled down on her.

She jumped to the ground and cleared her throat again. After she moved away, Walter dropped down.

"What are you laughing at?" He looked anxious.

"Nothing." She chuckled louder. His story was catching up with her. Little Walter, heading to the river in his sister's lace dress. Rolling in the mud. Standing in the river trying to wash the poor dress.

She sped up and jogged most of the way home. At the foot of the stairs to her apartment, she turned to Walter, who stopped.

Aurelia's mouth still struggled against a grin. "I'll see you later." She wasn't scared, not this time, but if she let him walk her to the door, he might think she wanted more of a goodbye—maybe a hug—or that she would invite him in. She wasn't ready for either.

He nodded. "See you."

She took the stairs two steps at a time and hurried to unlock the door. Then, finally, she shut the door behind her and let out a full laugh.

Meana shot her a dirty look from the couch, but Aurelia put her hands on her stomach and laughed harder—until she caught sight of the large man who sat on the other end of the couch, and her heart gave a sickening leap.

Meana turned back to her visitor as though the world hadn't just turned upside down. "I may not have the lead role, but I have a prominent part, and don't forget I got the lead last year." Her voice was petulant.

The large man Aurelia had seen only last night at the library was facing Meana, his arm slung across the back of the sofa. But his eyes were on Aurelia while he answered lazily, "I don't know why you even bother with theater. It's such a useless degree."

Meana paled and continued to ignore her roommate. "I'm good at it."

"Humph. Maybe that's a good reason." He situated himself more comfortably. "There aren't that many things you're good at."

Aurelia began to blush on Meana's behalf. But it made no sense that the man was here. In her apartment. Talking to Meana.

Meana tossed her head, her eyes fiery. "You saw one of my plays last year. You know I have talent. Everyone's impressed with me."

At the man's noncommittal grunt, Aurelia wished she could make herself scarce. She couldn't let this man out of her sight though. She had to know what was going on.

She walked to the kitchen and realized she was trembling. Trying to firm up her courage, she opened the spice cabinet, giving herself a reason to stay in the area.

"One of my teachers in particular adores me," Meana continued, as if desperate to convince this man she was worth something. "You should give me more credit, Uncle."

Aurelia dropped a jar of oregano, and the lid popped off, spilling seasoning all over the counter.

Heart beating fast, she looked around for a rag. Then she stiffened at movement out of the corner of her eye. The man, Meana's uncle, had gotten up and was coming her way.

She grabbed a piece of paper towel and wet it from the sink, her pulse beating ever faster while the man arrived at her side.

"Here, let me help," his deep voice said, and he reached for the towel.

Wordlessly she handed it to him and watched him wipe up the mess.

"I'm Stan, by the way. Meana's uncle."

Yes, that revelation was still sinking in. One of the mysterious men was seriously related to Meana? Her pulse pounded in her ears as she remembered the few bits and pieces she had overheard at the library. Someone had mentioned a niece, hadn't they?

The man was watching her, and she realized she needed to answer. Against her will, she returned the introduction. "I'm Aurelia."

He threw the mess into the trash can beside them. "You're the one who came out on top, aren't you?"

She blinked. "What?"

"Dating." He waved a disparaging hand at his niece, whose eyes were still fiery as she watched them from the couch. In fact, the edges of her eyes were turning red as though from strain. Aurelia returned her gaze to Stan.

"She's been trying to catch the eye of a guy you know. I got her tickets to a science symposium she could invite him to, but it sounds like you're the one he likes." He put his hand in his pocket and withdrew two strips of paper, dropping them on the table. "Why don't you take them? Meana can't interest a guy long enough to get him on a real date." He barked a laugh.

In that moment, Aurelia wanted nothing to do with the tickets or the man. She wasn't someone who engaged in confrontation, but she had to say something to stop his abuse.

She clenched a hand at her side to bolster her courage. "Meana can get almost any guy she wants." Her voice was shaky, but she forced herself to look into Stan's gray eyes. "You probably don't know what guys in our generation like, but Meana's gorgeous, and her style is amazing."

"That's true." Jackie added her voice to the argument as she sauntered into the room from the back hall. "Several of the guys in our ward are falling over each other trying to get her to notice them."

"Oh?" Stan looked over the girls as if he didn't quite know how to proceed. "Well, hopefully she has better luck with the next guy," he said and shot a look at his niece. "I need to get going. Good to catch up with you, Meana." He sounded more lofty than loving. After he gave the girl a half hug, Aurelia was relieved to see him turn to the door.

He left behind an awkward silence.

Aurelia turned to Meana, whose eyes were bright, although she didn't let her tears flow. "Are you okay?"

Meana jerked and glared at her. "Of course I am. There was no need for you to . . . *defend* me." She spat out the word. "My uncle adores me. He just doesn't show it the way others do. I can't believe you couldn't see that."

She turned on her heel and marched past Jackie with her nose in the air. In another moment, Aurelia heard her bedroom door slam.

"What's her problem?" Jackie exclaimed. "We stood up for her, and she gets mad at *us*?"

Aurelia worked a shiver through her body. The whole encounter had been more than unpleasant. "She's embarrassed. I think she'd rather we hadn't seen how he treats her at all."

Jackie huffed but, after another moment, sighed. "You were right about her. Her uncle's abusive. It doesn't excuse her behavior, but . . . I guess I understand her a little now. I was so uncomfortable when I came home and heard them talking. Can you imagine *me* hiding in my room to get away from them?" She shook her head in disgust.

"Jackie." Aurelia peered down the hall to make sure Meana wasn't returning. "That guy was one of the men that was at the library."

Jackie stood as still as the giraffe on the safari poster behind her. "You mean, one of the men you tried to spy on?"

"Yes. And they mentioned a niece last night." Aurelia clenched her hands and paced away from her roommate and the poster. "They said she was a distraction. But not a very good one."

"A distraction for what?"

Aurelia stopped in front of the counter where Stan had left the tickets. Her stomach churned. "What does he want with Walter?"

Jackie looked at her like she was crazy. "Walter?"

"Yeah. Stan was giving Meana tickets to take Walter to a symposium. Then he wanted me to take Walter there. This isn't about me or Meana." She thought back on the times she had seen those men. They hadn't been following Walter around then, yet today's visit seemed to be about him.

"Is there a reason they want him at this symposium?" She peered at the dates on the tickets. "It's on the twenty-first. In Salt Lake."

"I wouldn't go if I were you," was Jackie's prompt judgment.

"I won't." Aurelia pushed the tickets away with her elbow. "I talked to Confident Walter today."

"And? Did you get any answers?"

"The men are bad news, but we can't change anything they're doing or tell Comeback Walter about them."

"Are you still mad at him?"

"No. Barely, maybe. But one of him probably thinks I am." She winced at the memory of their sad parting. How could she have let their first date end like that?

She would have to talk to him, and soon.

Chapter Twenty-One

AURELIA CURSED Jackie's sudden slew of errands. Two more days had passed, and after being away from home more than she was there, she had seen neither hide nor hair of either Walter. Her information about Meana's relationship with Stan burned inside her, but most of all, she worried because she hadn't seen Comeback Walter since their first official date. What if he had come by while she was away helping Jackie? Worse, what if he *hadn't* come by? What if he no longer wanted to?

She dropped by his place twice and felt her heart sink when she didn't find him home.

Maybe Confident Walter would know where his other self was at. Aurelia arrived at institute that Friday, her pulse in her throat as she prepared to find out.

When she sat down, Walter looked up quickly, wide-eyed.

She blinked. "Are you okay?"

"Yeah. But you should know, I'm the other Walter. Walter told me to come in his place, because every time I've been by since Tuesday, you've been away. I'm not trying to deceive you or anything. I just want you to know it's me."

Relief flooded her, along with a sliver of disappointment that she would have to wait even longer to tell his other self about the uncle-niece thing. Comeback Walter *did* still want to see her.

"I'm sorry about Tuesday," he said, "and that our evening ended on a bad note."

"I'm sorry too."

"It was—wait, you are?"

Her heart melted. "Yeah. I still don't think it's quite fair, but—I guess I understand your reasons. And I feel like I've been bad-tempered and you didn't deserve it."

"You're not bad-tempered," he protested. "If anything, you're quick to forgive."

She smiled. "I'm glad you're here tonight."

The teacher got up and announced the opening prayer. Walter clasped Aurelia's hand between their chairs and gave it a squeeze.

Grateful for her newfound peace, Aurelia forced her anxieties about Stan and his companions into the background as she focused on the lesson. She had thought she would find herself comparing this Walter's comments to Confident Walter's comments, but instead, the things he said added on to the things she had heard the other him say in class and at church. Having him here tonight somehow made the two Walters more like one in her mind.

He followed her outside afterward and offered to walk her home.

"Sure," she agreed.

Poor Confident Walter. Why couldn't it be that easy when it came to him?

"I *am* bad-tempered," she grumbled.

"Why do you say that?"

"Because I've been mad at Confi—at the other Walter since this whole thing started." Of course, her caution had been more than justified.

"What did you call him?"

She cleared her throat. "I didn't."

"Okay, well, what did you *almost* call him?"

She looked the other way.

Walter walked close, touching shoulders. "And what's your name for *me*?"

"Uh, ha. I'm, uh, sworn to secrecy." Why, oh, why had she let part of his name slip?

"Wait, come on. How do you distinguish between the two of us? When you and Jackie talk, you've gotta have a way to refer to each of us." He hooked arms with her before she could move away.

"No comment." She giggled and tried to pull away.

"If it's unflattering, I'll try really hard not to be offended."

"Why, thank you. That is most gracious of you, kind sir," she said, still trying to extricate herself.

"Name?" he asked.

"The name's Aurelia," she said whimsically.

"No, no. *My* name."

She gave him a look of pity. "You don't know your own name?"

"I have a very serious question," he told her. "Are you ticklish?"

She screamed and laughed as he went for her. He grabbed her other arm but, stopping short of tickling her, let her pull free. She pushed him, making him swerve off the path before he returned to her side.

When they reached the place where she had seen one of the men last week, she hugged her jacket to her chest. After a quick inner debate, she pointed at the building. "Is that where you have your lab?"

"Yeah, do you want to see it? Well, actually," his face fell, "I'm not allowed to let you *in* the lab, so I can only show you where it is, which probably isn't exciting, but if—"

"That's fine," Aurelia assured him. Tonight, the walk to her home was too short for her liking. She wanted more time with Walter than that.

As he led her through the building, the halls soon became all too familiar. They walked the floor across which she had followed last week's visitor, and when Walter stopped in front of a closed door and pointed through the window to explain a bit about what was inside, Aurelia gulped.

All the doors looked the same, but she was pretty sure this was close to where the Boston man had entered—if it wasn't this very door.

"Who has access to this lab?" she asked. It must be limited if he couldn't even let her enter as a guest.

"Just my team and Dr. Jude. Actually, she consults with Dr. Jered and Professor Willington, so they're allowed in here," Walter said as they moved past the room. "I'm here a lot, so if you ever want to pop by—although Meana catches me here too." He frowned. "Sometimes I don't know how she finds me. I never told her I use this building, and most of my classes are in the Benson Building, which she already knows."

Aurelia peered down the hall they passed. This had to be where she saw Walter and Meana last week. She looked back at the door Walter had pointed out. It was either that door or the one beside it the Boston man had entered last week—and since access was so restricted, it must be the one beside it. After all, he hadn't broken in, right? He'd had a code. But what were the chances of Stan's associate using the lab next door to Walter's?

She tried to calm the queasy feeling in her stomach as they stepped outside. The air was cooling down, and the sky was a mysterious dark blue.

"I never did ask you," she said, ready to at least have her curiosity satisfied in one area, "what does your brand of time travel look like?"

His eyes looked darker in this setting. "My brand?"

"Yeah. I mean with your research project." Now that she had gotten past her disbelief about the time travel story, she was ready to learn more about it. "What methods do you use to try to make things go back in time?"

"You really want to hear about the science?"

She nodded. "Although I might not understand it."

"I'll make sure you understand it," he said with a touch of eagerness. "We're incorporating several astronomical theories and observations, but basically—there's this energy quality in the air, with differing degrees, all around us. You hear about atoms being bound together with negative energy, but what we're focusing on is a step further, an alternate layer of negative energy that you don't hear about in chemistry classes yet."

She raised her eyebrows but prodded, "Go on."

"There's talk of negative energy keeping wormholes open between different locations and times. We're trying to create sort of a mini version of a hole based on this deeper layer of energy, something that could be sustained in small areas on our own little Earth without messing up surrounding areas."

"You're creating a version of a *wormhole*?"

"Yes. We have a five-by-five-by-ten-foot polycarbonate enclosure in our lab that we shoot negatively balanced molecules into. It's very slow and careful work. We stop and measure the balance of energy with almost every shot, and until we can tell what effect our shooting session has had, we don't shoot any more into it." His eyes lit up further. "We've also found—or think we've found—a couple of chemicals that help maintain the artificially high energy. That might turn out to be key to the whole thing!"

Aurelia smiled at his enthusiasm and tried to make sense of her impressions of the picture he painted. Mad scientist laboratory or super cool experiment? "Does the air feel strange where you work on this?"

"You can't feel a difference. If there were a spot in public that was as strong in negativity as what we're playing with, you'd never know it."

"Except you'd get sucked into time and reappear who-knows-when," Aurelia reminded him.

"Possibly. We're not certain it would work as a time machine every time someone walked through the spot."

"Yikes." She chilled at the thought. "Are we seriously talking about a world in which I might walk through a time travel spot and not notice it, and I may or may not find myself transferred to another time and place?"

"No scientist would create these areas in random spots for people to walk across by chance," he reassured her. "*If* we manage to create our end product, those holes would only ever be created in secure locations. For now, of course, it's only done in the lab."

Aurelia looked up at the mountains ahead, shadows from the setting sun stretching across them. Did this amazing world really include the possibility of time travel for humans—for mortals?

"Did all of that make sense?" Walter asked.

"You explained it well. I just need to think about it." She appreciated that he hadn't used a bunch of jargon and names of chemicals and scientific instruments she didn't know.

He sighed. "For the sake of science, I would absolutely love to discover how to make this work. But in practice, it might not be so great to have the possibility of time travel."

Aurelia laughed quietly.

"At least I learn from my mistakes," he said with a crooked smile. "Or from *his* mistakes, but I guess they're going to be mine."

She shook her head. They crossed the street where they had stood, she now realized, during a series of traffic light changes. She had been engrossed in their conversation, and even now as her apartment building reared up ahead, she wished the walk wouldn't end so soon.

"What about *your* experiments?" Walter lifted his eyebrows. "Any new ones coming up?"

"Experiments?"

"For your books. Like the one with the pumpkin smashing. What happens in it, anyway?"

"Oh." She looked at him, gauging his curiosity as they walked. Should she tell him? It was nice to have a reason to keep talking as they reached the stairs.

She cleared her throat. "It involves a runaway princess and a rowdy group of children who take her in." His eyes widened, and she enjoyed the reaction. "Eventually they face her abductors."

"Cool. What happens then?"

"I can't tell you."

He did a double take. "You can't tell me?" He held her gaze, but she only smiled and kept her mouth shut. "Can you at least tell me if it has a happy ending?"

"All my stories do. When you think about it, that's the only realistic way to go."

"Really?"

"Yeah." She moved her hands, hoping she could help him see it. "Everyone's story ends happily, and even if it doesn't end well in *this* life, it does in the next. At least for everyone who chooses the right sooner or later. No matter what we go through, we all get a happy ending."

Walter looked at her in awe, if she wasn't mistaken. "True. That's very optimistic—and the best defense for happy endings I've heard."

"Right?" She thrilled at his words and turned toward her door. Her heart faltered at their impending parting.

"What time are you coming over tomorrow?" Walter asked.

Another question meant another delay in saying goodbye. She smiled. "Probably not long before the afternoon session. I'll come straight from lunch with Jackie and Kylie, but I don't know what time it'll be."

"Can I walk you home afterward?"

"Sure." She stepped away from her door. "Hey, look at the stars."

She leaned against the railing, and Walter leaned next to her.

Truth be told, there weren't a lot of stars out, but it was the first thing that had come to mind as she searched for another topic and a reason to stay outside longer with him. The twelve or so visible stars *were* pretty, and the clouds that nearly covered the dark sky looked ethereal.

She began humming "A Sky Full of Stars." A welcome breeze cooled her face. She half expected Walter to join in singing, but he remained silent. Then it occurred to her he wasn't watching the night sky.

She turned her head. As she had suspected, he was watching her.

She waited a moment. He didn't look away. "What?" she finally asked.

"What, what?" he returned, making her giggle.

"Yes, what?" she repeated, trying to sound stern.

He stepped away from the railing and raised a hand to the side of her face, his palm cupping her cheek, the effect slowing her breath.

"This," he answered, his brown eyes capturing hers.

She had two rapid-fire revelations. He was going to kiss her, and she was going to let him. Never mind that she had told other guys there would be no kissing until much further along in their relationship. Walter had driven her to distraction these few weeks, his adoration flattering, his good looks and his happy, mischievous demeanor equally alluring.

He bent his head toward her and searched her eyes, giving her time to stop him if she wanted to. As his movements slowed, her thoughts sped up.

She would do anything to keep his hand on her cheek like that and a sky full of stars spun in her mind while she remembered how she felt when he held her by the fridge and she really should . . .

Research, Jackie's sly voice sounded in her mind.

Of all the ridiculous things! With a huff of annoyance at the mental intrusion, Aurelia grabbed Walter's collar and pulled him to her.

Her mind went blessedly, peacefully silent. Walter's hand soft on her cheek, his lips on hers. Warm and gentle and . . . sparks inside her. Her fist gripping his shirt.

With a shock, she realized what she had just done. Pulling away, she repentantly loosened her grip and smoothed her hand against his collar. Judging by the dreamy quality in Walter's eyes, though, her brashness hadn't bothered him.

"You're captivating," he said quietly and closed the distance between their lips anew, making Aurelia thrill—

"*Walter*," a sharp voice rang out.

Aurelia and Walter sprang apart as though zapped by electricity.

Meana stood in the doorway, her face a storm cloud. "How dare you! Cheating on me," she screeched. "You *jerk*. I never want to see you again."

She disappeared inside, slamming the door.

Aurelia eyed the doorway as she and Walter stood in silence. She was half in shock over the kiss and half in shock over the rude awakening.

Their kiss already seemed a distant memory except for the feeling of sweetness that had settled on her lips and cheek. Her shoulders sank as she tried in vain to hold on to the feeling.

Walter rubbed the back of his neck. "Why does she keep acting like . . . She doesn't *really* think she and I are dating, does she?"

Aurelia shook her head. "I don't think so." She wanted to dwell on the kiss, not ponder Meana, but her thoughts wouldn't comply. Did the girl even like Walter, or had she gone after him in an attempt to prove herself to her uncle?

A muted bump sounded inside the apartment.

Walter shifted from one foot to the other.

"I should probably go in there," Aurelia said.

"Do you want me to go in with you? So you don't have to face her alone?"

Another, louder, crash sounded.

Aurelia bit her lip, then tried to smile at Walter. "No, I'm okay. But thanks. I, uh, good night."

Walter lifted his hand as though to detain her, but then he let it drop. "Good night," he said while Aurelia entered the lioness's den.

Once there, Aurelia saw no sign of Meana. She *heard* plenty—bumps and crashes and the sound of something dragging across the carpet in her room—but Meana blessedly left her alone.

Jackie, however, slipped into the living room and gave Aurelia a questioning look.

"What's up?" Aurelia asked weakly.

"You tell me. What happened?"

Aurelia winced at another crash. "I guess Meana decided Walter has been cheating on her."

"What did you do, hit her in the head with a fireplace poker?"

"What?" Aurelia stared at Jackie, at a loss. Whyever would Jackie think that?

"To get her to realize you and Walter are a thing? She's been terribly dense about it."

"Oh. Yeah, something like that," she said absently, looking in the direction of Meana's room.

"Something like that?" Jackie repeated, dumbfounded. "Really?"

"What? Oh no, *nothing* like that. She just . . . finally realized we're a thing."

"Oh. Okay." Jackie smiled knowingly. Far too knowingly. "Good for you." She turned and looked at the hallway. "I think the Cursed Room is about to be empty again."

Chapter Twenty-Two

IT WAS TOO bad Meana had chosen that particular day to leave. It might have been good for the three roommates to watch general conference together this weekend, although to be fair, Meana would probably have holed up in her room or gone elsewhere.

After the first session and a boisterous lunch with Kylie and Jackie, Aurelia drove home and then fairly skipped to Comeback Walter's apartment.

He pulled open the door before she could knock. "You're here," he said.

"I am." She smiled up at him and was reminded of their kiss. Quickly she lowered her head so he wouldn't think she was begging for another one. She would have to talk to him about that. Later.

"How are things with Meana?" he asked as Aurelia entered. He didn't touch her but stood close enough that she could feel his heat.

"She moved out."

"She did?"

"Yeah. The Cursed Room is empty again."

Walter looked thoughtful. "Cursed Room. It really does have a history, doesn't it? And the history continues. Well—I hope she'll be all right."

Her insides warmed. Though he had to be happy to no longer worry about running into Meana at Aurelia's place, his wish seemed in earnest and his kindness natural. That was much more important than brown hair. Well, technically, brown hair wasn't important at all, though it was a major plus. What Aurelia cared about was dating someone who was kind and trustworthy—and whose presence made her heart leap.

She cleared her throat and pulled a keychain from her pocket. "I brought you a general conference gift."

"What?" He laughed. "Is that a family tradition?"

"No. I came across a couple of keychains that reminded me of you, and I put them together and brought them today."

Walter took the chain and touched the dangling tags: a piano and a pumpkin. "This is great. Thanks. This is how our relationship started."

"It's how the *good* part of our relationship started," she corrected.

"We need a tree too." He looked up from the tags with a bright smile.

Aurelia returned his smile. Her heart fluttering, she looked around, and her gaze stopped short at the sofa table. A beautiful array of carrot sticks, broccoli, and apple slices adorned it, with a bowl of popcorn in the middle.

"Aurelia-snacks," Walter said. "And there's white chocolate popcorn, homemade."

"Wow. That looks amazing," she managed, honestly touched by the display. It proved Walter was getting to know her, not to mention the fact that he wanted to please her.

Before she could do something really silly, like cry over fruits and vegetables, Walter got down and pulled at a stack of papers under the sofa table.

"My notes are ready to go. Whoops."

Papers scattered when he pulled his notebook free. Aurelia bent to pick them up and wasn't surprised to find handouts from chemistry classes. A familiar flyer jumped out at her, showcasing the time travel lecture and a photo of Dr. Littlewater.

She remembered sitting there with Jackie, ignoring the conversations of students all around them as well as some older men on the left.

Stan. The image hit her like a punch to the stomach. *Stan and his cohorts. The Boston accent. The nondescript man.* All three of them had been there, hadn't they?

"Thanks." Walter accepted the papers, his hand brushing hers. "My notes *were* ready to go before I brought half my homework out here," he joked.

Aurelia nodded, her throat tight.

"Are you okay?" Walter asked.

"Yeah." She couldn't talk to him about those men, but she finally knew where she had first seen them. Again, they hadn't appeared to pay her any attention. They weren't stalking her. But they were . . . interested in Dr. Littlewater's presentation?

What did *that* mean?

* * *

TWO HOURS LATER, after the close of the second general conference session, Aurelia's thoughts were swirling. Her notes from conference were a mishmash of things that had stood out to her from the conference talks and theories about the men. Were they visiting faculty? Or professors she had missed seeing online? It could be perfectly reasonable for them to have a lab in the Eyring Center and to attend a scientific lecture—but in her mind, she saw again how the Boston man sped up by the hallway where Walter and Meana were talking, and she heard again how they talked at Macey's about not wanting their actions reported.

As she and Walter started the walk to her home, however, she knew she needed to focus on the topic that had held her mind captive before she saw the flyer.

Walter was sweet and smiling and rehashing one of the conference speakers' stories he related to.

At first, Aurelia found herself tongue-tied. Presently, she swallowed. She must get it out before they reached her doorstep, where Walter probably expected a repeat of last night's performance, minus Meana's dramatic contribution.

"About last night . . ."

Walter quieted and looked at her expectantly.

"I enjoyed our night, but, um, you should know I won't be kissing you again for a while. I have this rule," she hurried on as Walter's eyes widened. "I don't want to kiss a guy until I pretty much know we'll get married." She paused and held her breath.

Walter looked dismayed. "Are you saying I was too pushy last night? I tried to give you a chance to say no."

"I—well, chose to relax my rule."

"And you regretted it?"

She took a deep breath. "I liked it." The words made her blush, but she had to make that clear. Too often, she saw characters in romances apologize for their kiss, making the other person misunderstand and think their partner found it repulsive.

Here was another reason she wasn't romantic. She refused to follow the pattern.

"But," she continued, "I have my rule for a reason. It's my way of making sure I don't date—and I'm not being dated—just because one of us is physically attracted. I don't want to kiss just because it's nice." Until last night, she hadn't been sure it *would* be nice. "I want to wait until I know it means something, until there's really something there."

He looked as though he were trying to figure her out. After a moment, something cleared in his eyes, and understanding dawned in his face. "You're a romantic."

"Excuse me?"

He nodded as though everything made sense now. "You want that fairy-tale kiss, not the one that says 'You're cute,' but the one that says 'I love you.' And if I'm guessing right, you don't want to have kissed a bunch of guys before you find your husband."

She frowned. "That's true, but I'm not romantic."

He looked puzzled. "That's about as romantic as it gets."

Aurelia opened her mouth, then stopped and stared at him. He was right, wasn't he? Her wishes in the physical area of dating were in line with one of the most romantic ideals of the day.

Well, she certainly wasn't telling Jackie.

She swallowed. "Are you okay with my rule?"

He let out his breath. "Honestly, I didn't think I would get to kiss you that soon, but last night . . ." He gave her a sideways glance. "The stars seemed aligned."

She turned her head to hide sudden amusement, not to mention her reddening cheeks.

"Come on, that's a good one." He lightly bumped her with his shoulder. When she looked back at him, he was watching her with a smile that grew in tandem with her blush. Suddenly, a hopeful look spread across his face, and he straightened. "This rule of yours. We're talking kissing on the lips, am I right?"

She blinked. "Um, yes."

He cleared his throat. "Would I be allowed to kiss you elsewhere on occasion?"

Her heart sped up, as did her thoughts. Her words, not so much. "Um, well. Sure." She thrilled at the thought that he might kiss her elsewhere, maybe on the cheek. She would allow that.

He beamed. Then his gaze fell on her hands. "What about holding hands? I heard someone say once that it feels more intimate to them than kissing. How do you feel about it?"

She looked at him in surprise and hesitated.

"Tell me straight out," he urged. "I can take it."

His voice was less confident than his words, but Aurelia gathered her courage and spoke. "I think I'd like to have my hands free when I walk." Although she might find, just as she had with their kiss, that she enjoyed holding hands with the right person.

Walter nodded.

"But that doesn't mean we can't ever touch," she added, not sure how to explain what she wanted. Not exactly sure what she *did* want.

Walter's mouth quirked. "So if we were in the middle of a really serious conversation," he began and picked up her hands, "would I be allowed to do this?"

Where their fingers met, his firm ones appeared tanner than hers. She began to smile. "Yes."

He squeezed her hands. "Anything else? Other rules?"

She shook her head mutely.

"Are you free Wednesday night?" he asked as he let go and they resumed walking. "We could go on a hike."

Relief enveloped her. "I'd like that. You—you still want to date me?"

He stumbled. "Aurelia." He picked up her hands again. "Kissing or no kissing, I want to spend time with you. Am I bummed that I don't get to kiss you goodbye at the door? Yeah. Will I keep your rule now that I know about it? Yes. Being with you . . ." He sought for words and finally settled on, "You're worth it."

Delight sprang up inside her, making it hard to contain her joy as they walked on. Had she been alone, she probably would have started to dance. And sing something in Italian. As it was, she forced herself not to speed up her steps in spite of her sudden spurt of energy.

"Are we girlfriend and boyfriend, then?" she asked as they turned down the last street. "I mean, we've only been on one date, but—"

"It feels like much more." Walter finished her sentence with a grin. "I think we are. If you want to be."

She nodded. "I always feel good around you. Since karaoke, anyway." Not just good, but happy. She wanted more of that. "I wanted to leave that day, but you—you just did. That impressed me."

He ducked his head. "It was obvious you wanted to leave." His eyes met hers again. "As much as I didn't get why you treated me like a criminal at first, since then I've found you to be very transparent; not predictable—you keep surprising me—but transparent, and I love that. There's a light in you that draws me, and I want to keep getting to know you."

She caught her breath, feeling a little woozy as they walked up the stairs. No one had ever said anything that nice to her, or that romantic. Her heart fluttered. A little bit of romance never hurt anyone, did it?

When they reached her door, she turned to him, and he held out his arms.

Walter's embrace felt strong and solid and good, and it gave Aurelia butterflies.

She danced her way inside. Walter's reaction to her belated request was a huge plus in his favor. She had gone on dates with guys who turned out to expect a kiss on the first date, and when she told them no, they didn't ask her out again. She had gone on dates with guys who did *not* expect a kiss that early on but who did think they could start kissing by date three or four. When she had explained her philosophy, they hadn't liked it. She hadn't been "worth" it.

To Walter, she was worth it. He had said so. She even had the proof of his alternate, future self, who was still in love with her even though—well, surely she had told him the same thing the first time around. She must have had this very talk with him, and he had stuck around.

She closed her eyes and hummed an Indila song in the middle of the living room.

"That *wondersacious*, huh?" asked Jackie, peeking around the corner with a hairbrush in her hand.

"I think he likes me," Aurelia said happily.

Jackie slapped her own forehead. "I think you're right. Why didn't I notice that before?"

Aurelia sang out loud in French, drowning out her friend's sarcasm. Going to their room, she opened a drawer and retrieved her copy of her patriarchal blessing.

She remembered the day the patriarch over her church area had laid his hands on her head and given her that blessing. It was a guide for her life that detailed some of the hopes and expectations of her heavenly parents for her, dependent on her commitment to the gospel of Jesus Christ. She had been fourteen years old when she asked for her blessing, and she loved to reread it, especially the part that talked about her spiritual gifts.

That wasn't the part that drew her now though. Sinking onto the bed, she lay on her back and held up the paper, quickly finding the section that mentioned the man she would marry.

Your husband will love and respect you.

She read the words over dreamily, along with the surrounding sentences. For sure Walter respected her. And if it was a little early to use the word "love," at least he appeared to adore her so far.

* * *

THE NEXT MORNING, Aurelia and Jackie stepped outside between general conference sessions, only to catch sight of Walter heading up the stairs.

Jackie greeted him. "If there were five of you, I'd never turn a corner without running into you so long as I live with Aurelia."

"May there never, ever be five of me," he said with feeling. "Can I join you on your walk?"

Aurelia opened her mouth, but Jackie was quicker. "I'll just stay back a ways and let you two walk together," she said, already lengthening the distance between them. She affected a British accent. "I shall chaperone from back here."

Aurelia rolled her eyes. "Did we go for a walk the first time around?" she asked, certain she was facing Confident Walter.

He nodded. "We watched both sessions of Sunday general conference together and went for a walk in between." He held up his phone. "I checked with myself and found out it wasn't happening that way today, so I knew I wouldn't run into myself by showing up here. He got me this phone a while back, by the way. Good way to keep in contact with myself."

Aurelia chewed on her bottom lip and lowered her voice. "I know something new about those men."

He straightened, and his voice became tense. "What?"

"One of them was in our apartment this week. Visiting Meana. He's her uncle."

"*What*? What does *that* mean?"

"I don't know." She thought of the tickets Stan had given her. "He knows I'm dating you. He tried to give us tickets to a big science thing. But I don't want to go. I didn't like him."

"No." It was to his credit that Walter didn't seem interested in the event. "But he knows who you are, then."

They walked in silence. Walter was clearly concerned, but he didn't say anything about forbidding her to work on this mystery. He didn't warn her to stay clear of the men.

"They were at the lecture too," Aurelia told him. Somehow, this newest fact didn't sit well with her. "Are they interested in time travel in particular? Are they teachers?"

"No. Well, not teachers at BYU, anyway." They turned a corner and headed toward the duck pond and the surrounding botanical area. "I wonder if this guy, Meana's uncle, showed up at your apartment the first time around." He frowned. "But you wouldn't know. It's strange I can't ask you. You don't remember the first time."

She shook her head at how peculiar it all was, and Walter changed the subject. "Is Meana watching any of general conference with you?"

Aurelia's eyes widened. "Did she watch it with us the first time around?" Had that been messed up somehow?

"No, but she's been staying longer at your place than she did the first time, so I wondered if she might. At least that would be a positive change from the first time around."

"Yeah, but it's too late for that. She moved out."

Walter went still. "She did?"

"Yep. Friday night." All night long, and Saturday early morning. Really, it had been a six- or seven-hour process that spanned two days.

"She moved?"

"Yes." Why was that so hard for him to grasp?

Then she noticed the look of ecstasy on Walter's face.

"Does that mean we kissed?" he asked.

She caught her breath. Seriously? That was the way it happened before too?

"*You* and I didn't kiss," she told him sternly. "*He* and I kissed."

"That's great news," he exclaimed, and she could have sworn the sun illuminated him in that moment.

"We won't do it again," she warned him. "Not for a while."

"I know. It's a test of our relationship, and you don't want to kiss other guys than your future husband anyway."

She opened her mouth and closed it again. He had explained it perfectly. She watched him, noticing he didn't try to hold hands while they walked. Suddenly realizing she had a burning question and that she was looking at the one person who knew the answer, she asked, "Will he be able to stick to it?"

"Waiting?" Walter looked up at the sky. "Yes. It'll be hard for me, and at times I may find, uh, creative ways to show I'm attracted to you, but yes, I'll stick to it. I haven't messed up even once up to the day I—you know, went back in time."

Aurelia wondered at the situation she found herself in. Two Walters, one of them from the future. Both seemed perfectly devoted to her. She rarely wondered whether he might lose interest, which was an advantage so long as *she* didn't lose interest.

Walter gave her a sidelong look. "You know, I missed out when I let myself go to institute in my place two days ago. Is there any chance I could take you on a date this week?"

She nearly laughed. She should have predicted this.

"Because I'd really like to keep getting to know you, and while I'm super happy that things are moving forward with you and—Walter—I'm getting a little jealous of me, or him. Would you like to go roller-skating at the Classic Fun Center in Orem? Tuesday at seven?"

She looked at him again. He was as handsome as ever. Confident, but a tiny bit humbler than he had been. Hopeful. And one or both of him had, from time to time, shown himself to be amazingly respectful, sweet, and fun.

"I'll meet you there," she told him.

He smiled broadly even though she wasn't allowing him to pick her up. "I'll look forward to it."

Jackie came up from behind and slung an arm around each of them. "So, friends, are we making progress? I sure hope so, because I'm bored staying behind. Like it or not, you'll have to deal with me for the rest of our walk."

Chapter Twenty-Three

THAT AFTERNOON, Aurelia stared in bemusement as Walter lugged a spindly chair and a piano keyboard indoors while Brian followed with a music stand.

"You brought us a keyboard?" Jackie asked. "I hope that means you'll serenade Aurelia."

"Correction: Aurelia will serenade *me*," Walter told her.

"Even better." Jackie grabbed Brian's arm and pointed at the sofa. "Sit. I have paper ready for you."

"Paper?" He plopped down in front of the sheets of origami paper.

"Yes. Can you make an elephant?"

Brian's face brightened, and he reached out for a sheet while Aurelia wandered over to the keyboard.

Walter bowed, indicating the dainty chair. "It's all set for you, maestra."

She trailed a hand across the keys, resulting in a shy ascent of notes. Having had only two years of piano lessons when she was small and didn't want to practice, she wasn't eager to show off her skills, or lack thereof. "I don't play like you do."

He looked at her in happy anticipation, as though she could do no wrong. "Play it like *you* do."

She pretended to think about it. "I suppose I could get up on the piano and walk across it like I did when I was three."

His eyebrows raised. "If you did that, I'd have to grab you around the waist and lift you down." He leaned in close and whispered, "And then I wouldn't let go immediately."

The thought made her all tingly, but she managed to reply, "I think you should play something now."

He grinned and sat with a flourish. "*I* think *you* should sing something." He flexed his hands and started to play.

The opening bars were intriguingly familiar. Aurelia's jaw dropped. Was it really . . . ?

It was the song she had performed at the talent show! She listened in delighted surprise. "Did you buy sheet music for that?"

"No, I figured it out myself."

"By *ear*?" She hadn't realized he had that talent.

He sat up tall. "Did I impress you? I've got to do that more often. You'd better sing now. I memorized the words, but I'm afraid my French accent is awful."

Behind them, Jackie clapped her hands together. "Awesome. Now try a hippopotamus."

Aurelia felt a smile grow on her face. Touched by Walter's efforts, she began to sing, softly at first, because they weren't alone, and then with growing enjoyment.

When the song ended and Walter began another of Indila's songs, Aurelia couldn't hide her astonishment.

"Impressed you again, did I? I'm getting to be a pro at this," Walter said in a puffed-up voice, while behind them, Jackie squealed and promptly ordered an aardvark.

"Aurelia, look at this." Jackie soon beckoned both of them over and indicated a small pile of origami animals. "It's awesome."

"It's pretty cool," Aurelia acknowledged, watching Walter pick up the hippopotamus. He looked absentminded as he turned it over, a frown line appearing between his eyebrows.

"Awesome," Jackie repeated with a smile, and Aurelia couldn't help herself.

"It's not *awesatious*?" she asked.

"Nope." Jackie's enthusiasm didn't dampen in the least.

"Methinks Brian has a good influence on you, if you don't find yourself spouting nonsense words at him. I, for one, approve."

Jackie sniffed. "My English is *wonderfilious*. You've been jealous for years."

Aurelia rolled her eyes and looked at Walter, surprised that he didn't laugh. "Are you okay?"

He tilted his head at her. After a moment, he put down Brian's animal. "Yeah."

"Are you sure? You look kind of worried."

He started to shrug, then seemed to realize that all eyes had turned on him. "It's just some stuff at the lab."

"Like what?"

"I don't know. Some of our papers are getting moved around." He frowned. "Never mind. It's nothing."

"You're bothered by things being in the wrong place?" Up till now, she hadn't noticed any OCD tendencies in him.

"No, it's not that. It seems like they're getting moved and mislaid when nobody working on the project has been there. I honestly think—I want to say some of it's been stolen. Things get lost, but . . . I'd hope all of us would be really careful with our notes."

Aurelia opened her mouth, but she didn't speak. Was it possible . . . Was it too much of a stretch to think Stan's friend might have something to do with it? That he did, in fact, have access not to the lab beside Walter's, as she had believed, but to his actual lab?

"I know the feeling," Jackie commiserated, drawing everyone's attention. "When Aurelia puts my potato peeler with the ladles and spatulas instead of in the drawer where it goes, it's a nightmare."

"I only did that once," Aurelia protested, "and Walter's talking about something that messes up his research." *And possibly the world of time travel.*

"And I'm talking about something that messes up cooking," Jackie said, pulling a sad face. "Which in turn messes up life."

Aurelia reached over to smack her.

In spite of Walter's revelation, conversation during dinner ended up being festive. Like the previous week, Walter and Brian offered to do the dishes afterward. This time, Jackie stayed with Aurelia at the table and leaned in close. "We need a plan for when they leave. How's this? I'll distract Brian so you and Walter can say a proper farewell."

"I think your idea of a proper farewell and my idea are wildly different," Aurelia told her.

"More's the pity." Her roommate sighed. "Remember the day Walter ran inside, threw himself in front of you, and held your hands and asked if you were all right? I would love to see him burst inside and kiss you in the middle of the living room. Dip you and all that."

"You're addled," Aurelia said.

Walter and Brian finished and prepared to take their leave. "Is there anything else we can do for you?" Walter asked.

Jackie smirked. "As a matter of fact, you should—"

"Leave now but come back again on Sunday," Aurelia broke in, forestalling Jackie's request.

"Sure." He smiled at her. "But what else do I need to do, Jackie?"

Before she could answer, Aurelia blurted out, "You're picking me up on Wednesday for our hike, right? We'll see you then too."

"I'll definitely pick you up on Wednesday," Walter said warmly, his eyes alight as he looked at her. Something about his gaze was intimate enough that Aurelia wanted to just stare back and savor the feeling.

"Yes, that's a good beginning," Jackie approved. "Now if you'll move on to—"

Aurelia shook herself from her daze and steered Walter toward the door with both hands on his back. "Thank you both for coming. I can't wait till next week." Brian hurried to get out of the way before Walter got pushed out behind him. "We'll let Jackie get the rest of her evening back."

"Bye," Walter called in a too-innocent tone while a mischievous dimple played hide-and-seek at the corner of his mouth.

Aurelia shut the door.

Walter reopened it and stuck his head in. "My keyboard?"

Aurelia groaned.

"Can I leave it here? It'll be a lot of trouble to drive and carry it in every time I come by."

She liked the idea of having it in her apartment for him to play. "We can keep it here."

"Great. And I'm still curious about what Jackie would like me to do, because I totally didn't hear anything she said about me while I was in the kitchen."

Jackie chortled while Walter withdrew his head and Aurelia shut the door anew.

"That was fun," Jackie said happily and pretended to dust off her hands.

"I'm gonna start teasing you about Brian," Aurelia threatened.

Jackie flung out her hands. "Do! I can't wait till he comes again."

* * *

THE NEXT SEVERAL weeks were fun. Between dates with Comeback Walter and a tentative date or two with Confident Walter, which turned out to be enjoyable, all things considered, Aurelia was kept busy. She tried to think of places Comeback Walter would enjoy and had great success when she took him to the Loveland Living Planet Aquarium, where he filled her mind with science facts and growing inspiration for a science fiction story.

The weather turned colder, and the day of the science symposium, October twenty-first, came and went without incident and without Walter in attendance.

The following afternoon, Aurelia was eating celery.

"Why didn't I ask Brian for his phone number?" Jackie complained as she came into the living room. "I wanna invite him to something. What's up with you?"

Aurelia sighed and dropped her hands from her laptop's keyboard. "Tomorrow's my sister's birthday, but she doesn't have time to Skype with me."

"What's she doing, then?"

"School, a trip with the family, and hanging out with friends. I used to rate higher than her friends though." Aurelia bit into her celery stick with a noisy crunch.

"Maybe you can Skype the day before or the day after?"

"That's what I figured. She said we might as well chat on Sunday, as always, but I wanted to do something special. I guess it's not a big deal, but telling myself that and feeling it isn't the same thing." She managed a shadow of a smile. "I'm writing her an email though. One that mentions some of her qualities I admire. At least that's something."

"That's a good idea," Jackie agreed.

Unfortunately, the next day brought a new trial of sorts.

Maybe her family's email about celebrating Christmas once they got home should have cheered Aurelia, but instead, it depressed her.

Following a meeting on campus, she wandered outside, where the autumn sun tried and failed to warm her. The few students who stood around in scattered groups only served to make her feel lonelier.

Then she caught sight of a familiar polo shirt. Walter sat bent forward on one of the benches, engrossed in his textbook.

She made a beeline for him.

He looked up with a start when she sat next to him. His surprise gave way to a broad smile. "Hey."

At her lack of answer, his smile dropped away. "Are you okay?"

She looked down and fiddled with her hands. Admitting to being sad would make it worse, more real.

"What do you need?" Walter's voice was soft.

She shrugged, but the movement loosened something inside her. To keep the sudden tears at bay, she quickly put an arm around him and hid her face against his shoulder.

Walter put both arms around her. "What's wrong?"

"Nothing, really," she mumbled, her voice muffled. She may as well tell him now. "I wish I could spend Christmas with my family."

His hold tightened. Aurelia listened to her own breathing and his for a minute.

"I'm sorry," he said into her hair.

She let out a shuddering breath. "It's not a big deal. Their last Christmas in the mission won't be normal anyway. They want to hold a delayed Christmas with me after they get home the first week of January. That sounds cool, right?" Her voice was pitiful.

"But it's not what you wanted," he said in understanding.

She sniffed. "I'll get over it." She sniffed again.

Walter rested his chin on the top of her head. "You miss them."

She nodded against him. "I'm okay having Thanksgiving without them. It was actually fun last year to get together with faculty members and students for dinner and pies. This year, I'm going to Jackie's for Thanksgiving, and that'll be fun too." Her voice faltered. "But Christmas is different."

"I'm sorry."

She wondered if he was uncomfortable sitting the way he was. It felt good to her, but he was twisted sideways, and his arms were probably getting tired.

If only her thoughts would turn off the way they had during her first and, at her demand, only kiss. Worrying about Walter's comfort ruined some of the peace she felt in his arms.

She sat up, and he let go.

"Thanks," she told him, looking into his vibrant eyes. "I should probably go home. I have a project I need to make some last changes to."

"If you let me gather my things, I'll walk with you."

She waited while he put away his books.

As they walked, the concern in his eyes both warmed her and made her feel guilty. She shouldn't be upset. Her parents had talked before about the possibility of holding Christmas after they got back, since Christmas and their return date were so close. Now Walter was all worried and sweet because she couldn't pull herself together emotionally.

He spoke up as they left campus. "You know, I remember the Christmas when I was twelve years old and my older sisters decided to convince my parents to believe in Santa."

Aurelia blinked several times in quick succession. "Come again?"

"Yeah, they hid notes from Santa all over the house and put gifts in my parents' Christmas stockings. Oh, and truffles in my little sister's everyday socks. I got to help them with the milk and cookies—and the acting."

"What acting?"

"Acting out Santa and his reindeer, of course." He smiled as they stopped at a traffic intersection. "At a totally acceptable time for people to get up on Christmas morning—like, three a.m. or so—Miriam and Louisa turned into Santa. By the way, they're awful actors. You should have heard them bump around in the living room, speaking in deep girls' voices: 'Oops, I dropped my sack. Merry Christmas to all and to all a good night. Mmm, I want the recipe. Five stars.'"

Aurelia giggled as the silly story unfolded. She hadn't known his sisters were such characters.

"Meanwhile," Walter continued, "I was climbing the roof."

"What for?" Aurelia blurted out.

He looked around furtively and lowered his voice. "They had bought some antlers from a classmate, and they needed a rooftop scene."

She gaped at him. Walter pointed at the light, which had turned green, and stepped forward. Aurelia followed, intent on hearing the next part of the story.

"While they bumbled around downstairs, I ran around on the roof, making as much noise as possible until the family got out of bed. As soon as my little sister, Polly—she was seven years old—came running, my sisters yelled, 'Santa! Catch Santa, Polly!' I climbed inside through the window and ran around the tree to join the search. Then when my parents appeared, Miriam yelled, 'Check the roof, Polly! There was something on the roof! Go see!'

"Maybe my parents would have protested if they had been more awake, but my sisters didn't give them time to think. Polly was super excited, and Miriam rushed her outside and helped her climb up on the rooftop, where she found the antlers."

"You guys are crazy," Aurelia exclaimed, her eyes dancing.

Walter laughed. "My parents stood stunned while Polly shouted about the antlers and hearing Santa in their living room and hearing reindeer gallop on the roof. When we finally calmed down enough to open presents, they found their gifts and notes from Santa in their stockings. By the end of the day, they had discovered the gifts in their everyday socks as well."

"Your sisters go all out, don't they?" Aurelia asked in admiration.

"Pretty much. Polly loved it. My sisters had planted more notes than I knew about. Dad found the TV remote wrapped in a note: 'You watch *Elf* if you watch anything. Santa.'"

Aurelia gasped with humor, but Walter wasn't finished.

"A week later, when it snowed and we took out our sled, we found a note taped to it: 'You call this a sled? My training sled was five times as big and flew fifty times as fast!'"

Aurelia burst out laughing. "Who *are* these people?"

"Nutcases," Walter answered promptly.

She wiped away tears. "Walter, that's amazing." They reached her apartment, Aurelia still smiling, her despondency gone. Walter had chased it away completely, and even remembering her upcoming Christmas now didn't bring it back.

"Thank you," she told him, "for cheering me up. I really appreciate it." She wished she didn't have to get to work now. "I'll see you soon."

"Definitely." He smiled at her. "Not that it's soon enough."

She didn't tell him he was being sappy or corny. At the moment, she felt the exact same way.

Not until she sat down with her laptop did it occur to her to wonder which Walter she had just been with. The thought came as a small shock. Her fingers paused above the keyboard as she considered the last half hour.

She couldn't tell. This was the first time she couldn't tell which Walter she had been with and the first time she hadn't thought to differentiate. The realization left her stunned. Up till now, she had never let Confident Walter walk her all the way home, and yet she had just allowed a Walter to do exactly that without her questioning who he was.

Jackie walked in, laden with bulging plastic bags. "Have you seen Brian around anywhere?"

Aurelia stood, struggling to tear her mind from her revelation. Jackie's words slowly made their way through her brain. Once they registered, Aurelia cracked a smile. "It's a pity you didn't get his phone number." She paused and noticed the groceries. "Let me help with those."

"Thanks. It's a humongous pity, and he's not even on social media. Did you see the email?"

"What email?"

"Our newest roommate has signed the contract. She's coming on Monday." Jackie put chicken in the fridge. "Took her long enough. It's been weeks since Meana left. We don't usually have such a gap."

"Oh cool," Aurelia said halfheartedly. "What's her name?"

"I don't remember. From now on, I rely on you to remember names when it comes to our Cursed Roommates. It just isn't worth the effort anymore."

Aurelia didn't give the new roommate much thought either. Her mind returned to Walter and stayed there until it was time for institute. Upon her arrival, she returned his greeting and carefully looked him over. He wore the same shirt, but that had happened before.

"Did you walk me home from campus today?" she asked him.

"One and the same."

She had to be sure. "You're the Walter that has gone back in time, right?"

He nodded. "Is that okay?"

Confident Walter had comforted her. Confident Walter had walked her home and entertained her with a family story. Confident Walter had cheered her up.

She smiled at him. "Yes, it's okay."

After institute, she let him walk her home. It was the second time she had given Confident Walter that honor and the first time she had consciously done so.

Chapter Twenty-Four

THAT SUNDAY, Walter and company were unusually late, prompting no small complaints from Jackie about boys and phone numbers.

When the bell rang, Jackie tore the door open and stuck her head out past Walter. "Where's Brian?"

"I don't know," Walter answered. "He said he might arrive a little later today, so he wanted to come separately."

Jackie groaned and pulled her head back in. "He's late," she announced.

"Are you sure? I could have sworn you guys told us we should be here at, um . . . Hold on. Maybe you never did tell us a time."

"Ha, ha," said Jackie.

Walter and Aurelia kept the impatient Jackie company until Jackie had the brilliant idea for Walter to text his friend and ask when he was dragging his sorry self over.

He sent a text and held up his phone. "I didn't put it quite like that," he said, "but I've asked him now." He turned to Aurelia. "By the way, can I get your phone number? I keep forgetting to ask while I'm with you, but I hope we're way past the point when you didn't trust me."

They were, and yet she hesitated. Somehow, she had managed to get this far without sharing it, and she didn't love the idea of his surprise visits changing. "Will you stop coming by unannounced?"

He watched her carefully. His lips quirked upward. "No."

She smiled in relief. "All right, get out your phone." She liked those visits. She wouldn't have if she didn't like him, but because she did, they were highlights of her week.

A knock sounded on the door.

"I'll get it!" Jackie flew to the entrance and slammed the door open, making it hit the wall as it revealed Brian, the object of her attention for the last half hour.

She paused and leaned nonchalantly against the doorway, catching herself when the door moved. "I need your phone number."

Aurelia and Walter looked at each other, suppressing grins. Walter's eyes twinkled. "Would you like to go to a Halloween dance this week?"

Aurelia cocked her head. Dances weren't really her thing, but Walter looked eager, and if it were with him, she would look forward to it. "Yes."

"Super." He raised his voice. "How about you guys?"

Brian cleared his throat and looked at Jackie. "I don't know if there'll be slow dances, but if there are—would you save one for me?" His shoulders tensed before she answered.

"Of course." She looked up from her phone to flash him a smile, and Brian brightened. "We can all be third and fourth wheels for each other. It'll be *delightable*."

* * *

The dance was all Jackie could talk about the next few days, and apparently it was on both Walters's minds, as well. Confident Walter brought it up when Aurelia spent the evening at his aunt and uncle's place, learning family history with him. Shortly after she returned home, Comeback Walter called.

"I came by unannounced like you wanted, but you weren't home," he said. "How was your evening?"

It was a new experience talking to him on the phone. Aurelia settled back on the couch as she described her visit. Had she been using a landline, she would have been twirling the cord like a grade-school girl. It was fun to hear Walter's laughter as she shared some of the jokes his aunt had told.

"What about the new roommate?" he asked. "When will I get to meet her?"

"There's no sign of her so far." She sat forward, dropping her feet on the floor. "By the way, Walter asked me to go to the Halloween dance with him." She rubbed her head. That had been the only awkward moment of her night. "I told him I already told you yes."

There was a pause on the other end. When Walter spoke, he sounded curious. "Would you go with him if you could?"

She frowned. "Are you asking me to choose between you and you?"

"Not at all. Just wondering. If I were out of town, would you want to go with him?"

"Well, yeah." She no longer had any qualms about Confident Walter, which meant . . . that she liked him. She finally liked both Walters. She finally liked all of him, no matter which timeline he was on.

Actually, *liked* wasn't quite the right word, but—

Walter was definitely smiling now as he said, "Well then, I can't wait for the dance."

* * *

IT WAS Jackie's idea that she and Aurelia would meet the boys at the dance rather than walk together. That way they could look for each other without knowing how each had dressed up. When the girls arrived, the crowd was sparse but growing, the size of the ballroom making it easy for the hundred or so people to spread out and dance the "Thriller," which was in full swing.

"Now, where could they be?" Jackie wondered out loud. She was dressed as a whale, complete with a blue head pulled on top of her own head like a hood.

"They might not be here yet. Maybe they wanted to be fashionably late, like you." Aurelia wore Hogwarts robes, and her hair was curled in imitation of a blonde Hermione, although she wondered how long the curls would last in her naturally straight hair. She had debated carrying a stack of books in her arms, but it wouldn't have been practical.

Jackie opened her mouth dramatically wide and raised her voice, startling everyone within thirty feet as she imitated whale-speak from *Finding Nemo*. "OoooWwwwheaaaare aAAAare theEYYy?"

Aurelia covered her mouth to contain her giggles.

"Found you," announced a familiar voice, and she whirled to see Walter step toward her in a white lab coat and huge black glasses that nearly obscured his face. His chocolate-colored hair was pomaded in crazy swirls on top of his head. Funky as it looked, the sight wreaked havoc on Aurelia's insides as she imagined trying to pat it all back into order. Even the lab coat, which completed the dorky costume, fit his frame nicely and made her think "firm" instead of "dork."

"It wasn't difficult," said Brian's amused voice as he approached from the girls' right.

Jackie elbowed Aurelia. Aurelia thought it was to make her stop gawking, but then she noticed Jackie's eyes fixed in admiration on Brian. He wore a dinosaur head, followed by a zebra-striped shirt with sleeves ending in hooves, followed by furry pants with a curled monkey's tail. Aurelia was reminded of a mix-and-match children's book.

"Brilliant," Jackie declared. "This'll be your next origami project. Now let's see you dance this one before it ends." She grabbed his arm and tugged him into the mass of zombie dancers.

Walter knelt with a flourish in front of Aurelia and took her hand. "Hermione? You look magical, as always."

Aurelia smiled and shrugged. "Jackie did the makeup."

Walter kissed her hand. "It's not the makeup," he said in a voice several shades deeper than usual.

She blushed. Then she snorted and felt her face go red with the effort not to laugh. Having this wild-haired, handsome scientist spout compliments wasn't among the events she had expected from tonight.

Vincent Price's maniacal laughter announced the end of "Thriller," and Walter returned to his feet, his hair making a little *swip* sound as it bounced. Aurelia's laugh rang out like bells, uninhibited. Walter stepped close, his eyes brightening at either her reaction or the next song. "Seeing that a slow dance has begun, may I have this dance?"

She felt breathless up against him. At her nod, Walter's hands slid to her back, and they stepped slowly back and forth. Aurelia put her arms around him and buried her face in his chest.

How had it come to this? How had she come to like him so much?

"Like" wasn't a strong enough word. It was weak and feeble in comparison to how she felt. Her pull toward him ran deep, and there was much more to it than the physical attraction he inspired in her.

She was disappointed when the song ended and Walter let go. Then he began to dance with vigor to the next crowd-pleaser. Aurelia watched his bouncy, swirly hair in awe before joining in, smiling and not caring how her mediocre dance moves might look to others. She could hardly look as strange as Mad Scientist Walter.

When the song ended, to her surprise, another slow song started. Before she could comment on it, Walter turned and walked away. She took a step to follow just as a familiar voice sounded behind her.

"May I have this dance?"

She whirled around and stared at the pirate before her. Long black braids; white collared shirt and brown vest; old-fashioned trousers; and a dark tricorn hat.

Heavy black makeup reminded her of Jack Sparrow and made strange changes to Walter's kind face, which was partially covered by the hat and the wig.

She threw a look behind her shoulder and felt a jolt at the sight of Scientist Walter's still-retreating back. As she turned anew to the pirate, her heart sped up significantly. Both of him were here. She was actually seeing both of him.

Mutely she let the pirate take her hand and begin the dance.

She found herself swaying to the music. Walter twirled her out and back in front of him, and her black robe swirled about her.

"But—you can't both be here," she whispered.

"Can't we?" He looked around the room, and she followed his lead. "Some of the people here know me. A lot of them don't. Even those who do might not pay me any attention. Besides, while we're not allowed to wear masks, there's still a lot that can be said for Halloween disguises."

She gasped, seeing the humor of the situation. He was right. Unsettling as it was to her, it was as perfect an opportunity as he might ever get to have both of him in the same place at once. There was a risk, yes, but one had to look close to recognize this pirate as Walter, and even the scientist with his large glasses could go unrecognized if he didn't draw attention to himself.

Walter grinned. "I think the person we have to be most careful around is Brian, and he's plenty occupied right now."

Aurelia scanned the crowd until her eyes landed on a blue-and-white Jackie who, as cheerful as ever, spoke nonstop to Brian as he led her through some impressive swing dance steps, his hooves slapping against his forearms.

"Shall we?" Walter asked.

When she looked back at him, he was closer than before. She involuntarily reached for his shoulders for balance, and he put his hands on her back. Her heart pounded, and she wanted to shake her head at herself for getting all twitterpated twice over two different—well, one different—well, the guy she was dancing with.

She frowned. Which one was she dancing with?

And who had she been dancing with before?

"I hope that frown doesn't mean I've done something wrong," Walter said.

"I was just wondering—which Walter are you?"

His expression cleared. "I can't tell you that." He led her into a series of steps she didn't know well, but with him leading, they went smoothly.

"You can't tell me?" she asked, pretending outrage and then gasping as he dipped her and stopped, looking down at her.

His voice lowered. "I'm Walter."

She opened her mouth to reprimand him, but he pulled her to a standing position and twirled her outward, stealing her breath.

When she returned to him, she found herself in his arms, her hands on his chest. She moved a hand up and fingered a bundle of the black braids as she and Walter stepped to the music. Looking at his makeup-clad face, his brown eyes ringed by black, she was just beginning to grow hot at their proximity when her eyes widened at a new thought. She dropped the smile that appeared with her idea and instead glowered at Walter. "Unhand me, you rogue."

She had always wanted a chance to say that.

"Unhand?" His ringed eyes widened with delight. "Now that I have found me a maiden, I can hardly be expected to unhand her, now can I?"

"Protocol demands it," she said, raising her chin and pulling back for a moment.

"Hang protocol. It can walk the plank," was his pronouncement as he tugged her closer, raising her heart rate.

"You knave," she said, keeping her voice down in case someone overheard and worried something might actually be wrong. She let go of the braids and thumped her hands on his chest, once, twice, not very hard.

"Aaarr," he growled, and before she knew it, he had swept her off her feet, one hand under her bent knees and the other behind her back, leaving the bottom of her robe trailing toward the floor.

She began to shake with laughter in his arms. Walter chuckled and lifted her higher, decreasing the distance between her face and his.

She caught her breath on a smile, and her eyes traced his face, trying to see Walter behind the pirate. If this were a movie, he would have kissed her next.

"I can't kiss you," he said in a low voice, his eyes gleaming. "A refined lady told me I must not do so."

"She must be daft," she said quietly. "But wise," she added quickly.

But daft.

Still, as much as she wished in that moment that she had never made the stipulation, she would stick to it.

"She *is*"—he teased, and she narrowed her eyes, waiting to see whether he would pick the word "daft" or "wise" to complete his sentence—"refined," he finished.

"Does this lady hold a part of your heart?" Aurelia asked, her heart beating faster underneath the golden Gryffindor crest on her clothes. Normally, she wouldn't be so bold, but something about this night, or their costumes, or Walter, held magic.

"Every piece of it." He lowered his face closer, creating a small, warm space with just the two of them. Then he gently returned her feet to the ground.

"You're the Walter who has gone back in time," she said, trying to slow her affected breathing. "Right?" Surely only Confident Walter, who was already at the point of proposing two months ago, would express such a strong sentiment as to claim she held every piece of his heart.

A hopeful part of her prayed that Comeback Walter felt just as strongly about her by now.

"Do you think so?" he asked, meeting her eyes squarely. Then he bowed and stepped back as the song ended.

A white lab coat appeared at Aurelia's side, and Scientist Walter held out a hand. "May I have *this* dance?" he asked while the pirate walked away.

Aurelia stared again, forgetting to breathe, amazed at the evidence before her. She had accepted the fact that there were two of him, and yet she had never experienced the fact quite this way. She smiled weakly at this change of the guards.

"How do you like my pirate costume?" the scientist asked.

She shook her head. "Which Walter are you?"

One of his spiraled locks dropped to the side, drawing her gaze.

He grinned. "That's for you to figure out. Or to wonder about for the rest of your life."

She pouted. "Not fair. Wait. How come there are so many slow dances tonight?"

"I went and asked the DJ if we could have a lot of them," he confided. "It turns out his best friend is at the dance and had already made the same request."

"Huh." She caught a glimpse of Pirate Walter dancing, and she craned her neck. Who was he with?

Scientist Walter followed her gaze. "I was taught to dance with others besides my date. I hope that doesn't bother you."

She pondered with a tiny frown and then shook herself. His behavior was perfect. It meant there would be fewer girls sitting out, and Aurelia was used to sitting out dances. A lot of guys stayed on the sidelines during slow dances, and she often wondered if those who did ask girls to dance thought her too reserved. Either way, she was glad Walter kept to what he had been taught. "So long as he doesn't flirt with her."

"I won't. You and I are practically . . . I'm very committed to you, Aurelia."

Practically . . . engaged? She squinted at him. "*You're* Con—the Walter who has gone back in time."

His lips quirked and he watched her, saying nothing, making her doubt her guess.

"How about we make a deal?" He pushed his glasses further up against his nose. "You tell me your nicknames for us, and I'll tell you who's who."

"You're the Walter who *hasn't* gone back in time," she said. "He's the only one I've let that slip to."

"Yes, but he and I communicate sometimes," he said calmly.

Just as they must have communicated about tonight. One Walter had melted away when the other Walter approached. He hadn't been surprised to see himself.

"Deal?" he asked, smirking.

"Nope." She smirked back. "I'll just keep guessing."

Truth be told, while it was normally helpful to know which Walter she was with, tonight, it didn't matter. She loved—um, enjoyed—maybe was entranced by—both of them.

What was the right word at this point?

"Where have you been?" Jackie exclaimed, grabbing her and disrupting her musings at the end of another dance. "Stop hiding. If you and Walter are going to have a private romantic moment tonight, then have the decency to have it out in public where I can see." At Aurelia's snort of amusement, Jackie turned to Walter. "Come on, dance with us." She bounced to the music, her whale head slapping against her back. "Now would be an opportune time for a romantic scene."

"I'm not sure this party song is conducive to romance," Walter called out, bopping along to it.

"Yeah, I doubt these dance moves will do the job," the mix-and-match Brian said as he followed Jackie's lead.

"What? There's nothing that says romance like . . ."

Aurelia didn't hear the rest of Jackie's words. A black-haired pirate had joined their growing circle, and he now danced across from her.

Somehow, Aurelia kept moving, but she felt like she did so in slow motion. What was he thinking? She couldn't even ask him, for fear that Brian would notice. Hadn't Walter the Pirate told her earlier that he needed to watch out for Brian?

Beside her, Walter the Scientist did a double take. She gave him an anxious glance as he kept going, trying not to let on that anything was amiss. The room seemed to swim with emotions as he regained his composure. Then, to Aurelia's consternation, he smiled at himself as if all were well with the world.

Jackie went into the middle of the circle, and Aurelia gasped as Pirate Walter entered from the opposite side, joining arms with her and turning in a circle before facing off and matching her moves. Jackie laughed, enjoying herself with the seeming stranger. When he was about to leave, she suddenly choked and coughed.

Hand over her mouth, she returned to the edge of the circle in between Aurelia and Scientist Walter.

"Someone's playing with fire," she told Aurelia behind her hand. Then she turned to Walter on the other side. "Well met."

He tried to look innocent but failed completely. Jackie grinned.

Jackie probably wouldn't have recognized the pirate if she hadn't looked straight into his face from close up. Maybe the risk was low that Brian would notice his friend was twice in attendance.

Anyway, Aurelia wouldn't let it scare her. If Walter was willing to risk it, then it was his problem.

"Here comes another one," said Brian when a piano and flute duet signaled the beginning of a slow song.

The pirate moved away, and the scientist claimed the dance with Aurelia.

"They're playing a Disney song?" Aurelia asked when the melody of "Beauty and the Beast" became clear. "They never do that."

"They should do it more often," Walter said. "Or host Disney dances. There'd be a market for it in Provo."

She nodded and looked around, lowering her voice. "Isn't it weird to see yourself here?"

Walter let out a mild huff. "When I see pirate me dancing with you, I start to get jealous. Then I remember it's me, and I'm happy about it. But still a little jealous." He reached out and stroked her hair, his fingers grazing her neck and raising goosebumps. "I'm not jealous now."

She swallowed. "The curls are coming out already, aren't they?"

"Mostly," he grinned, running his hand through them again.

The crowd shifted. People stopped dancing and pressed together in the east end of the ballroom. Soon, Walter caught sight of what they were staring at and found a place where Aurelia could see it too: a dressed-up Belle and a dressed-up prince dancing near the front.

"I guess it's some sort of performance," he said.

Aurelia imagined dressing up as Belle herself and dancing to this song. That would be fun. "That's way cool," she said just as a rush went through the crowd.

She looked but could only see Belle above everyone's heads, her hands pressed to her mouth. A young man's voice magnified by a microphone asked, "Julie Miner, will you marry me?"

Belle, or Julie, squealed, "Yes!"

The prince stood up, reappearing in Aurelia's line of sight, and then both were obscured by clapping, cheering people.

Walter was amused. "That prince has to be the DJ's friend, the one that asked for all those couples' dances."

"Oh. That would make sense." Feeling awkward, Aurelia shifted her weight. "I wouldn't want it done like that."

Walter cocked his head in question.

"In front of all these strangers. You know? It'd be weird to have complete strangers congratulate me and cheer me on. Or ignore me because they don't know who I am and don't care. But, um, I guess a lot of people like this kind of thing," she amended, hoping she didn't sound critical. "People get proposed to in large public spaces all the time. It's just not me."

"You like your privacy," Walter concluded, and Aurelia nodded, relieved that he understood. He picked up her hand and absentmindedly rubbed it, sending thrills through her while he continued to watch the couple. "My older brother proposed to his wife in front of both our families."

"That's nicer." At least in her view.

"Nicer? But is it nice or just better than this?"

She watched his thumb move across her hand. "Well—getting engaged means you'll be part of each other's families, and of course you'd want your family to share in your excitement, but . . . it's kind of a private moment. If the family's there, they'll tease and talk up a storm at a time when all you really want is to be with that one person."

"That makes sense. If you're alone, you can kiss to your heart's content," Walter said, grinning widely behind his jumbo glasses.

"All right, wise guy," Aurelia scolded, pulling her hand from his. The next song began, and her eyes widened in dismay.

Walter struggled not to laugh at the song choice. "Let's check out the refreshments."

She was quick to agree, and they walked to the table while the crowd bounced to her least favorite song, the one Walter had played on repeat on his phone what seemed ages ago.

Chapter Twenty-Five

AURELIA'S DAYS after that were filled with Walter. Ever since her family history date, she had had both Walters's phone numbers, and whoever didn't get to spend time with her on any given day would compensate by calling her if she didn't call first.

Comeback Walter started attending the temple with her on Saturdays, bringing names of ancestors his other self had researched so he and Aurelia could perform their ordinances for them one at a time. On weekdays, he took to doing homework at her apartment while she worked on editing. One such afternoon, he again expressed frustration about his project.

"I have proof that someone else is accessing our equipment," he said, leaning his elbows on top of his textbook. "I dusted our papers and tools for fingerprints, and there are prints from two more people than those who are on my team. The others have started noticing things that are wrong too."

"You're sure?" Aurelia put down the flash cards she had been quizzing him on, unsure whether to encourage him in his detective work or not. "What'll you do about it?"

"For now, we're keeping track of when any of us are there. The other me might know something about this, but he pretty much limits our conversations to making sure we won't be in the same place at the same time, so I'm on my own." He rubbed his head. "Anyway, I'll wipe our tools of fingerprints whenever I leave the lab, and then I'll check for new prints when I get back. That way, we'll have a better idea of how often and when they come."

It was crazy that Aurelia knew who it might be, and yet she couldn't tell him. She mustn't mess up anything that might keep him from traveling back in time when he was supposed to.

She changed the subject to her new ghost roommate, Janna, who had bought the contract but had yet to show up.

On her next date with Confident Walter, however, she let him know about his current self's suspicions.

"He dusted for fingerprints, and the team are all aware someone else has been there. Is that a problem?" she asked in the darkness of the movie theater while opening credits lit up the screen.

Walter looked cheered. "No, that's good. I did that the first time around."

Aurelia pursed her lips. "So it's okay for him to know something's wrong, but we can't tell him it's those men who are doing it?"

"He can't know yet—wait, how is it *you* know?"

"I followed one of them to the lab some weeks ago." She held up a hand to ward off his protests. "You're sure I didn't know about them before, right? I didn't say anything that helped you figure out at the right time what's going on?"

He took her hand. "You often say things at the right time that are helpful to me. But in this case, you're free of responsibility. Let me flounder on my own till there's only one of me."

"Only one of him" was both a dream and a scary prospect. Aurelia sat as close as the divide between their seats allowed during the movie, and when she got home, she carried the image of his parting smile inside with her.

"CB brought you flowers," Jackie said from a yoga pose on the floor. She had taken to trying out various exercises between homework assignments when her workload became too heavy. "He was sad to miss you. Said he looks forward to tomorrow." She grinned, looking a little too much like the Cheshire cat and making Aurelia wonder what Jackie had done now. Then she saw the flowers, and a happy sigh escaped her.

The vase on the counter held gorgeous star-shaped pink flowers flanked by yellow roses and small sprigs of blue. She touched them reverently, and Jackie came over to look at them with her.

"Your romance is blooming, my friend. Just look at them. Aren't they ostentatious?"

Aurelia smelled one of the roses. "I don't think they're overdone. They're very nice."

Jackie pointed at her. "Marry him. His flowers are turning your head. How long will there be two of him again?"

"Who knows? In what way are his flowers turning my head?"

"They put you under a spell. You didn't even flinch at my lovely new word, 'ostentatious.'"

"Um. You do realize it's a real word, right?" Aurelia asked slowly.

Jackie blinked. Then her eyes widened in horror. "You're right. It sounded just like one of mine though."

The rest of her words were drowned out by Aurelia's laughter.

* * *

EVEN SO, Jackie's question about how long there would be two Walters stuck in Aurelia's mind the next morning while she went for another jog with Confident Walter.

He couldn't tell her, she reminded herself as she huffed her way through the park, and she didn't want him to, not since he had been ready to propose the day he went back in time. Knowing the timing would spoil the surprise, so instead she asked, "Do you think time travel will be a thing from now on? After it's worked once?"

Walter kept up an easy jog. "Well, first we'll have to see if we can duplicate the event, but preferably under different circumstances."

"Was anyone around when you appeared?" If anyone had been in the laboratory, it must have been a shock for them. Then again, if they had seen him appear, they would have had to spread the news about their success.

"No, fortunately. The street was empty."

She stumbled. "Street? Weren't you in that enclosure Walter told me about, in the lab?"

He stopped and opened his mouth but didn't speak immediately. "Ohh," he faltered. "Well, no, I wasn't."

Aurelia's heart sped up. "But he was telling me how you do your research, and he said it's all contained in the lab. No one has to worry about walking across a spot that'll transport them through time. Yet you were out in the middle of the street?" Her voice went high-pitched.

"Well, the entry location was known and, uh, attended, so at least no one could have gone through unknowingly."

"*Entry* location," she emphasized. "The exit was in a different spot, then. You did something to that spot on the street to turn it into an exit?"

"*I* didn't," he answered reluctantly.

"Then who?"

He raised a hand to her face and cupped her cheek. "I promise I'll tell you once there's only one of me. I won't worry then about messing up the future, and I won't worry about me somehow not going back in time, leaving two of me here. I'll explain everything I know to you then."

She held on tight to his hand and took a deep breath. "Just tell me this. Your negative-energy spots won't be harmful for anyone to come across, will they?"

"No." His voice was full of sincerity. "We're very careful about shooting and measuring bit by bit, making sure the air doesn't become dangerously unbalanced."

"You better be," she mumbled. Comeback Walter had reassured her they didn't create wormholes anywhere besides in the lab, but it sounded to her as though that was going to change. "What would happen if you weren't careful?" She couldn't help her anxiety. "If you kept shooting negative energy at the spot without measuring the air quality or whatever it is?"

"If we didn't balance it between the energy and the two different chemicals," he began thoughtfully, "and maybe if we did too much too fast and didn't give it time to settle, worst-case scenario, the air would . . ."

He stopped talking. His eyes glazed over, and his hand dropped from Aurelia's face, leaving her cold.

"I've gotta go to the lab," he blurted.

Aurelia's mouth fell open as he raced away from her. In another moment she started after him. "Wait! Walter, wait."

He kept running. Aurelia sprinted through the park but soon had to stop to catch her breath. What was so important he couldn't have finished their conversation first?

As he disappeared in the distance, she shook her head and straightened, her breath still coming fast. The cartoons had it right. She could easily imagine a cartoon-Walter with a speech bubble: "To the lab!"

She did wish she could have heard the end of his sentence though.

* * *

WHEN COMEBACK WALTER showed up for their date that afternoon, Aurelia picked up the picnic basket she had prepared for them and forced aside thoughts of the wormhole-exit on the street. This wasn't something she could discuss with him.

Walter smiled at her in the doorway. "Are you ready to play tennis?"

"Sure." *Forget the wormholes. Think about—*

"Good," he said, rubbing his head as though it was itchy. Aurelia's gaze flicked to his beautiful hair, but she forced it back down to his face before he spoke again. "I bet it'll come back to you quickly. Here, let me take that." He hefted the basket. "Thanks for preparing dinner."

He carried it to his car and put it in the trunk. Aurelia smiled at the sight of the keychain she had given him at General Conference. It had two new tags now: a tiny fir tree and a milk jug he had found online to commemorate the rather flirtatious day he was mean to her.

When they sat down in the front, he combed a hand through his hair, then leaned forward and shook out the strands before putting on his seat belt. Aurelia swallowed and turned to look out the window. His hair didn't usually distract her these days, but it was another story when it was so— active. He really did have glorious hair.

And glorious green-flecked eyes, she reminded herself as he backed out of the parking spot.

"Thank you so much for the flowers," she told him. "They're beautiful."

His eyes twinkled. "Shall I say it?"

"What?"

He leaned over in his seat. "Not as beautiful as you."

"Oh, haha. Corny." At least when he said it jokingly, it didn't make her blush. "Are we going to Kiwanis?"

"No, Riverview Park." He took a hand off the steering wheel to rub his arm against his hair.

"Are you itchy?" she asked, her eyes again drawn to the hair while butterflies swirled in her stomach.

"Not much. I only brought two racquets. I hope one of them will work for you."

Her gaze was slow to leave Walter's hair. When she forced it down to his face, he was smiling so broadly she felt like she had been caught doing something. She cleared her throat and answered, "I'm sure it'll be fine."

When they arrived, Walter pulled out the racquets and a tube of tennis balls while Aurelia looked around the park where they would play and picnic. It held spacious, grassy fields, a gurgling stream, and a playground.

She accepted her racquet and skipped toward the court, Walter keeping up beside her. He grinned at her enthusiasm and shook out his hair like a dog, letting the breeze play with it. Aurelia bit her lip but refused to let her gaze linger for—what—the fifth time since he had shown up?

She raised her chin. For this next hour, she would focus on tennis and only tennis.

As they played, Walter got a kick out of yelling "Love!" whenever it applied to the score. Aurelia rolled her eyes at first but soon started to beat him to yelling it whenever one of them had zero points.

Something both exhilarating and torturous she hadn't anticipated was how often the breeze and the exercise caused Walter to toss his head or run his hands through his hair. The more he touched it, the more hyper-aware Aurelia became.

It was actually a relief when they stopped playing and picked out a tree to picnic under.

"You know what we should have done?" Walter asked as they set out the food: chicken burgers and plenty of Aurelia-snacks. "Since you love climbing, I should have scouted ahead for a tree to picnic *in*. Maybe we can do that in the spring, when the leaves are new. What do you think?"

"I'd love that." She especially loved hearing that he expected her to still be in his life come spring. For her part, she hoped they would last much longer yet. The glaring obstacle of the last many weeks had been removed. She was every bit as happy and comfortable now around Confident Walter as around his counterpart.

She ate herself full as they talked. Then, lazily, she snacked on the veggies.

Walter lay down on his stomach, his elbow bent and his hand supporting his head, absentmindedly fingering through his hair. It was strange how much he ruffled it today. He had never touched his hair half as much as he had this afternoon. Aurelia should know. She would have noticed.

Walter spoke up in a quiet voice. "Do you ever wonder if there was a reason I went back in time? Or . . . turned back time, since we all kind of went back?"

"Like what?"

"I don't know. Something orchestrated by God. Maybe something should have happened differently than it did."

She frowned. "But the other you wants to keep things the same as they were."

"Yeah, but it could be something that's barely even related to us. Someone else gets a chance to do something differently. Maybe a small thing we do this time around changes things for them. We might never even know about it."

The air smelled of grilled chicken and grass and soil. Aurelia picked at the grass, pondering. She was curious about God's purpose, but Walter was right—she might never know. People went through trials and didn't realize until years later how it worked out for their good.

She sighed when they stood to carry the remains of dinner to the car.

Walter closed the trunk on the basket and looked out over the green landscape and lengthening shadows. "If you're okay on time, we could sit and watch the sunset. I have blankets if it gets too cold."

She paused and looked around for a bench. "Sit where?"

He clapped a hand on the back of his car.

She brightened and was quick to pull herself up. The bulky steel body was nothing like the slender branches she normally climbed. Walter sat beside her, and they leaned against the sun-warmed windshield. She looked toward the orange sky, but Walter reached for his hair once more and made a noise. "Do I have a bug in my hair?"

Aurelia blinked and asked stupidly, "Do you?"

He lowered his head toward her. "Can you check?"

She bit her lip. That hair had teased her ever since she met him. Still, she held back, scanning it closely with her eyes but not touching it. "I don't see one."

"Are you sure?" He ran his hand through it again, and Aurelia smothered a sigh.

"Yes. Is something wrong though? You've been acting strange all day."

He looked at her with innocence. "How?"

"You keep touching your hair."

"Well, it feels nice today." He shrugged but couldn't keep a grin from his face. "You should feel it."

"You want me to touch your hair?"

"Sure. It's really soft"—his impish look became even more impish—"and *brown*."

Aurelia jerked upright. "Did Jackie tell you?"

He looked surprised—too surprised for it to be genuine. "Tell me what? I do seem to remember your younger sister complimenting me on my hair once. I have to wonder if you have similar taste."

"I'll . . ." Aurelia stopped herself from saying "kill her." Or maybe "kill you." It seemed too violent, and she wasn't sure who to exact her revenge on: Jackie, Rachel, or the Walter who had knowingly thrown his gloriously brown hair about all evening.

"I figured if you like it, why not let you touch it? Maybe you can even tell me what it smells like," Walter teased.

Aurelia huffed and tried to get her thoughts under control. "Actually, I *would* like to touch your hair," she conceded.

Walter blinked. "All right. Here it is."

She scooted closer and reached over, behind his head, letting her hand settle on the nape of his neck.

Walter sat still with a smile of—mirth? Triumph? Pleasure?—as he waited for her to move her hand to his hair.

Instead, she shoved his head forward, then let go and sprang off the car to run away.

In a flash, Walter was beside her and caught her by the wrist, lifting her arm.

Aurelia squealed and laughed and meant to pull free, but his lips touched the inside of her wrist, and she froze, electrified.

If ever there were a time she blushed pink in her life, this was that moment.

Walter gently fingered her wrist. He took his time raising his head to look at her, and his words came out long and slow and baritone. "I'm not allowed to kiss you, kiss you. This is how I'm keeping myself from doing it right now. Is this all right?"

"Yes," she said, but it came out a whisper.

He smiled and lowered his head again, kissing the softest part of her wrist for the second time and making thrills race up and down her arm and through her entire system.

"I'd like you to meet my family." He sounded breathless. "They're coming through Utah this weekend and spending Saturday with me. With us. Will you join us?"

"Of course," she breathed. At this point, he could ask her to stand on her head and she'd do it.

Then again, that would rebalance her circulation and let her think clearly, at which point she might not be so willing to play acrobat.

He returned his attention to her wrist, and all she could think was that she must have given the correct answer.

Then he slid her arm through his hand and slowly let go. Aurelia wavered between continued pleasure from the last minute and regret that he had stopped.

Walter spoke. "I better take you home now."

"Why?" she asked. The sun was nearing the mountaintops. Its colorful show was still going.

He heaved a sigh. "Because you're driving me crazy."

"Huh?"

"Shall we?" He held out his arm.

They were mostly quiet on the way home, but it was a good kind of silence.

When he walked her to the door, her thoughts returned to his rascal hair displays during their date.

She snorted. "I can't believe you did all that with your hair to make me go crazy. You dork." She pushed him, and he pretended to stagger for a moment before regaining his balance and flashing her a smile.

"I love you," he said and leaned in, kissing her on the cheek. While she stood frozen at his words, he gave her a body-melting hug and moved back to look at her.

She stared into his eyes, her thoughts bouncing around the fact that he —loved her? Truly?

"I mean it," he said, his voice gentle. "But don't feel like you have to say it back if you're not sure."

She was far too entranced by his words to even consider sorting through her own feelings for him.

He put a hand to her cheek. "I won't pressure you. I just want you to know."

She swallowed and nodded against his hand.

He stepped away and smiled at her. "I'll see you soon."

Aurelia stood still, breathing deeply, trying to get herself past the watch-Walter-leave-and-sigh-again-and-again stage. As he descended the stairs, she, still looking in his direction, forced herself to open the door behind her and step backward inside.

"I have a question," Walter's voice said right behind her.

She shrieked and whirled to face him, her hand clutching her chest.

"What?" Her date came plowing back across the walkway with a yell and stopped short at the door. "What are *you* doing here?" he asked himself.

"Scaring me to death," Aurelia said.

Confident Walter looked regretful. "Sorry, I didn't mean to scare you. I figured you'd be home soon. Jackie let me in."

"Why are you here so late?" Comeback Walter asked in accusation and braced his hand against the doorframe while Aurelia tried to catch her breath.

Confident Walter just looked at him. After a moment, Comeback Walter's face turned red, and he dropped his gaze.

"Would you mind leaving?" his future self asked.

"Fine." Comeback Walter started down the walkway anew, muttering.

"Who got murdered?" Jackie asked, appearing in the other doorway with her phone at her ear.

"No one," Aurelia answered.

"That's a relief." Jackie returned to her room, continuing her phone conversation.

Walter looked at Aurelia. She put her hands on her hips and asked, "What's the question?"

He blew out a breath. "Sorry again. I was wondering if you could take me to your friend Kylie's place."

"To Kylie's?" She gaped at him.

"Yeah."

She narrowed her eyes. "Not until you tell me why. *And* tell me what got you so excited this morning that you had to run away."

He knit his brow. "Oh, right. Sometimes I get carried away with these things. Sorry. You asked me this morning what would happen if we didn't pace ourselves and stop to measure and rebalance the energy."

Aurelia nodded.

"If we didn't, the air in the space we were working on could become unstable and explode."

"Explode?"

"Yes. As far as I can tell from my reading and some minor experiments today, it would be a small explosion, concentrated over maybe a few square feet. Things in that area might get singed and possibly knocked over, but nothing more than that."

"Like my incident at Kylie's," Aurelia said, her eyes wide.

"Yes. And, I'm thinking, like various other unexplained explosions around town for the past while. I think they were all hot spots that had negative energy pumped into them—possibly without any chemicals to stabilize them."

"Pumped." Her voice was strangled. "I knew those men had probably set off the explosions, but I didn't realize they—they're experimenting with time travel?"

Walter stared at her as though she had grown two heads. "I knew they were experimenting, but I didn't realize until today that they were responsible for the explosions. How . . . ?"

She crossed her arms. "We have got to work on our communication. They were at Kylie's home and Macey's before each of those explosions. I guess I didn't tell you about Macey's or why I was following them." Her shoulders fell as she ran through what she knew about them. They had been at the time travel lecture—not as vaguely interested faculty members but as fully invested researchers. They had been in Walter's lab too.

"So the explosions are . . ." She let her voice trail off, and Walter finished for her.

"Failed experiments." He shook his head in wonder. "They got into Kylie's home and possibly others under the guise of bug sprayers, like you told me, but they were really there to try to create a travel hole."

"Why in the world would they do that in someone's home? Or in a store?"

Walter blew out his breath. "I don't get it either. It's so irresponsible. I think they're picking places that have strong negative energy to begin with in the hopes that those spots are more conducive to time travel. I can't believe they'd be so careless in their work though. It's one thing to kidnap and threaten me, but it's quite another to conduct experiments without making sure—"

"*Kidnap?*" Aurelia shrilled. "They're going to kidnap you?"

He opened his mouth and looked like a deer in the headlights. "I shouldn't have said that."

"You get kidnapped?" she shouted again, grabbing his shirt.

"Not for long! It was over pretty fast. It's fine, really."

Aurelia's bottom lip trembled. "I don't want you to get kidnapped." Her vision swam.

"Hey, hey, I'll be fine." Walter took hold of her arms. "Don't cry. It'll be less than an hour. Don't worry." He sounded almost panicked at her reaction, but as tears started down Aurelia's cheeks, Walter wiped them with gentle hands.

"This is stupid," Aurelia insisted, her tears still rolling. "Knowing the future and not being allowed to prevent the bad parts."

"We can't—mustn't—do anything about this part," he affirmed. "But hey, maybe there's a reason I went back in time, something God wanted to have happen that didn't happen the first time around. God's in the details, right? I promise I don't get hurt. You already know it ends well."

New tears welled up in her eyes, but they didn't spill over. "I guess."

"You guess? Okay, what did I look like when I showed up on your doorstep with a ring in my hand?" he asked with an encouraging smile.

She sniffed. "A little dusty. Your jeans were ripped. And you had stubble."

"I'm not sure how the stubble happened." He grew thoughtful. "It must have been a side effect of passing through time. But see, I wasn't hurt, was I?"

She stared at him, her eyes finally starting to dry. "Are you saying you went straight from getting kidnapped to going through time?"

He chewed on his lip. "Well—I'm saying I came through it just fine. So please try not to worry."

"Ugh. I can't tell Walter any of this." She reached up and wiped away the remaining moisture.

He touched her cheek again, his beautiful brown eyes searching hers. Then he leaned in, kissing her on the nose. "We'll be okay."

Aurelia began to giggle.

"What's funny?" he asked with a slight smile.

"You kissed my nose."

He looked dismayed. "You think that's funny?"

She was still giggling. "I know it happens in romantic stories, but—I never thought someone would do that to me."

"Ah. Well, when you lay down rules, I have to stick to them, right? I can't kiss your lips, but I can do this." He put a hand on the back of her neck and kissed the top of her head. "Or this." He kissed her forehead.

"Good night, Walter," she said quickly, trying to forestall any more "or this's." As much as she liked them, she would turn into a tomato at this rate.

"Or this . . ." He went for her cheek.

She put her hands on his chest and kept him at bay. "Good night."

He folded his hands over hers. "Okay. Good night."

She withdrew her hands and hugged him. "Be careful."

He planted a last kiss on her hair. "I will."

"I'll talk to Kylie. See if we can come over tomorrow."

Walter nodded, touched her cheek, and left.

Aurelia let out a shaky breath, holding on to the sensation of Walter's lips on each of the various places they had touched, including her nose.

"For a practical, unromantic person," she murmured to herself, "you're turning into a complete sap."

Chapter Twenty-Six

"Here we are," Aurelia said as she pulled up next to the curb in front of her friend's white brick house. Kylie had given them permission to visit, and Aurelia had picked up Confident Walter since his other self had his car. Aurelia opened her door, feeling a little shaky. This Walter's kisses last night and Comeback Walter's declaration of love pressed on her with happy but unsettling intensity. She cleared her throat and tried to focus on the present. "Are you ready to meet Kylie?"

"I'm so ready," he said, taking her hand and facing the walkway, "and I'll act like it's the first time."

She had forgotten he had already met Kylie "the first time around."

Kylie flung the door open at the first knock. "Come on in! You can keep your shoes on. Come on." She thew appraising looks at Walter and practically bounced in place as he entered. "So *you're* Walter."

"Guilty." He grinned.

Her answering smile was bright. "I'm glad to meet Aurelia's guy, even if it *is* due to a scary explosion."

"I'm glad to meet Aurelia's friend. What is it you do?"

After a minute of conversation, Aurelia and Kylie pointed out the spot near the glass door where Aurelia had met her downfall.

Walter eagerly knelt on the carpet and started asking questions. Had Kylie vacuumed it since then? (Of course she had.) What nearby objects had been affected, falling over or ending up with any bit of dust? Had she washed or dusted off the nearby shelves?

He put on gloves and pulled a thin silvery instrument from his bag to scan the area. It looked like a glorified tuning fork, except it had little buttons and a screen that showed changing numbers.

"Is that the thing that measures negative energy?" Aurelia asked.

"Yes. It's more basic than what we have in the lab, but I can't remove our instruments from there. I made this at my uncle's house."

"You made it?" Aurelia was flabbergasted.

"What does it do, again?" Kylie asked.

"It reads the balance of energy in the air," Walter explained. "An imbalance could create a benign explosion like what you had. The negative energy here *is* rather strong, which makes me think it might have been a lot stronger just before the air exploded. But don't worry," he added quickly, "there's no way it'll happen again at this point."

"*That's* a relief."

Walter took out various materials—fabric, small containers, bottles. Kylie asked a few more questions, but Walter kept his answers deliberately vague. He couldn't let on that the men who were supposed to have sprayed her house for insects had likely caused the explosion. If she were to report them to the police or make a phone call to the company about it, Walter's upcoming time travel could get messed up.

In fifteen minutes, he was ready to leave. "I'll study these samples on campus and get back to you," he told Kylie and placed the last bottle in his bag.

"Thanks for letting us come," Aurelia said.

"Anytime. I don't mind seeing you and your *boyfriend* around," Kylie said, wriggling her eyebrows.

Aurelia cleared her throat, growing warm. "See you later."

She took Walter's hand and walked him outside. Her last glimpse of the doorway showed her friend clapping her hands and hopping up and down. It would appear that Kylie approved of Walter.

"I hope you have a great time with my family tomorrow," Walter said as they got in her car.

"You know about tomorrow, do you?"

"Know about it? I've been *plotting* tomorrow."

"You've been plotting for me to meet your family?" she repeated with a frown. "How?"

"We've had a lot to figure out," he began while she drove. "I live in two different places full-time. My family's dropping by to visit my aunt and uncle while they're here. They've had some contact during the semester, fortunately *after* the other me and I began communicating, so my parents have been given the story that my apartment accommodations fell through and I'm living with my uncle. They've also been told something happened to my car, because so far as Uncle Frank knows, I haven't had it all this time."

Oh yeah, that would all make it complicated.

"How will you make it work?" she asked, now feeling anxious.

"Walter and I are switching places. I'll be at the apartment with the car, and he'll be 'living' at my aunt and uncle's house and spending the day with my family and you. But I don't want you to worry about all that. Have fun tomorrow. I can't wait for you to meet them."

* * *

THE MORNING SUN found Aurelia walking nervously from couch to window to her bedroom to the bathroom, and back again to the living room. Walter had called five minutes ago to let her know they were on their way over.

"Antlers," she muttered to herself. If she kept his Christmas story at the forefront of her mind, that should make his siblings less scary.

Walter had been surprised last night when she told him she had already gone to the temple for the week and would be available whenever he wanted her to join the family. Now, she second-guessed that decision. Maybe it had been presumptuous of her to clear her day.

"Peas," she mumbled, pacing to the fridge and pulling out a bag. "Don't stress eat," she admonished herself and put it back.

She still hadn't had the chance to tell him she loved him. It had been two whole days, but they hadn't seen each other in person yesterday, and it wasn't something she wanted to tell him over the phone. For that matter, did she really, truly *love* him? The one guy she had dated in high school had told her he loved her, and she had been quick to echo back his words, but she realized later she hadn't actually felt it. She had said it because she didn't want to leave him hanging and because she did, at least, like him.

The possibility of her and Walter being sealed in the temple for time and eternity popped into her head. She swallowed hard. She could see it in her mind's eye, and the image planted a light inside her, a growing light that made her smile. They would have an inexpensive but sweet reception in a chapel afterward. Jackie could be the best woman and Brian the best man if he was the one Walter would pick. Did the fact that she felt joy when she imagined it mean she was ready for it?

The sound of steps outside broke into her thoughts, and she flew to open the door.

"Hey." Walter looked like a hero illuminated by sunlight. Unaware of her ponderings, he put his arm around her and kissed her cheek, then turned to the young woman behind him.

His tone became teasing. "Aurelia, this little high schooler is Polly. The others are coming in a separate car. Polly," he addressed his sister grandly, "*this* is Aurelia, my girlfriend."

Polly grabbed Walter's free arm and leaned toward Aurelia. "Did you totally smash a pumpkin with my brother, and was that your idea?"

Aurelia coughed and tried not to laugh. "What else has he told you?"

"All good things," Walter promised, letting go of Aurelia and holding up his hand as if in a solemn vow.

"Better than what you've told *her* about *me*, I'm sure," Polly broke in. "You always make me sound like a little girl even now when I'm a senior in high school." She looked at Aurelia. "Walter's in love with you."

Although the words were probably meant to embarrass Walter, Aurelia paused and looked at him, her heart fluttering. Could she confess to the same feeling later, when they were alone? She thought so. She hoped so. For now, she tried to put all her admiration for him in her gaze so he would know how she felt. "I know." Her voice wavered with emotion.

Maybe he understood what her eyes told him, because his own lit up, and he kissed her cheek again.

"Really?" Polly huffed at the public display.

"That's right. You'll have to work harder to tease me," Walter said. "Now, how about we go to the parking lot and wait for the others?"

"I don't have to work hard at all," Polly argued as they headed downstairs. "I have lots of stories—"

"Here they are," Walter hurried to interrupt as a white Hyundai pulled into the parking lot. "Meet the Caspers."

A tall, broad-shouldered man with Walter's complexion and light brown hair exited from the driver's side. "Hello. You must be Aurelia."

"Nice to meet you," she said, feeling shy as several other people left the car. "You're Walter's dad?"

"I am, but you can call me Walter's dad." He winked. "It's a pleasure to meet you."

"Jeremy," scolded his wife, a middling-tall tan woman with blonde hair that fell in waves. "Aurelia, I'm Janet, and you may call *him* Jeremy. These are Louisa and Miriam, and you've already met Polly."

"I have." Aurelia looked at the two older girls. "You were the geniuses behind the Santa Claus gig, right?"

Louisa, whose eyes held more green than her siblings', let out a surprised laugh. "That's right. I'm glad to hear Walter still appreciates our creativity."

"That was a great Christmas," Miriam said with satisfaction.

Aurelia turned to Walter, who gaped at her. She elbowed him softly. "Don't you remember telling me that story?"

He closed his mouth and nodded slowly. "Um, yeah."

Walter's dad—Jeremy—rubbed his hands together. "Let's get going. We'll meet up at the park. Have fun being a third wheel, Polly. Maybe you can break up the romantic mood in your car."

Polly turned to Walter. "Ha, ha—"

"We'll give her a run for her money," Walter vowed.

"Don't you dare get kissy. They've already kissed twice," Polly complained to her dad.

Aurelia and Walter spoke at the same time.

"Scandalously," Walter grinned.

"On the cheek," Aurelia clarified.

Jeremy laughed a full belly laugh. Aurelia shook her head in long-suffering.

Walter offered her the front passenger seat, while Polly took a back seat in the red Kia.

"Whose car is this?" Aurelia asked while Walter started the vehicle and headed out of the parking lot.

Polly answered. "It's our parents', but they let us take turns driving it.

Louisa drove it here, and now they're letting Walter take over, even though, apparently, he totaled his own car."

"I didn't total it," Walter smirked, refusing to be baited. "I'm keeping it at a friend's place because of problems."

"I hope you're up for a fun day, Aurelia," Polly told her. "We'll play Kubb at the park, and after lunch we're going hiking, and we're browsing BYU Store and getting a tour of campus, and we'll barbecue with Uncle Frank and Aunt Ilia . . ."

"It's a big day," Walter said, his grin growing along with his sister's list.

Polly's enumeration had the opposite effect on Aurelia. This was obviously quite the family outing, and Walter's parents and siblings had come to spend time with him. Though she wanted to meet them, maybe she shouldn't have planned for the full Saturday. They might not be excited about having a stranger along for everything.

"I don't have to come to all that," she blurted. "That is, if you don't want me to."

"Of course I do." Walter looked perplexed.

"Yeah, we do," Polly agreed. "Did you have something else you needed to do?"

"No." Aurelia squirmed. "But I don't want to impose. It's Walter you're here to see, not me."

"I can always see Walter." Polly sounded almost offended. "My screensaver's a picture of Walter. He's hanging upside down from the roof of a beachside ice cream shop, eating a cone. Not much of it made it into his mouth, by the way."

Walter's cheeks turned red. "We, uh, tend to have our own experiments in my family. We don't exactly do dares, but sometimes we take an idea and run with it."

Aurelia giggled. "Point taken. I still don't want to get in the way though."

"You'll be one hundred percent in the way," Walter said firmly. "I'll keep you so close to my side that no one can look at me without seeing you as well, and when they come over to talk to you, well, they might just stumble over me."

Now it was Polly who giggled. "Stay with us through the day, Aurelia. We all want to get to know you. Maybe we can take more pictures of Walter in case we ever miss him and need something to look at besides the ice cream photo." She sighed dramatically. "I so wish we had gotten a picture of him in my—"

"Don't you dare," Walter warned, drowning out her words.

"Your lace dress?" Aurelia guessed, and the two siblings gasped.

"How do you know about that?" Walter cried, while Polly asked, "He *told* you about that? Are you trying to scare her away, Walter?"

Walter glanced at his sister through the rearview mirror and revised his question to Aurelia. "I *told* you? What had I done to deserve that?"

Aurelia raised her eyebrows at him. "You kicked me out of a library."

He blinked. "Oh. Okay."

"You kicked her out of a library?" Polly punched the back of his seat. "That's terrible. She's a writer, Walter."

Walter shook his head. "Maybe you don't know, Polly, but writers tend to be the most unruly people in libraries."

Aurelia huffed and raised her eyes to the ceiling.

Walter reached for her hand, putting an end to her pretend annoyance as his voice softened. "I don't want a day with my family to mean I don't get to spend time with you."

Her heart warmed at his words.

"If you hadn't joined us, I'd spend every second missing you," he continued, melting her further.

"I love you," Aurelia blurted, shocking herself with her own surety, with the strength of her feelings, and with the sudden realization that she had spoken out loud.

Walter's eyes flew wide open, and Polly gasped.

"You do?" Walter asked, his voice several notes higher than usual.

"I said that?" Aurelia asked, a sudden sense of panic making her own voice rise.

"Walter," Polly cried out as the car swerved. "Watch the road."

"You did," Walter said, a smile playing on his lips as he looked at Aurelia.

"In front of your sister." Her thoughts were going a hundred miles a minute.

"Who cares." His voice was soft, as though he didn't notice what he was saying. His signature grin came out like the sun and took Aurelia's breath away.

"Walter, that's a stop sign," Polly exclaimed. "I think I should drive."

"Yeah," he said, slowing the car without taking his eyes off Aurelia.

Polly groaned. "Pull over. If you two are going to make declarations of love, I need to be behind the wheel." He reached the curb and stopped the car. "Good, now get out of your seat."

An effectual change of seats took place, and Polly restarted the car while Aurelia and Walter gazed at each other from diagonal spots, Aurelia still in the front and Walter now sitting behind Polly.

Polly tried to pull them into conversation, but Aurelia felt too warm and happy for words.

When they finally arrived and parked, Walter ran around the car, opened Aurelia's door before she had the chance, and pulled her into a hug, whispering, "I love you too."

She drew a small breath, not wanting the movement in any way to distance her from his firm hold. "Thank you for not pressuring me. I had to know for sure."

"I was almost certain you loved me back." She could hear the smile in his voice. "You just needed to realize it yourself. If I hadn't been so sure, I would have gone crazy waiting."

Polly jumped out of the car and yelled to the family members milling out of the vehicle opposite them, "Guess what? Walter told her about my lace dress!"

With regret, Aurelia stepped back. She did need to get to know his family, and it appeared that now was the time, beginning with lawn games.

With Walter and Polly's reassurances that the Caspers were happy to have her around, it wasn't hard for her to feel at ease around them.

"Aurelia, what do you call an angry carrot?" Jeremy asked as soon as he had thrown his wooden cylinder sticks and it was time for the other team to make their move.

Walter groaned beside her, and Louisa protested, "Dad, she doesn't need to hear that one."

"A steamed veggie," Jeremy forged on despite his children's objections. "Have you ever tried to catch a frog?"

"Are you going to tell her *all* your jokes?" Miriam asked from the other end of the playing field, but just then, Janet's stick whacked down one of Aurelia's team's rectangular blocks, and Janet and Polly screamed and hopped up and down, high-fiving and hugging Miriam and each other.

"Mom always wins this game," Louisa whispered to Aurelia while Janet grabbed the next stick and did a victory dance.

Aurelia enjoyed every moment of the day. Even the barbecue went well. She had worried that Walter might say something wrong or get confused if his uncle mentioned something only the other Walter knew about, but her queasy feeling soon passed. As she reminded herself, no one would randomly guess he had traveled back in time just because he acted strange. Besides, she could tell he did his best to minimize conversation with Frank and Ilia without appearing to avoid them.

When it was time to go home, Walter's mom grabbed her up in a hug. "It was good to meet you, sweetie."

Aurelia's eyes suddenly filled with tears. She hadn't known the motherly gesture would make her miss her own mom all over again—and she wasn't even sure it had, because she didn't feel sad, exactly—but even so, her throat choked up.

"Aww." Janet gave her another hug. "You come to our house for Thanksgiving if it doesn't work out with your friend Jackie, you hear?"

"Thanks." Aurelia sniffed.

Walter put his hand on her back. "If not Thanksgiving, then how about—"

"Christmas," his mom interrupted brightly. "Of course. We want you over for Christmas, dear."

They did. It felt as though a thousand-watt lightbulb had turned on, shining on Aurelia's near future. The Christmas she had dreaded and expected to cry through was now something to look forward to. In fact, it might become one of her best Christmases yet.

She stammered out a thank-you and got in the back of the Casper's Kia with Walter. Polly drove them to Elite and stayed behind the wheel while Walter walked Aurelia to the door in the dusk.

Aurelia sighed. Earlier she had worried about spending the whole day with Walter. Now she wished they didn't have to part ways.

"Do you really love me?" Walter asked quietly.

She reached up and linked her hands at the back of his neck. He put his arms around her and pulled her close.

"I do," she murmured, leaning her cheek against his chest. If every day could be like this . . . No, that wasn't feasible. But if she could be with Walter every day . . .

She sighed. She didn't want to release him, but she knew she had to. "I'll see you tomorrow," she said, hoping the words would help her let go. Or better yet, they might induce him to step away first so that she didn't have to.

He hugged her gently and moved back.

"Did you say good night yet?" Polly's voice yelled from the parking lot.

In the dark, Aurelia could see one side of Walter's mouth pull upward.

"I wish we could kiss right now just to scandalize her."

She responded with half a smile.

Walter shook his head. "Actually, I wish I could kiss you because that's what I want to do."

She smiled more broadly.

"I have a curfew," Polly howled.

"She's a lot more mature when she isn't with her family, or so I've heard," Walter said.

Aurelia smiled impishly. "I want to say the same thing about you, but I'm not sure that's true."

His eyes widened, and Aurelia hurried to turn and unlock the door. She flung it open and was caught in a bear-hug from behind. "I'm not mature?" Walter half growled.

"No." She tried to step inside and only managed a couple of steps as Walter allowed himself to be dragged along.

"I'm not mature?" he asked again.

"No." She heard noises from the back of the apartment and wanted to laugh, or hide, or both, before Jackie came out.

"Would you like to reconsider that answer?"

"Oh, you want a different answer? Well, sure, you're mature," she indulged him.

He let go, and she turned around.

"You drive me crazy, Aurelia," he said, his voice a mixture of exasperated and amused, his expression adoring. "And you know what?" His voice changed to match his expression. "I love you."

She breathed slowly, taking in the moment, loving the echo of his words, the silence, and the look in Walter's eyes.

"So dip her in a kiss already," Jackie demanded from the doorway.

Walter and Aurelia jumped. Before Aurelia could do anything, Walter turned to Jackie with a grin and saluted her. "You'll just have to come to the wedding to see that," he said and walked out.

In a flash, Jackie was at Aurelia's side, grabbing her hand. "Wedding? Where's your ring?"

"No, no, he hasn't proposed."

"Oh, sheesh." Jackie dropped her roommate's hand. "You don't mess with the word 'wedding.' There had better be one soon."

Aurelia stood still, her limbs weak as she tried to imagine a wedding, *her* wedding, hers and Walter's.

She didn't hear the rest of Jackie's rant, but the word "soon" sounded good to her.

Chapter Twenty-Seven

The next day at church, Aurelia was animated as she told Confident Walter all about her day with his family. Later, in her afternoon Skype session, she told her family about it while Walter, sitting beside her, added his own comments. He had his arm around her, and she often turned to gaze at him, blushing with pleasure when he smiled at her. Her parents and siblings reacted with knowing grins, nudging and winking at each other.

Dinner was at Brian's place that night. Jackie left early to help him, and after the Skype session, Aurelia and Walter went to join them.

"That's a lot of green," Aurelia said, staring at the walls and couches when Brian let them in.

"Yeah, I thought I might as well get green furniture to match the paint."

"It actually looks good," said Walter.

Jackie made a sliding entrance across the floor to greet them, her arms out for balance and a touch of drama. "Brian thought you guys might like to work on a puzzle while we finish prepping dinner."

Aurelia raised her eyebrows. "You don't want help? Or should I say, you want to be alone in the kitchen?"

Jackie ignored the second question. "We're fine. Go build a galaxy." She pushed a Milky Way jigsaw puzzle into Aurelia's hands and sent her off toward the jungle couches.

Walter started to sort the pieces, but Aurelia was more interested in watching her roommate and Brian's interactions until Walter picked up her hand and drew circles on her palm. When she turned her gaze on him, they both forgot about the puzzle.

Little ticklish thrills spread through her hand while she wondered at how far they had come together. When she spoke, it was in a murmur. "You know, Jackie and I used to call you Reticent Walter. After the way I turned you down, you were nervous about somehow doing something that would offend me for no reason."

"Flattering." He grimaced but continued to trace her palm.

"You made such a comeback in confidence that we renamed you Comeback Walter."

His smile came out like the sun. "That sounds better. In fact, do you ever say it like a command? 'Come back, Walter,'" he intoned in a pleading voice, batting his eyelashes.

She chuckled. "That wouldn't make any sense. I call you Comeback Walter when I talk *about* you, not when I address you. I can't very well command Jackie, 'Come back, Walter.'"

"True. Besides, it would be more to the point for you to say, 'Stay, Walter.' You could address me that way if you like," he said magnanimously.

Aurelia leaned into him. "Stay, Walter," she repeated in dulcet tones.

Twin bursts of laughter broke out in the kitchen, and Aurelia looked over to see Brian gripping the counter and Jackie bending over with laughter.

"Jackie, you're hilarious," Brian said when he could speak again.

Jackie beamed like a spotlight.

"What do you think?" Walter whispered. "Are they a match made in heaven?"

Aurelia cocked her head, considering. "If they are, heaven sure went to a lot of trouble to make it happen. Apparently, they didn't meet before you traveled back in time."

He sat up straight. "Really?"

"Yeah."

Walter shot a glance at the couple, a light in his eyes. "I guess we'll have to see how it plays out."

* * *

IF THERE WAS one thing that wasn't working out though, it was the roommate situation. Aurelia huffed her way home from an afternoon internship meeting a few days later and called out as soon as she entered her apartment, "Jackie, have you seen the email?"

She was met with silence.

"Of course you're not home. That's right, you're on a date, aren't you? This is ridiculous." She let out her breath in one last huff. Their newest roommate, the one who had bought Meana's contract and never showed up yet, was now trying to sell the contract.

She entered the hall and stopped short. The door to the Cursed Room was festooned with a crisscross of police tape and a bold, diagonal sign that read, *Condemned*.

Oh yes, Jackie had seen the email.

"That's a little passive aggressive." Aurelia fingered the tape. Then again, what was the point of pretending another roommate might come and, heaven forbid, stay? She was so done with the whole seesawing roommate situation.

Thunder rumbled, and she hummed in agreement. She wasn't in the mood for work, that was for sure. The sound of raindrops began to patter on the roof above her, and before she knew it, it was pouring outside.

She retrieved a notebook and turned off the nearest lights, then shook out a blanket on the floor. She sat down cross-legged and closed her eyes, listening to the rain, blending the sounds of the storm with the memory of one of her trips to the California coast.

A roaring wind. Sand blowing everywhere. The tangy smell of seaweed.

She wrote, and when the storm outside stopped, she kept writing, drawing on the one in her mind.

The story she had wanted to create with a setting in Iceland took shape with one haunting beach scene. She would have to do some serious research for this, but for now she just wrote, running the song "Husavik" through her head.

Finally she leaned back with a sigh and looked over her notes.

The front door opened, jerking her back to Utah. Jackie strode inside, flipped on the light, and put her hands on her hips. "Never go hiking during a thunderstorm."

Before Aurelia could reply, Jackie strolled past. She turned around in the doorway and paused. "But if you do, make sure you're with a cute guy."

She disappeared into the bedroom.

Aurelia craned her neck in Jackie's direction, wondering if that was truly all her friend would say about her date.

The bedroom door reopened, and Jackie sprinted into the living room, now backpack-less.

"Okay, I'll tell you what happened," she said as though Aurelia had regaled her for details. "So Brian and I are in Rock Canyon, and it looks like rain, but how often do we actually get rain in Utah, right? Then it thunders and starts to drizzle, and he goes, 'There's a cave nearby.' Perfect, right? So we sit down in our dry cave and the thunder gets worse, and I don't like thunder—but don't you dare tell anyone—so I'm all quiet and he just holds me and he's all comforting and tries to distract me with conversation. And the rain stops, but the thunder keeps going and going.

"Then it finally stops and I feel a little better, and we talk some more and I feel a *lot* better, and he's been really nice and cute and sweet, so I kiss him. And I get up. Then he's like, 'Wait a minute,' grabs my arm and pulls me back down, and then he kisses me for real! It was so good!" Jackie clapped her hands and then pressed them to her face, squealing.

Aurelia knew she was supposed to say something or squeal with her, but she was still stuck on the fact that Jackie was afraid of thunder. She would never have guessed it. "That sounds Hallmark-worthy," she finally said, and a smile spread across her face.

"I know, right? And I *like* him." Jackie flung herself onto the couch and looked at Aurelia with shining eyes. "He's a great kisser," she added. "Maybe we should kiss regularly in front of you to give you inspiration for your bestselling romances."

Aurelia made a face. "Does that mean I don't have to kiss Walter anymore?"

"Do you want to?" Jackie asked, narrowing her eyes.

Pictures of Walter filled Aurelia's head, her mind lingering on his tall brown hair, his intelligent, often mischievous eyes, and the warmth she felt when he held her. "Yeah, I do." Her voice sounded dreamy and faraway.

"You're long gone, Aurelia," Jackie said in amusement. "Speed things up. Let me know if you want me to kick him into action—I mean, if you want some pointers," she said modestly.

Aurelia hesitated. "I've known him for less than three months." Still, she already loved him. Did he realize that when she said she loved him, that meant she was ready to marry him? Or did he think he should wait another few months, half a year, or even longer to propose?

Did he feel the need to wait longer for his *own* benefit?

Hopefully not if he was already telling her he loved her. Still, if he wasn't ready to get married, she couldn't exactly push him into it.

Downplaying her hope to move to the next step soon, she said, "I mean, what would be next? How many people get engaged after knowing each other two or three months?"

"Half of BYU," was Jackie's response.

"I doubt it's half. Maybe a fifth or a tenth. Maybe not even that much," Aurelia said thoughtfully.

"Statistics. Who cares?" Jackie threw her hands in the air. "'Wait a minute,'" she quoted Brian in a deep voice and bounced on the couch, apparently reliving the climax of her date again. Then she jumped up and skipped to her room, singing.

* * *

AURELIA AND WALTER had one last date before Thanksgiving. She hated how final that sounded, but it helped that he had promised to make it longer than usual.

Even so, they were running out of time. She could feel it. As she stood in the sunshine on campus watching leaves blow across the ground and waiting for Comeback Walter to finish his noon class, she thought of how tense Confident Walter had been of late, of how much damage Meana's uncle and his friends might be doing in Provo with their experiments, and of how ready she was to hear the words "Will you marry me?"

And that was before she caught sight of Meana walking toward her across the lawn.

Her stress turned into a desire to flee, but it was too late. Meana's eyes locked on hers. Firming her shoulders, Aurelia reminded herself of her determination to be nice to Meana at all costs.

The girl didn't miss a step. As she drew close, Aurelia mustered up her courage and tried to smile. "Hi, Meana."

Meana kept going—kept going—and stopped right in front of her. She surveyed her ex-roommate without a word.

Aurelia tried for another smile, but it didn't fare much better. The question "How are you?" got stuck in her throat. Maybe it was best to wait and see what Meana wanted.

Meana raised her chin. "You know what I've realized?"

Aurelia held her breath.

"My uncle manipulated me regarding Walter."

Aurelia's eyes widened. Whatever she had expected to hear, it wasn't this.

Meana did a cast with her head, and her tone turned mocking, as though she were quoting someone else. "'You can't get him to take you out, not even for a milkshake. He wouldn't go with you tonight.' My uncle said that a couple of times, you know. 'Your boy's too busy with his homework. I bet if you went and found him in his little science building right now, he wouldn't go with you.'" She put her hands in her jeans pockets, the model of casualness. "Reverse psychology. I can see now how pointed it was, how it wasn't just random mockery. Uncle Stan was using me to occupy Walter at some very specific times." She paused. "I thought you should know."

Aurelia stared at her, designer jeans and jacket and all. She had known Meana was supposed to be a distraction. One meant to keep Walter busy—that is, to keep him away from the lab, right?

The men wanted access to the lab without Walter and his team around. They had been sneaking in to steal notes and to check out equipment. With a start, Aurelia realized what Stan and his cohorts had meant when they mentioned "the kids'" instruments at Macey's.

"The kids" had never referred to grade-schoolers but to college students. Stan's tickets to the science symposium were supposed to ensure an evening of a Walter-free campus. Had Stan's friends kept a similar eye on the other research team members and tried to make sure they were away on some of the same days?

Meana changed topics without warning. "Did you mean what you said about my style?"

"What?" Aurelia jerked in surprise. Meana's voice was almost frosty, as though it didn't matter to her, but Aurelia wasn't fooled. Her ex-roommate wouldn't have asked if she didn't care.

She swallowed. "Of course I did. I liked seeing what you wore every day. And you're beautiful." The compliment felt awkward, but she meant it.

Meana tilted her head. "And I could get a lot of guys?" Before Aurelia could answer, her voice hardened. "But not Walter or other nice guys, right?"

What could she say to that? Aurelia felt like she was walking through a mine-field as she began her honest answer. "I think if you tried to be more like the kind of girl a nice guy wants . . ." She broke off as Meana's eyebrows shot upward. "Sorry, that was mean."

"Ha." Meana sounded amused. She looked down at her pink nails as if unconcerned. "People say *I'm* mean."

Aurelia bit her lip and waited.

"If I could let go of my . . . defensiveness . . ."

Did she mean her rudeness? Her meanness? If she did, Aurelia had been right all along to see it as a front and a shield.

"Do you think there's a Walter who would like me?"

Aurelia pushed out her breath. It seemed Walter had become a symbol to Meana. Someone nice. Someone she wished she could date.

"I think so. But don't let go just for the guy," she pressed on, hoping it wasn't heavy-handed of her to say. "Do it for yourself." Meana deserved to feel good about herself, with or without a guy in her life. Everyone did.

The brunette's stare was long and pensive, but she gave no argument and showed no anger.

She turned her head, and Aurelia followed suit. In the swirl of students leaving their classes, Walter was coming toward them. A hitch in his step revealed his hesitation when he saw Meana.

The girl spoke again, and her voice was low. "Uncle took a pointed interest in Walter, getting me to take him places. My guess is he's keeping an eye on you now. He'll know exactly where and when you two are going places."

A chill raced down Aurelia's spine.

"Now you know." Meana tilted her head at Aurelia as if that was the most she could do in farewell. She sent another look at Walter, another farewell. "Well, I'll get going. Have a good time." Meana's mouth moved into a smile that transformed her face. Dimples Aurelia had never seen came out. Her eyes shone in a way that made Aurelia wish, just for a moment, that she was an artist who could capture it.

Then Meana turned and walked away into the milling crowd of students on their way to and from classes, leaving Aurelia feeling like she had been doused with water.

Her skin prickled as she imagined Stan and his associates all being aware of her, all keeping an eye on Walter and knowing more about today's date than she did. Maybe planning to steal more of his research during their date.

And there was nothing she could do about it, because Walter needed them to be free to do whatever they did before he traveled back in time.

"Are you okay?" he asked when he reached her. His shirt was green-and-black striped, the same as on that long-ago day she saw both of him in the campus library, and he smelled like aftershave.

She swallowed. "I'll be fine."

"Did Meana say anything?"

"Nothing—well, she was being—positive," Aurelia decided on.

Walter watched her. "That's good, right?" Her hesitation probably wasn't reassuring.

"It is," she said, but again, she couldn't put any confidence into the words.

It wasn't Meana who worried her. If anything, Meana was at last going through a transformation that boded better days for her.

But that didn't change the fact that her uncle was up to something very suspicious and that Aurelia had to keep it secret.

She strained to smile at Walter. "I'm ready for our date."

* * *

WALTER OBVIOUSLY FELT HER TENSION, and he did his best to help. Aurelia did enjoy the movie he took her to. It was fun, cute, and innocent. She alternately laughed at the scenes and remembered anew her worries about Meana's uncle.

She had to let it go. With a sigh, she leaned her head on Walter's shoulder. He put his arm more firmly around her and scooted closer in spite of the divide between their seats.

At the end, they stayed and listened to the closing-credit songs while the people around them got up and began to leave.

A slow, sweet song was playing when Walter turned to Aurelia and brushed back a lock of her hair. His eyes traveled her face. Hand in her hair, he whispered, "Aurelia."

Her heart sped up, and thoughts of Stan and experiments fled her mind. This was the Walter who had told her he loved her. The Walter who had kissed her wrist in the middle of a sunset. "Yes?" she whispered back.

His gaze was unwavering, and his thumb stroked her cheek. She forgot to breathe. He leaned forward and kissed her temple.

When he stood and picked up their empty popcorn bag, Aurelia let out a breath. She had thought . . . But no.

She stood. "Where are we going now?" she asked, swallowing back disappointment from—whatever had just happened. Or rather, from whatever hadn't happened.

"To the Museum of Art on campus. You like portraits, right?"

She did, and she enjoyed it when they arrived and walked through the exhibit, hand in hand. There was so much inspiration, so much story material, to be gained from looking at paintings of people: elderly Native Americans with lined faces, nineteenth-century railroaders in dusty clothes, and frontier women parading in varying stages of solemnity or merriment.

Aurelia paused to study their expressions and imagine being them or meeting them. She felt Walter's eyes on her often enough that she had to smile at the thought that he looked at her more than at the paintings.

Next came the landscapes.

Walter pointed out a picture of the sun shining through forests and forests of pine trees. His voice was soft. "That's what it looks like near my home in Colorado."

"I guess I'll be there come Christmas," Aurelia said, turning to him. Her words were casual, but it was something she truly looked forward to.

"I guess you will be." He picked up her hands. "There'll be snow," he said, but it didn't sound like he was paying attention to his own words.

It occurred to her that one of him wouldn't be able to spend Christmas with his family. She almost mentioned it, hoping he had some plan in mind to switch places with himself. Then she realized how intense his gaze had become, and the thought fell away.

Time slowed as she stood with Walter, her hands in his. She tried to read his eyes and wait for his lips to tell her what he was thinking.

After an eternity, he smiled, squeezed her hands, and let go.

Aurelia felt her shoulders slump.

Walter put his arm against her back. "Do you need more time to look around?"

She bit her lip. She was fine leaving the exhibit but didn't want to go home just yet.

"Do you want to go find a piano?" he asked.

"Yes," she said in relief. "Let's."

Aurelia had grown fond of the Wilkinson Center piano over the course of the semester. They found the piano bench empty and were quick to claim it.

"Requests?" Walter asked as usual.

"Anything you like."

He began a song she quickly recognized as the party song she hated. "No," she exclaimed, but already he was changing the tune—to the "My Little Pony" theme song.

She laughed and listened in growing amusement as he played the song to the end while nearby students tittered.

Aurelia closed her eyes and relaxed during the next few songs. Then Walter turned to her.

"Aurelia."

She opened her eyes and waited.

"Do you know . . ." He picked up her hand.

Her breath caught.

He turned her palm over in his. "I could use another song request."

She blinked. Her imagination had run away with her again. Annoyed with both herself and him, she pulled her hand free. "How about *Pirates of the Caribbean*?"

"The Caribbean it is, love," he said in a grating imitation of a pirate.

Several soundtracks later, he stood and extended his hand to her with a dramatic bow. "May I escort you home?"

With a sigh, she let him raise her from her seat. Their date had come to an end, and they would only see each other a few more times before Thanksgiving.

On the way home, he kept up a discussion of the artwork from the exhibit. Aurelia's heart sank when they proceeded up the stairs to her apartment.

"Can I have some water?" Walter asked while Aurelia unlocked the door.

"Of course," she said, glad to have him stay. "Come in."

"Thanks."

She walked to the sofa table and dropped her purse on it. "I'll get you a cup."

A foghorn-like alarm sounded behind her. She whirled around as it blew again, and then again.

Walter was scrambling to pull out his cell phone. He must have stumbled, because he straightened as though he had been on the floor. "I'm sorry. So sorry. I have to go." He turned off the alarm, looking thoroughly chagrined.

"It's okay." She hadn't expected him to stay long, although she wanted him to. "What's wrong?"

"I just . . . have to go take care of something. Aaaugh." He rubbed his face. "I'm really sorry, Aurelia."

"It's no big deal," she tried to reassure him, but he still looked upset.

He stepped forward and gave her a hug. "Thank you for today. I gotta go." Ducking his head, he hurried out the door.

Aurelia's shoulders lowered with a sigh. After a moment she walked to the window, thinking she might at least wave goodbye. Walter was already in his car, starting the engine. The vehicle pulled out, turned the corner, and disappeared. Whatever was going on, it was urgent enough to make him forget about his cup of water.

She returned to the living room, wishing their afternoon hadn't come to so abrupt an end, but happy to think back on it all the same.

She got water for herself before a knock sounded. Putting down the cup, she went and opened the door.

Walter stood there. Of course, who else? He held a knapsack in one hand and wore a green-and-white polo shirt instead of the green-and-black shirt he had worn on their extended date.

Confident Walter looked straight at her and asked, "Would you like to see what happens next?"

Chapter Twenty-Eight

AURELIA STARED DUMBLY AT HIM. "What do you mean?" she asked at last. "What's going on?"

"There's a *lot* going on," he said with emphasis. "Can I come in for a moment?"

She let him enter.

Walter shut the door and turned to her. "I—meaning he—put trackers on some of the equipment in the lab, and I rigged alarms to go off on my phone if anything was moved around during the hours nobody on my team would be there. The alarm went off just now, didn't it? It went off, and the tracker showed a couple of things leaving the laboratory."

Aurelia's mouth fell open. "You're saying those men are stealing your research stuff right this moment? And Walter ran off to—what, stop them? See where they take it?"

"Yes."

A sense of urgency coursed through Aurelia. "Can we call the police now? Or should we go stop him, keep him safe?"

Walter shook his head. "All we're going to do is watch what happens. If you're up to it. I've installed video cameras in the main location, both so we can see it happen and so we can show it to the police afterward."

Aurelia nodded and said tightly, "Let's go, then." Finally there was something she could do.

She followed him outside, tension humming through her veins.

Soon she was driving through the city, following Walter's directions and throwing him regular sidelong glances. She gritted her teeth as construction and heavy traffic slowed them on University Parkway.

"Why was he so frustrated when he had to leave, when the alarm went off?" she asked. "I know he was worried about the equipment getting stolen, but he kept apologizing. Was it because he wouldn't tell me what was going on?" It *had* been rude of him, sort of, not to let her in on it. Shouldn't he have told her about the trackers and let her come along?

It was like the day he told her to leave the library. He was fine going off to apprehend a group of thieves on his own, but he wouldn't want to risk her safety by letting her come along.

She looked at Walter, realizing he hadn't answered. "Well? Do you know why?"

"Yes. Turn right at this light."

She turned.

"Keep going a few blocks."

"Walter. Why did he keep apologizing?"

He fiddled with his shirt collar. "I'd better not tell you while we're driving."

Her eyes widened. What was so bad that he didn't dare tell her until she parked somewhere? She drove quietly through the neighborhoods, her heart thumping.

"Here's good," Walter said, and Aurelia pulled up next to a small park. She turned off the engine, her mind in turmoil as she wondered what was about to take place. The thought of staying inside the car in this seemingly tranquil spot was suffocating.

"Can we go outside?" she asked, struggling to control her voice.

He looked at the deserted playground and the grassy hill behind it. "So long as we stay on this side of the hill and don't make too much noise."

In a flash Aurelia was outside, slamming her car door and running for the hill, ready to release some of her tension and at least get close to the action.

She stopped at the bottom and turned. Walter had followed at a sprint. He halted in front of her, breathing hard. "We're staying on this side, right?" he implored, eyes wide.

"Yes. Sorry, did I go too far?"

He swallowed. "We can go a little farther. Near the top, but not far enough to see the other side." Taking her hand, he began walking uphill.

"Because you're about to arrive on the other side?" Her heart was beating fast. Just what was about to happen?

"Yes, in a little bit, and so are the people I'm tracking. There's a warehouse on the other side that they'll all enter after they park. No one will be outside for long, but we can't risk them seeing us."

Aurelia frowned. "Where are the electronics you were talking about? You said we would watch what happens."

"I'll get the screen up and running in a few minutes. Let's stop here."

She dropped unceremoniously to the grass. "What made Walter feel so bad about leaving?" she repeated her earlier question. "I expected him to leave anyway. It wasn't a big deal, but he seemed to think it was."

Walter sighed and sank down, dropping his knapsack beside him. "I was about to propose."

Her breath lodged inside her. "You were? When?"

His eyes gleamed. "We had just been on a long date, right?" When she nodded, he asked, "Where did I take you first?"

"To the movie theater." Didn't he know that?

He smiled as if at a fond memory. "Right. And there was probably a moment toward the end when I could have chosen to propose, right?"

She nodded. She had thought he was about to propose during those closing credits. It had been a sweet, private moment—for the most part. People were picking up their things and walking out, chatting. She had partly managed to tune them out.

"But there were people around." Walter dismissed the scene. "Not the place for your proposal, and not where I planned to do it. Did we go to the Slate Canyon trailhead next?"

The question shook her. "No."

"Oh. Where did you go then?"

"To the Museum of Art."

"Okay." He nodded. "I remember considering that. Again, there were probably moments in there that we were talking, we were focused on each other, and I could have gotten down on my knee. Right?"

There had been. She had been so disappointed when he didn't.

He continued, "But again, there were people. Where did we go next?"

"Where did *you* go next?" she asked.

"To the Wilk to play the piano."

"That's where we went too."

He smiled. "And we had a good time, right?"

"But there were people," she finished for him.

He smiled wider. "Then I took you home. Jackie wouldn't be home from classes for another while, so it was just the two of us. I found an excuse to follow you inside." His smile faded, and he pulled a hand through his hair. "You were ahead of me, with your back turned, for just a moment. By the time you turned around to face me, I would be down on my knee holding out the ring."

Aurelia clapped her hands to her mouth. "I would have loved that," she whispered. With just the two of them there, and just as she was wishing their already long, three-stage date—which had included several moments she had thought he would get down on one knee—hadn't reached its end yet.

His expression became pained. "But as I was getting down and reaching for the box in my pocket, the alarm on my phone went off."

Aurelia looked down, sharp disappointment filling her.

"I got up fast and pulled out my phone instead of the ring box." He made a noise of disgust. "I was *beyond* frustrated. Two of our measuring instruments were leaving the laboratory, and—you're infinitely more important than that research project, but I couldn't knowingly let someone walk off with our things while I proposed and stayed at your place. Besides, the moment was ruined. It would have been weird to turn off the alarm and then get down on my knee. I'd have to find a different way, a different day."

She stared at him. "So you apologized again and again because, even though I had no idea what you had planned—"

"I felt like I was letting you down, big-time," he finished for her. "It was absolutely rotten timing. I'm sorry, I really am."

She gripped his hand. "But now you're running off to clash with a group of men all three of us have spied on at different times." The thought was terrifying. "Can we take a look now at what's happening?"

"Yes. I'll turn on the video feed." He squeezed her hand, then stood and pulled a tablet from his bag, attached by a cord to a smaller electronic gadget.

Aurelia stood as well and leaned in to look.

Within moments, the screen flickered on, showing a spacious room with crates and boxes stacked against the walls and two men standing in the middle of the floor.

Walter clicked around, and the screen split between three scenes. Two showed the large room from different viewpoints, and the third showed the outside of a warehouse and a man slipping through the entrance.

Aurelia held her breath. "That was one of the men from Kylie's place, the guy from the East Coast." Had there been someone ahead of him? It seemed to her that she had seen part of another silhouette, but maybe it had been his shadow. "And in that room are the other two. The big guy is Stan, Meana's uncle."

She looked closer at the scenes of the room. The men stood in shadow behind an area of dust motes illuminated by sunlight. The sun must be coming through a window outside the camera's range. Walter zoomed in while Aurelia focused on the men.

Cold rushed through her at the sight of a clumsy-looking gun in the nondescript man's hand. It reminded her of a water gun, except it was black and made of metal.

"What's he holding?" she asked in a small voice.

"We call it a negatizer. It's the tube that shoots negative energy—a deeper-level cathode ray tube. They have their own. They didn't steal that one from us."

Was that the metallic object she had seen disappear into one of the men's bags at Macey's?

The fact that it wasn't a gun should have reassured her, but Aurelia's lips trembled. "You're about to travel back in time, aren't you?" She looked up at him.

His face softened. "It will work," he said firmly, but Aurelia saw lines of tension at the corners of his eyes. He was worried.

They watched in silence as the man they had seen slip indoors entered the spacious room. Walter turned on the sound, making himself and Aurelia privy to the three men's conversation.

"Thorn's taking care of it. Let's see what these tell us," said the thief, showing the others the instruments he had stolen—two objects like the silvery tuning fork Walter had used in Kylie's living room. "This is how the field read ten minutes ago when we stopped by."

"Let's see how strong it is here," said Stan, taking the second reader and directing it at the sunny, dusty spot in front of them.

A car drove into the parking lot. Walter's car. Aurelia grabbed Walter's arm, careful not to compromise his grip on the screen.

He spoke in her ear. "I didn't want to follow right behind the thief's car. With my trackers on the instruments, I was able to stay behind a few minutes without fear of losing them."

Heatedly, she whispered, "Why didn't you just call the police?"

"I wasn't one hundred percent sure it *was* a thief. Maybe, just maybe, my professor had taken the equipment for some reason or other, even though I was pretty sure she had something else on her schedule that would keep her from the lab at this time. Maybe whatever she had got cancelled. It's almost Thanksgiving. She could have been removing the equipment for safekeeping without telling us."

On the screen, Comeback Walter got out of his car and slowly approached the back door. He tried the knob, found that it turned, and let go without opening the door. Instead, he pulled out his phone.

"What are you doing now?" Aurelia's voice was breathless.

"I told one of my project teammates that I think someone stole readers from our lab and that I followed them. I'm sending him my coordinates and asking if he'll call 911 and send the police here if I don't text him back within ten minutes."

Aurelia gave a tense nod. That seemed like a good idea.

He continued, "I know those men have found ways to manipulate the video cameras in our lab, or they would have gotten caught already. They've probably done something similar with the security cameras in the warehouse today, but obviously they didn't find the cameras I placed there. After we watch it all unfold, we'll have a recording to show the police when they arrive."

The on-screen Walter still stood by the door. A soft *ding* sounded, and he checked his phone before putting it in his pocket.

"That was my friend's answering text. Now I'm going in," Walter narrated beside her.

The man with the gun-shaped negatizer was pumping energy into the sunny, dust-swirling spot in front of him.

"Wait a minute." Shock crawled through Aurelia. "That sunny spot in front of them—"

"It's not dust floating in the air," Walter said quietly.

She looked at him. "I thought you couldn't see anything different about a highly negative area."

"This time you can," he said, his voice strained. "It's the only time I've seen it be visible."

She hushed as he added another scene, showing himself walking through a hallway.

"One of them is putting more chemicals into the area," he said, confusing her until she looked back at the men. One directed a long, snake-like instrument at the hot spot, spraying liquid chemicals that quickly evaporated. The other two checked their newly pilfered measuring instruments. "Stop," Stan commanded with a gesture. "Now, negatizer. And—stop."

"Don't be scared," Walter said in a warning tone, but when the on-screen Walter in the dark hallway was grabbed and forced against the wall, Aurelia screamed and clapped a hand to her mouth.

"Sorry," the Walter next to her said quickly. "Maybe I shouldn't have shown you that. I promise it's not that bad."

Not that bad? She wanted to scold him, but all she could do was stand frozen, watching the scene continue, watching the stranger shove a gun into Walter's ribs.

"Don't move," said the man's unfamiliar voice. "I'll shoot you if you do anything besides what I tell you to."

Aurelia shook all over as the man directed Walter along the hallway.

"I didn't know it would be so bad to watch," Walter said beside her, putting his arm around her shoulders. His face had gone pale.

Soon, the man pushed Walter into the large room at gunpoint and approached the other criminals. "Here he is."

"You're on the research project," said Meana's uncle as he towered over Walter. "You programmed a tracker into this?" He held up his stolen reader. "We noticed it on our way here."

The other two men sent dark looks at the new arrival. The featureless man stepped closer to the other, and Aurelia barely heard the murmur, "What do we do about him?"

Comeback Walter set his jaw and looked around. His gaze fixated in sudden awe on the spot before him. "You made that? A travel hole?"

"We did. We're considerably further along in our research than you. This spot will allow time travel an hour into the past."

On-screen Walter's eyes widened, but the Walter next to Aurelia scoffed. "If I had known they were responsible for the clumsy trials that caused explosions around town, I wouldn't have been so quick to believe their confidence," he murmured while Walter in the warehouse said, "Then why ransack our notes and steal our equipment?"

"Because some of your research fills in gaps in some of ours," the Boston man answered brusquely.

"How did you manage to break into our lab?"

"Never mind that," Stan said and stepped closer, shoving his reader into the hostage's line of sight. "Tell me your cutoff number for the green digits. How far have you been able to go without having the air collapse?"

Walter took his time answering, causing the man with the gun—Thorn?—to shift his weapon menacingly.

"Ten more digits, and I'd say it's gone too far."

Stan stroked his chin and stared at the silvery object. "And the overall readings? What would you say about the current state of the hole?"

Walter shook his head. "I've never seen it get that far. We've never had the change in the air be visible for longer than a millisecond."

"But the numbers," Meana's uncle persisted. "Are they balanced?"

"They look right."

Stan turned to the Boston man. "How were the field's readings?"

"The numbers were close enough when we dropped by. As long as the air hasn't collapsed, it'll work."

"You better go back to that field and make sure it's still good before we send the box through," said the nondescript man.

"What field?" Walter asked.

"We created an energy spot an hour ago in a field that already had strong concentrations of underlying negative energy," the man explained, looking smug. "All we need to do now is send this box through, and it'll show up an hour ago in the field. Those two will be ready to pick it up. They were there an hour ago, energizing the spot."

Confident Walter shook his head in disgust. "It wasn't the field that became an exit spot. It was a street a bunch of blocks from your place."

Aurelia didn't answer. *A box.* They were planning to send a box through—for now. She waited with clenched teeth for the men to realize they could send a live person through their hole for the experiment. Any moment they would decide to push Walter through instead of their box.

"Does the other spot look like this?" On-screen Walter asked, indicating the glittering air two yards from him and gazing at it with intensity.

"No, but it'll work as our exit."

"Thorn has to stay here with him," Stan directed, indicating Walter and the man who held him. "He has experience with this sort of thing."

"He was supposed to be on the receiving end with me," the Boston man protested.

"I'll come along in his place. Tie up the boy if you need to. Make him analyze the readers if anything changes with the energy field here."

The men divided up, two of them to stay behind in the warehouse with a reader, a negatizer, and the snake-like chemical sprayer, and the other two preparing to leave with one each of the same three instruments. Somebody retrieved a rope, and the nondescript man, who was staying, pulled out a gun.

"How many of those do they have?" Aurelia whispered vehemently.

The new gun wielder addressed Walter in a threatening tone. "You'll help us, won't you?"

Aurelia thought of how the men couldn't possibly be planning to let Walter go after this, not once they no longer needed his cooperation. They couldn't let him go home now that he had seen them and could turn them in. Walter himself must be terribly aware of that fact.

A *ding* sounded, echoing through the large room.

Thorn handed his gun to one of the others and reached into Walter's pocket, pulling out his phone. "We'll take that," he said, turning on the screen.

Aurelia knew that Comeback Walter's phone required a password. However, it always showed the first line of an unread text even before the screen was unlocked.

Thorn looked up, his face livid, and flashed the screen at the person next to him.

"Calling 911," the man read out loud, his eyes widening with horror.

"Shoot him," Thorn ordered.

Aurelia gasped.

"What?" the Boston man exclaimed, but the nondescript man turned his gun on Walter, not waiting for discussion, and Walter, with no time for second thoughts, threw himself into the glittering cloud and disappeared.

Chapter Twenty-Nine

AURELIA CLAMPED her hand on the arm of the Walter next to her and gasped as he swayed.

She would not let him disappear. If this whole thing somehow resulted in all of Walter disappearing, she would disappear *with* him before she would let him vanish into thin air.

"Walter, are you okay?" she cried.

He shut his eyes and gingerly reached up to touch his temples. His balance remained unsteady as he leaned on her.

"Walter?" she asked in a tiny voice. An eternity passed as she waited.

The lines of pain in his face smoothed, and his shoulders relaxed. He didn't speak though. Aurelia kept her death grip until his eyes popped open.

"I proposed?" His voice was hoarse. "I had no idea. No *wonder* you wouldn't have anything to do with me."

Aurelia's mouth fell open, but before she could say anything, Walter winced, making her fear for his life and his existence.

"Ouch, your rejections were painful." He paused. "Yeah, I know now why I deserved them, but I had no idea at the time."

Had the Walter next to her switched places with Comeback Walter? But no, this sounded like Comeback Walter who suddenly knew the things Confident Walter knew, and vice versa.

He shook his head and muttered, "I proposed before the talent show. I don't believe it."

She reached out cautiously with her other hand and touched him. At least he was still there.

He tilted his head as if listening to something. "You went to the karaoke night? I took her kayaking that evening. She won't have any memory of it though." He shook his head sadly.

"Walter? Can you hear me?" Aurelia asked with trepidation.

With that, his eyes cleared and focused on her. Warmth sparkled in them. Placing his hands on her arms, he completed their little circle. "Yes. I think I'm all right. I'm here, all here."

"Both of you?" she asked, just for good measure.

"Both of me. All of me. I went back in time, but I guess this time, the world's resuming where it left off, and so here I am! It's fascinating. My mind is flooded with memories from both of me."

He looked much more enthusiastic about the process than she felt. At the moment, all she cared about was that he was safe.

"You had better stay one person from now on," she said and tightened her lips to keep them from trembling.

He looked down at her, shaking his head. "You've been through so much in this whole confusing mess." His voice was filled with both regret and wonder.

"I'm glad," she said fiercely. "I'm glad I've gotten to know you. *All* of you. *Both* of you, future and past."

He held her tighter. "Still, I'm sorry I put you through it."

"Don't be sorry," she demanded. "Just . . . stay. Stay, Walter." She laughed shakily at the phrase he had come up with. He was here to stay. He had gone back in time, and finally there was only one of him—not two as they had feared, and not zero, as she had suddenly feared a minute ago. She hadn't lost any part of him. CB and Confident Walter had combined.

Her chest rose and fell as she stared up into his green-flecked brown eyes. A world away, it seemed, sirens sounded.

Walter smiled. "Aurelia Michelle Jackson," he said as if tasting each syllable and finding it better than anything in this world. "Will you marry me?"

Heart thudding, she pressed her hand to his cheek and watched his eyes shine down at her.

"Yes," she exclaimed, and Walter dipped his head and kissed her.

She held on, not breaking the kiss until she felt tears in her eyes and drew back to blink them away.

Walter pulled out the ring box she had seen once before and snapped it open, kneeling before her.

Starry-eyed, she held out her hand and let him put the ring on her finger. His touch sent warmth up and down her arm. She looked at the ring, a beautiful gold band with a small, sparkling diamond. Then she looked at Walter. "I love you."

He claimed another kiss and whispered against her mouth, "I love you too."

She felt whole, filled, blissful. Threading her fingers through his, she asked, "When will we get married?"

His gaze caressed her face. "Your family gets back the first Friday in January, right?"

She nodded, watching him in adoration.

"I was thinking the day after."

She gasped with laughter. "They'll be exhausted that day."

"Then when?" He smiled.

She pondered. She wanted this next step, and yet, as short as their courtship had been, maybe they ought to have a somewhat longer engagement.

She sighed. "I suppose we need a few months to plan the reception. Although maybe Mom can do some of the planning from Costa Rica."

"Maybe she can." He buried a hand in her hair and moved his lips to within a whisper of hers. "Aurelia."

"Yes?"

"What are our rules on kissing now? Is there a limit on them before we get married?"

She stilled, feeling his breath. Walter waited, the air around him charged with intensity.

"Well." She forced herself to speak. "We can't scare our friends away before the reception. And too much kissing will make it too hard to wait to get married."

She felt undercurrents of energy coming off him.

"Other than that, though, I think we should be free to kiss now," she finished.

Walter straightened. He didn't need to be told twice. He put his hand on the back of her neck, and with a beautiful smile and a look of admiration in his eyes, he lowered his face to hers and . . . stopped, a strange expression crossing his face.

"You have a thing for brown hair?" he asked in disbelief. "You mean, I've had this arsenal the entire time? How did I not know this?"

"Oh, sheesh." Aurelia pressed her hands to her cheeks and stepped away.

Walter's hand caught her wrist. "Guess what?" he said, capturing her in his gaze.

"What?" she asked breathlessly. Sirens sounded on the other side of the hill, and the landscape behind Walter flashed red and blue as police cars pulled into the warehouse parking lot below.

"I love you," he said and kissed her again.

* * *

WALTER PULLED AWAY SLOWLY, regretfully. "We'd better go talk to the police."

Aurelia nodded. Walter took her hand, and they crested the hill and started down the other side.

"When you went back in time, you went straight to my place to propose?" Aurelia asked in wonder.

"I thought I had gone back one hour," he explained. "I was still stuck on the fact that I was supposed to propose, and when I realized the timing and the place where I appeared near your house worked out so I could return only minutes after I ran off, I went for it. I'm sorry if that was a dumb thought—if that was unromantic."

Aurelia squeezed his hand. "If going back to me was one of your first thoughts after you narrowly escaped getting shot and you went through a mini wormhole, then I'm flattered." She paused. "Did you realize it was suddenly summer?"

He groaned. "I obviously wasn't thinking straight. I guess I was pumped up on adrenaline from getting kidnapped and all."

They neared the parking lot, where two police officers disappeared inside while two others covered the outdoors.

"Hey, what are you kids doing here?" One of the policemen asked, approaching them.

"My friend was the one who called you," Walter explained. "The men in the warehouse stole equipment from our science lab."

Aurelia gripped his arm and added, "They held Walter hostage and meant to shoot him."

"They have guns?" The intensity in the man's eyes grew.

"Two that we know of," Walter said. "Here, I can show you pictures and help you find out where those guys are right now."

On his phone, he pulled up pictures of three of the men. Then he scrolled through video cameras on his handheld screen, looking for the various hallways and rooms each criminal-scientist was sneaking through or hiding in. He also pulled up a screenshot of Thorn taken during the warehouse scene today.

"We'll use this," the man told Walter, who passed the electronics to him. "You two get behind that cruiser over there. We don't want you getting caught in the crossfire if those guys come out here and things get ugly." Without waiting for a response, the man moved briskly across the parking lot, relaying information over a walkie-talkie.

Walter and Aurelia hurried to the police car farthest from the warehouse door. It was parked with its back to the building, so they crouched in front of the hood. Aurelia regretted no longer being able to watch the proceedings on video.

Here and there, an order was called out. Aurelia tensed when she heard a gunshot inside the building, and Walter put his arm around her. A second gunshot sounded.

Within minutes, an officer called out, "We have all four."

Cautious, Aurelia and Walter stood to watch as officers escorted the men outside and hustled them toward a jail car.

"I'd never seen that man Thorn until today," Aurelia said in a low voice to Walter.

"Me neither. I think he's more of a hired man for the dirty work than a scientist."

The prisoners caught sight of Walter. The three men Aurelia had spied on stared at him, and she could almost see their scientist minds churning, their need to know about his time travel trip etched in their faces. The last man, Thorn, didn't share in their curiosity. He glared evilly first at Walter and then at Aurelia.

She glared back with a vengeance, furious with the man who had first held Walter at gunpoint and then ordered him shot. Her blood boiled as she stared him down.

He looked taken aback, forgetting to glare in his confusion. Before he could recover, he was directed into the back of the police car.

"How dare he," Aurelia ground out and tightened her grip on Walter, who looked at her with a question in his eyes. "How dare he try to hurt you," she clarified.

Walter's lips pulled into a faint smile. He smoothed her hair back and began to stroke it, soothing her.

"We need to ask you some questions," an officer said, stepping up to them.

"Of course," Walter told him, continuing his comforting movements. Then he pulled Aurelia close, and she tucked her head beneath his chin, breathing deeply. She loved the firmness of his chest and the beat of his heart, the feeling of security and belonging in his arms.

As she looked down, her gaze was drawn to a glint of light from the diamond in the gold ring encircling her finger. The sight made her smile. Joy and gratitude welled up inside her, edging out and finally overshadowing the fears of the last hour.

Chapter Thirty

"THIS IS what the criminals used to find prime places for their experiments," Walter said, sitting beside Aurelia at the police station and holding up a rounded device that fit in his hand. Aurelia leaned subtly against him, still feeling protective. "It seeks out spots with concentrations of negativity above a certain threshold. When they found such a spot, they'd prime it further and try to create a time travel wormhole, even if it was in a public place or someone's home."

"Time travel." The officer beside Aurelia shook his head, looking harried. "Whatever that disappearing act in the warehouse was—"

"That's not the question we need answered. Leave that to the—uh—science community." The one who had interrupted sent a sidelong look at Walter as if doubtful the scientists would think today's event anything beyond quackery.

The officer on the opposite side of the desk shuffled through his notes. "The GPS coordinates we found among their papers correspond to the explosions we know of as well as several other places, but we haven't heard reports from any of the homeowners about someone forcing their way in."

"They didn't force their way in," Aurelia said, drawing everyone's attention. Her cheeks heating, she swallowed and forged on. "At least not at Kylie's place." She explained about the pesticide visits, setting off another flurry of phone calls and an assignment for two officers to investigate the company the men might have used as their cover-up.

Meanwhile, Aurelia turned to Walter, feeling a pleasant swoop in her stomach at his smile. His eyes shone, and hers probably did too. They were helping the police with an investigation. She was getting first-class material for her books. And she was engaged to the love of her life, who was currently staring into her eyes and wrapping his fingers around hers.

The policeman in charge cleared his throat and picked up the negatizer. "Is this the one that would have caused the explosions?"

Walter turned back to him. "Yes. That's not its purpose, but if you add too much energy with this, the air explodes." He sat up taller, his voice eager. "I can show you in our lab how it works."

"Let's wait for a demonstration until your professor gets back after Thanksgiving," the officer hurried to say. "In the meantime, you can help us go through their notes. We want you to identify the pieces that were stolen from your lab. Depending on the amount of info that came from your research, we may eventually release the notes to your team."

"Then we can find out what they did beyond our own methods to make time travel work." Walter looked like he was in seventh heaven.

The officers exchanged glances in various stages of disbelief. Aurelia couldn't blame them. She squeezed Walter's hand. "Just don't send a person through. You and your team will keep things safe, right?"

* * *

"It's no good," Walter said after a week of intensive testing in the lab. The criminal-scientists' notes had been released halfway through December, prompting a flurry of work and explosive anticipation for Dr. Jude's team. Aurelia had waited for Walter outside the laboratory, and so had a reporter, but Walter's professor demanded the journalist's attention while Walter steered Aurelia from the building.

Campus was layered with white, and Aurelia's breath was visible in front of her. With her hand snug in Walter's, though, she wasn't cold.

"Those guys' notes don't add much value to ours," Walter said in dejection. "We haven't been able to recreate the shimmering time travel hole the men made, and as far as I can tell, they didn't do anything different in particular this last time. It's like they experimented with whatever hot spots they found, hoping something would work out at some point. Dr. Jude doubts they'd be able to recreate their own success a second time around."

"And the video hasn't helped?" She knew he and his team had pored over the video from the warehouse, which showed part of the creation of the hole he had gone through as well as his disappearance into it.

"No. What we need are measurements throughout the process, and they didn't get hold of our readers until after they created the hole." He looked as though he very much wished the men had stolen them earlier. "But we'll keep working on it." He brightened. "Other institutions are showing a lot of interest, at least those who don't think our story's a scam. We've been offered three different grants already to help us continue our research."

"Not to mention an interview on the *Today* show, as well as an interview with *Insane, Insaner, Insanest.*" Aurelia pursed her lips in annoyance. Somewhere along the way, the video had been leaked to the public, and the world didn't know what to do with the information. "What does your family think about your time travel journey at this point?"

"They're still in shock. But they've been comparing notes with Frank and Ilia and my roommates, and I think they're starting to believe it. Hey, Jackie."

Aurelia looked up just as her roommate joined them, her ponytail swinging and her mouth spread in a grin.

"I dodged another paparazzi." Jackie had her own way of referring to the reporters. "I think someone's making a friend," she said in a lowered voice and pointed.

Aurelia turned and caught sight of two female students walking along the length of the study abroad Kennedy Center. One of them wore an adorable faux fur-lined coat and designer jeans.

Hope fluttered in Aurelia's heart. She had wondered how Meana was doing, especially since her uncle had been arrested. Her eyes moved to the other girl. "Do you think that's her new roommate?"

"Could be." Jackie squinted in their direction.

"They look like they get along," Walter commented.

"Yeah." Aurelia thought she detected some hesitation in the two of them as they walked and talked. On the other hand, Meana had never so much as walked and talked with Aurelia or Jackie. It would have been a huge step forward if she had.

"All right!" Jackie clapped her hands together, making Aurelia jump. "You better be done with work, Walter. Finals are over, and next semester, Aurelia rejoins the test-taking, homework-laden world." She rubbed her hands in delight. "Let's go celebrate her doom with hot cocoa."

Aurelia let Jackie drag her and Walter to the Wilk, where they bought steaming hot cocoa and fell to talking about the upcoming Christmas holiday.

* * *

WHEN AURELIA and Walter arrived at his home three days later, the family welcomed them with open arms.

"I can't believe you didn't tell us what was going on all semester," Janet said while she squeezed her son.

"Aurelia, come see our Christmas tree," Louisa said and grabbed her arm.

Walter tried to free himself. "Can I come too?"

"You'll have to get past me first." Polly blocked his path with her arms out like a basketball player.

The break passed in a blur of laughter, Christmas lights, and questions about Walter's time travel experience. It was fun, animated and, during quieter moments, cozy. At the end of their time together, Aurelia was sad to leave.

Still, now she could have more one-on-one time with Walter, and she found herself growing more and more excited about certain upcoming events.

* * *

"I FINISHED MY THIRD DIARY," Walter said, standing next to Aurelia in the airport with flight information screens flashing above them. Her family's flight had landed, and Aurelia was bouncing in place.

"Third?" She planted her feet on solid ground and considered. "One for Comeback Walter. One for Confident Walter."

"And one for the first time around," he finished. "Our love story has been well recorded. You know, when I tell people stories about our early days and you say, 'That's not how it went, dear,' I can claim I'm sure that's how it happened the first time."

"Sure." She smirked. "But you won't be able to do that with anything that's happened after the two of you merged."

He made a regretful noise. "I'll figure something out."

She patted his arm in mock sympathy. "It'd grow wearisome for you to claim to be right all the time."

As she removed her hand, he captured it and leaned down, nuzzling his face against hers. "I don't think I'll care who's right and who's wrong, so long as we're together."

"You will," she mumbled, "once some of this infatuation fades."

"Maybe," he mumbled back. "But when I do, just remind me of what matters."

She slid her hand up into his hair. "We'll figure it out."

"*This* is what we come home to?" Her younger sister's voice cut through their bliss. "I don't think she missed us at all, do you?" Rachel shot her dad a grin. "I think—"

But President Jackson only said "Oomph" as his college daughter launched herself into his arms.

"Dad, welcome home, welcome back," Aurelia cried, and then all the Jacksons were hugging and getting in each other's way.

"It's good to see you, Aurelia," Dad said with moist eyes, "even if we did find you in a shockingly non-missionary embrace with your young man."

Aurelia grinned, only blushing a little. "I'm not one of your missionaries, Dad."

"I missed you so much, sweetie," Mom said, squeezing her.

"You did it," Rachel told her. "You're marrying a brown-haired guy."

Aurelia scoffed. "Rachel, there's a lot more to Walter than his hair." She turned and was surprised to see her dad pull Walter from a handshake into a hug. When had her family become this affectionate? Was it the Costa Rican culture that had rubbed off on them?

"Yeah, there's mystery and science fiction in him," Rowan agreed with shining eyes.

"Walter," Rachel called out, "is your dad bald?"

"No." He sounded confused.

"What about your grandpa?" she persisted.

"No." He looked to Aurelia, who narrowed her eyes at Rachel.

"Aren't you lucky?" Rachel smirked. "You'll have that hair for a long time, Aurelia."

"I'm not marrying him for his hair," Aurelia said in exasperation.

"No, indeed," said Dad. "Now, can we hear a little more about this time travel . . . stint? I know we've talked it over some on Skype, but maybe in person it'll be easier to understand."

Aurelia was suddenly at a loss for words. So was Walter.

"Uh," Aurelia began.

Mom put a hand on Dad's arm. "Let's get home first. We appreciate Walter coming to meet us and give us a ride home, don't we?" She gave Walter an understanding look as he took her suitcases, eager to table the time travel discussion with the parents.

"It's the coolest thing ever," Rowan said, falling into step with Walter. "You've gotta figure out a way to make it work again. I'm telling all my friends I know a time traveler."

"I hope we can make it happen, now that we know it can be done," Walter responded with equal fervor. He slowed his steps, trying to make it back to Aurelia's side.

For her part, Aurelia was trying to speed up in spite of one of Rachel's suitcases in her right hand and one of Rowan's in her left, but Rachel impeded her, catching her arm and hooking elbows. "Will you play games with us tonight? Every night this week? It's been forever since we've all played."

"Definitely. Uh, in between wedding planning," Aurelia said when she noticed Mom's frown. She was glad to hear that Rachel wanted to spend time with her. Although she had just started a new semester—a semester with actual classes and homework—she would make time. "Did you hear that, Walter? If you want a date night this week, you'll have to come to our place and play games with the family."

"I'd love to," he said, finally making it to her side. Aurelia felt content to walk beside him, even though they couldn't touch because their hands were full. Rowan, trotting ahead of them, turned and made a crazy face, his tongue sticking out and his eyes rolling.

"It's good to have you back," she told him and felt that all was well with the world. "Mom, are you ready for Christmas seven days from now?" she called to the front of their group.

In light of the upcoming late holiday, Walter and Aurelia had prepared the house, complete with a sparkling Christmas tree in the living room and lights along the roof. Dad had never let Aurelia help hang the lights before, but Walter, privy to her tree-climbing passion, had walked all over the roof with her while they worked on the lights.

"I will be," came Mom's determined answer. "Are you ready for your wedding in two months?"

"No, no, no." Aurelia shook her head. "Mom, Christmas is in seven days. Our *sealing*," she looked at Walter, "is in fifty-nine days, twenty-two hours, and"—she looked around for a wall clock— "sixteen minutes."

"Is that how it is?" Dad asked in amusement and exchanged glances with his wife.

Aurelia and Walter exchanged glances and smiles of their own. "That's how it is," they chorused.

Rachel wriggled her eyebrows at Aurelia. "It's amazing how good you can be at math when you have the motivation for it."

"I think you and my sister Polly will get along famously," Walter told her.

"Good. I like making friends, and it'll help to have someone to cry with when you take away my sister, from whom I have been separated e'er so long." Rachel raised a hand to her head in a pathetic gesture.

"I think you *will* like her," Aurelia said, ignoring the dramatics. "*I* like her."

Her younger sister looked pleased at the prospect.

"I'm excited for Christmas number two," Walter said in a low voice to Aurelia.

"I'm excited for them to find all the notes," she whispered back. There was still time to think up more good ones to plant that upcoming "Christmas" night.

"I'm excited for them to meet the reindeer you rented."

"Sssh," she said and laughed under her breath.

Her family was going to have a good old-fashioned Casper-inspired Christmas.

Epilogue

Two and a Half Years Later

"WE'VE BORED THEM TO SLEEP," said Jackie and leaned back against the plush couch with feigned affront.

"They wore each other out," Aurelia corrected, looking at the two toddlers who had fallen asleep on the rug in the midst of their toy cars and ponies. The girls, Liz Casper and Elly Roper, were inseparable when they got together.

Jack Casper, the baby, wriggled on his blanket and reached for Elly's hair, which he proceeded to pull.

Walter was quickest to leave the couch and kneel down, gently prying his son's fingers open. "This one still has plenty of energy." He lifted Jack into the air, raising peals of laughter from the boy.

Aurelia reached for her baby, but Walter gave her his hand instead and reclaimed his seat beside her. Jackie reached across her to take Jack, who greeted her with a happy gurgle and smiled up with blue eyes and chubby cheeks.

"Hello, handsome. You love your Aunt Jackie, don't you? Hey, Aurelia, if you don't want to write a romance, I forgive you, so long as you write *something*. I'm desperate to read a book from you. How about *Chronicles of Jack and Jackie, pacifier edition*?"

"Actually, I *have* begun to write again recently," Aurelia confessed and looked at the closet where she stashed her notebooks. "I never thought I'd have time as a mom, and I really don't, but I started to feel like I should take the time anyway."

"That's great." Jackie's eyes brightened with mischief. "You'll need a babysitter, then, so your kids won't be ignored when you write. I know how distracted you get."

"No, I don't. What, baby?" Aurelia tilted her head at Jack as he caught her sleeve and then sucked on it. A two-tone melody rang out from the hallway. Aurelia extricated herself and stood in response to the doorbell. "I'll get it."

A feeling of déjà vu came over her as she walked down the hall, passing between wedding pictures and baby pictures that more than once included Jackie and her little girl. The entrance hosted little shoes and big shoes and a shoehorn she had been gifted last month.

She opened the door and gasped. Jackie, wearing a decidedly different shirt than the one Aurelia had just seen, stood on the step. With faint lines in her cheeks and a broad smile, she held out her arms. "Miss me?"

"Hey, friend." Aurelia spun around to see Jackie walk up behind her, carrying Jack. She grinned at Aurelia. "She showed up this morning. Isn't this great?"

"Wha—Jackie!" Aurelia exclaimed but was ignored as Younger Jackie and the newcomer, who looked about ten years older and a few pounds heavier, exchanged hearty hugs.

The slightly lined version of Jackie beamed at the little boy. "My favorite namesake. Oh, you're so *little*. I've always felt honored that your parents named you after me."

"I know, right?" Under Aurelia's accusing gaze, Younger Jackie handed over the boy, who blew raspberries at his new admirer. "They keep saying they named him after someone from Walter's family history, but we both know the truth."

"What's going on he—" Walter entered the hall, and his question turned into a choking noise.

Mature Jackie stepped forward and pumped his hand up and down. "*There's* the scientist. Congratulations! Oh, Jack wants you now. Fine. Anyway, keep experimenting and all that, because this is so much fun."

Aurelia opened her mouth in protest just as Walter blurted, "Wait, do I —my team—how do we do it? Because we've been looking into laser—"

"Oh no, no cheating." Mature Jackie wagged her finger. "I can't tell you about the future. Besides, I'm only here for a couple of days, so I don't have time for a disserta—"

"A couple of *days*?" Walter interrupted and bounced Jack. "How are you getting back? Do you have an entrance spot, or are the chemicals from your travel enough to—"

Aurelia interrupted. "What *I* want to know is, why are you here?"

"To torture you, of course," said Mature Jackie. "Write a book about me, and I'll stop." She paused. "Actually, just write a book about me. No promises from my end. And give me a cool, *significal* name from another language. Your audience loves your linguistic touches. Hey, why don't we all go inside? I think I hear the girls in the living room."

"Let's." Younger Jackie turned to a stunned Aurelia with enthusiasm. "My daughter's already seen both of us together, and it didn't freak her out. Liz should be all right, too, don't you think?"

"Dude, Liz *loves* me," Mature Jackie exclaimed and hooked arms. "Let's do this."

Younger Jackie shrugged and started toward the living room, arm in arm with her other self. "She'll probably just think you're an older aunt."

"Whoa, 'older'? I haven't aged a bit, I'll have you know."

"Oho! Tell me, have I always had that wrinkle in my cheek?"

Aurelia helplessly followed the Jackies into the living room, where both proceeded to fawn over the now awake Liz and her playmate.

Walter came up behind her, placed a wriggling Jack on his blanket on the floor, and put his arm around Aurelia's waist, shaking his head. Aurelia stared at her friend—*friends*—her mind galloping over the slip about her writer's audience. She had readers in the future. She was an *author*.

Liz screamed with laughter as Mature Jackie flew her through the air.

Walter kissed Aurelia's cheek. "Just remember, one day we'll laugh about this."

She rolled her eyes but melted into his side, enjoying his warmth and his nearness. This was how life ought to be: full of Walter and children and, for better or worse, time travel.

She turned and gave Walter a long, slow kiss, the kind that sparked awe and familiarity and left both of them breathless.

Younger Jackie looked over at them. "You're such a married couple," she said with pride, as though their relationship was all her doing.

Mature Jackie grinned. "Speaking of which, I can't wait till Brian gets back from his business trip tomorrow. This is one anniversary I won't let him forget."

Terms Relating to The Church of Jesus Christ of Latter-day Saints

EXPLANATIONS BY THE AUTHOR

Temples: The focus of temples is Jesus Christ. Members enter the temple to perform ordinances that bind them to him and to each other so that their families will last beyond mortality and forever. They also perform baptisms and the other ordinances in behalf of those who have passed on, knowing their spirits will then have the choice to accept those ordinances for themselves before they are judged and resurrected. Clarity and a feeling of love abound in the temple, and many members love to go not only for the ordinances but to have a sacred, quiet place to commune with God.

For more information about temples, see
churchofjesuschrist.org/temples

Patriarchal blessings: Each member has the privilege of receiving a patriarchal blessing that tells them which tribe of Israel they belong to and gives counsel from their heavenly parents. Members are encouraged to ask for this blessing early in life so it can be a guide and a source of hope through many of their trials, joys, and decisions.

For more information about patriarchal blessings, see
churchofjesuschrist.org/study/manual/gospel-topics/patriarchal-blessings

Dear Reader

Imagine getting proposed to by a stranger! When I got the idea for this story, I knew I had to explore it. I don't often engage in science fiction, but this hilarious time travel idea gave me a surprisingly beautiful opportunity to reconcile science with faith in God, our Creator. I hope you enjoyed this adventure with two Walters and one very concerned Aurelia.

I would love your help in spreading the word about this book. If you're willing to rate and review *Walter Times Two* on Amazon or elsewhere, it will help other romance readers know you found it worth your time.

Thank you for reading, and I can't wait to share my next novel with you!

About the Author

Annika Champenois grew up partly in Denmark, partly in Utah, and wholly in the world of books. She studied statistics at Brigham Young University and Data Analytics at Western Governors University and lives an exciting life, splitting her time between data analysis and giving voice to the stories that dance around in her imagination. When she isn't immersed in fiction, Annika loves to go for walks, study languages, and spend time with her family and friends.

www.annikachampenois.com
facebook.com/annikachampenoisauthor
instagram.com/annikachampenois